■ □ ■ □ ■

THE THIRD SHORE

Writings from an Unbound Europe

■ □ ■ □ ■

THE THIRD SHORE

WOMEN'S FICTION FROM
EAST CENTRAL EUROPE

Edited by Agata Schwartz and Luise von Flotow

NORTHWESTERN UNIVERSITY PRESS

EVANSTON, ILLINOIS

Northwestern University Press
Evanston, Illinois 60208-4170

English translation copyright © 2006 by Northwestern University Press.
Published 2006. All rights reserved.

Printed in the United States of America

10   9   8   7   6   5   4   3   2   1

ISBN 0-8101-2309-6 (cloth)
ISBN 0-8101-2311-8 (paper)

Library of Congress Cataloging-in-Publication Data

The third shore : women's fiction from East Central Europe / edited by Agata Schwartz
and Luise von Flotow.
    p. cm.
Includes bibliographical references.
ISBN 0-8101-2309-6 (cloth : alk. paper) — ISBN 0-8101-2311-8 (pbk. : alk. paper)
    1. East European fiction—Women authors—Translations into English. 2. East
European fiction—20th century—Translations into English. I. Schwartz, Agata,
1961– II. Von Flotow-Evans, Luise
PN849.E92T44 2005
809'.89287'0947—dc22

                                                                        2005013707

CONTENTS

COLLECTING AND TRANSLATING

Making a book of texts from East Central Europe for a North American audience involves challenges at every stage—collecting the texts, selecting the most appropriate, and translating them. We began this project in 1997, when the immediate shock waves of the changes of 1989 had begun to settle and organizations and journals such as *Pro Femina* in Serbia or *Aspekt* in Slovakia or the *Women's Forum* in Albania had been founded and were eager to help. Numerous congresses on literature in this new age and seminars on "new writing" in general were being held, and women's texts were appearing in larger numbers. Many of the women academics from the region were cautiously exploring different forms of Western feminism, and the atmosphere was one of excitement and collaboration and renewal. Further, English-language translations of some individual writers had been appearing in somewhat obscure literary journals in the United States, Canada, and Great Britain for some time as well as, toward the end of the 1990s, in bigger anthologies, often in German. These selections were predominantly by male writers. Finally, both editors, Luise von Flotow and Agata Schwartz, mobilized their extensive connections in East Central Europe—through family, friends, and academia—in the interests of presenting a wide selection of short texts by contemporary women writers of the region.

All these networks and sources were tapped for materials, with the only criteria being that authors were to be born after 1945 and their text published after 1989. And so the work came in: in French translation from Albania, in German translation from Slovakia, in English translation from the literary journals and few English anthologies we scoured; from women's organizations, from literary groups in Poland

and Latvia, from academic colleagues we encountered at conferences in Budapest and Oslo or whom we approached directly in Bulgaria, Romania, Macedonia, and elsewhere. We read as many texts as we could in the original languages (between us, we know six) and verified the writers' backgrounds and reputations in their own cultures, as far as we could, but we were also grateful for the suggestions and submissions of English translators such as Adam Sorkin, Andrée Zaleska, and Celia Hawkesworth. They showed us again that translators are *the* mediators of foreign materials; they not only know what is happening in the cultures where their languages are spoken and written, but they make the immense effort it takes to translate and then publish their work. In the English-language publishing environment this is usually a thankless and often an unpaid task.

We tried to maintain a foreign sound in the translated work and not adapt them into too glib a form of English. When we couldn't get a copy of the original (Albanian, for example), we did what is normally frowned upon (but happens regularly)—we translated from a translation. Sometimes our networks supplied us with English translations that had been done in Macedonia, for instance, but sounded too strange for even our generous threshold of foreignness. These we revised—using the original text and other speakers/writers of the language, which is why multiple translators occasionally appear.

Much of this collection is the result of chance encounters or word-of-mouth communication and Sunday-afternoon sessions of joint translating and revising. A number of graduate and undergraduate students have helped—as researchers and translators and word-processing geniuses. In every way, this has been a collaborative effort—an effort that may, for a moment, create the impression of having produced a solid collection of texts, but that has really been a constantly revisable, uncertain affair.

■ □ ■ □ ■

ACKNOWLEDGMENTS

The editors wish to thank the University of Ottawa for its generous support toward the realization of this project. We would also
like to acknowledge the contribution and precious help of our research assistants, Michèle Healy, Mara Bertelsen, Bernard Aladdin,
Brent DeVoss, and Ruxandra Lungu. We are particularly indebted
to the following contributing editors, who helped us with their advice and the selection and translation of authors and texts from the
different countries: Edi Bregu and Delina Fico (Albania); Elizabeta
Bakovska (Macedonia); Dubravka Djurić (Serbia); Asja Hafner and
Celia Hawkesworth (Bosnia); Zrinka Stahuljak (Croatia); Dr. Darja
Završek and Dr. Metka Zupančić (Slovenia); Dr. Miglena Nikol-
china (Bulgaria); Jozefina Komporalj and Adam Sorkin (Romania);
Jana Juránová (Slovakia); Andrée Collier-Zaleska and Dr. Bernadette
Higgins (Czech Republic); Dr. Alois Woldan (Ukraine); Dr. Eva
Hausbacher and Dr. Tatyana Barshunova (Russia); Irina Pivnick
and Ela Rusak (Poland); Dr. Cheryl Dueck (former East Germany);
Dr. Ausma Cimdina (Latvia); Barbi Pilvre and Dr. Leena Kurvet-
Käosaar (Estonia).

EDITORS' INTRODUCTION:
WOMEN'S SPACE AND WOMEN'S WRITING
IN POST-COMMUNIST EUROPE

The present anthology is a selection of prose written by women authors after 1989 from countries that were previously referred to in the West as Eastern Europe. The term East Central Europe is geographically and historically more adequate, which is why we use it in the title and throughout this introduction. Literature by women writers from East Central Europe in English translation has been either underrepresented in existing anthologies, such as *The Eagle and the Crow: Modern Polish Short Stories* (ed. Teresa Halikowska and George Hyde, Serpent's Tail, 1997), *The Day Tito Died: Contemporary Slovenian Stories* (ed. Drago Jančar et al., Forest Books, 1994), and *Estonian Short Stories* (ed. Kajar Pruul, Darlene Reddaway, and Ritva Poom, Northwestern University Press, 1995), or collected in anthologies dedicated to literature by women that focus on one or, at most, two national literatures, such as *Allskin and Other Tales by Contemporary Czech Women* (ed. Alexandra Büchler, Women in Translation, 1998), *The Veiled Landscape: Slovenian Women's Writing* (ed. Zdravko Duša, Slovenian Office for Women's Policy, 1995), *Present Imperfect: Stories by Russian Women* (ed. Ayesha Kagal, Natasha Perova, and Helena Goscilo, Westview Press, 1996), and *Russian and Polish Women's Fiction* (ed. Helena Goscilo, University of Tennessee Press, 1985). *The Third Shore* is the first anthology in English to offer a selection of women writers' prose from eighteen countries and sixteen different languages, thereby covering most of the region, from the south to north: Albania, the now independent states of former Yugoslavia (Croatia, Slovenia, Bosnia and Herzegovina, Serbia and Montenegro, Macedonia), Bulgaria, Romania, Hungary, Slovakia, Czech Republic, Ukraine, Russia, Poland, former East Germany, Lithuania, Latvia, and Estonia. The only country missing is Belarus, for the simple reason that no texts from this country were available. The volume thus aims at filling a gap in the knowledge about contemporary literature by women from this region; as such it is also a contribution to the writing of East Central European women's literary history.

We have used the term *women's writing* or *women writers* despite some methodological considerations that need to be addressed. In the European context, the term *women's writing* is not unproblematic. It has often been used in a derogatory sense to refer to women's literary production, which, measured by a male-dominated literary establishment, was considered of a lower aesthetic value and therefore unworthy of being included in the literary canon. In the West German context,[1] the term was linked to feminism, to the women's movement of the 1970s. It was used in West Germany to refer to writings that openly supported the goals of the women's movement and, therefore, carried an obvious political message pertaining to "women's liberation." The flip side of such a definition of women's writing was that it often ignored texts of the highest quality simply because they were not explicitly political. In East Germany, just like in the rest of the region, on the other hand, since "gender" in the sense used in Western scholarship was an unknown category, women's writing was not even acknowledged as needing a different reflection or presenting different issues than literature written by men. By the same token, for the longest time, literature written by women in East Central Europe was not considered as something in need of special consideration. In this respect, it is noteworthy that in many countries there were few women who wrote prose; poetry was *the* feminine genre. This fact reveals the stereotypes that defined women's writing, which was often considered emotional or lacking the capacity to produce larger literary forms of quality, such as the novel. If women wrote prose, the authors most recognized were those who remained closest to the literary standards considered as "high" literature. These, again, were set by a male-dominated critical establishment.

Another concept of women's writing was developed in France under the term *écriture féminine,* which has remained somewhat problematic to translate into English.[2] It referred to the capacity of women's writing to disrupt ingrained assumptions about aesthetics and literature and extolled qualities that were traditionally considered weaknesses—such as lack of coherence, rationality, and logic—to undermine those very same "qualities" considered as the norm in a phallocentric order of things. *Écriture féminine* claimed the power to subvert the system that confined the manifestation of the feminine to the opposite or lack of the masculine—and to do so by using those very same "missing" qualities.

Neither approach to women's writing quite corresponds to the profile and background of the texts gathered in this volume. The texts presented here are mostly by already established authors; only a few are at the beginning of a promising literary career. By no means can their texts be qualified as "women's writing" in the sense of lacking literary quality. These texts do not necessarily address issues of women's liberation either, although they often reflect or deconstruct prevailing patriarchal attitudes. They may have an open or a hidden feminist message, or they may not; in some, one may identify similarities to *écriture féminine* aesthetics. Our selection was based on texts that we collected over the course of several years with the precious help and suggestions of a whole network of scholars, writers, and translators from Europe and North America. It thus reflects both our personal preferences as well as those of colleagues and friends who have contributed to this selection with their knowledge and expertise and who made this anthology possible. Our intention was to maintain in our selection a variety of different literary styles. We also wanted to let the authors speak on various topics and from the point of view of their diverse national and cultural backgrounds so as to underline the distinctiveness and, often, innovative character of literature written by women from East Central Europe. As Alexandra Büchler remarks, there is still "little understanding of the specificity of women's writing" in the Czech Republic and other post-Communist countries as there is little understanding of women's issues or the need to theorize them.[3] By talking about women's writing, and particularly women's prose from East Central Europe, we as editors of this volume also wish to make a statement concerning the lack of a literary history of women's writing, especially prose, from this region.

The texts selected in this anthology are different not only in their style but also in their literary aesthetics, some carrying a stronger referentiality to recent historical events (such as the texts by Ljiljana Đurđić, Alma Lazarevska, Carmen Francesca Banciu, Jana Juráňová, Kerstin Hensel), others less (Zsuzsa Kapecz, Renata Šerelytė) or not at all (Sanja Lovrenčić, Nora Ikstena). They can and should be read and understood, on the one hand, in the context of their own literary and sociopolitical history and, on the other, as products of the authors' different backgrounds and aesthetic approaches. Our selection thus offers a wide range of topics that women's literature of the 1990s has dealt with across the region. What Harold B. Segel claims is a dominant trait of the literatures of these countries, namely, that they are "undeniably bound up with the political history of the region,"[4] is only partly true if we look at the variety of subjects explored in these texts. This variety of content and aesthetics was produced despite the fact that the region for half a century shared a similar political system and its discourses; therefore, these texts by no means "thematize in a recognizable way mere variations of a given common."[5]

Former Communist Europe may have conveyed the impression of a unified political and regional entity. However, we agree with Susan Gal and Gail Kligman that regional boundaries are constructs cultivated both in the West and the East rather than a self-evident consequence of historical developments and even less of cultural resemblance: "The apparent separation of regions was and is a consequence of political economic relations and discursive interactions among them."[6] Historical and cultural differences among the eighteen countries presented here were vast, particularly in regard to their statehood as well as their cultural and literary developments, not to mention their linguistic diversity.[7] While traditions in these countries differed widely, most of them share a long history of several centuries of foreign rule on their respective territories under different empires. Even though they were governed for nearly half a century by the same Communist ideology, the operations of the Communist system in each individual country differed from each other. The year 1989 brought liberation from Soviet controls to most of Communist Europe. Former Yugoslavia, however, two years later plummeted into an atrocious civil war, as did parts of the former Soviet empire. These few facts may convey a brief impression of the complexity of this region. The texts gathered in this anthology speak from these different backgrounds and histories, often carrying a local color that is sometimes easily recognizable but may also remain hidden between the lines. We therefore added notes to the texts in order to help the reader who is unfamiliar with certain geographic or historical references or local customs.

Part of the common experience of having lived under the Communist regime was the fact that many intellectuals and artists left their respective countries for the West, thus choosing a life of emigration and exile. Due to the totalitarian character of the Communist system and often the lack of, or serious restrictions on, freedom of movement, strong intellectual diasporas from Romania, Bulgaria, Hungary, and other countries started to build in the West as far back as the 1950s. We have included in this anthology three writers who have been living in emigration: Carmen Francesca Banciu from Romania and Natasza Goerke from Poland, both living in Germany, and Gabriele Eckart from former East Germany, living in the United States.

All the previously mentioned differences notwithstanding, we can agree that the year 1989 brought significant changes to this part of Europe, not all of which were necessarily positive. The collapse of communism in most countries forged the term *transition* in its different local variations. The ups and downs of the "transition" have been particularly palpable in women's lives. Regarding the Bulgarian women's situation, Dimitrina Petrova says that "the 'revolution' of 1989 left the patriarchal system of power intact, transforming its more superficial manifestations from bad to worse."[8] This can be said for the rest of the region as well. The word *emancipation* itself carries a stigma from the Communist period. The so-called women's federations that existed in the Communist countries in lieu of a women's movement were little more than state-controlled entities with no scope for any questioning of women's real position in the Communist system; this was considered unnecessary given the fact that communism officially supported women's emancipation.[9] In the 1970s, there were feminist groups and some forms of feminist grassroots activism in former Yugoslavia and Hungary, and a women's peace movement emerged in the 1980s in East Germany,[10] but one cannot talk of a large-scale women's movement. The apparent benefits that the Communist system put into place for women—full-time employment, free day care, job security during maternity leave, support for single mothers—in reality reinforced women's double burden and did not alter their traditional role in the family. It is undeniable that communism did ensure women's equal participation in the labor force with equal wages for the same work. However, on the average, women still earned about 30 percent less than men for the simple reason that they worked in less prestigious jobs. They were also virtually absent from any important political and decision-making positions. Women were considered the second breadwinner to help the family make ends meet, and they also carried the main responsibility for housework and childrearing as communism did almost nothing to change the traditional gender roles in the home. Olga Tóth from Hungary calls this a "no envy, no pity" situation.[11]

Another aspect of women's "emancipation" during communism was, in most countries, free access to abortion. Romania was the starkest exception here, where abortion was illegal unless pregnancy threatened the woman's health or if she was over forty and had ful-filled her "duty" to the state by giving birth to at least five children.[12] In most other countries, abortion had been either fully legalized by the end of the 1960s (Soviet Union, East Germany, Yugoslavia) or made available under certain restrictions (Bulgaria, Poland,[13] Hungary). Although to many Western women this may seem an enviable freedom over one's reproductive rights, one has to look more closely at this aspect of women's "emancipation." Free (or relatively free) access to abortion in most countries compensated for the lack of contraceptives on the market and was a consequence of nonexistent public sexual education. Reproduction thus became the sole respon-sibility of women while it was regulated by the (father) state.

With the "transition," another way of controlling women's sexu-ality emerged. Not only have the abortion laws been toughened in several countries, but it can be said that "women and femininity are currently mobilized throughout the region to reanchor national and sexual essentialism."[14] Along with the back-to-the-hearth currents in politics, pornography is flourishing, poverty has driven many women into prostitution, and the trafficking of women has reached alarming proportions. "Romanian women are prostituting them-selves for a single dollar in towns on the Romanian-Yugoslav border.

In the midst of all of this, our anti-choice nationalist governments are threatening our rights to abortion and telling us to multiply, to give birth to more Poles, Hungarians, Czechs, Croats, Slovaks."[15] Because of the negative and double-standard connotations associated with the notion of women's "emancipation" under Communist rule, it has been difficult to publicly criticize state policies developed after 1989 that have negatively affected women's lives and led to the loss of certain positive aspects of Communist "emancipation" policies, such as full employment and job security or child-care facilities.

Women's organizing and feminist activism have developed slowly after 1989. They cannot be measured by Western standards and expectations. Instead of seeking a unified women's movement in East Central Europe, it is more appropriate to talk about women's groups and activities that influence and improve both women's political and media representation. Although there are many women's groups with different ideological orientations and goals, there are few organizations that call themselves "feminist," such as the Polish Feminist Association or the Feminist Network in Hungary, and they are usually very small. Feminism carries a negative stigma in most of East Central Europe, and there are reasons why even those women who are involved in activities or research that in the West would be considered feminist like to say, "I do this although I am not a feminist." The word itself "conjures up an array of pejorative associations: one can be accused of being a feminist."[16] The post-1989 political discourse reveals a lot of back-to-the-hearth intentions. Perestroika-father Mikhail Gorbachev wanted to return women to "their purely womanly mission," and Czech writer and political leader Václav Havel said about feminism that he "assumes that it is not merely the invention of a few hysterics, bored housewives, or rejected mistresses."[17] On the other hand, there are many reservations among East Central European women themselves toward Western feminism. It is often perceived as too normative, rigid, and humorless. Given the Communist past, which was all about prescriptive discourses and behavior, "with its prohibitions on certain words and thoughts,"[18] the source of such perceptions of certain aspects of Western feminism may be clear. Many East Central European women also have a different attitude toward chivalry, which is often welcome as a nostalgic return to pre-Communist forms of cultural interaction between the sexes.[19] Many women also perceive the emphasis on one's "femininity" as liberation from a totalitarian body image. The consciousness that the image of "femininity" imported through the Western media may be just another form of oppression has not gained much ground yet.

However, in spite of the above, much feminist activism and awareness can be noticed in the 1990s, such as the opening of shelters for abused women and children, the publication of feminist magazines, and at certain universities, the offering of courses with a focus on gender. There have also been gains in uncovering a feminist past and women's contributions to the national cultures and literatures. What Ruth Zernova claims for the literary scene in the former Soviet Union, namely, "that literature in the USSR was a man's job,"[20] can, without exaggeration, be said for the rest of the countries included here as well, regardless of their cultural differences. A writing of women's literary history still has a long way to go in East Central Europe. What is still true for the writing of literary history in the West, namely, that the literary canon is measured by standards set by a male-dominated establishment, is even more true in this region. The efforts initiated over the course of the past decade to begin the writing of women's literary history and to recognize women's particular cultural contributions in the past and present have come both from within East Central Europe as well as from scholars living and writing in the West.[21] The present volume intends to make a contribution in this direction as well.

The stories by the two Albanian authors, Diana Çuli and Mira Mekşi, in many ways reflect the contradictions of contemporary Albania, a country at a crossroads of modernization and still prevailing, strongly patriarchal customs. To Albania, which in many ways was still a medieval country in the first half of the twentieth century, with high rates of poverty, illiteracy, blood feuds, and the subjugation of women, communism brought some radical changes. Under Enver Hoxha, radical modernization took place, which also gave women legal equality. However, under Hoxha, Albania also increasingly became isolated from its previous allies. After Hoxha's death in 1985 and more so after 1989, the country started opening up again. In 1994, the Women's Center was created in Tirana as a documentation and support center for women and women's NGOs.

Çuli and Mekşi are both actively involved in contemporary Albanian women's issues and literary life. Çuli is an active member of the Independent Women's Forum founded in 1991. Her story, "Plaza de España," reflects the life of an Albanian woman intellectual who travels the world in the 1990s while civil war in former Yugoslavia is tearing apart the peace in the Balkans. What gives the story its particular actuality is the inclusion of this external political reality mingled with the reality of contemporary Albanian women's lives, where an emancipated lifestyle for some intertwines with the burden of a traditional morality and sometimes deadly customs for others. Mekşi, editor of the literary magazine *Mehr Licht*, in her thrilling story "The Shears," mixes Albanian reality and imagery with a poetic universe inspired by her background in Spanish and Latin American literature, in particular J. L. Borges and G. G. Márquez.

Literature from Croatia, Serbia, Bosnia, Slovenia, and Montenegro cannot be fully understood without reference to the larger context of Yugoslav literary history. Officially, former Yugoslavia recognized four national literatures: Serbian, Croatian (written essentially in the same language, Serbo-Croatian), Macedonian, and Slovenian. Literature written in the languages of national minorities was also recognized, the largest being Albanian and Hungarian. Because of Yugoslavia's particular position among the Communist countries and its independence from the Soviet Union, post–World War II literary history was also shaped differently than in the rest of the region. The socialist realist aesthetic canon that left its mark on the other countries' literatures was not dominant in Yugoslavia: "Yugoslav literature never experienced the rigors of the *socialist realist* canon. . . . It developed almost without political obstructions throughout the postwar years to the present."[22] Despite the sharing of the same group-oriented discourse that was characteristic of communism in general, in the 1970s and 1980s a conscious female voice entered both the Serbian and Croatian literary scene, changing the way women were represented in literature. This process in literature was closely linked to the emergence of fairly strong feminist circles both in Belgrade and Zagreb, the capital cities of Serbia and Croatia, a phenomenon that was unique in the region. Some prominent authors also known to English-speaking readers, such as Slavenka Drakulić, were directly linked to a feminist group in Zagreb.[23] Topics that authors of this generation explored include women's sexuality, the body, gender roles and stereotypes, and mother-daughter relationships from a new angle. Postmodern narrative strategies were also used for the first time, particularly by Dubravka Ugrešić, another well-known author. Women of this generation were breaking with long-standing patriarchal traditions, which were alive and well under communism, by asserting their subjectivity and individualism. It is not surprising that Yugoslav feminists were accused of propagating bourgeois individualism, something that should have been overcome in a socialist society. Following the outbreak of the civil war and the nationalist propaganda war that accompanied it both in Serbia and Croatia, several of these authors wrote against the current in the Croatian political landscape. As a consequence, the Croatian media accused them in the most vulgar terms of being witches, and both Drakulić and Ugrešić, along with a few others, had to leave the country.[24]

The Croatian author selected for this volume, Sanja Lovrenčić, belongs to a younger generation of writers. We chose her so as to bring in a voice from this new generation who remained and wrote from within the country, relatively unknown to an English-speaking audience. Lovrenčić's prose is characterized by the presence of parallel realities, which often envelop her stories in a fairy-tale-like aura. She thereby reclaims the space for the fantastic threatened by the harsh external political realities. She has explored this sensibility, this "seeking refuge in the fantastic, absurd, ironic, macabre"[25] through her work with the GONG group, a group of young writers (five women and two men) who have written twenty-five short plays together.

Slovenian literature had its own trends within former Yugoslavia. According to Nina Kovič, in the post–World War II period, there were quite a few women writers, but she also stresses that these writers were poets rather than prose writers.[26] The modernism of the 1960s and 1970s was also reflected in Slovenian women's poetry. The past three decades saw the emergence of several interesting women writers and poets, among them Berta Bojetu and Maja Vidmar. The end of the 1980s not only redefined the concept of national art in Slovenia, together with Neue Slowenische Kunst and retrogardism, but also reflected on the militancy of the Yugoslav geopolitical region before it plunged into the disaster of the civil war, which, luckily, touched Slovenia only briefly.[27] Lela B. Njatin, one of the most important and recognized younger Slovenian writers, thematizes these topics in "Why Do These Black Worms Fly Just Everywhere I Am Myself Only Accidentally." In an experimental style, Njatin talks about the Yugoslav civil war from the perspective of the generation who grew up with tales about World War II from their parents' generation, thus stressing the absurdity and omnipresence of war, death, and decay.

The civil war brought infinitely more destruction and suffering to the people of Bosnia and Herzegovina. It comes as no surprise that the war figures prominently in contemporary literature from this country. Alma Lazarevska's award-winning story "How We Killed the Sailor" is a beautiful and powerful account of a couple's life in besieged Sarajevo. It is told from the perspective of day-to-day conversations in their room, through which the reader witnesses the effects of the war on their daily life and the terrible destruction of human lives in the besieged city as well as the deeply seated human need and desire to prevent such destruction, be it only on a symbolic level.

In Serbia, the civil war has not been adequately and sufficiently thematized in literature. Reasons for this denial are multiple and still being reflected on by progressive Serbian intellectuals, such as the circle around the feminist magazine *Pro Femina*. Of the two authors representing Serbian literature in this volume, one is an ethnic Serb (Ljiljana Đurđić), the other a Jewish Hungarian (Judita Šalgo) who chose her second language, Serbo-Croatian, for literary expression. Đurđić's "20 Firula Road" is a nostalgic remembering of the old Yugoslavia, abundant in historical references, while it also hints at the terrible way in which the country later fell apart. Šalgo's story, on the other hand, does not offer any particular historical references. The editors preferred that not all narratives from the former Yugoslavia center around the topic of the civil war because this would not adequately represent recent prose production. There is, however, some geographic referentiality in Šalgo's story to her city, Novi Sad, including some local customs, such as making sauerkraut. Intertwined with this are elements of the fantastic. The author also offers a subtle reflection on writing and being a woman.

Macedonia gained its independence without major skirmishes. Macedonians, like Slovenians, had their own national language and literature within former Yugoslavia. Some contemporary Macedonian writers add archaic Church Slavonic language as an expression of national pride about their cultural contribution to the creation of the Old Slavonic script and language in the tenth century. Many contemporary Macedonian writers, on the other hand, offer a critical approach toward the traditional, including folklore, which they often integrate into their writing. This can be seen to some degree in Jadranka Vladova's narrative, "The Same Old Story," which abounds in imagery full of Macedonian local color. She takes a critical distance from this Garden of Eden type of mythical idealization of her country—something Macedonia did carry in the minds of the Yugoslav people[28]—by adding some quasi-surrealistic elements.

Post–World War II Bulgarian literature largely adhered to the doctrine of socialist realism. However, there were Bulgarian writers who opposed the schematic postulates of this doctrine. Women's contribution to Bulgarian literature has been acknowledged in regard to their poetry, but no literary history has yet been written about women's prose and fiction. One of the reasons for this is that poetry, by men or women, has always dominated Bulgarian literary history. Another reason can be found in the use of the femininity myth by Bulgarian women poets. The myth of the "eternal feminine" they explored is anchored very strongly in Bulgarian culture as well as in mythical ideas about the mother-daughter bond. In fiction, women were recognized as writers of historical novels because this form was never perceived as particularly "feminine" and in need of special recognition. The first recognized post–World War II female novelist, Blaga Dimitrova, emerged in the 1960s and brought in a female point of view along with textual experimentation against the socialist realist current. The 1980s are characterized by the emergence of an *écriture féminine,* followed by a certain stylistic simplicity in the 1990s. Despite this simplicity, the younger generation of women writers manages to bring in unusual, sometimes even shocking topics. Hristina Marinova is one of these young writers. In her award-winning story "The Herbarium," she deconstructs powerful myths inherent in Bulgarian society, such as the above mentioned mother-daughter bond, when she writes about the devastating and finally lethal impact an incestuous mother has on her daughter's life.

Romanian fiction after World War II, under the Soviet regime and the dogmatic aesthetics of socialist realism, was cut off from its traditions. Many writers emigrated, and a diasporic Romanian intellectual community developed in several Western countries. During the 1960s, following Ceaușescu's takeover of the Communist leadership, socialist realism was replaced by the somewhat more vaguely defined Socialist Humanism, which made the appearance of literary experiments and avant-garde movements possible.[29] However, following a visit to China and North Korea in 1971, Ceaușescu launched his own "cultural revolution," which meant total control over cultural production. This resulted in a new wave of emigration of Romanian intellectuals. Those writers who stayed, such as Gabriela Adameşteanu, chose photographic realism to expose everyday drudgery in Ceaușescu's "Age of Light." Censorship in those years prevented many authors from publishing or allowed them to publish only parts of their work. It was not until after 1989 that postmodernism and textualism reestablished the link between Romanian literature and the rest of the world.

Of the two Romanian authors selected, Carmen Francesca Banciu is one of the many writers living and writing in exile, in her case Germany. She now writes both in her native language, Romanian, and in her adopted language, German. Her text "A Day Without a President," which is an excerpt from a novel with the same title, raises a number of the philosophical and existential questions faced by the generation that knew both the pre- and post-Ceaușescu period. The fragmented sentence structure reflects the loss of a solid point of reference. Daniela Crăsnaru, one of Romania's most prominent writers, in her story "Everything's OK," fuses the topic of the Romanian living in emigration with the topos of the Oedipal son. The story could also be read as an allegory of the emigrant's ties with the motherland, ties that can never be completely cut, a theme also present in Banciu's text.

In Hungary, women writers have been generally marginalized and underrepresented in national literature.[30] *Women's writing* is still a term used with disdain, even among women writers themselves. Women's place in literature is generally somewhat better acknowledged in poetry, but even there, Ágnes Nemes Nagy is recognized as the most prominent poet to date for representing a "'masculine' type of objectivity, the only publicly acceptable approach."[31] Prose writers, such as Erzsébet Galgóczy, Magda Szabó, or Anna Jókai wrote about women's realities in Communist Hungary in the 1960s, 1970s, and 1980s. The transition after 1989 opened the space for women writers, but it also meant a decline in subsidized publishing and smaller edition sizes thus forcing women writers to find secondary sources of income, usually in translation, children's literature, editing, or even nonliterary professions. A more positive aspect of the transition was that interest in Hungarian writers living and writing in the large diasporas of neighboring Romania, Yugoslavia (now Serbia), and Slovakia increased. Women writers in those diasporas thus also received more attention and recognition. In the 1990s, a new voice emerged among young women writers, which talks very openly and in a language unheard of during communism about female sexuality and gender relations. Dóra Esze's work is an example from this trend. In her intricately composed narrative "Like Two Peas in a Pod," from which we are presenting an excerpt, she chooses her characters from among a new class of Budapest city youth whose values and lifestyle are not only far from what the communist ideal would have preached but also strangely reflect the lack of guidance and role models in their parents' generation. Zsuzsa Kapecz, on the other hand, in her fluid short prose "South Wind and a Sunny Day" looks at posttransition Hungary through the eyes of the generation born in the 1950s, who lived their formative years under communism and are thus able to compare the old with the new from a different angle than the generation Esze refers to.

Slovakia and the Czech Republic, although both parts of former Czechoslovakia, each had their respective languages and literary histories. However, they both shared the same political fate after World War II. Following the Communist takeover in 1948, literature, and art in general, became an ideological tool. Many writers either went underground or into exile. Not many women published in the 1950s in the Czech part of the country, and those who did served mainly as a "token for the proclaimed equality of gender."[32] In Slovakia, most women writers of this generation opted for socialist realism.[33] In the 1960s, which culminated in the Prague Spring in 1968, there was a cultural renaissance "where experimentation was once again more welcome and literature was passionately debated."[34] After the brutal crushing of the Prague Spring, censorship was renewed, and once again, writers went underground or into exile. Thus there were writers who published in the official publishing houses, another group who published in samizdat, and the third group in exile. Among Czech writers, several important female authors became samizdat authors, such as Eda Kriseová and Lenka Procházková. The latter gained the reputation of being a typical author of "women's literature" for her treatment of male-female relationships. As in many other countries in the region, *women's literature* was and still is considered a pejorative term to describe romantic novels, and good women writers, although too numerous to even list here, are simply being ignored by the literary establishment.[35]

Not much has changed since communism regarding the perception of women's issues and women's literature both in Slovakia and in the Czech Republic. Similarly, the question of women's rights was and still is ignored. As Büchler remarks, referring to the women's movement at the turn of the century, "it is ironic that the 'women's question' was raised far more rigorously almost a hundred years ago."[36] In Slovakia, emancipation is still often viewed, even by women writers, as a fusion of an ideal of the woman devoted to family duties and only partly actively involved in public life. A further reason for this reserved attitude toward feminist ideas, besides deeply rooted patriarchal values that remained unchallenged under communism, is the deep distrust toward any ideology that may be perceived as polarizing. It is, of course, ironic that whereas the issue of human rights has been such a hot topic among those who opposed the post-1968 regime, not much has changed regarding the treatment of women in society to date.

Slovak writer Jana Juráňová, who is also a feminist activist and editor of the feminist journal *Aspekt,* points out precisely these contradictions in her hilarious "A Little Bedtime Story." She exposes the hypocritical and sexist attitude of her countrymen toward women through her comic portrayal of a human-rights activist. Juráňová criticizes the double standard in post-Communist Slovakia when it comes to human rights, which don't seem to include a woman's right to be taken seriously in her intellectual work and ambition. Besides sexism, she also touches upon another ignored topic, namely, homophobia. Etela Farkašová, the other Slovak author, already attracted attention in the 1970s with a prose that was quite different from other women writers' at the time. A central character in her prose is the educated woman "who tries, or has tried, to achieve something in life."[37] Her story "Day by Day" is a young, educated mother's tale of her relationship with her handicapped son. This first-person narrative not only undermines myths of happy motherhood but also draws attention to the socially marginalized. Farkašová's account of the draining repetitiveness of this young woman's life, one that has destroyed her relationship with her husband, despite some rare moments of happy bonding with her son, reflects her hopelessness regarding any change for the better.

Daniela Fischerová represents Czech women's literature in this volume. Fischerová belongs to the middle generation of Czech writers. Her story "Far and Near," just like the plays for which she is mostly known, presents an "existential puzzle"[38] and follows in the footsteps of Czech literary tradition with "its inclination toward the fantastic, the absurd, the grotesque, and the surreal, its penchant for political allegory and satire, its sense of irony and black humor, its lopsided view of reality."[39]

In Ukraine, Stalin's takeover resulted in a decimation of the Ukrainian intelligentsia and a "cleansing" of the Ukrainian libraries. Following Stalin's death, the 1960s brought a period of national and cultural revival where a new generation, known as the "Sixties" wrote against the black-and-white portrayal and cast a critical look at social and national issues.[40] As a consequence of a new wave of repressions between 1965 and 1972, an underground literary life was established. In the 1970s and 1980s young authors who found inspiration in Ukrainian mythology and the country's historical past entered the literary scene. Today's literature consists largely of historical novels and prose that deals with the social as well as the fantastic and folkloric. Much of the most interesting younger Ukrainian literature can be described as postmodern in its playful and parodic demystification of national values. "This literature reveals and challenges the structures of political, social, and cultural power that prevailed in the Soviet period and enjoy an afterlife in post-Soviet times."[41] The deconstruction of power structures is particularly present in prose that explores the erotic. However, Marko Pavlyshyn remarks that the "heterosexual male point of view" has hardly been challenged.[42] Oksana Zabuzhko, one of the most interesting and provocative younger Ukrainian writers, certainly writes against this current, in particular in her brilliant and witty novel "Field Studies in Ukrainian Sex" (*Pol'ovi doslidzheniia z ukrains'kogo seksu*, Kiev: Vidavnitstvo Zgoda, 1996). In her brilliant short narrative "I, Milena," she again speaks from a woman's point of view. By adding elements of the fantastic, she investigates her character's identity crisis within the context of the new power of the visual media, thus endowing her text with a particular actuality.

In the Soviet Union, despite the fact that women had equal access to education and were active and equal participants in the labor force, including technical fields and industry—"the Soviet Union boasts more women engineers than all other countries combined" [43]—they were not present in the decision-making bodies and were virtually absent from the political elite; this once again confirms the hypocrisy of the Communist espousal of gender equality.

This gap between the theory and the reality of women's lives was expressed in the now classic novella by Natalia Baranskaia from 1969, "A Week Like Any Other Week" (*Nedelia kak nedelia*), which for the first time discussed women's lives in the Soviet Union and their double or—as some say—triple burden: that of mother, wife, and working woman. [44] The 1980s brought the "new women's prose" (*novaia zhenskaia proza*), with Liudmila Petrushevskaia as one of its major representatives. Her prose is a good example of how "the 'new prose' has reconstituted woman's perspective as subject and object: her purview is not confined to domestic and professional matters, nor her existence reduced to that of a stock character in the stale tragicomedy of contemporary *byt*. Her week is *not* like any other." [45] Ljubov' Romanchuk, on the other hand, is a young author who experiments with science fiction. She writes against the current in Russian science fiction, including science fiction written by women, that reflects "misogynist or stereotyped views about women." [46] Her story "The Cyber" is the only piece in our collection from the genre of science fiction. Romanchuk's ironic narrative style ridicules and deconstructs the arrogance of a reductionist approach to science that excludes women and everything associated with the feminine, thus offering a criticism of institutionalized knowledge.

In Poland after 1945, under Soviet rule, women were assigned full equality with men in all spheres of life. However, just like in the other parts of East Central Europe, this equality was applied more in theory than in practice. Two famous women from contemporary Polish literature are poets Julia Hartwig and Nobel Prize laureate Wisława Szymborska. Writer Jadwiga Żylińska is the first Polish writer with a consistent interest in Polish women in history, mainly those in positions of power. The first interest in feminist theory dates back to the 1980s and resulted in a five-volume collective publication with the title *Transgressions,* coauthored by a group of young writers over the period of several years. "The books helped to introduce and strengthen new tendencies which developed in the literature of the early 1990s when the question of the understanding of a woman's identity, expressed by women themselves from within their existential experience, came to the forefront of intellectual life." [47]

Currently, a whole still fairly young generation of excellent women prose writers is present on the Polish literary scene. Many would argue that the most interesting literature coming from contemporary Poland is written by women. Olga Tokarczuk, one of Poland's most popular writers, and Natasza Goerke are only two examples. Tokarczuk has been praised for her original style and choice of subjects independent of literary fashions. Her novel *E.E.,* from which this volume presents an excerpt, is set in Wrocław at the beginning of the twentieth century, "when the fame of Freud, working in neighboring Vienna, was spreading in ever wider circles." [48] In the excerpt, Tokarczuk tells the story of a young girl and the transitions in her psychology and body as she gets her first period. Goerke, who for years has lived abroad in Hamburg, Germany, has been writing in Polish and publishing in Poland. Her story "The Third Shore," which provided the title for this anthology, uses bitter humor about exile to explore a young woman's experience of living torn between exile and nostalgia for the homeland.

The present volume includes two authors from former East Germany, even though the country stopped existing in 1990. Both Gabriele Eckart in her story "The Men and the Gentlemen" and Kerstin Hensel in her narrative "Dance by the Canal" are good examples "that it is possible to write GDR [East German] literature even after the demise of the GDR." [49] The historical distance now acquired allows for a critical reevaluation of East Germany and has opened up the space for previously unexplored or taboo topics, such as child abuse and lesbian love (Hensel) or the many facets and dealings of the Stasi, the infamous secret police (Eckart).

During the forty years (1949–89) of the country's existence, East German women writers were an important part of the country's literary establishment. Although East Germany, just like the rest of the region and unlike West Germany, did not have a women's movement in the

1970s, East German women writers started to address issues that their Western sisters would label feminist. Thus Christa Wolf in her now classic novel "Cassandra" (*Kassandra,* Darmstadt: Luchterhand, 1983; English translation, New York: Farrar, Straus & Giroux, 1984) rewrote the story of the Trojan War through the eyes of the Trojan princess and prophetess Cassandra. Irmtraud Morgner (1933–90) has been called *the* East German feminist. In "The Life and Adventures of Trobadora Beatrice as Chronicled by Her Minstrel Laura" (*Leben und Abenteuer der Trobadora Beatriz nach Zeugnissen ihrer Spielfrau Laura,* Berlin: Aufbau Verlag, 1974; English translation by Jeanine Blackwell, Lincoln: University of Nebraska Press, 2000), Morgner not only created a novel mostly innovative in its form but wrote a critical *herstory* of women's condition under various forms of patriarchal oppression from the late Middle Ages through the alleged liberation of the 1968 student movement to "socialist paradise" East Germany.

The cultural histories of the three Baltic states, Lithuania, Latvia, and Estonia, have at least one thing in common, namely, that "the history of the Baltic states has been one of occupation and suppression."[50] Under Stalin, 300,000 Lithuanians were deported and only about 30,000 survived. Life under the Soviets trained Lithuanians to use a language full of verbal nuances and to speak and write in codes. Under the socialist realist dogma no underground literature was written in Lithuania. In the 1960s, experimentation with stream-of-consciousness techniques entered Lithuanian literature. Women writers emerged in the 1970s. Renata Šerelytė is a promising young writer who started publishing in the 1990s. Through the eyes of a young female protagonist living in the countryside, her story "Lady with Cowshit" reflects, in a succinct way, life in the country and socioeconomic issues after the end of the Soviet empire.

Latvian literary history proudly mentions Zenta Maurina as a great female intellectual from the first half of the twentieth century, even though she wrote most of her works in German during her exile following World War II.[51] In 1940, Latvia was first occupied by the Soviets, and as a consequence 35,000 people were deported to Siberia. After 1945, 90 percent of the Latvian intelligentsia emigrated, and the Latvian diaspora spread over many Western countries, including the United States and Canada. Poet Veronika Stērelte and prose writer Ilze Šķipsna belong to this generation. Until the end of the 1950s, Latvian literature developed mainly in the diaspora. In Soviet-occupied Latvia, literature was placed under very strict ideological control. However, certain literary innovations were tolerated between the 1960s and the 1980s. After 1991, a young generation of women writers entered the literary scene, among them poet Maira Asare, playwright Lelde Stumbre, prose writers Gundega Repše, and Nora Ikstena, whose story "Pleasures of the Saints" we have selected for its dreamlike atmosphere, full of the fantastic.

Estonia's fate is very similar to that of Lithuania and Latvia. Following a brief period of independence between World War I and World War II, Estonia fell under Soviet control. Estonian writers had to adhere to the doctrine of socialist realism. However, unlike their Russian colleagues at the time, Estonian authors enjoyed more freedom, given Estonia's position as the Soviet "'display window' to the West."[52] By the end of the 1960s, modernism, greatly influenced by the absurd, began to permeate Estonian literature. The writers in the 1970s, such as Mari Saat, wrote about social problems. Maimu Berg, who published some unnoticed short stories in journals in the 1970s, entered the literary scene in the mid-1980s. Her story "The Mill Ghost," where she relates the tribulations of a female writer whose writing block lifts after she meets her (male) muse, is considered by some as "the seminal work and starting point for feminist issues in Estonian prose."[53] Kärt Hellermaa is an author of the 1990s whose novel "Alchemy" (*Alkeemia*) describes male-female relationships from the perspective of a woman in her forties who falls in love with a much younger man. Hellermaa deconstructs and ridicules not only the internalized prevailing social attitude that condemns such love affairs but also the representation of passion as a paroxysmal force.

Referring to Yuri Lotman, Roumiana Deltcheva talks about a shift in the East Central European historical and cultural paradigm. Instead of the revolutionary "recipe" to destroy the old and rebuild everything while denying the past, Lotman proposes a "gradual evolution and integration."[54] The title of the present volume, *The Third Shore,* was chosen because it reflects the contents and aesthetics of these texts, which were all written in the 1990s. The women writers from eighteen East Central European countries, despite their choice of different styles and topics, share similar concerns and an often unique openness for new forms of literary representation. They all evoke a "third shore," a third way that is not the way life and creativity used to connect before 1989 and not the way of the West either. While these writers may still be struggling with old patterns and a controversial Communist legacy, they are at the same time exploring new paradigms and claiming their own space in a new Europe.

Notes

1. We will be using concepts of women's writing developed in the Western European context since no similar theorizing of women's writing existed in Eastern Europe in the 1970s.

2. Moira Gatens, "Psychoanalysis and French Feminisms," *Feminism and Philosophy: Perspectives of Difference and Equality* (Bloomington, Ind.: Indiana University Press, 1991), 100–21.

3. Alexandra Büchler, ed., *Allskin and Other Tales by Contemporary Czech Women* (Seattle: Women in Translation, 1998), viii.

4. Harold B. Segel, "Introduction: The Literatures of Eastern Europe from 1945 to the Present," in *The Columbia Guide to the Literatures of Eastern Europe Since 1945* (New York: Columbia University Press, 2003), 7.

5. Gordana P. Crnković, "That Other Place," *Stanford Humanities Review* 1, 2–3 (Fall/Winter 1990), 133–40.

6. Susan Gal and Gail Kligman, *The Politics of Gender After Socialism: A Comparative Historical Essay* (Princeton, N.J.: Princeton University Press, 2000), 6.

7. Segel, "Introduction," 3.

8. Dimitrina Petrova, "The Winding Road to Emancipation in Bulgaria," in Nanette Funk and Magda Mueller, eds., *Gender Politics and Post-Communism: Reflections from Eastern Europe and the Former Soviet Union* (New York: Routledge, 1993), 27.

9. Chris Corrin, ed., *Superwoman and the Double Burden: Women's Experience of Change in Central and Eastern Europe and the Former Soviet Union* (London: Scarlet Press, 1992).

10. Ingrid Miethe, "Women's Movements in Unified Germany: Experiences and Expectations of East German Women," in Silke Roth and Sara Lennox, eds., *Feminist Movements in a Globalizing World: German and American Perspectives* (Washington, D.C.: American Institute for Contemporary German Studies, 2002), 43–59.

11. Olga Tóth, "No Envy, No Pity," in Funk and Mueller, eds., *Gender Politics and Post-Communism,* 215.

12. Herta Müller in her essay "Hunger and Silk" gives a gruesome account of the Ceauşescu era, especially regarding anti-abortion policies and their effect on women's lives. Herta Müller, "Hunger and Silk," trans. Luise von Flotow, *Delos* 21–22 (January 1998), 15–32.

13. Małgorzata Fuszara, "Abortion and the Formation of the Public Sphere in Poland," in Funk and Mueller, eds., *Gender Politics and Post-Communism,* 242.

14. Anikó Imre, "Gender, Literature, and Film in Contemporary East Central European Culture," *CLCWeb: Comparative Literature and Culture: A WWWeb Journal* 3.1 (2001), 4.

15. Slavenka Drakulić, *How We Survived Communism and Even Laughed* (New York: Harper Perennial, 1993), 132, quoted in Imre, "Gender, Literature, and Film in Contemporary East Central European Culture," 4.

16. Ewa Hauser, Barbara Heyns, and Jane Mansbridge, "Feminism in the Interstices of Politics and Culture: Poland in Transition," in Funk and Mueller, eds., *Gender Politics and Post-Communism,* 258.

17. Zillah Eisenstein, "Eastern European Male Democracies: A Problem of Unequal Equality," in Funk and Mueller, eds., *Gender Politics and Post-Communism,* 312, 314.

18. Hauser, Heyns, and Mansbridge, "Feminism in the Interstices of Politics and Culture," in Funk and Mueller, eds., *Gender Politics and Post-Communism,* 268.

19. Larissa Lissyutkina, "Soviet Women and the Crossroads of Perestroika," in Funk and Mueller, eds., *Gender Politics and Post-Communism,* 274.

20. Ruth Zernova, "Reflections on Women's Literature in the Soviet Union," in Albert Leong, ed., *Oregon Studies in Chinese and Russian Culture* (New York: Peter Lang, 1990), 207.

21. A few examples are Anna Fábri, *A szép tiltott táj felé: A magyar írónők története két századforduló között (1795–1905)* (Budapest, 1996) [*The History of Hungarian Women Writers Between Two Turns of the Centuries*]; *Contemporary Women's Literature in Serbia* (special issue of *Pro Femina,* Beograd, 1997); Zdravko Duša, ed., *The Veiled Landscape: Slovenian Women's Writing* (Ljubljana: Slovenian Office for Women's Policy, 1995); Marlene Kadar and Agatha Schwartz, eds., *Women and Hungary: Reclaiming Images and Histories* (special issue of *Hungarian Studies Review,* XXVI.1–2, Spring–Fall 1999).

22. Slobodanka Vladiv-Glover, "Post-Modernism in Eastern Europe after World War II: Yugoslav, Polish, and Russian Literatures," *ASEES* 5.2 (1991), 135.

23. Cf. Jasmina Lukić, "Women-Centered Narratives in Contemporary Serbian and Croatian Literatures," in Pamela Chester and Sibelan Forrester, eds., *Engendering Slavic Literatures* (Bloomington, Ind.: Indiana University Press, 1996), 223–43.

24. Cf. Nadja Grbić, "Freiheit und Gefangenschaft im Exil. Kroatische Autorinnen im deutschsprachigen Raum," in Sabine Messner and Michaela Wolf, eds., *Aus aller Frauen Länder: Gender in der Übersetzungswissenschaft* (Graz: Universität Graz, 2001), 143–51.

25. Celia Hawkesworth, "Croatian Women Writers 1945–95," in Celia Hawkesworth, ed., *A History of Central European Women's Writing* (London: Palgrave, 2003), 276.

26. Nina Kovič, "Women Writers in Slovene Literature, 1840s–1990," Hawkesworth, ed., *A History of Central European Women's Writing*, 303.

27. Zdravko Duša, "Landscape Unveiled," in Duša, ed., *The Veiled Landscape*, 132.

28. A popular Yugoslav rock song from the 1970s talks about Macedonia with the following words: "Where the sun eternally shines / there is Macedonia / there is the country that I love."

29. Florin Manolescu, introduction, in Georgiana Farnoaga and Sharon King, eds., *The Phantom Church and Other Short Stories from Romania* (Pittsburgh: University of Pittsburgh Press, 1996), vii–xiv.

30. Andrea Pető, "Hungarian Women's Writing, 1945–95," in Hawkesworth, ed., *A History of Central European Women's Writing*, 240–55.

31. Ibid., 214.

32. Veronika Ambros, "Czech Women Writers After 1945," in Hawkesworth, ed., *A History of Central European Women's Writing*, 202.

33. Dagmar Kročanova et al., "Slovak Women's Writing, 1843–1990," in Hawkesworth, ed., *A History of Central European Women's Writing*, 290.

34. Büchler, *Allskin and Other Tales by Contemporary Czech Women*, ix.

35. Büchler mentions the compilation of Czech literature *Český Parnas: vrcholy literatury 1970–1990* [*The Czech Parnassus: Literary Highlights 1970–1990*], edited by a collective of academics and published in 1993, which out of sixty writers includes only five women.

36. Büchler, *Allskin and Other Tales by Contemporary Czech Women*, viii.

37. Dagmar Kročanova et al., "Slovak Women's Writing, 1843–1990," in Hawkesworth, *A History of Central European Women's Writing*, 295.

38. Ambros, "Czech Women Writers After 1945," in Hawkesworth, ed., *A History of Central European Women's Writing*, 213.

39. Büchler, *Allskin and Other Tales by Contemporary Czech Women*, iii.

40. Anna Halja-Horbatsch, *Die Ukraine im Spiegel ihrer Literatur: Dichtung als Überlebensweg eines Volkes. Beiträge* [*Ukraine in the Mirror of Its Literature: Writing as Survival of a Nation*] (Reichelsheim: Brodina, 1997), 4–12.

41. Marko Pavlyshyn, "Ukrainian Literature and the Erotics of Postcolonialism: Some Modest Propositions," in *Harvard Ukrainian Studies* 17, no. ½ (June 1993), 125.

42. Ibid., 125.

43. Helena Goscilo, trans. and ed., *Russian and Polish Women's Fiction* (Knoxville, Tenn.: University of Tennessee Press, 1985), 20.

44. Zernova, "Reflections on Women's Literature in the Soviet Union," in Albert Leong, ed., *Oregon Studies in Chinese and Russian Culture*, 217.

45. Helena Goscilo, "Women's Space and Women's Place in Contemporary Russian Fiction," in Helena Goscilo., ed., *Fruits of Her Plume: Essays on Contemporary Russian Women's Culture* (New York: Sharpe, 1993), 342–43.

46. Diana Greene, "An Asteroid of One's Own: Women Soviet Science Fiction Writers," in *Irish Slavonic Studies* 8 (1987), 133.

47. Małgorzata Czermińska, "Women Writers in Polish Literature, 1945–95: From 'Equal Rights for Women' to Feminist Self-Awareness," in Hawkesworth, ed., *A History of Central European Women's Writing*, 238.

48. Ibid., 236.

49. Anna K. Kuhn, "Women's Writing in Germany Since 1989: New Concepts of National Identity," in Jo Catling, ed., *A History of Women's Writing in Germany, Austria, and Switzerland* (Cambridge: Cambridge University Press, 1999), 241.

50. Thomas E. Kennedy, "Baltic Literature after Communism: Contemporary Prose and Poetry from Lithuania, Latvia, and Estonia," in *Cimarron Review* 104 (July 1993), 9.

51. Viesturs Vecgrāvis, "La littérature lettone entre la province et l'Europe" [*Latvian Literature Between the Province and Europe*], in *La littérature lettone au XXe siècle* (Riga: Nordik, 1997), 5–11.

52. Tiit Hennoste, Kajar Pruul, and Darlene Reddaway, introduction, in

Pruul and Reddaway, eds., *Estonian Short Stories* (Evanston, Ill.: Northwestern University Press, 1996), 3.

53. Ibid., 13.

54. Roumiana Deltcheva, "Post-Totalitarian Tendencies in Bulgarian Literature," in *Revue Canadienne de Littérature Comparée* 22 (1995), 853–65.

■ □ ■ □ ■

THE THIRD SHORE

■ □ ■ □ ■

PLAZA DE ESPAÑA

Diana Çuli (Albania)

I MET ZANA BROKO IN A CONVENT. I DIDN'T GO LOOKING FOR HER, I didn't even know that there was a woman by such a name. Nor that she was precisely the woman that the man who had approached me in the airport in Rome wanted to kill. I had other worries at the time and was trying to come to terms with the tedious pressure of comparisons that inevitably surged into my consciousness every time I left Albania in order to travel to some city of Western Europe, waking up in one country and going to bed in another; every time I crossed the snow-covered mountain ranges of Bohemia I would start yearning almost painfully for the tiny beach near home, on the edge of that warm sea that I dreamed about every night.

On the other hand, though, I could not help but think about Virginia Woolf, who during her entire life did nothing but write, think, and write some more—not even fry an egg—and about the fact that that was why she was Virginia Woolf. It was bothersome, even embarrassing, to spend more than a moment thinking about this, but this detail had been circulating in my head for the last three months, ever since I'd read a biography of the famous writer. As for Simone de Beauvoir, who at thirty-eight discovered the truth about the female condition before she sat down to write her famous *Second Sex*, I couldn't get her off my mind either—because of the fever that the discovery of her work had set off in me, the astonishment and wonder it had triggered. And now, on the banks of the Seine, as the twilight gilded the waters of the river, I thought about Mrika's wedding. It hadn't taken place so long ago, in the summer of 1991 in the courtyard of a house located on the edge of a cliff, a house built as though to offer its residents the option of throwing themselves over the edge when they'd had enough of life. Mrika had just turned nineteen, was as beautiful as an ancient statue, and on the day of her wedding she kept her eyes fixed on the ground or turned toward the cliff. It was the height of summer, the cicadas were crazing in the trees, the guests were dancing to the music they made on the lahute.

I was on my way home from Poznan. Among other things, I'd visited the Gothic cathedral where Walesa's union activists had once held their secret meetings; I don't know why but it had given me cold shivers. Maybe because of its crypt or its gray nave where the lonely echo of the least little word reminded me of my own social condition, which was rather vague—in fact, quite undefined. So I looked out the window of the plane to contemplate the landscape and try to understand whether the connection between man and nature is one of intellect or simply naive intuition.

Finally the white clouds, well-defined fields, and joyful sun typical of the Mediterranean appeared. Planes landing out of a welcoming sky, windows where the white light broke into a whole spectrum of colors! . . . I could choose to live like many of my compatriots, with only the smallest intellectual effort. Go up the escalators the way they do, in the direction of VOLI DOMESTICI, ignoring the VOLI INTERNAZIONALI. Carrying a handbag and another bag slung over my shoulder, I could stop at the information desk and, like the other passengers, politely ask for the gate for Bari. Go there, sit down, and leaf through a fashion magazine. Even dare to have a coffee; there was no reason not to, since at Poznan, at the Council of Europe conference where human beings are treated as such, they'd paid me for an interview.

The coffee made me feel better, and I put the fashion magazine back in one of my bags. A woman sitting nearby looked exactly like a pianist I'd known in Tirana. I stared at her, intrigued as I always am by doubles, but she did not like being observed and turned her back to me. So I had to look somewhere else—that girl for instance, with the slim tall body who was just pushing back a strand of hair with her delicate white hand and sipping her Orangina through a straw. At the same time I had to control my anxiety, prevent it from gaining the upper hand over my body, from coming out of the hiding place deep within me where it had been confined for so long, behind my heart and my stomach, or maybe my lungs. Probably there, nowhere else, definitely nowhere else.

And then I realized it was my turn to be observed. Behind me someone was staring holes into my back. My plane was leaving in half an hour; the night sky stretched blue and mauve beyond the big windows. The man watching me was still there, two meters away. He was leaning against a slim pillar and scrutinizing me with eyes full of malice. I was sure it was malice. I was also sure he was an Albanian, with his rather hollow cheeks and the tanned skin of a harvest worker. Maybe he was an immigrant who simply wanted to give me a letter, a message . . . or someone applying for asylum, a latecomer, without papers . . . or a counterfeiter of visas and passports . . . a businessman of some kind still working in the public sector who wanted to talk a bit to kill time till takeoff. . . . In any case, he was an Albanian who had doubtless also been conditioned by the comparatist method that is currently being applied to different social, political, economic systems . . . an Albanian with a body haunted by anxiety, just like me. . . .

"I know you," he said, speaking our language. He was not unattractive, no older than forty with graying temples. He had a narrow, wasted profile, thin lips and evasive eyes.

I didn't respond. Any silence between two Albanians who meet in a foreign airport is loaded with meaning.

"Are you going home?" he continued. "Or staying in Bari?"

"I don't know yet. I may spend a few days there." I stopped talking with the sudden, unpleasant impression of participating in a long-ago meeting of the only union that ever existed in my country.

"I'm a chemist," he said, "and I work in the lab at Hospital No. 2 in Tirana."

"Glad to meet you . . . but you're going to miss your flight. It's taking off in a few minutes; they've just announced it."

"I've got time. Just listen to me for a moment."

Two nuns walked by speaking Serbo-Croatian. Their gaze, flattened by the practice of their spiritual life, turned me into a swirling cauldron of sin.

Staring at me, he touched my hand and I forgot where I was. There was something dangerous in his eyes, and I can't say I was completely composed when I felt his hand and his piercing gaze.

CREEP! "Listen," he said, "my wife left me. She's here in Italy but I can't find her. She thinks she can get away from me, but she doesn't know me. I've been looking for her for a month. I've got nothing but debts; I sold everything I had to pay for my trips here and back, but I don't care. I heard she was seen in Milan, a week ago. In any case, if she's gone south where you're going and if by chance you meet her, tell her I will never give up. Tell her I'll kill her. . . ." The plane for Milan is leaving in five minutes. . . . "Tell her I'll kill her, hear me?"

And he disappeared into the colorfully dressed crowd pushing through the endless halls of the airport. But he might reappear, pull his revolver out of his pocket, and take two or three shots at me until I collapse on the tiles in a pool of blood. Then he'd turn toward the policemen and say, "Arrest me, please. . . . I can rest now. Mission accomplished."

I shook out my hair as though it were covered with a thick layer of dust. The night before I'd dreamed I was hoeing a field of corn together with some other people. Everyone had their row, but mine was the longest; the sun was burning down on us, and everybody except me finished their work quickly. I raised my hoe, I planted it in the ground, but it was very strange, I couldn't progress even an inch. I was still there, hoeing on the spot, in the middle of an endless field, burning in the sun, and with the leaves of the corn plants scratching my forearms. I often had dreams that were too horrible to try to remember afterward; sometimes I dreamed that I was eating nettles, but in no dream had anyone ever tried to shoot me as I imagined it now, in broad daylight with my eyes open.

The plane cut through the night, and as though he wanted to complete the series of my failures, the passenger sitting next to me began reading a book with the title I had chosen for my next novel. Ideas were circulating in some inexplicable way in people's minds all around the world, and this last idea suddenly seemed small and powerless. Everything reproduced and repeated itself in an unhappy spiral. Often it even seemed that the world was rolling through space obliquely, groaning and deformed with the effort.

When I met Zana, I was still floating in waters that gave me the impression of hovering above a void. The void of the skies I'd been flying through for a year, the void of the streets of the big cities, buzzing with lights, cars, and hurrying people.

That week there was a long break in the electricity supply in Tirana, and I phoned from a well-lit and heated hotel room. I was washing my hair with Elsève de l'Oréal and taking a bubble bath perfumed with Camay. But I returned to my loneliness after the receptions, the dinners, the roundtables, and the speeches I was invited to. In my loneliness I was surrounded by a void, and I had the impression that the white sheets of paper in my bag were taunting me, daring me to entrust them with at least a few lines of writing.

At night I couldn't stand the silence and was afraid that in my dreams I might be witness to killings carried out at the edge of certain cliffs in Mridita. The menacing mountains rose before me and I could see transparent water sprites flitting about the waterfalls.

There was always the same void about me. It echoed, all alone, as though hemmed in by walls of metal.

I could not understand why the woman had locked herself into the church near the convent for the past week, only coming out to eat and to sleep. Especially since her family name was clearly Muslim. "Actually," I thought, "it's not something I need to worry about. It's the job of priests and nuns to ask why a Muslim woman prays in a church; as someone with at least three thousand years of Albanian heredity, I couldn't care less."

Like most of the people born in Communist Albania, I'd never believed in God. And like most other Albanians of my age, I had never under the old regime called upon God in expressions such as, "Dear God, please help me to make ends meet this month without going into debt," or "Dear God, please chase the informers out of my neighborhood," or "Dear God, spare me some disease or other; there's no medicine in the pharmacies," etc. Like any Albanian compatriot in the street who might suddenly find himself in a damp, dark, ancient, silent room, covered with inscriptions or frescoes of saints with enigmatic expressions on their faces, whether this were a church, or a mosque, or a synagogue, I would find nothing surprising about an Albanian Muslim praying to God in a church or an Albanian Christian taking off his shoes to kneel down in a mosque.

The region has many churches and baroque cathedrals. And beyond the white houses with the colorful shutters, the sea sparkles. "Come on," I said to her one morning, "let's go take a swim in the sea. I do a better job of cleansing away my sins down there than in any church." She looked at me with the eyes of a lost bird, "I can't," she said. "I can't walk on the beaches where I once walked with him."

"Get a grip on yourself," I said, "and try to get away from here. You know your husband's looking for you everywhere."

"He'll never find me," she answered. "I feel safe here."

She'd barely escaped death, and little by little, timidly but with some curiosity, and trembling with desire as she waited feverishly, more desiring than ever, she was nearing the ardent source she'd dreamed of. She often thought about what happened to Icarus when he became intoxicated with the sun, and she placed all her bets on the side where death seemed to have a different quality.

"Death is the same everywhere," I tried to tell her. "It has only one face."

"No," she said. "There's death and there's death. Mine can come now. It was worthwhile going to meet it."

I had the impression that Zana didn't take her husband's threats seriously. Maybe she knew it would come one day, and so she waited, enjoying every minute of life that remained to her, as a reprieve. Her life only had meaning in the memory of the few hours her single true love had lasted, and she said, "Now there's nothing else important. I'd like to live another month just to be able to remember the streets I walked with him."

Pablo Garcia caught sight of me as he was slowly making his way across a square in Valencia called the Plaza de la Virgen, enjoying the view of the trees with the leaves changing colors. I was drinking an orange juice, gazing at the fountain across the way with my mind on the war raging in the Balkans. The morning before at the beach we'd laughed; in the evening we'd cried after straining our minds all afternoon at a press conference on human rights. Pablo Garcia was one of the local journalists.

He hoped to see me on my last night in his city. That's why he'd come across the plaza that led to the Asttria Palace, where I had taken a room a week before; he was probably hoping to run into me through some lucky coincidence.

He could not have known that on the evening we met, not as a couple but among a number of other friends, on that evening when the moonlight silvered the sand, the sea, and the sky, pouring a magic light over my hair and into his eyes, that that night was placed under the sign of fate. No, he couldn't have known that. And I couldn't either. He couldn't have known that that night I forgot my origins, my attachments, the comparative methods, social parameters, and my scruples about being poor; I'd run across the sand, wet my feet in the sea, just like him, like the others, thinking that human rights were not just phrases pronounced in conferences, thinking that the moon was shining for the whole world far above the still mountains and the quiet seas, and I'd forgotten the moaning of the lahoutes on the slopes of my country's menacing mountains, the terror of young brides at home on whose hair the moonlight turned soft and white like goats milk.

High up above the Balkans, the moon grew sad, like a human face.

One day everything fell prey to continuous anxiety, everything became an unbearable to and fro. He left for Sarajevo with a group of pacifists while I went to Germany to write about Albanian refugees. "Can't you come and join me in Sarajevo," he asked in the brief messages I found in my hotel room after a full day. "Please, come and spend just one day with me in Sarajevo," he begged on the phone. "They won't give me a visa," I said.

With his camera on his shoulder, Pablo Garcia filmed the killed in the Balkans. "A child shredded by an exploding shell," he wrote, "just died in front of me. How can I continue living when I've just seen him die? Do you know what it looks like when the light in a child's eyes flickers madly and then goes out?" He suddenly stopped sending messages and the hotel rooms, those nests of loneliness, were also obstinately silent. . . . Raped women went crazy. Raped women had abortions. Thousands of women wanted to see their future children die. On her wedding day, Mrika, far away in Mridita, dreamed of throwing herself off the cliff.

I thought about Otrante, the convent where Zana Broko had taken refuge. About the white beaches where she'd walked with the man who had conquered her heart. About the blue skies of Italy.

Zana Broko fell passionately in love with a man whose name she had so far not revealed to me. She even loved the skies and the seas that surrounded him. "My life no longer has any meaning since he left me," she wrote. "I cannot ask him for anything since he didn't promise me anything; it was a mad journey across beaches and down the streets of Rome, where past and future were dimensions I didn't know. Did we ever, in the afflicted Tirana of years ago, did we ever think we might fall in love in other countries? I've lost him, but I also knew happiness with him. And what is happiness after all? A comparison of two different realities."

I imagined the two of them, Zana and the stranger, kissing on the beach in the twilight. The setting sun was gilding their tanned shoulders. . . .

Pablo Garcia was in Sarajevo. He was filming the moments when children died, and at the same time, his brain cells, so many sources of enthusiasm, were dying in clusters, forever. I saw him hasten along in the spray of shrapnel, laughing and trying to avoid it in order to stay alive.

I suffered from not being able to run through the cruel snow too, through the cruel winter, with the soles of my feet bloody, in that distressed line of women, terrorized, spurned, covered in spit, stumbling into the damp trunks of trees, the hostile stones in the road, those distant ice-covered roads that led to the Croatian border.

For the first time in my life I was curious abut the stranger that Zana Broko couldn't forget, and I reopened letters from her that had accumulated in the drawers of my desk in Tirana. "Oh, no, my dear," I sighed as I reread them and finally understood. "I don't think you will ever see him again. You were interesting for him, but one day you stopped being interesting. Because the interest you aroused ended up exhausting him, given how weighed down he was by our cliffs. You should have remained forever interesting for him."

Suddenly I shivered and Pablo's unbearable absence almost materialized into a tangible shape in my room.

"Come," he insisted from far away. "Why are you so hesitant? Come on, we're free individuals. . . ."

One day at the seaside when I asked myself whether I should go—Pablo Garcia had won first prize at an international film festival for the film he'd made that winter and kept calling and inviting me—a sudden gust of wind suddenly spread a page of the *Albanian News* out in front of me. Headlines slipped past and only at the last moment did I realize what I'd read: "Attempted murder in Otrante. Perpetrator arrested."

Round about me, seagulls strafed the surface of the water.

Remembering the man with the anxious face who traveled from airport to airport with rather unpleasant ideas, I thought that he might now have found peace. "The shot he fired has probably erased any desire to kill his wife."

I dived into the water following one of the lines of gold the setting sun etches into the sea. The ripples and warm rays of the sun caressed my face, and it was at precisely that moment, when I had the well-known sensation of being one with the air and the sea that I knew what I needed to do. My place was at the side of Pablo Garcia.

He was waiting for me in his hometown of Valencia, for, as he wrote, "Valencia is a symbolic city." He added, "We have to celebrate the anniversary of our first meeting. Your feverish wait on the Plaza de la Virgen. And the night by the seaside lit by the bewitched moon, that night of hearts from which broke the irresistible spark that changed the course of our lives. . . . And you'll see my film too."

I decided to spend a day in Otrante before leaving for Spain. Zana Broko's voice on the phone told me she'd lived through a real trauma. "It's my fault," she said in tears. "It's my fault my husband's in prison." And she asked, "How was I allowed to go too far?"

When I met her in her small but cool room, she was drawing up lists of humanitarian aid that Caritas was sending to Albania; in her eyes I thought I could discern fragments of the scene in which her husband had pointed his revolver at her. She must have raised her thin black eyebrows like two question marks. "Are any of them our refugees?" I asked. "I'd like to write one last piece on them."

She did not really answer my question. "I am waiting for signs now," she said. "For signs that will help me understand the meaning of what I did and explain why all that had to happen to me. Pablo told me our meeting was not mere chance. He wanted to understand too, by interpreting certain signs in his life."

"Pablo?"

"Yes, I never told you. His name was Pablo. Pablo Garcia."

The blue expanse of the sea broke neatly against a further limit-less blue. Boats floated peacefully on the water, and people wandered slowly by on the shore. "I'm going in," Zana said. "I want to pray."

That evening I took a train to Rome. I had enough money to pay for a dark little hotel room, not far from the Termini station. But once in the hotel I felt I was suffocating in the tiny space. I went out for a walk through the noisy streets, the streets Zana Broko's husband must have strode along with vindictive steps and where Zana Broko and Pablo Garcia had toured the Coliseum, the old bridges, the Roman ramparts, St. Peter's, and Valentinos.

It was May, and the Plaza de España was scented with azaleas. It was May, and young people were sitting on the sidewalks unaware that I was pursuing the shadow of Pablo Garcia as it stopped for a moment to buy a slice of coconut from them. He walked tirelessly, and I was sure Zana must have felt breathless beside him.

It was May, and night was falling slowly, there was perfume in the air, and a young man, a few steps away, was coaxing a soft tune out of his guitar. Pablo Garcia's shadow invited me, "Come," it said, "we're free individuals."

Suddenly I felt like Mrika, down there in Mridita, who wanted to throw herself off the cliff the day of her wedding. Then I thought I absolutely had to go join the women who were out on the roads, desperate, trying to escape the obsessive specter of rape. Then I thought I should return to Tirana and wander along its tree-lined streets to discover new socioeconomic problems that might supply material for another book that would never be published. Or I could fill in some application form in the offices of the Council of Europe and go off to Africa, or India, or Brazil, or somewhere else; anywhere where malaria, floods, and AIDS are rampant, anywhere where there are abandoned children; to Somalia, to Arab countries to militate against women wearing the veil and then get killed by fundamentalists; anywhere where there was no limit to suffering; maybe it was all pure madness, because I could just as well go home to my mountainous country where there are still young girls like Mrika, and contemplate the Balkan moon, sad as a human face, and listen to the lonely lament of a lahoute above silvered rivers, or simply sit down at my desk in Tirana and not stop writing. . . . Or forget everything, including Zana Broko, and go to Valencia.

That's what I was thinking about that evening in May when the Plaza de España was more beautiful than ever and I wanted to escape the suffering of the world, and I couldn't.

Translated from the French by Luise von Flotow

■ □ ■ □ ■

THE SHEARS

Mira Mekşi (Albania)

OF COURSE, THIS STORY WOULD NEVER HAVE COME BACK TO ME IF one rainy afternoon in a park I hadn't seen a pair of gardening shears lying beside the broken branch of a rosebush. Over time, the story had buried itself in a remote corner of my memory, and shears or rosebushes alone, or even roses with broken branches, could never have unearthed it.

Only the association of these two images was able to pull those events out of the mud of forgotten things into which they had sunk, and they came back to me little by little, through the eyes of an eight-year-old girl.

He used to follow us like our shadow. As soon as I saw him, I would pull on my mother's sleeve. At this signal, she would cast a few furtive glances, spot him, and then put her natural pride on display.

This show of pride, so blatant, was our only weapon against him, our only way of warning him, sternly, to keep his distance: my mother would raise her chin and fix her stare upon some far-off horizon, which could not compete with the blue of her eyes. She would thrust out her chest, expanding her magnificent décolleté, and as she walked along, the skirt of her dress would swish magically, fanning her arrogance all the way down to the devil.

I would wait for that moment impatiently; maybe I even looked forward to it? In any case, I took part, eagerly, in that little ritual of pride. Her eyes fixed on the horizon, her body tensed, I admired my mother, who seemed to show off her beauty for me and me alone.

We never spoke of Him. His name would never be uttered, at that moment or ever. We had an unspoken understanding. If I saw him first, I would pull on her sleeve. If she was the one to catch sight of him, she would let me know in her own way, but never with words.

One day, as the two of us were walking along hand in hand, unsuspecting, I heard a voice close to me, a voice deepened by cigarette smoke, a voice at once punishing and calm:

"May God strike you blind!"

I turned and saw a woman, bent over with age, passing between us and Him—the man staring at my mother with famished eyes. I was frightened and squeezed her hand. She appeared to have seen and heard nothing. A second later, I turned again, but the old woman had already vanished. For years and years afterward, the voice of Fate continued to echo in my mind.

Madame Ephtiqui's house, where we went nearly twice a week, was on a quiet lane that seemed isolated from the rest of the world, even though it opened onto the city's busiest street. It was a small house, built low and shaded all around by rich vegetation. On hot summer days, the cool, shaded lane leading to the porch made one believe that both house and yard were set against a backdrop of dark, green forest. Behind the house was a garden of rose trees, whose branches and leaves were left to grow thick against the windowpanes. I liked to sit near the window on a small stool. I would sit there whenever my mother, in front of a tall mirror in the next room, was trying on the dresses that Madame Ephtiqui had made for her.

From time to time, when my mother asked me how a dress looked, I would glance through the half-opened door, and then I would lose myself once again in the green door of the church, the only thing that could be seen through the roses and the small garden gate.

That's where, for the first time, I saw those eyes up close, in the garden, at the open window, hidden among the roses, which the evening air had made heavy with dew and perfume.

They were still eyes, terribly mild and imploring, so much so that once the initial terror had passed (it was one of those heart-chilling terrors that strike one dumb), I became his accomplice. Yes, I became his accomplice. I allowed those eyes to admire my mother, my radiant mother, as she tried on her dress for the first time, as she instructed her seamstress to cut the neck lower, to widen the sleeves at the shoulder.

THE SHEARS

15

My mother as she dressed and undressed, lifting her long, thick hair because—who can say?—the gesture made her more beautiful. This game of watching, this understanding between us, lasted a very long time, until the day we went to Madame Ephtiqui's to pick up the summer dresses that were ready and waiting. Burning with curiosity, speechless with impatience, I took my seat in the little corner by the window, waiting for those eyes to appear in the rose garden.

There they were, looking tortured from having to wait. Those two eyes were mad, sick with love.

As the two women stood in front of the mirror, inspecting the dresses, seeing about last-minute alterations, I felt like speaking to those burning, imploring eyes. I hadn't yet found the words; I only wanted to tell them that this was our last meeting. . . .

My attempt to break our supernatural pact cost me dearly: I had betrayed it in spite of myself.

Whether it was a terrible stroke of Fate or an unfortunate trick of the mirror, it is all the same. Madame Ephtiqui, the wise and gentle Madame Ephtiqui, suddenly turned around, her face contorted with fear and rage. Like lightning she ran the distance between the mirror and the window and hurled the shears with all her might.

I felt my heart stop and I squeezed my eyes shut.

I heard a faint cracking sound and that was all.

When I opened my eyes, I saw only the broken branch of a rose-bush and Madame Ephtiqui close beside, her face fallen and pale with anger. She was distractedly wiping the bloody shears on her apron.

I never saw him. Neither did Madame Ephtiqui.

More than twenty years had passed when, in that grim, forgotten little park, I suddenly set eyes upon the broken branch of a rosebush and a pair of gardening shears. That was long ago. I was living in another city and would have been about the same age he had been at the time.

It was then that I felt an urgent, an irresistible need to see Madame Ephtiqui. I didn't know whether she was alive or dead.

I lifted the iron knocker and gave three knocks at the door. The house was still there, isolated, forgotten by the world. Then I knocked another three times with my ring, like my mother used to do. I saw her suddenly appear in the doorway, Madame Ephtiqui, bent beneath the weight of the years and beneath the secret buried deep inside; only her chignon hadn't changed.

"My name is . . . ," I tried to introduce myself.

"Come in!" She took me by the arm and led me across the porch that smelled of forest, still the same, untouched by time, like the entire house.

As I went in, I saw the little stool up close by the window, still waiting for me there after . . .

"Exactly twenty years today," said Madame Ephtiqui with a loud, clear voice.

I couldn't believe my ears. By what chance could that woman suspect that of all those fleeting childhood memories, it was precisely that one? What force had led me to this house on exactly this day?

Madame Ephtiqui seemed to possess extraordinary powers. It appeared to me that it was she who held in her hands the threads of Fate, she who had kept everything unchanged, even the perfume of the roses flooding through the open window. It was she who had placed before my eyes, in the forgotten, grim little park, the broken branch and the shears; it was she who had brought me here so she could confess and finally find peace. . . .

"He had become my nightmare," Madame Ephtiqui began, while I still struggled to believe.

"Every day, he would appear on my doorstep like a ghost, and then begin turning the house upside down."

I felt my eyes leave their orbits.

"Oh yes, they used to watch over all the artisans, all the tailors who had a private clientele, and hit them with heavy fines," she rushed to explain, "but I had to raise my daughter, and my husband was in jail as a political prisoner. He was the devil in person. A monster. Every seamstress with private clients was afraid of him, and it was my misfortune that he came after me more than the others. Even when I went to my clients' houses to have them try on clothes, he was at my heels. I hid my clients' fabrics up in the attic. It was no use. He managed to find them even up there, the devil. Once he found two of your mother's dresses that I had just finished. For a while he stood there smelling them, then he took them both. Oh, what was I to do? I had to spend all my savings making two more dresses for your mother. But that evening . . ."

Her voice had deepened and smelled of cigarette smoke. Her tongue was thick like set custard. She spoke half Albanian, half Greek—Madame Ephtiqui was raving. . . .

"That evening, yes, I had seen his tracks in the rosebushes before . . . that evening, then, I saw in the mirror the desire burning in his eyes. He wanted . . . he didn't just want to steal the dresses, but your mother too, whom I . . . whom I adored."

I started, as if waking from a nightmare and ran for the door.

Madame Ephtiqui's raving voice followed me:

"He lost an eye, but he didn't turn me in. . . ."

My legs carried me, I don't know how, to the rose garden. I had great trouble opening the little rotted-out garden gate. I rushed out into the lane facing the door of the condemned church.

Translated from the French by Ryan Fraser

■ □ ■ □ ■

THE DANCER IN THE WINDOW

Sanja Lovrenčić (Croatia)

I STILL ENJOY WRITING LETTERS. RETIRING FROM ALL THE NOISE, closing the bedroom door, and lighting the lamp on the small white table. It is always night. And I always find my way to the table in the darkness even though it is not real darkness. The window looks out over one of those narrow courtyards, squeezed in between whimsical protuberances of inner staircases, small balconies, and bedrooms. As if that abyss of a courtyard had no bottom since it ends at the wavy blue roof of the garage. But the strangers' windows covered with light fabric shine at night. The space imprisoned by the rear walls of the house is larger than it seems at first: the faces in the windows across from mine are too far away to be recognizable anyway. . . .

Maybe these letters are boring, and maybe that friend of mine was right when—toward the end of our not-particularly-close friendship—she asked me for permission to destroy them, because they were in the way in her drawers and she certainly wasn't going to read them again. I don't describe many happenings in them, and those I do talk about are stretched out across time to the point of losing the character of an "event." . . . I never write letters during times of high excitement, and maybe here, when I sit down in the circle of the small light of the bedroom, I am looking for something else: some special time that has slowed down, or a reflection of myself. I write slowly, with many interruptions, and then—the table being next to the window—the unchanging picture of the courtyard keeps invading my consciousness: three vaulted windows placed diagonally, I believe there is a staircase between them, a well-lit staircase, so it seems. . . . The four

19

balconies belong to the other building; their exterior lights are never lit, nobody ever passes through their doors, and their closets of different sizes seem to be sealed, enclosing their unfathomable courtyard legacy.

Part of the facade is in bad condition, and bricks peer through the mortar. Two narrow twin windows have grayish frames; it is through them that I recognize the old woman in the shadow that sometimes slips by the curtains. . . .

On the other side there is a set of wide three-winged windows that may belong to the same apartments as the balconies. I never watch them during the day, but I can recall their nocturnal light patterns whenever I close my eyes.

In the third wide three-winged window—the third counting from below, counting the way you count the lines in musical scores—the dancer appears. She turns on the light, pulls the curtain aside, and her figure is outlined in the three-winged frame, not big but clear, in a black leotard. Of course it is not possible to hear the music. It is not possible to foresee whether the dancer will appear or when she will finally appear. . . . In an attempt at some big all-encompassing recollection, or in a dream, or if I could read those letters scattered all around and now out of reach, I could perhaps remember exactly—I think I really could—how many times I have seen her. Fifteen? . . . Twenty? . . . Twenty-three? . . . Sometimes several evenings in a row, then a pause of several years. Sometimes for many weeks in an almost settled rhythm—Thursdays or Saturdays?—but as soon as the expectation starts to solidify in a foreboding of certainty, she disappears, for a long time. Maybe there has been some mistake in that attempt to grasp time. Still, is it possible to believe that my life has lasted only a few evenings?

During those evenings there is always a moment when someone approaches my bedroom door—my mother? my husband? the children? my children's children?—stopping as if they were about to enter but then going on, through the small corridor, toward the kitchen, or through the big corridor toward the other rooms or the exit. None of them has ever noticed the dancer, her body dressed in black that always looks the same. But the dance changes somewhat.

If I were to think of describing her in one of my letters to whom would that letter be addressed, whom could I write to about the dancer? It would be difficult for me to find the words to describe the diversity of her dancing movements. They are seldom quick and yet sometimes sudden. In the first scenes, I remember—if I remember correctly—they were gentle and brisk, like a melody, full of turns, and with some bizarre pirouettes that suddenly broke off and changed into something else. . . . She didn't seem to be following a regular rhythm. . . . Several evenings in a row, she danced perhaps the very same dance, bending backward in a bow in the same unexpected way and toward the end always stretching in the same way, on her toes, her arms up. . . . Still, the end itself came with no warning. She would suddenly stop in front of the three-winged windowpanes and, with both hands, pull the light and then the dark curtains.

Later, much later—and in the meantime she would seldom appear—when she seemed to be coming at regular intervals, her dance acquired gymnastic features, as if it had somehow become open to the public, as if she wanted to tell those who might suddenly burst into the room: "Just watch, I am not doing anything strange. Any doctor would recommend a few minutes of evening exercise." And yet, in the mechanical repetition of simple movements softer gestures shone through, hands pleasantly folded above her head.

Now she shows up again almost every night, and my family is puzzled and asks me to whom I am writing all those letters, and I answer that it is all the same long letter I don't manage to finish. . . . Unpredictability, which had always been present, has never been so obvious: when the lights in her window are turned on, she is already standing there in a bent, painful position that she suddenly abandons for a series of regular, classical movements that, for some reason—but why? because of a hint of fragility? or a precision that hides her total surrender to desire?—provoke tears. Her body in black hasn't lost the least bit of its perfect flexibility, but it is as if her dance were in a dilemma, continuously falling into bitter tragic gestures and short bursts of ballet-school exercises.

And now, while I am trying to write a letter to the person whom—unless there is really an error in the calculation of time—I haven't seen for several decades, I think: It would be good if this time it could last. It would be good if she could leave her three-winged window, the third one from the top, and appear in the other ones until she filled them all up. Perhaps other frames—like the vaulted one or the one with the gray crosspieces—could give her other rhythms . . . and then her dance, more constant than my letters and my longings, would never come to an end.

Translated from the Croatian by Agata Schwartz and Luise von Flotow

WHY DO THESE BLACK WORMS FLY JUST EVERYWHERE I AM MYSELF ONLY ACCIDENTALLY

Lela B. Njatin (Slovenia)

MY CHILDHOOD WAS FULL OF STORIES ABOUT THE WAR. PAST WAR, whose heavy blow never ceased to suffocate my mother. her stories were no hymn to heroism, she escaped from torture, fled from the wall of hostages, survived the concentration camp, and yet she was always retelling her own disbelief about having deluded death.

the fear of violent death, arising out of hatred and vengeance, was the only fear i could never live with. i wrote in the school paper: "my biggest wish is there will never be a war." but my mother has always asked me to burn her body after her death. "i can't stand the thought of being devoured by worms," she explained her vision of the inevitable absurd. i felt this absence of reason during my entire life as an unfinished though invincible wall of intolerance and as impenetrable glasses of unconcern. now i don't even know anymore when the absurd adopted a face and began to walk around here. i remember the most persistent was my bulletproof jacket, when on the street next to mine a helicopter was shot down; persistence was my helmet, when there was gunfire under my window; persistence dragged me away, when a missile exploded above me; persistence protected me from the panic of people i had been spending hours and hours in the shelter with; later on persistence became a filter in front of a tv screen. persistence is just a rampart against the emotions that try to break through into me like a mountain torrent, to tear me up and drag me

23

away into the flood of war. on friday goran and his friends came from osijek. they were showing off videotapes of the destroyed town, they were displaying pictures of dead bodies, they were reciting missives of the attacked ones, they were singing. . . . "to document, not to interpret," he said, composed and submissive as never before. he is also persistent. he travels incessantly through the enemy encirclements, taking the war from osijek to zagreb, rijeka, hungary, czechoslovakia, germany—and afterward he goes back.

to persist.

we were facing each other, two empty mirrors, from which the images were erased by persistence, we were exchanging speechless words and just feeling, how slowly, but in persistently increasing numbers, we were being eaten by worms. our encounter was simple, short and completely inexplicable, like death.

Translated from the Slovenian by Krištof Jacek Kozak

■ □ ■ □ ■

HOW WE KILLED THE SAILOR

Alma Lazarevska (Bosnia)

I

If I mention it, he'll say I'm being petty and that's unworthy of me. He'll close his eyes, and as though he were speaking of someone who wasn't in the room, he'll say:

"I'll count to three to make it go away. There, she didn't say a thing. One, two, three. Forgotten."

That's what he did when I pointed out that he was spreading the margarine too thickly on his slices of bread; when I remarked that he had given away almost the entire contents of the packet the inhabitants of the besieged city occasionally received. He had left us only a little bag of green mints. I once told him they reminded me of my grandmother who had died long ago—my mother's blue-eyed mother who was never hungry. It's true that we still had the cardboard packing. It burns well, but we won't use it. The inscription on it and the list of contents may one day feed some future story.

He closed his eyes and counted to three when he noticed . . . but I won't say what. Maybe I'll use that too, when the shame passes, to feed some bitter story. For the time being, let it be forgotten.

The room is losing its box shape. The light of the thin candle doesn't reach its corners. It creates a dim, uneven oval that shifts lazily if an unexpected current of air happens to touch its tiny wick. There is a transparent, trembling film over us. The few objects that are bathed in dim light, and the two of us, make up the inside of a giant amoeba. We are its organs, pulsating in the same rhythm, but not touching. Is an amoeba that single-celled organism covered by a transparent film we saw through the school microscope? If you touched the drop of water it was floating in with the tip of a needle, it would slowly curl up. Right now in the besieged city, where tonight no fiery balls are falling and no whistling bullets are being fired from the other side of the encircling ring, there are thousands of films hovering like this. The people in these bubbles of light are silent. Frightened, tired, or indifferent, they are silent. Or listening. Hoping for sleep. To overwhelm them and spare them this vigil.

He lit five cigarettes this evening, and each time he used a new match. He put the dead match down in the saucer by the candle. In the ashtray lay cigarette butts and the thin red band from the cigarette packet.

"Why are you doing that?"

I sense that sleep won't come for a long time yet. But as I utter the question I'm aware that it's unworthy.

He doesn't reply.

Now I have a reason to be angry and speak.

"Why are you doing that?"

I don't care what's worthy of me and what isn't. He looks at me and waves his hand, as though removing invisible headphones from his ears. He'll put them down for a moment and focus on me and my impatience.

"Doing what?"

"Using matches to light your cigarettes!"

"What am I supposed to use?"

Now he is prepared to put his invisible headphones away. He is interested in learning something new, something he hasn't heard before. He is expecting me to tell him where the sun could rise other than in the east. That someone is killed every day on his daily route through town, that he already knows.

"The candle! You know yourself that we don't have enough matches. They're hard to find. The candle's burning, so use it to light your cigarettes."

There are already too many words in our mute bubble. Added together and expressed like this, they are all unworthy. Without them, we are just two organs pulsating to the same rhythm until they are overcome by sleep.

He looks at me as though he had stopped beside a stupid child who understands nothing and who has to have everything painstakingly explained.

"I can't!"

"You can't . . . what?"

"Light cigarettes with a candle!"

"Why not?"

"Every time you do that, someone dies somewhere in the world."

If he had said this in daylight or with a light bulb on in the room, I would have laughed. I like it when a room is lit up like an operating theater. I would even have remembered some images from films in which He lights cigarettes from the candle illuminating a dinner for two. First for Her, then for Himself. Gazing the whole time into Her eyes while the audience sighs deeply in the dark, in unison.

Besides, whatever he does, at least one person dies somewhere in the world every second. There are cold statistics about that. In books that the candlelight doesn't reach. That is why, suddenly and unexpectedly, his answer begins to engage me like a holy law whispered into the ear of an unwilling novice.

2

Maybe one day I'll scatter all those matches into his hand and say:

"That's how many people you've saved from dying!"

Then red-hot balls will no longer fall on the besieged city, and people in it will not die with tiny pieces of hot iron in their bodies. They will die of illness and old age again. There will be light bulbs again, and no one will be obliged to light cigarettes with candles. That will only happen in films.

I've been collecting the dedicated matches for three days now. I put them into an empty Solea cream tin. It says "contents: 250g." But even if it didn't, I can assume from its size that it can hold another hundred matches or so. Sometimes I miss one and it ends up in the ashtray. In the morning I dig it out from under the butts. After that the tips of my forefinger and thumb stink all day, and the child frowns when I touch the tip of his nose.

The matches he puts beside the saucer with the candle don't stink. There is even something agreeable about the slightly piquant smell from the phosphorous tip that remains even after it's extinguished. When I take the lid off the tin and count the matches, I'm aware only of the leftover smell of the cream. It is sweetish, like a woman's deodorized armpit in summer. Crouching among them rest the souls that have been saved. There are twenty-five of them for now. When I close the tin, they come to life. I listen to the sounds they make while the tin rests on my hand. There are twenty-five saved souls in my hand. Today in the besieged city fifteen people died from one fiery ball (sent from the dark hill where the bad people went). No one wanted to save them. I'll see their faces tomorrow in the newspaper obituaries. What about these saved souls in my hand? How old are they? What do they look like? How much good is there in them? Do they know there is a besieged city somewhere in the world with the saviors of their souls in it?

3

I found out where this thing with the candle and the cigarette came from. The morning was calm, but as though damned. At such times I reach frantically for books from the shelves. I open them, leaf through them, put them down. . . . An old bill fell out of one of them. On the page it slipped out of, in the last line, it said that every time you light a cigarette from a candle, somewhere in the world a sailor dies. This was a book by Dario Dz., our former neighbor. He smoked a lot, lighting each cigarette from the last. Now Dario Dz. is somewhere out there in the wide world. And the sailors are in a harbor, somewhere on the sea, in a ship, in a tavern, in the bought embrace of some lady of the harbor. . . . Are there any sailors where Dario Dz. is living now? On the other hand, if you were to throw that sentence published long ago back at its author, perhaps he wouldn't remember he had written it.

Like in that film . . . was it called *Night*? A man and a woman come out of a house after a long, barren night that has made them strangers. They sit down on the grass. Dawn is breaking. She takes an old letter out of her handbag. She reads it out loud. Emphasizing every sentence. Declarations of love, words of tenderness, swearing devotion till eternity. . . .When she has folded the letter, she puts it back in her bag and looks enquiringly at the man. He asks:

"Who wrote you that?"

"You!"

Dario's "somewhere in the world" is now America. Everyone has his troubles, even if he isn't in a besieged city. But he doesn't have to think about matches and candles. He can switch on ten light bulbs and turn the room into a dazzling operating theater with no dim corners nibbling at the space, where painful questions nest. He lights his cigarettes with a lighter. The first one in the morning and then, through the day, each one from the last. When he uses up his lighter, he buys a new one. He can choose a new color and trademark every time. And he's left the sailors' souls to us. He has off-loaded all their weight onto our weary souls, which even sleep no longer spares.

"Do you know Dario's address in America?"

"Which Dario?"

"The writer Dario, Dario the writer."

"The writer? No, I don't. Why do you need it?"

"No reason."

4

This morning I put only three matches in the tin. All three stank of old ash. There's still room in the tin. When I toss it from one hand to the other, I hear cheerful sounds, the sounds of tiny souls sliding and bumping into each other. They are enjoying their loss of weight. When the boy saw me playing with the tin yesterday, he said:

"You're a child now. You've got a rattle. A really ugly one!"

Now I have to find another tin. Until I find a better one, I'll use the empty box that once held long thick matches with yellow phosphorous tops. It says "Budapest" on it. I was there once, but I don't remember the building in the picture. It isn't ugly. But it wouldn't be worth going back to that city to see it.

This box won't last long. It's already worn at the edges. For the moment, there's a ball of paraffin wax resting in it.

While we sit beside the candle, he makes three or four of them in the course of an evening. He collects the dripping wax with his fingers. The hot touch isn't enough to burn him but quite enough to make the chilly room cozier. Some of the wax slides onto the saucer. He forms a little ball from what remains between his fingers, with the tips of his thumb and forefinger. When it's half formed, he puts it on his palm and rolls it with the forefinger of his other hand. Taking my arm, he holds it by the wrist and drops the little ball into the palm of my hand, it's quite cold now and smooth. There's no trace even of the short-lived warmth it picked up from his hand.

He touches the little ball in my hand with his forefinger again. Now I feel the touch of his fingertip as well as the slight tickle of the little wax ball. In the morning I collect the little balls from the table and place them in a glass jar with the words *Kompot svetsky* on the label. Under the first word is a picture of two blue plums. When I have collected a lot of little balls, I melt them into a narrow candle.

But this morning I also placed one wax ball in the box with "Budapest" written on it. That's when it happened!

Nothing particular preceded it. It had been an ordinary day. He came home late. With no sign of particular tiredness. That mute film already covered the room. At around midnight he took a cigarette out of the half-empty packet, put it to his lips, but before he had separated one lip from the other, he made the face people make when their nose is itching and their hands are full. He moved his lower jaw upwards, and his lips moved toward the tip of his nose. His upper lip, comically pinched, touched his nose. Nothing special.

I don't remember a single film scene where an actor does that before killing someone.

He reached for the candle with his right hand. He raised it, on its saucer, to which it was secured by a broad wax base. The saucer has a picture of a rococo lady in three colors on it. Gray, violet, gold. The lady is sitting on a swing and a long arc separates her from the young gallant who has, presumably, just given her a push and is now waiting for her to swing back. The wax base covered part of the picture. Part of the lady's face was hidden. You could see her wig, with its comic curls. And the lady's legs. They are painted violet and gray. Her feet are separated one from the other and have little narrow shoes. The little golden shoes of a rococo lady. When the picture is completely revealed and daylight reaches into the room, everything looks somehow different. Deprived of color and action.

The candle in his hand was raised to the tip of the cigarette. A trickle of wax ran down the thin stalk out of the hollow round the wick. It covered the lady's left leg. For a time the leg could be made out under the little transparent pool of paraffin, until it cooled, solidified, and became an opaque blot. Musing on the lady's leg, I forgot the sailor standing on the deck of a ship sailing from one continent to another. He was pressing tobacco into a pipe with his broad thumb. He had turned his back to the wind. Did he strike a match? He raised it to his pipe. And fell. As though struck down. Like when one player's pawn knocks out his opponent's and it is no longer in his way.

5

He is smoking. He was away for three days and two nights. In the besieged city men have duties that keep them out of the house a lot. Should I tell him that the night before he left he killed a sailor? I'll tell him. I'll tell him tomorrow:

"Put out your hands. Palms up."

I'll put the tin on his left hand, and the box that once held long matches on his right hand. I'll step away and say:

"Those are the souls you've saved and one you didn't."

Will he feel their different weight? God, in these giant amoebas, in their mute membranes, words and games acquire a weight that should be forgotten with the morning.

"Give me a cigarette!"

"Since when have you been smoking?"

"Since this evening. . . ."

He taps the packet and a cigarette slides out of it. I take it with the fingers of my right hand, with my left I lift up the saucer with the candle. A trickle of wax runs down the thin candle and in an instant the rococo lady's other leg disappears as well. Just the tip of one little shoe peers out, no bigger than the tip of a needle.

The lady is completely smothered by the wax base. Beside her, the smiling gallant is waiting for her to come back to him on the swing. . . . There, he's vanished. His charming game has been stilled by the hard wax pool.

Now we are still. For a moment at least. I inhale the cigarette smoke awkwardly and cough. There are no more sailors whose lives and souls depend on our tiny actions and decisions, weariness and forgetfulness. There are no more ladies and gallants whose game is in our hands. Just the two of us, alone, waiting for sleep. Today more people died in the besieged city. Perhaps their names and pictures in the obituaries will one day feed some future story. Like wax that you shape into a little ball and when it cools drop onto someone's open hand.

I won't throw away those two boxes. I won't empty them. I'll leave them somewhere, in one of the dark corners that gnaw at the square shape of the room. When this is all once again brilliantly lit up one day, will I find them?

Will I ask:

"Who left this here?"

Will I be able to say:

"I did!"

Translated from the Bosnian by Celia Hawkesworth

■ □ ■ □ ■

20 FIRULA ROAD

Ljiljana Đurđić (Serbia)

THIS IS AN AUTOBIOGRAPHICAL STORY. I HATE SUCH STORIES, AND
for this very reason, to avoid any speculation, I want to make that
clear from the very beginning. Childhood is full of different kinds of
love: for birds, worms, smells, regions, pine resin, certain men and
women. Depending on where the parachute of fate drops you and
how its lines and cords are gathered afterward, you may end up at the
seashore or at the edge of a large swamp. In my childhood I ended
up at the seashore, in Split, Spalato, in the part of town known as
Firula. 20 Firula Road.

I owe no debt of gratitude for this to anyone in particular: it is a
complicated thing, a family matter. Mine was of one of those sizable
families that never really were, in which the cars of one worn-out
train attached themselves to another that was already made up of
assorted cars from other worn-out trains. Ethnic mixing is not at all
unusual in such families, at least not in this part of the world. The
train travels along and, all things considered, it is often less tiresome
inside than in other trains that stick more rigorously to Greenwich
time, that stop more regularly and only at major stations in order to
cast off worn-out cars and hook up brand-new ones with certified
pedigrees. It was one such slapped-together train that would drop me
off at the Split station every June, all beaming and intoxicated by the
fragrance of the Dalmatian vegetation that floated into the car somewhere around Perković and heralded the dreamed-of blue expanse;
the same train would pick me up every September, wet with tears,
and take me far inland, to Belgrade, to await the following June.

At the age of five or so, I was already in love with everything: the house in Firula, the garden with its thick carpet of pine needles, the two half-naked plaster statues that guarded the stairs cascading down to the sea, even the caterpillars that fell in abundance from the tamarisks and pines after the rain and whose crawling, hairy bodies turned into disgusting green mush if you happened to step on them. The love notes we carved into the leaves of the gigantic agaves that formed a rim around the garden would be found the next year as scars that had dried and wrinkled along the sutures, destroying the names of the loved ones. There were a lot of us, children and Them, the old people, the forty-year-olds, who would go shopping and bring us food in the morning. The sea was in front of us, from morning till evening; just the stone steps, a little iron gate, and the sea with three reefs and a small pier from which we first jumped and then dived the whole day long, until echoing voices called down from the garden: "Mićo, Lidija, Tonko, Lila, time to come ho-ome!" In the evening, under the tamarisks, we would hear murmuring and the clinking of glasses in the dark, with the smell of pine resin and salt, and in the distance the island of Brač would send secret messages to Split from its many twinkling inhabited inlets.

I can see myself at dawn—a thin, long-legged little girl, tanned and slippery as a seal, knee-deep in the water hunting for little snails, shellfish, crabs, anything the evening tide had bestowed upon Firula. The surface of the water was an enormous magnifying glass, revealing the sparkling, magical underwater world that lay hidden in the convolutions of sand and the clumps of seaweed. There was no one in sight. The sunbathers didn't come until noon, and until then it was a secluded South Sea paradise. Bit by bit the sun, with the help of this magnifying glass, would set the world on fire. By noon, the sea and the rocks would be burning. The immense joy of those mornings inundates me even today: it is untouched for the most part, unsullied by the other images that have accumulated in the years since, polluting the Firula sea with algae, garbage, refuse, oil slicks, and human excrement.

The crayfish that we sometimes ate were from the river Cetina, not from the sea. Granny Jerka brought them from the market and shook them like a pile of slippery rocks onto the table among the intoxicating aromas of the Dalmatian kitchen; a little later, they emerged from the boiling water, red as bricks. They were deader than dead, but their long pincers and feelers still moved as we stared, mesmerized, forgetting the pangs of hunger in our stomachs. Live crayfish from Cetina for lunch! Every evening Granny would take her little folding chair to Zenta to look at the "campground"—the first foreigners to come to Split with their multicolored tents and water-sports gear. She repeated insistently that no film could beat the "campground." We preferred to jump over the fence that separated us from the Bačvice, the outdoor summer movie theater, and stare at the screen: first the enormous five-pointed star announcing the newsreel would burst right at us, and then, depending on the program, there would be men and women in passionate embraces or soldiers in a wide variety of uniforms wandering foolishly from one side of the screen to the other. In the surrounding darkness unbearable swarms of gnats and mosquitoes flew about, mingling with the stars, and periodically blocking the beam of light from the projector.

Just as I sneaked out at dawn to hunt for snails and shellfish, so did ninety-year-old Modul; he would secretly leave the house with his deck chair in order to grab the best place in the garden to observe all the bare female legs and buttocks that paraded before his cataract-clouded eyes throughout the day, as he muttered into his beard, "Wonderful!" That garden was a real menagerie! The tenants and their visitors, swimsuit in hand, who came to swim, oarfish Željko, a ball boy at the nearby tennis courts who, in years to come, would be a world-class tennis ace and own a yacht, and his rustic sister Vinka from Blato on the island of Korčula; pudgy, good-natured Mario and his feebleminded brother Tonko; slick and handsome Vice—the Latin lover—who would become famous wailing national songs and his ugly buck-toothed wife, Dijana; then there was the long-legged Belgrade architect Pantović, the spitting image of Monsieur Hulot on holiday. Many years later, he would hang himself in his bathroom one harsh Belgrade winter. There was Grandpa Pave with his glass eye; enormous Božićka and tiny Božić; Mićo and Lidija; and greater than them all—Aunt Juga, born in 1918 of a father who belonged to the Sokols, her full name being Jugoslavija, a traveler who had been to Al Shatt, a coquette sheltered in the comfortable nook of long widowhood, a woman for all times who told her small children, "Come on, show me how you kiss. Your whole life depends on that!"

Aunt Juga did not prepare crayfish from Cetina. Once or twice every summer, with glory and pomp, a magnificent lobster from the very depths of the Brač Channel would appear on the table. The lobster was served in the evening, in the garden, with candles and amber-colored wine from the island of Vis, accompanied by the chirping of crickets and the sound of the waves as they splashed against the little pier at regular intervals. Aunt Juga entertained—drugged, we said—tourists, foreigners from England, Belgium, Italy. Enticed by the aromas and Juga's lavish hospitality with which she offered them all of Firula and the entire Brač Channel, all the way to Supetar, they repaid her one hundred percent. Frequently her children, Mićo and Lidija, spent their winter school holidays in London, Brussels, or Milan. So I too, one Christmas, ended up on the sandy beaches of Sheveningen, frozen, with a runny nose, as colorless, shivering Lane Jansen asked me to repeat over and over again what it was like in Firula at that time. My memory of Holland lies right beside an Italian doll whose eyes opened and closed, kilograms of silky candy, and a small gold ring with a flat part where my name had been engraved—presents brought by Aunt Juga when, once a year, she came to Belgrade to stroll through her capital.

Thanks to Aunt Juga and her undeniable diplomatic skills, the house and garden were filled with the spirit of a departed member of the family, Duško, the first officer on a ship—no one remembered the name—that was part of the Yugoslav merchant marine in convoy PQ18, sunk by German submarines in Arctic waters in 1942. According to eyewitness accounts, the entire crew was saved except for the captain and Duško, who stood in a formal salute on the bridge and went down with the ship. Duško, in a tropical helmet, surrounded by glaciers and Jan Mayen Island. The helmet, which floated to the surface after they sank, was returned to Firula by the survivors, and Aunt Juga wisely placed it among the other souvenirs that Duško had brought from his trips to the Far East and which we were allowed to use freely. The Chinese and Japanese vases whose curves we brushed against in passing, and which by some miracle remained intact, were stuffed with the most unbelievable things, from umbrellas and old shoes to lost buttons and wet bathing suits. On the outside, the vases clearly kept their gracious but shatterproof Chinese or Japanese beauties and old men with long beards and pigtails. The bamboo cane that stood in the entrance was used to beat the sand, brought in by our bare feet, out of the rugs, and the pith helmet served more than once to protect the head of a wandering and forgetful visitor from the August sun. The only thing missing was the little monkey that Duško had brought from Borneo. All that remained of him were the stories: how skillfully he had climbed trees, making no distinction between pines and palms, and how, at about the same time that Duško disappeared in the Arctic waters, he was allegedly eaten by the Italians when they entered Split; they thought he was a cat. This is how Firula, Duško, the Far East, and the man who wrote of *Jan Mayen and My Srem* were forever linked in my young heart.

And that love is still there, along with an aversion for the nasal voice like that of a eunuch that would periodically reach us, like a ball from the tennis courts, across the wall separating us from the house next door. It belonged to the austere figure of a bespectacled man who used to visit our neighbor, Aunt Maja Čulić. Every time Aunt Maja's guest appeared I would jump as though hit by lightning and run to the other end of the garden; from afar I would observe his slow movements that deadened and immobilized the space in which he moved. Once, early in the morning, I saw him standing at the very edge of the garden, leaning against a pine and staring at the sea; he had taken off his glasses and his face was softer, almost feminine. On the other side of the wall, I automatically took up the same pose—a funny, scrawny little girl who had just begun to wear the top part of a bathing suit—and I knew at once that we were not seeing the same thing. To this day I am still not sure whether the gentleman staring at the sea in our neighbor Aunt Maja Čulić's garden was Ivo Andrić. Everything indicates that he was, which is all the worse for me, as his appearance was like a crack that ruined the oil painting of my childhood with its pine trees and the sea in the distance. There is nothing about the sea in his work. He simply did not belong there.

Aunt Juga's youngest brother, Rade, often stopped by our garden. He was a tireless womanizer and tennis player who carried army boots wrapped in newspaper around with him all summer long; he would put them on whenever he got on a crowded bus so that the swarms of tourists would not step on his feet. He suffered from corns and told everyone that since the "Let's all go to the coast" campaign

had begun, the problems with his feet had grown worse. The story of his tumultuous love life culminated late in his life, when two of his children from different marriages almost fell in love, having met on some excursion where they found out only by accident that they were brother and sister. His daughter didn't even go to his funeral, saying that he was an old donkey, that whenever he had run into her around town with one of his new girlfriends he would only greet her politely with a tip of his hat, and that he did not deserve to have a single handful of earth thrown on his coffin. But her clear blue eyes that would darken whenever she saw him arrive in Firula with his parcel under his arm were his eyes. Granny Jerka had found the boots he used to protect his aching feet when she was rummaging through a pile of junk—her personal treasure trove. She handed them to him triumphantly with a remark she made to herself, but more or less aloud, that human suffering is infinite, but divine grace unattainable. And she was right.

And then it was all over. It did not burst like a bomb—that came later—it died out slowly and imperceptibly, as things go to ruin, as human life dies out: wrinkle by wrinkle, tooth by tooth, hair by hair. The train that dropped me off at the Split station every summer picked up speed. It was no longer fun to take the "fast" train through Bosnia. Only the shadows of the former inhabitants wandered through the garden at Firula. One summer Mrs. Elvira, a pile of bones held together by the coquettish elastic of her swimsuit, who kept an eye out all day long for strong male muscles to take her down for a swim, was no longer at her old place under the oleander; she had faded along with the fragrance. Another elderly lady was already sitting in her place.

Aunt Juga moved away. She, whose name Jugoslavija had saved her children from the stigma of their father's Italian surname in the Al Shatt refugee camp, would live to see those same children disown her and change their mother's name to Jugana on their new documents. But she knew little of that, immersed in bridge and old photographs on the thirteenth floor of one of the huge buildings of the Chinese Wall, with Firula behind her, in an apartment full of Chinese and Japanese vases that had miraculously made it to the present undamaged, the only things to have kept that little aura of silence and mystery that once enchanted the writer of these lines; the far-off seas of Java, China, Japan, the tropical pith helmet forgotten in a closet whose owners had long since removed the fish and algae. The old woman who addressed me sleepily, still provocatively swinging her hips, behaving indulgently toward both male and female members of the human race, still looked better than her namesake, our shared homeland Yugoslavia: "For Christ's sake, they're unsheathing their swords up there, reaching for their battle gear. Everything will go to hell!"

That was the last time I saw Firula and my childhood garden. That intoxicating, special aroma of the Dalmatian kitchen owed its character to the gas they cooked on, rarely used where we lived. It had nothing to do with magic. And the house, oh, the house! The garden, the old paraphernalia, that picture of decay, the twisted pines, the decapitated plaster statues on the facade, the loose, sadly drooping trim! I saw the house fly off into the past, simply rise up off the ground and fly like some wondrous object made by Spielberg, off to the great warehouse of the past filled with unneeded, used-up things, smells, and pictures. Criminals, like lovers, always return to the scene of the crime, knowing that is the only way to break the spell of the moment; nothing, revisited, has that original power that binds us for all time. Déjà vu emerges as the only true yardstick by which to judge the course of those circular, convex images: when the surface of reality is touched again, they often fade in an instant and vanish forever.

Sometimes I dream of Firula, and if I strain my ears in my sleep and look from the polluted beach up to the house hidden among the pines, I can hear Aunt Juga calling: "Mićo, Lidija, Tonko, Lilo, time to come ho-ome!" Then we climb out of the water and run toward the house, but the old steps are gone; before us is the cliff that we cannot climb. We split up, each going his own way, and Tonko, feebleminded Tonko who died young, goes back into the water, wades into the shallows, and waves at us for a long time. But we don't turn around and wave back; we leave. And we never see each other again.

Translated from the Serbo-Croatian by Alice Copple-Tošić

■ □ ■ □ ■

THE STORY OF THE MAN WHO SOLD SAUERKRAUT AND HAD A LIONESS-DAUGHTER

Judita Šalgo (Serbia)

"WHAT SHALL I WRITE ABOUT?"

I had already asked the same thing a little while ago. I've been trying to write for years. I've got the words all ready. I've got something to say, but I don't know what to write about. Whenever I ask my husband he says something nonsensical. I'd like to write something that makes him happy, based on an idea of his. Maybe it would mean something to him.

We left the car at the edge of the village and headed down a dusty dirt road that skirted a beech-covered hill. Around the first bend we were assailed by the acrid odor of decay. In the middle of the road lay a large, moldy, pickled cabbage. My husband kicked it and it rolled heavily, soddenly to the side. We left the road and took a shortcut along the ravines cut into the steep slope.

"I saw an amazing woman yesterday. Tall, lean, and powerful, dark-skinned. Her movements were rapid, controlled. She walked as if she were dancing. A cat."

We were standing on a plateau, in pasture. The grass was short, tough, steppe-like, so the sheep, accompanied by conscientious but indifferent dogs, made their way quite quickly, at the same speed and in the same direction, like a small woolly cloud. The sky was clear, there was no sign of the weatherman's "late afternoon thunderstorm," and everything was clean, clear on the evenly trampled ground. Anything anyone said or did there was important, worthy, and in its place.

But I can't write about a woman he has seen.

"What shall I write about?"

I took my husband's arm and leaned my head against his shoulder. He stopped, turned toward me, and drew me close. He was straight, with a flat stomach, solid as an oak. He squeezed my shoulders, patted them lightly, then let me go with a gentle shove.

"Write about a man who sells sauerkraut and has a lioness-daughter."

We headed down the southern slope of the plateau along a path through orchards divided into small plots. The slanted rays of the afternoon sun fell on his face. His right cheek was still warm, his left one already cold.

This was not such a pointless task. Or difficult. It would be quite easy, even, to describe an ordinary girl, the daughter of a man who sells sauerkraut, a few words about her life, begin the plot, and then, in passing, add: by the way, she's not a girl, but a lioness. Or: describe a beautiful powerful lioness, her silent, springy footfall as she paces nervously back and forth in her narrow cage, rubbing against the iron bars, slapping them with her flank, and then at one point, when the sentence has almost ended, mention in passing (once again, only in passing!) that, incidentally, she's not a lioness, but a girl, the daughter of a man who sells sauerkraut, and therefore quite an ordinary, run-of-the-mill lioness-girl.

The two of them, father and daughter, live alone in a garden apartment on Futoška Street (her mother died of septicemia after giving birth, without saying a word about her unusual child); between opening the door in the morning and closing it in the evening they live like everyone else in the neighborhood, and only her heavy, half-closed eyelids and her sleepy look indicate that the girl is a lioness. On the other hand, only her bewildered, sad expression indicates that the lioness is actually a girl. Her nature is almost completely without bestial traits. She never seems to long for the company of real beasts (like other young people, she likes dogs and cats); it has never occurred to her to attack a goat, a sheep, or a child: she is nothing like those notorious panther-women in the fables that the homosexual Molina tells to the revolutionary Valentin in their prison cell in Puig's novel *The Kiss of the Spider Woman.*

Her father, who makes and sells sauerkraut, does not bemoan his fate. He has never reproached his daughter for having been born a lioness unlike all the other womenfolk in his family, unlike the dozens of new little girls who come crawling out of the neighbors' apartments year after year. Father and daughter talk about business: how things are going at the market, how much has been sold. During the summer, the daughter helps her father bring the cabbage (from Futog, of course, that's the cheapest); she cleans it, cuts it, salts it, and packs it in plastic barrels (this causes a lot of friction with the neighbors, as they take up half the shared basement); she brings water and pours it over the cabbage. From mid-October, with her father's help, she takes the barrels out of the basement and loads them into his three-wheeled cart, only one each market day. She rarely goes to the market, however. They don't talk much about anything else, least of all themselves. Her father silently strokes the back of her head, pats her on the back, and mumbles to himself. Only sometimes does he rouse himself and says more clearly, "Don't worry, my girl, things will get better. . . ."

It would be simple to say that she was a lioness in her sleep and when awake a girl. Or vice versa. Because, awake or asleep, she was both: a lioness-girl. In fact, the girl would sometimes wake up as a lioness, and the lioness, particularly after a long afternoon nap, toward dusk, would sometimes wake up as a girl. The girl would come face-to-face with herself as a lioness, and the lioness, seeing her reflection from time to time in a bucket of water or in the puddle in the middle of the courtyard on a rainy day, would face herself as a girl. She was both human and beast, and therefore self-sufficient.

There was a time when I really liked Rousseau's painting *The Sleeping Gypsy.* The dark-skinned girl (her face, hands, and feet seemed to be made of sooty baked clay) sleeps on the bare ground of the wasteland. The light, multicolored dress she is wearing seems to be made of porcelain, next to her on the ground lies her guitar, a little further away is a jug, and above her, opposite the clear sky, which grows darker and darker toward the top, stands a lion, already touched by the gathering twilight, dark, but with his luxurious mane lit by moonlight. His bright, round eye is fixed sternly on her; he sniffs her, but does not touch. In the distance (which does not exist, as everything here is without perspective), parallel with the girl lies a narrow strip of water, separated from the sky by just a whitish wreath of sandy or misty mountains. The landscape is dreamlike, but the girl belongs to reality. She is real because of her heavy, deep, earthy sleep. The moment she wakes and tries to get up she will simply disappear. She will become (remain) the lion.

And now I really wanted the lioness-girl to be credible, authentic, real in my description. The request that I speak about her must have been made with some purpose. I had to make something out of nothing, create something compelling, essential, out of something purely random. Only if she were real would the rest of it be real: her deep devotion to her father, her simultaneous fear of and longing for the neighborhood children, the kind of children that—she has suspected for some time—she will never have; only then will her father's harsh life as a market trader be real, for whatever he puts on the counter to sell, fresh or pickled cabbage, onions, carrots, leeks, or potatoes, he always has trouble with the market inspectors or with the other vendors, and most of all with the fat women, red-cheeked in their youth and bluish in their old age, who, at the first sign of autumn, stuff their large breasts and stomachs into sheepskin coats over which they put white aprons, wet in front from the brine; it is only then that it will be real: the girl's heartache over her father's misfortune and humiliation, her deeply hidden yearning for revenge, her desire to let out a tremendous roar as she chases and tears apart those wretched market people who buzz like flies around rotting leaves and roots, touching, nibbling, tearing to pieces, and devouring like rats those tasteless, miserable substitutes for life, for raw meat.

It is only then that we will be real, my husband and I and this latest futile conversation of ours.

"I have to tell you something," he said.

Both of them, the man who sells sauerkraut and his lioness-daughter, live in a world apart, squeezed between the house and the market stall, each dependent on the other. It is not very likely that anything new could happen, such as the lioness-girl falling in love (and if that did happen, her love would have to be unrequited, unhappy from the beginning, and unalloyed misfortune does not make

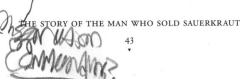

a plot); it is not very likely that some day, after all kinds of problems, she could get married, have children, be happy, worry, suffer, that she could meet and leave various people, welcome people she cares for and wave them good-bye, mourn for anyone, cry over anyone. Neither could the old man's life consist of anything but the daily, painful but calm progress toward death. So a story with two such characters can have no plot. It is only the shortest path between the beginning and end; it separates the narrator from his audience by only the briefest possible moment. While the girl was waking up and confronting herself as a lioness, my husband simply wandered off. When she opened her eyes, he was gone.

Having walked in a large circle, we were now on a path lined with blackberries, already bare, climbing once again to the open plateau. My husband was walking lightly, with pleasure. I was dragging my feet, dead tired. It was just getting dark. The sky was still light, but the moon was already up in its place, round, magnificent, in all its glory.

If I sit down, I thought, I'll lie down. If I lie down, I'll fall asleep. If I fall asleep, my husband will pass, give me a stern, astonished look, and leave. He won't even hurt me. But I didn't want Rousseau's picture to be repeated right now. I didn't want anything to be repeated. Bad things always look like art. Off-the-hook art. When I weep, I have the feeling that it has already happened somewhere. Suffering should not be exhibited.

My husband was twenty steps ahead. Then, in the middle of the plateau, he stopped, dropped the canvas bag from his shoulder, and as though suddenly overcome by fatigue, sat down and stretched out on the ground. I thought he would close his eyes and I would be able, unobserved, to lie down next to him.

But he watched me approach with wakeful eyes. I stopped, closed my eyes. I breathed in his smell. I wanted more than anything to lick his hard, tight mouth.

"But I don't even know how cabbage is pickled," he said.

"What cabbage?"

I didn't have the courage to touch him, or even leave. His damp look slid down my cheek. That's all I need, I thought. But the salty drops I tasted on my tongue didn't come from my eyes; they came from somewhere above. The sky was clear, only a damp film covered the moon. The wind was getting stronger and stronger. Who knows where it was bringing those drops from?

"Brine?" I said, wiping my cheek.

The moon had already been dipped in cloudy white juice. Wrinkled, with a sour expression, it was draining like a pickled cabbage.

Brine! Brine from a clear sky!

It was a miracle. I knelt and buried my face in my hands. The brine fell harder and harder.

"This is real," he said. "Real."

My husband looked at me calmly, seriously, from a great distance. He was absent, unreal.

But wet.

Translated from the Serbo-Croatian by Alice Copple-Tošić

■ □ ■ □ ■

THE SAME OLD STORY

Jadranka Vladova (Macedonia)

IT TAKES MY FATHER A LONG TIME TO WALK UP THE TWO STEPS. He hooks the handle of his cane into his pocket, pushes the door open with his right hand, and stoop-shouldered and panting, enters the kitchen. He carefully sits down in his chair and says, catching his breath, that we have a turtle.

My mother looks up with eyes red from chopping onions and through a veil of tears looks at him admonishingly.

It all sounds familiar to me: he has talked about nuns in brown dresses with bluish purple haloes over their heads, the monastery for the construction of which my grandfather collected a thousand gold coins, the water splashing below the bedroom, unknown people with swollen faces who stand in the garden at full moon staring into our windows, pictures you can enter (even more easily than mirrors!) by simply stepping high into the frame, travels that only require cold-dim-blue darkness behind closed eyelashes. . . .

But so far my father's stories have never included animals. In his visions of healing, there have been winged horses for the angels. . . . And yes! Once, as he walked in from the street (wearing a thick sweater over his striped pajamas) he said ten donkeys were waiting for their tailor. But all this was at the beginning of his illness, and we took it as a successful joke about Uncle Risto—the saddler.

That's why I ask him, "What kind of a turtle?"

"Very pink," he says, and calmly inhales the smoke of his lit cigarette.

My mother wipes away her tears with her right wrist and, only for a moment, glances at my father's wrinkled and misty face whose expression inspires my second question:

"Where did you see it?"

"In the garden," he says with an insecure tremble in his voice that, like so many other times, promises secret nests for miracles like those I find in my favorite books. I often make the wrong choices, as I do this time interrupting my father before he gets a chance to explain. I return to my book, all the while thinking about a turtle appearing in our garden; although it is unusual, it is not a big enough miracle for me to listen to my father going on and on. He will be sure to mention the old monastery, whereupon my mother will raise her voice: "What monastery! And in our garden!" and the magic will vanish and turn into an ordinary family fight.

My father, oblivious to all external influences, becomes self-absorbed. He strokes his powerless, stiff arm with his other hand making slow, measured movements that are his only remedy against the pain and stretch the thin, transparent string that still connects him to the *ordinary* world. He opens his mouth to say something; this scares us because we expect him to start moaning. The ritual of stroking his arm is usually accompanied by moaning and the "nonsense" about a big worm drilling holes into his elbow.

My mother used to yell at him often before, annoyed with "this stupidity": "What worm? What worm?"

And he would answer, staring indifferently at her wide pupils, "A white one."

This time around, this scene is omitted. And my father whispers the reason for it, "It's not too bad. There's a lot of greenery. . . ."

It took us a few days to get used to my father's new story. Everybody knew there was a turtle in our garden. Some people mockingly asked questions about it. (What does it eat? Where does it go? How does it sleep? Where did it come from?) Others just agree, nodding, disinterested, whenever my father starts talking about it—in his calm, monotonous voice with an undertone of worry for the "poor, unprotected, and gentle creature under the shell. And you can smash the shell if you step on it accidentally."

My mother, rolling her eyes, gives a long sigh; then it passes and she starts making jokes. "Your turtle" from her screaming monologues turns into "our turtle" in a gentle feminine mocking tone that she uses to provoke her apparently sexless husband in those rare moments when a thin smile displaces the stable set of wrinkles on his dark face. But even in this new mood, he stubbornly sticks to his claim: we have a turtle in the garden!

Our garden is truly miraculous. Everybody entering it for the first time strains their necks to look up at the Big Tree. And with loud exclamations they admire the feminine faithfulness of the ivy winding its way up to the top of the tree. Exhilarated, they take in the air, breathless from the fragrance of the flowers, and make vulgar noises with their tongues as they imagine the salad growing in the vegetable beds — tomatoes, cucumbers, and peppers — that they would love to devour.

But the biggest miracles in our garden, says my father, are upside down. As though in a mirror, the top of the monastery bell tower reaches as deep as it reaches high to the top of the Big Tree. These flowers share their roots with those even prettier ones on the other side. Under the marble basin of the former Turkish bath (where my mother has planted petunias) there is a gurgling spring that you hear in the deep silence of the bedroom at night. No, there aren't any tomatoes or peppers that can measure up to these. That's the way it is. There aren't any. The guests know how to admire the underground image of our garden. But for the sake of most of the guests, my father stops his story and lets their noisy munching cause us goose bumps, a sure sign that there are a few of us who know how to differentiate between important and unimportant things.

Our guests breathe in the fragrant air with nostrils wide open. With stooped shoulders my father sits in the chair that doesn't obstruct the frequent to and fro to the kitchen. My mother brings out the dishes that our succulent garden has produced.

My father gazes into the distance; his eyes follow the concrete path and, like a magnet, draw the dark spot out of the parsley bushes. Slap-slap. Staring fearfully, he lowers his eyes toward the niche of light and follows the turtle's clumsy movements along the path. The guests sit with their backs turned. I stare at the turtle with my mouth open, and my mother, as she steps over the kitchen threshold and faces the miracle on the path, drops the bowl (probably the salad bowl).

I follow the turtle with my eyes. I catch a glimpse of my father's frozen silhouette; his eyes protectively push it into the safety of the thick shade among the okras and eggplants. In the kitchen, my mother lets out her rage over the freshly sliced vegetables and whispers to me sharply, "It's not pink, did you see! And I'm sure it's the small turtle we brought from Vodno when you went there on a summer vacation. With the children from the kindergarten. I'm sure. S-u-r-e! It's just grown. Nothing strange, after such a long time."

The case of the turtle inspires me to listen to my father with a new kind of attention as he tells the old stories with a new vividness. My mother follows our conversations suspiciously and from time to time mutters, "Pink turtles only exist in cartoons!"

Many days after the encounter with the turtle, my father woke me up in the morning touching me with his cold healthy hand. His hair tousled and his pajamas open, he could barely lean against the bed. His shiny eyes were asking for help, and he stuttered that I had to save it. . . . She had thrown it into the garbage. I'd have to get up. He was sorry, but the garbage collectors would be coming.

I walked, freezing, through the thick fog in the garden. And it was true; my mother had thrown the turtle into the garbage, and it was trying, helpless, struggling with the five openings in its shell and using the round shape of its back to turn over. . . . I looked at it closely—its whitish, smooth belly and dry, scaly legs with the sharp claws, its awful head from which shone two dark little eyes begging for help. But . . . but I couldn't touch it while the five little snakes were slipping in and out through the openings of its shell. . . .

Breathing heavily, I walked back through the yard yelling to my mother that she had to take it out *immediately*. Yawning and barefoot, she sauntered down the trail and returned slowly to sip her hot coffee. After a short question, my father slowly limped to the barn as though weighed down by a great burden. He peeked through the crack in the old door for a long time and then came back the same way we had gone, but more slowly. He whispered, stuttering, that it was awful. I should never leave him alone. He couldn't break himself in half to help the poor pink creature. Yes. It looks like a snake at first, but you have to overcome that. You have to reach out and turn it over, you can't be disgusted by the shell or afraid of the claws. . . . And then it will turn pink.

THE SAME OLD STORY

49

My father died one night while I was sleeping soundly either because I had read late or because of the predetermined human destiny to die alone.

The next day I looked at his body in the coffin, shocked. His crossed hands, now symmetrically immobile, had long, uncut, curved nails. The fine capillaries on his forehead and cheeks created bluish shadows on his blurred face. . . . The sleeve of his sick arm had a big hole on the elbow. My mother whispered as she followed my glance, "Moths have been eating our clothes."

But I knew that the big white worm had left through that hole. Now that the pain had become completely meaningless.

The night after the burial I dreamed of a huge turtle on the path in our garden. It was turned over on its back. And had enormous claws sticking out through the openings for its legs. Its head was showing. Just like a snake's head. Disgusting. But it looked at me with eyes filled with the familiar sorrow that begs for help. I was sweating as I turned it over. I had to work as though I were moving a paralyzed man. But after I turned it, it disappeared, pink, like a movable bush into our garden.

I woke up to my own weeping and was drawn to the window; it was pushed half open by the cold air and was rhythmically banging its glass wings. Leaning over the teary, dark garden I yelled to the top of the Tree-Bell Tower, "Fraaaanz! My father has turned into a turtle."

Translated from the Macedonian by Elizabeta Bakovska,
Agata Schwartz, and Luise von Flotow

■ □ ■ □ ■

THE HERBARIUM

Hristina Marinova (Bulgaria)

"YES, I'M THE ONE THAT FOUND HER. LYING IN THE MIDDLE OF THE
room. . . . She was barefoot. Facedown, yes. No, I didn't touch her.
I got really scared and went downstairs to the doorman right away.
No, she had no boyfriend. I don't remember her telling me whether
she was expecting anyone. I don't know. I don't remember. No, we
weren't close. Just roommates."

Tuesday never brought me anything nice. When I came back from
class, I found my roommate murdered. She was strangled. I didn't
love her, I didn't hate her, I often didn't even notice her. Mira . . .
They had her move in with me in November. Until then I had lived
alone. She came from far away—from the country, just like me.
First-year student. She seemed scared, humble, quiet, closed. Several
times I tried to get closer to her, but she simply didn't want to know.
Our contacts were limited to greetings, short expressions of polite-
ness on my part, and none on hers. A pretty girl—tall, dark-eyed,
and dark-haired. All I can remember about her is her death.

When they took away the body, I washed the floor, tidied her
bed and her clothes. I expected parents frantic with grief who would
gather their daughter's belongings with teary eyes. I could not sleep
in the room so I moved in with a friend. I left my condolence note
for Mira's parents. I came back a month later and everything was still
there. I called the police. I wanted to get rid of her things. I was told
the body had been collected by the mother, who did not ask about
anything else at all. They gave me a phone number. But it rang without an answer for days. All this angered me. I felt no sadness about

51

her death, I asked myself no questions, and I did not even want anybody to speak to me about this. I decided to throw everything out and ask for a new room. They did not give me one—they said they had none available. Of course, no one wanted to move in with me. Everyone was afraid of the dreams they might have sleeping in the bed of the deceased. So I went on living with her things as I had lived with her. Weeks went by and her mother didn't show up.

I didn't know she kept a diary. No one ever looked for it. I probably wouldn't have opened it if it hadn't been so beautiful—with fine, pale blue pages. I began by peeking at the dates on the first and last pages—November 2 and March 14—four days before the murder. I was in no rush to read it. I was afraid it would be quite boring, all sorts of romantic dreams and greetings of the "Dear Diary" sort. I was sitting and stroking its exquisite cover. I thought about Mira, who had written it in secret. But my condescending smile melted with the first line.

November 2

I came here to be what I am. A whore. All men will want me, and I promise they can have me. Now I am far away, and I will get what I was born for—lots and lots of sex.

I swallowed the saliva gathering in my mouth and quickly turned the page. There was a detailed drawing of male genitalia.

November 7

Around thirty. Not tall but decent looking. He did not believe I was a virgin and that made him nervous the first time. Then I seduced him many more times. He got more and more aggressive but not perverse enough. He paid me without me having to ask. On my way out of the hotel I took a yellowed birch leaf with me. I will start a herbarium collection. Every man will remain inside me, dried up and hidden.

Yes, I remember! I had seen her arranging some leaves. My heart began beating madly. I continued to read.

November 8

I was sitting in the park, on a bench. My uncle's age, two. 40–50. I paid no attention to them at first. I wanted to check whether they were serious. We went to the apartment of one of them. It was great! They fucked me all day long—from 9 in the morning until 8 at night. Fantastic! One of them bit me on the neck pretty hard. I'll have to be careful for Dora not to notice. They wanted my address, but I cannot give it out. I told them I would call them. Oh yes, I will call them.

November 9

Around 25. For now he's my youngest. And the most boring one. I asked for money. He didn't give me any. Just hit me across the face and told me to go away. Full of hang-ups. I went too quickly with him. From now on I will wait to be offered money and then . . . I won't make a living out of this, but somehow if they pay me, I will feel professional. I want to write to Mom, but I don't have the strength to pretend at the moment. I'll wait.

I closed the diary. My heart was throbbing with surprise. And excitement. How could I have been so blind? I wanted to read more but my hands trembled. I shoved the diary under my pillow and relaxed on my bed. I closed my eyes but could not escape what I had read. I imagined Mira in the arms of all those men. Then I remembered her on the floor—dead. I opened my eyes and was startled by her things on the empty bed. I went outside to forget and hide. I should not read more of the diary. It was painful because I was beginning to know and love her. Now that she had died.

My curiosity prevailed and at night I again opened the pretty notebook. I flipped the pages quickly and with appetite. She hadn't missed even one day. Every time—at least one man, often several. For each one of them she gave the approximate age, no name, but often a rating such as "was no good," "fucked me senseless," "little boy with a penis the size of a cocktail sausage." . . . Some more detailed descriptions even turned my stomach. On some pages there were pictures from pornographic magazines. They illustrated the positions described. I was most surprised by the care with which everything was done. No crossed-out words. One and the same pen, even and beautiful handwriting. . . . I turned each page very carefully and with a sort of respect. All the men were different—in age, size, imagination. I had not suspected such things could be written this way, without shame. I wondered why Mira had done it. Not why she had slept with them, but why she had documented everything so carefully. On some lonely nights, she had probably read her stories, masturbating, excited by her memories. Or maybe she expected me to find her diary and she wrote it for me? I was flattered by the thought that she might have wanted to tell me, to share what she felt uncomfortable discussing. I read on, and all of a sudden I froze.

March 10

Today I wrote to Mom. I described the last one. In his forties. I like those best. I wrote that his was quite big and that he did it to me three times, anal. I told her everything in detail, even how he held me and what he had said. She'll like it. I wrote a lot. I am expecting an answer.

I closed the diary angrily. I felt ashamed for her. I got up and started walking around the room in circles. I was furious that I had not guessed, that I had not talked to her. One of those perverts must have found her and killed her. He wanted more than she could give. But her mother would have never found out the truth about her daughter if Mira had not written to her. I realized I was speaking out loud, that I was scolding and lecturing her. I was very angry, but decided to finish reading the remaining pages. I opened the last one immediately and found . . .

March 14

I got an answer from Mom. Exactly the one I was expecting. She'll be here on Tuesday. I am expecting her, I want her, I feel her.

There was nothing else. I felt dizzy. Her mother had come the day of her murder! I could barely wait until the morning to go to the police. I took the diary. I found the policeman who had interrogated me and, stuttering, began to explain. He interrupted me.

"We've got him already. Serial killer. He operated on campus. He attacked single girls, raped and strangled them. Your roommate was an exception—she was not raped. She must have put up a stronger fight. Don't worry. It's just a product of your imagination."

I shoved Mira's diary in his hands:

"Oh, silly girl stuff! I would advise you not to show it to anyone. After all—if you have nothing nice to say about the dead, you better not say anything at all." A polite smile slid across his face. I was already outside when I remembered I should have taken Mira's address. I went back. He copied it down for me just as politely, and patronizingly told me to be careful. Had he slept with her too? I returned to the residence to pick up my things and went straight to the train station. There was a train in two hours.

The death notice was attached to the door, and I didn't dare ring the bell.

"Mrs. Nikolova has been gone for a few weeks." A woman in a bathrobe was peeking from the apartment across the hall. "What is the reason for your visit?"

"I was her daughter's roommate. Mrs. Nikolova, when will she be back?"

"I think she is selling the apartment and is planning to live in the country. Come on in, let's not talk like this, in the hallway."

I went in and sat down without taking my coat off. The neighbor happily began telling the story.

"She had such a difficult time surviving little Mira's death."

"And Mr. Nikolov?" I interrupted.

"There has been no Mr. Nikolov for twenty years now. Oh, you didn't know? I think that is why they were so attached to each other. She, Maria—Mrs. Nikolova, I mean—after his death cared alone for the child. She went crazy spoiling her and admiring her. She bought her everything. Never had any contacts with me or anyone else in the building. . . ."

"What about Mira?"

"Neither did she! She was a big girl, ten years old, but she'd start crying if she was separated from her mother even for a little while. I'm telling you, it was a little too much. And the fights before she let the child apply to university! They yelled for days, they cried. The little one then pulled herself together and got her way. I didn't think she would let her go. Then, for the placement tests and all, they went everywhere together. But when the school year started it couldn't go on. Who could have imagined such a fate! To be murdered, the dear girl. . . . What a beautiful child she was. . . . Maria, when she came back, kept on repeating, "My little girl—my beauty!" Always the same . . . Her hair went white. I have never seen anything like it before!"

In the train on my way back I couldn't stop crying. I did not believe that she had killed her. The neighbor offered to call me when she saw her so I could come back. But there was no point. I was already not so sure. Maybe it really was the serial killer, and I had imagined all this nonsense.

In the night I woke up because of the rustling of the leaves. Mira's herbarium. It was on the table—a shoebox that had always been there, but it was as though I saw it for the first time, I turned the light on and drew the box closer to me. A lot of dust had already accumulated on the lid. I opened it. The dried leaves inside almost filled it. I felt like crying. I carefully emptied the contents on the table. At the bottom I found what I had expected. Her mother's letter.

"My little girl, why are you doing this to me? Why are you killing me? I miss you. I want to nurse you, I want to kiss your feet. I want you to press yourself against me. I need to see you bathing in the morning, my dear! Why did you abandon me, why do you think that by doing these ridiculous, foolish things you would forget about me? Only I can make you happy. I will come on Tuesday. And I will take you with me forever. I love you! I believe everything you have written to me, and I want you to know that I do not care. Do not expect jealousy from me. I know that you do it because you miss me as much as I miss you. You cannot exist without me. You will not exist without me. I kiss you all over!"

Translated from the Bulgarian by Spaska Siderova and Luise von Flotow

■ □ ■ □ ■

EVERYTHING'S OK

Daniela Crăsnaru (Romania)

THIS WAS THE FOURTH TELEGRAM HE HAD RECEIVED IN THE LAST
two years. The first was brought to him by a boy in hotel livery, on a
silver tray with a white carnation beside it. The hotel's custom.

Must be from Horst, from Bern. Maybe they changed the concert
date, he thought with immediate displeasure. Any modification in
his schedule irritated him, and every irritation raised his blood pressure. It was only two hours before the performance, and Wagner isn't
child's play.

COME HOME. MAMA ILL.

When Luigi arrived to take him to the concert hall, Luigi found
him still in the armchair holding the telegram, the carnation clenched
in his fist.

"Che succede, maestro? Sta male?"

"No, niente, niente. Andiamo."

He doesn't even see the orchestra. The opening phrases have liquefied
his brain. For the first time in thirty years of conducting, he hates the
music. The final applause, the taxi in the rain, the airport. And in the
plane, who knows why, after more than ten years, the words of that
little half-crazy girl from Madrid who calculated for him the fixed
stars and the ephemerides: strong life foundation, a rich psychic underground, the house of matrimony ineffectual, sensuality reinforced
by a vigorous imagination, financial and emotional detachment, ex-
ceptional gift for music, powerful influence of his mother, powerful
influence of his mother, powerful influence . . .

She was as beautiful as ever, the elegant nose, the thin lips, the royal cut of her gray-green eyes. Only very pale.

Uncle Aurel: "She had the grippe. Now she's all right. But at her age anything could have happened, even to . . . We both thought, I and your brother, that you had better come. But those good caramels from abroad, you know which ones, have you brought us some or . . ."

After the joy that overwhelmed him because he saw her alive, because he could pat her unnatural white hands deformed by rheumatism, because she too responded with tormented gestures to caress his hands in turn, he didn't care about anything else. Neither about Uncle Aurel, her younger brother, who was self-installed as head of the family after the death of her husband, nor about Victor, his own brother, the "normal" child of the family, the taciturn engineer, whom she used to love "normally"—"I could never love him as I love you, but he doesn't mind, he forgives me because you are my light and my joy and my life"—nor about Victor's two children, his nephews, sneaking more and more insistent glances at his luggage.

She caressed his hands as in his childhood, when she used to say to him, "It's gone, you don't have a fever anymore, tomorrow I'll make you a rich chicken soup with tiny stars shimmering on top, and after tomorrow you can take out the new sled."

That room smelled of antiseptic alcohol now, of medicines, of old age, of the end, but he was determined to identify her scent from long ago, the best smell in the world, and look, he isn't able to, these others won't leave the two of them alone, and he'll never let himself cry in front of them because . . . "You distanced yourself from us, Gelu." And, "With all these journeys of yours, you've already forgotten you still have a family here. . . . You've forgotten where you started from. We're tormented with everything here, and you, God knows, I can't at all imagine, Gelu, how an insensitive and stone-hearted man like you can make music, boy. . . ."

He went on caressing her hands, weaving his fingers into her twig-like fingers, touching palms, the same way he used to do in those short moments of emotional paroxysm with the women he loved, whom he felt he possessed fully only that moment, the bitter moment when their hands joined together. That gesture, look, look where it comes from, but he didn't think about this then, not about this.

The second telegram with identical contents confused him more than the first one. Oh God, maybe this time! Maybe this time. Oh God! He told himself, It clearly must happen one day. It's part of the course of nature. He tried to encourage himself, but his words weren't enough to stop the waves of weakness which inundated him. In his hurry he forgot the score of *Walkyrie* in the Zurich airport, and on the flight he tried to picture the score, to decipher the notes in his mind, remaining immersed in it with closed eyes while waiting for the landing, but in fact it was *her* he thought about, her shrunken aged body, her gnarled hands.

When he entered the house, an indescribable bustle, a gaggle of biddies from the neighborhood fussing about, carrying pots and trays from here to there.

"He's come, Madame Iliu! The boy has come!" And then, from the kitchen door, *she,* an apron on, her hands full of dough: "Oh, Mama's Gelu." And he, stupefied, trying to understand yet powerless to understand, and, above all, no longer even capable of feeling joy.

"I didn't want them to summon you, oh your Mama's dearest boy, but you know tomorrow it's Aurel's daughter's wedding, little Lia, your cousin, and, oh Mama's dear boy, your uncle Aurel said that if he doesn't write that I am sick, you aren't going to come. They want to boast about your being at the wedding because you know, you — oh, your Mama's pet — you're the pride of our family, and . . . well . . . Mama's little chickie, I'm glad you've arrived. Go with your uncle, dear son, and take some money from that special account of yours, too, you know which one, and buy what's necessary from the hard-currency shop, because look at us, we're struggling to do our best, because, you know, they need a lot of things, Mama's sweet child, because only once will your cousin marry, our dear little Lia."

He let himself be dragged where they wanted, he smiled politely, he docilely answered the questions put to him by the unknown people who stared with poorly masked curiosity:

"So, are you making a lot of money, Mr. Conductor?"

"Yes."

"And do you also give some money to our country?"

"Yes, the percentage provided for by contract."

"Oh, that's good, Maestro, good. Because it's true, too true, our little country has a lot of need."

"It has."

"Good for you that you don't forget your country and your family and your poor, helpless old mother."

"Yes, yes."

After more than four years he went to the cemetery where his father lay buried. In the silence of autumn, he thought about his father, about his manner of being so alone and withdrawn, about the fact that he passed away with no noise, just the way he used to live his whole life long, about those days when, after the family gatherings, he retreated silently to a corner of the garden to smoke a cigarette and think intensely about something. About what? No, he won't ever learn because he never tried to become close to his father, to know him, to discover what was inside him. It was too late. And only here, finally, did his tears fall in quiet grief, the tears that he had to pay in debt for this journey.

As he flew back on the plane, the words of that girl came into his mind again: life foundation, powerful influence of his mother, of his mother, of . . . oh, God! This sordid farce affected him so disagreeably. That he could rejoice that *she* is on her feet, that she is healthy, that *she is*!

Anyhow, something inside of him began to putrefy. To become detached. To wear away like old silk, which you can rip to shreds merely by looking at it.

The third telegram read this way:

SERIOUS FAMILY PROBLEMS. COME AT ONCE.

It was very curious that nobody said a thing to him on the telephone. And he used to call them every two weeks. They protected him, so to speak. More like, Yeah, you with your life and we with ours. Everything is the exact same way you know it to be. He couldn't find out anything, either from Uncle Aurel or from his brother, Victor.

What could it be now? he asked himself, somehow already anes-
thetized, immune. Turned to stone? It was clear he *had to* help them,
whereas they had no obligation to understand him, for the simple
reason that they couldn't. "The devil alone can understand you artists!" And Uncle Aurel underscored the word *artists* with a gentle
mockery, meaning, How come? Don't you have the same mother and
the same father as your brother, Victor? It's simply that you had all
the luck, that's how come!

But did they know his genuine torments, his loneliness, masked
by applause? (The women, as many as they were, could understand
almost nothing, and if they wanted him, they wanted just him, not
his music as well, a realization that was impossible for him to bear.)
His fears, his insomnia, the ominous test results of his medical check-
ups, this engine in his chest which chugged along more and more
arbitrarily, contrarily, exhaustedly. At least it's not the beginnings of
Parkinson's. Deaf, I could continue to conduct a year, perhaps two.
But not with tremors in my hands. And he watched his hands like
strange wild animals, filled with autonomous life; he watched them
with suspicion and worry, almost spying on them.

He'd done a lot of shopping. In order to satisfy them. At home,
Uncle Aurel: "Your mother's in the hospital. She fell and they put a
pin in her leg. Go see her, but don't stay long. We have some business
we must attend to."

He stood at the gate of the hospital grounds about three quarters of an hour before a nurse came to let him in. He didn't ask
this nurse anything. He advanced toward the hospital building, and
he felt guilty. Guilty because he didn't feel himself able to tremble
with worry anymore, to be frightened for her as before, because he
couldn't *feel* as before, because . . . his mother is lying somewhere
nearby, on a hospital bed, his old mother who . . .

"In here, Mr. Iliu."

He opened the door. In the room, only two beds. One empty,
and there in the other, *she,* and beside her on a chair, the attending
physician. "I kiss your hand, Mama. Good morning, Doctor, I am
Gheorghe Iliu."

"So? You came at last? You let them throw me here in this
hospital, like a dog, completely alone, in this room? Why did I
give birth to two children and raise them and make men of them?

Why? Tell me why? For them to throw me out, to put me in a hospital?"

"Don't be upset, Mr. Iliu," the doctor told him, almost whispering, leaning over him. "That's the typical reaction of old people. They feel they're being rejected. To them, the hospital is where ungrateful children abandon their parents, get rid of them. They hardly understand that certain illnesses cannot be cured at home. But they want to be at home because they want to die at home among their own. Please understand her and forgive her. Anyhow, in a week, she can be taken home. The operation went very well. Her psychological recuperation will be more difficult."

"Do you have your car with you, Gelu?"

"No, Mama. You have to stay here a while longer."

"Not even in chains. Call a taxi and, if you don't have money, *I'll* pay it. Maybe you don't have any, boy—that's why you travel all over the world, not to have any money! Call a taxi, and your mama will pay for it."

He went out dazed and humiliated, followed by the condescending smile of the young doctor.

Uncle Aurel: "What more do you want, man? She's eighty-four. She's afraid to die there. Try to understand her. What do you mean, to make yourself into a joke? Well, that's a good one! My, my, how sensitive you've become, Gelu! But look, let's be practical, let's look at our real problems, in fact. Lia and her husband cannot stay with me anymore. So tomorrow you'd better go and visit some big shots and ask them about arranging for an apartment for them. And in addition, while you're there, see what can be done to speed up the official approval of your brother Victor's buying a car. Got it, Gelu? Please don't be upset, but, you know, you come so seldom, the problems keep increasing, you know, you're the sole hope for all of us, and . . ."

He stood up, lit a cigarette, and surprised himself by heading out to the garden toward that corner of his father's loneliness.

This was the fourth telegram. It had already been opened. He didn't know that the management from the hotel had sent the telegram to the clinic, and the staff from the clinic had sent it to the embassy to be translated in order to determine whether they should show it to him. Nurse Maggie, the one who brought him the music journals every day and who used to change not only his IVs but also his CDs, released his right hand, disconnected and removed the tube, and, leaving him hooked up to only the central monitor, held out the telegram for him to take in his hand and read.

"Don't worry, sir, please don't worry. It's all right. Everything's OK." She hurried to communicate this, speaking English, smiling reassuringly, adjusting his pillow. "Read it, please. Everything's OK."

APR. 25 — MAMA'S 85TH BIRTHDAY.

Translated from the Romanian by Adam J. Sorkin with the author

■ □ ■ □ ■

FROM A DAY WITHOUT A PRESIDENT

Carmen Francesca Banciu (Romania)

IT WASN'T A DAY LIKE ANY OTHER DAY. IT WAS THE DAY THEY STARTED numbering the years again. As if he, Artur, had lived part of his life in one world. Then. A cataclysm. And the world started again from zero. And he who had hated the world he had lived in. Who had struggled to find a way out. Now found himself locked out. Exiled in a tree.

For good? Nonsense, Sandra had said at the time. Someday he'll get down of his own free will. He'll understand that you can't rise above your condition. And Maxim had sulked. Looking at her like a child. From under his brows. His head bowed. You don't know Artur, he had said. You are too young. And Maria-Maria wanted to understand what he meant.

My dears, Ilina says. We are our own children. But who can come to grips with Maxim being a child. Sometimes her child. Other times his own child. And at other times a parent. At other times Sandra's parent. Or somebody else's. How can you come to grips with that? Maria-Maria herself could not grasp it. And yet she did. How come Maxim was her child? And sometimes he was not. At those times he was Maxim, a man in his prime. A pillar. And yet he was the Maxim who had lost Artur. Or who knows how things stand. Maybe Artur had lost his own self. And thus all of them had lost Artur. But before anybody else they had lost Toma.

Before anybody else they had lost Toma. It's not the same thing, Varvara cries. Or she would have cried if she had still been there. It's not the same thing. And she knew it best. Although this is not clear either. For Toma it was a fulfillment. But even this, I mean. They had gone too far. That even this was questioned. By Ilina. The one who should have known it best. By Ilina herself. Here Maxim was firm. He wanted to be firm. For how can you look at the world otherwise? How could you raise your eyes from the ground? From the bottom of the glass? How could you walk? Move? Believe that anything has any importance in this world? If nothing has any importance. If everything is relative. If everything is called into question. If everything changes. And is no longer what it used to be. If nothing remains what it was. So nothing is what it is. Then how can you know if something is anything in this world.

Maxim feels that the world slips away before his eyes. That it slips away from under his feet. That love is called into question. Happiness is called into question. That Maria-Maria calls him into question. The children. Life. Death. Fear.

Where is this going to take us? Come to your senses.

Maxim was firm in his belief. That they had all lost Toma. But especially that Toma had lost himself so that they could find themselves again. That Toma had done it knowingly. Toma. Who had let his blood flow into the rich earth? A hero. A martyr. These are not empty words. Motherland. Love. Freedom. No myths, Ilina says. To hell with the myths. That's what brought everything down onto our heads.

Ilina can afford to say these things.

I have no idea why Maxim said this. But it was clear that he turned his eyes away from Ilina.

Maxim said we have nothing if we don't have myths. We are nothing. Who are we?

Maxim turned his eyes away from Ilina. And Ilina turned her eyes away from Sandra. It got cold. So Maxim said if we no longer have myths I'm afraid. Maxim was afraid to look at Maria-Maria. For fear she might have turned her eyes away from him. Away from the children, too? No. Not from the children. Never from the children. Like hell! But . . . if everything is relative . . . Forget it. Forget the myth of relativism. Everyone has gone astray a little. Relatively astray. Relatively little. Something like this wouldn't have been possible in former times. When they were all together. When they had come together without planning it. As if in response to a signal. A signal each of them had felt. They had come together because they were one. Or for what reason. And why this sharp pain now. The loneliness.

Treason. Artur had said. A butterfly said. Dreaming a bird's dream.

Without myths. No. Nothing. Who are we?

Varvara had retired long before. When they had lost Artur and all hope about him. Valer was in Berlin. On the way back from. Or on the way to. It didn't really matter. It meant he wasn't. Valer's endeavor was the wide world. Valer was in Berlin. Because he had lost Artur. Or Ilina. Or. Maria-Maria says he hadn't found himself again. Valer. And he wouldn't come back until he had.

Valer thought he was in Berlin. But he was always here. Obsessively here. Says Ilina. So far away and yet so much here. He can't do even this. He can't even run away into the world. To hell with him. Why doesn't he let me alone. With his hiccups. His undecided spasms.

And Maxim. He needs living myths. He looks to the right. Then to the left. He always needs something. He smokes. Drinks. Gets into a rage. He. Becomes individualized. In a way. Through his need to belong somewhere.

Maria-Maria says I am. Whether you like it or not. I live. Breathe. Suffer. I hit my head against the walls. Day after day I'm born again. I get round. I get whole. I become what I am. Maria-Maria.

Ilina says, My reason. That's what Ilina says. My reason for living is to find out. And Sandra says, Like hell! But Ilina says, We shouldn't look like two fighting cocks. Ho-ho-ho. Ha-ha-ha. Says Maxim. And he tells only Maria-Maria whatever else has flashed through his mind. Heavyweight fighting flyweight. Or something like that. But Maria-Maria doesn't like the joke. Ilina says, My reason for living is to gauge myself. To find my limits. To know my force. My strength.

As for Sandra. She wants pure power.

It wasn't a day like any other day. But for it we'd have been entirely different.

■ □ ■

It wasn't a day like any other day. That's what Radu Iosif says while listening to the tape. But for it no one would have found out so many things about themselves.

Only Varvara kept silent. For Varvara had shut herself up in her own self. She had gotten up from the table. Pushed the chair back into place. Gone away. A long time ago. She had left the field. Shut herself up in her own self. Only her silence could be recorded. The silence she interposed between Varvara and the one who had been Varvara to Artur and the others.

It wasn't a day like any other day. Radu Iosif could be heard saying these words on the tape on which he was commenting on tape number 49. Varvara was silent. Because she had shut herself up in her own self. Her silence could be heard on the same tape. Tape number 49. On which Radu Iosif said, It's clear, while listening to the talk in question. All of this could be heard clearly. Radu Iosif listening. Interpreting. Interrupting the recording. Saying it wasn't a day like any other day. And all the rest. Maria-Maria had accidentally found the tape among the things Artur had left in her care. But the tape didn't belong to Artur. It had shown up later, Maria-Maria said. I won't start investigating now. Won't become a detective. Accidental. I can't call it anything else. Said Maxim.

But why at my place, said Maria-Maria. Nothing is accidental. She turned the cassette player on. Pressed the button. And then voices came on. Ilina's voice. Her own. Maxim's voice. The voice of each of them. And then the interruption. And Radu Iosif saying, It wasn't a day like any other day. And all the rest.

But it's not clear who he's saying this to. Because you can't hear an answer. Only silence. The swish of the blank tape. Running on. And their voices on file. How in hell had Radu Iosif gotten hold of them. And how in hell had the other one gotten hold of Iosif's voice commenting on their voices. And how had the tape ended up among Artur's things at Maria-Maria's place.

How in hell had the other gotten hold of it.

Whoever the other may be. He's one of us, Maria-Maria said.

And Ilina repeated. One of us.

Sandra. And Maxim. And Ilina. And Maria-Maria. All of them lowered their heads. Then they raised them. Looked the others in the face. One by one. Looked into the thoughts of one another. Far away. Into Artur's eyes. Who was no longer Artur. He was a cocoon that had dreamed a bird's dream. They looked into Toma's eyes. Who was no longer. In Varvara's eyes. Who had thrown down the chair. No. She had put it back in place. They cautiously looked into each pair of eyes. The blue eyes. The violet ones. Valer's eyes. Who was and wasn't. That's why they looked at one another. And then silently at Ilina. Ilina lowered her head and looked into her own self. She said, No, not him. But her voice trembled. She would have given anything to be able to hold her head up. Braving the others' eyes. She would have given. Everything.

She would have given anything to be able to speak to the others as before. To stay together with them and debate. To be afraid. Afraid of the same thing. To look for the same solution. To find out. Who. Where from. Why. And that it couldn't be him. Him of all people. Could she say her Valer? But that was exactly it. She could no longer leave things in the hands of chance. She had to make a decision. Now or never. It was a matter of life and death. With Valer. On her right. Or she on his right. Through fire and sword. But how could one do this to Valer? To a person like Valer? Or. Well. Without Valer. Through fire and sword. To defend herself from Valer. And from everything that was attributed to Valer.

How could one do this? To someone like him? To whom one could attribute everything? Loyalty. Friendship. Honesty. Discretion. And other things. And many. Other things.

Now she had to decide. She felt that life wouldn't let itself be lived randomly. No. She. Ilina. A woman like her. Phew! A human. A person. A being. An entity. A what? Whatever. Had to decide her own fate. Take her life in her own hands. Live her own life. With. Or without Valer. Of her own will. But apparently also of his.

The doorknob!

Valer doesn't know what he wants. Doesn't know whether he should want. He would like not to want. He'd like not to be responsible for what he wants. He'd like to be pushed by fate. Actually, Valer is afraid of both wanting and not wanting. He's afraid he might not want to want. Or want not to want. Dammit. This is the most difficult thing. To say no. Or yes. To say no to Ilina is very difficult. It's extremely difficult for Valer. He says. It's inhuman. Moreover. He knows it's good to want what Ilina wants. Only we'll again have questions without answers. Or with two. Three. Multiple. Answers. If it were that simple. Everybody would know.

And it would be. Or wouldn't be. Fine with the world. Or everything would be fine. And for balance. It would also be bad. And the world would be divided into two. Into four. Into angels with tails and devils with wings. And in the sky above. Everyone would be flying. To the sound of lutes. To the clinking of lilies. You see what I mean? And a perfume would be hovering above the world. A stinking perfume.

Dammit. It's inhuman to say no. It's beyond Valer's power. That's why he keeps going to Berlin. That way he doesn't have to deal with it. Say yes. Or no. He drifts with the current. With fate. With Ilina's decision to wait for him. Or not. With Berlin's decision to receive him. He has the others say no. Or yes. He sets Ilina's decision to wait for him beside Berlin's decision to receive him. Ilina's decision not to wait for him. And Berlin's decision to reject him. He plays with all these decisions. For fear of making his own.

Ilina is the one who has to take the bull by the horns. She knows it. But not yet. She's still pondering. Weighing things. Analyzing. She knows. Even if she doesn't know that she knows. She knows which is the best way. And Valer counts on it. Valer who runs away from himself. To look for himself out in the world.

But maybe things are different. Says Sandra. To put it bluntly. She has never had patience with Ilina. Nor has Ilina with Sandra. While Maria-Maria has had patience with both. That's how people are. Complicated. And we must be patient with them. She almost felt like quoting donna Amara. We are all the children of a mother.

Stop playing the saint, Maria-Maria. We know only too well who we're dealing with.

But maybe things really are different. Even Ilina admits that things might be different. After all, she knows Valer so well. That she doesn't know him at all. But no one else can know a person who runs here and there not to get caught.

She knows him so well that . . . She lowered her head. Looked into her own self. And said, It's not him. Then she looked into his eyes. Faraway. But his eyes were closed. Covered with an impenetrable mist. And then her voice trembled. She said things might be different. Perhaps. No one knows which of Valer's stories is true. Unique and true.

And Maxim said, Leave Valer alone. Now you're attacking him too. Maxim knew. That there was not a single story. He knew that Valer had more than one story. And that he, Maxim, didn't know them. Although. He had known Valer for ages. Ilina too. And when the Revolution broke out. How extraordinary! They had come together spontaneously. All of them had come together. He always went back to the history of that day when he wanted to learn something about someone. As if that day were essential.

■ □ ■

That's true. All of them said. It was an essential day.

Even Radu Iosif said, For me it was essential that I didn't participate.

I learned something essential about myself. They say Iosif had said that on another occasion. Essential about each of them. And each of them about themselves. But apparently Varvara had said, Nonsense! None of this is my business. I won't let events. Distract me from my routine. You call them history. I call them accidents. I won't let accidents manipulate my life. Maxim needed myths. The myth of friendship. Of cleanliness. Of human solidarity.

To hell with you. This is what you call myths!

Anyway. Maxim needed Valer. The Valer of that particular day. He didn't know that people are not always what they are. And that on that day many of them were different from what they were. On that day many of them had become luminous. Witnesses to the event had seen a bright cloud hovering above the plaza. Above the demonstrators. Each of them seemed enveloped in smoke. Each one had restive wings with which they produced light. Many of them were different from what they were. But many of them had to be different. They had been told to.

What?

They had received orders. If you want to know.

Maxim felt the ground run away from under his feet. He had lost Toma. And Artur. And he had never had Radu Iosif. Now he clutched at Valer. Hey, you can't tell me that Valer had to take that guy to the embassy. In his car. That he had orders to expose Ilina. You can't tell me that it had been arranged for us to gather. That we received specific orders. You can't tell me that they kept me in prison for a while. And then let me out purposely. So that it got to you. For why would they have let me out. Maybe my task was to lead them to the plaza. But I didn't know I would go to the plaza. And I don't know why I went. Where we all met. Spontaneously. I know we came together spontaneously. Out of human solidarity.

Maxim needed living myths. He drank. Smoked. A lion in a cage of air. An invisible cage. In his fear of losing Valer he was on the point of saying, Don't judge people by their facts. Judge them by their goals. Ilina stared at him. Maria-Maria said, You have lost your mind. She hugged her children to her breast. To protect them from Maxim's thought. And Maxim got red in the face. Looked down. Said, You're right. Dammit. I surrender he would have liked to say. But he only said, You're right: the end justifies the means. Doing good by force. A lot of blood was shed for this. He again saw Artur at the top of the tree. Saving the cat. That didn't want to be saved.

You can't tell me that Valer was exposing Ilina to carry out an order.

Ilina avoided the answer. She said, Toma. What about Toma? This time Sandra's eyes became moist. You're going too far Ilina.

Toma writes: The soil of my homeland. Ilina shivered. She said there are words that should be banned. Abolished. Words that incite to hatred. Words that divide.

But interdiction also divides. Said Maxim.

Maria-Maria said, We all are one. Part of a whole. We are God. God has no homeland. Love is our homeland.

Toma! What about him. Said Ilina. Losing Toma may have affected her the most. For her that was the real loss. She had reread his letter dozens of times. He had written it for her. And for the others. Still Valer had no reason to be jealous. Ilina could be the nucleus. The possibility of communication. With Sandra. Maxim. Valer. Artur. Varvara. And many others. Radu Iosif? No. Not him. He was only trying to find out. But Ilina knew. And so did Maria-Maria. They knew without knowing that they knew. One day. After the pain. The sadness. Despair. Fear. Loneliness. After all this, doubt would come.

And doubt came. Like lightning. Oh, dear. Did it insinuate itself? No. It got accepted.

Ilina said. How naive we were. And vain. I'm ashamed. You're wrong, Ilina. These were Maria-Maria's words. You're right. And also wrong. Our lives are parallel. And multiple. The choice is up to us. Up to us only. We know this. We can also decide for the others. What I'm saying makes me shiver. A dictatorship of the good? That's not what I mean. I don't know how to remove this accusation. I mean it's up to us. To each of us. And to all of us together. The future is up to us. And the past, Maria-Maria. Can we interpret it any way we like? That's not what I mean, Ilina. The past is. We can't exploit it. Our past. Call it revolution if you will. Select what you wish from it. Distort it if you can afford it. It will only turn against you.

everything differs

■ · □ ·

Maybe it is different. Maybe it really is different.

Sandra says, You shouldn't ask me. I've always had the impression that Valer was hiding something. And Maxim said. Each of us is hiding something. Maria-Maria looked at him with wondering eyes.

Just like that. One day you learn that Valer is not Valer. And that Maxim. Who you can read through as if he were a book . . .

To hell with it all.

One day you find out that Valer isn't the son of his father. That he was adopted. That in reality he's the son of a father who has no sons. And lives far away in the world. And Valer is afraid to say all this. For fear he might stop being Valer. For fear that the others might not believe he is who he is. And who is he if he can't even say where he comes from and whose he is? Also, he might have put his mother at risk. She might no longer have been who she wanted to be. Or who she was. After all, before anything else she was his mother. And he. Was Ilina's husband. He would have preferred Ilina to be his husband. But that's how things are in the world. Sometimes you belong to someone. You are contained by that someone.

Ilina believed that he was contained by their love. But he knew nothing about their love. He was in search of a shelter. He was searching for something that Ilina couldn't provide.

CARMEN FRANCESCA BANCIU

Why in hell? said Sandra. Why in hell does Valer need complicated stories? Ilina said, What stories? What do you know about Valer? And Maria-Maria said, That's true. He never tells. He does, said Maxim. But never about himself.

Valer is the universal observer.

What are you talking about. Said Sandra. He has no personality. Valer never says, I.

Valer seeks a fixed point. Valer has a brother who isn't his brother. Who abandoned him although he isn't his brother. Valer has a mother he no longer has. A father who isn't his father. And a father who gave him to someone else. Valer also has Ilina who wants to be Ilina.

And Ilina says, How on earth can no one understand? That I'm ready to become one with him? If he is one with me. The problem is he wants himself to be himself. And I should be part of him. And no one can ask that of me. Not even Valer.

Who has a brother who isn't his brother. Who gave him away. So that he could go out into the wide world. To forget about himself out there. He exchanged him. For. I mean. I know what you mean. And it's unfair. Everyone has a right to his or her own freedom. Including Valer.

Valer can expect nothing from half a brother. Or from anyone else in the world. He must expect everything from himself. He has to give. But this is hard. That's exactly what Ilina says. Lowering her head. And everyone knows that Ilina is afraid. She's afraid for Valer. And of Valer. She's afraid Valer might be afraid of himself. And thus he might get lost in the world forever.

That's what Ilina says. And Sandra understands. And Maria-Maria bites her lips. Closes her eyes. So that she won't hear any longer. Not to mention Maxim. But Sandra won't stop. Or maybe you think that's why. Maybe he did and didn't have a brother. One who abandoned him. Who took the liberty of leaving him imprisoned. Trapped. This was Valer's weak point. Which made him expose Ilina. That he had had no choice. You can't be someone when your brother defected. Even if he isn't much of a brother. After all, a personal file is a personal file. And a personal file speaks.

Thank God. That these are nothing but speculations. And stop it, for God's sake. My head is spinning. I feel sick. I'm getting dizzy. It wasn't a day like any other day. And we came together. All of us. As if in response to a signal. And that's it. There's nothing to call into question here. Says Maxim.

But Sandra won't stop. Valer didn't give in she says. Ilina would like to get up from the table. Push the chair back in place. Button up her overcoat. Wipe her glasses. And go away in the world. Maria-Maria is afraid she might lose Ilina.

Everything is lost, says Sandra.

Maxim looks around him. He clutches at a cigarette. At his children. At everything that used to be his. But what is his? Children grow up. Love comes to an end.

What are you saying? Not Maxim's love.

Maxim is carried away by a whirlwind. By the wineglass. By life. Maxim knows he has lost Ilina. That Ilina has lost Valer. That Valer is lost.

Everyone is lost. Says Sandra.

Maria-Maria says, I don't know what's the matter with you. You're shut up in a nightmare. How can I help you? How can I liberate you? Give me your hands. I'm here. Ilina. And Maxim. And Sandra. What's the matter with you? What mirage is clouding you?

Everyone is lost. Says Sandra. She gets up from her chair. And leaves. She doesn't have glasses.

It wasn't a day like any other day. It was a day when they started numbering time again. But for that day no one would have learned so many things about themselves.

And all these were. On Radu Iosif's cassette. Thirty-three years old. Unmarried. Radu Iosif who didn't participate. Who was a loner. As he said. And Artur said he knew more things about Iosif. Who detested himself.

Why did Iosif detest himself?

Everything they know about Radu Iosif is uncertain. They don't know even his real name. Or anything about his father. Artur used to say that Iosif's father. Apparently. Was the albino man with the notebook. Who filled the cups of coffee that Ilina drank. And Maria-Maria's abortions. After all, a profession is a gold bracelet. It gets handed down from father to son.

Translated from the Romanian by Georgiana Farnoaga

SOUTH WIND AND A SUNNY DAY

Zsuzsa Kapecz (Hungary)

"I'D LIKE TO TURN A SOMERSAULT," SAID MY MOTHER AND STRETCHED out her numbed legs, then pushed herself up on her side and winced in pain as one of the five thin golden needles poked into her hip. The narrow sheet covering her slid aside, and my mother lay there like a puppy huddled in its den.

"Pardon?" I woke from my thoughts. I was huddled next to the bed on a chair with an uncomfortable back that had been put there for family members in a part of the room where the sun shone most intensely. I was pondering my sister's new marriage. She had married a rich businessman; our family had no idea what kind of business it was exactly. I would have spent a raucous weekend with a guy like that, at most. Mother was coughing gently. "I wonder if I could still turn a somersault. That would certainly do my spine good, don't you think?"

"Yes . . . of course," I answered, looking at the worn-out beige sandals carefully set next to the bed. Mother has small feet, as small as a child's, and I realized that I tend to wear down my shoes in the same place she does.

The Chinese doctor came in with her permanent smile and swift movements and adjusted the pillow of the patient lying in the corner, plucked the shining needles out of his body with lightning speed and started rubbing his shoulder blade. My mother pushed herself up again and massaged one elbow.

"Ask her how much time is left," she whispered to me. The doctor quickly turned around and nodded encouragement. "Soon, soon . . . only ten more minutes."

Mother lay back with a tormented face. In these moments I always felt guilty. I was the one who had talked her into treating her back pain at one of the acupuncture clinics in the Chinese suburbs of Budapest. We suffered through the trip on the packed subway two or three times a week and then waited for the bus at a stop surrounded by factories and neglected apartment blocks. At the terminus, there was always the beggar with the thick glasses and both legs missing who sat across from the escalator, always in the same spot on the mosaic floor, so immobile that a cynical sculptor could have modeled him after Buddha. When the bus turned onto the railroad bridge, mother always swept a look across the bleak landscape cut into sections by rails and iron pillars, and only to annoy me, she said, "I've had enough. I am not coming anymore."

I looked at the bed. Mother had fallen asleep, she was heaving and moving in her sleep; the sun was pouring into the room through the plastic lace curtains with oblique stripes shining into my eyes. I pushed my chair back and leaned against the wall. I sat like that for a while, wearily wiping the sweat off my forehead. As if outside everything were ablaze, hoarse and deaf and panting with all hope lost in the heat, in a space filled with mirages and framed by the asphalt and the fleecy clouds.

I remembered a summer day a long time ago, when mother woke me early because she had decided to have arch supports made for me. She had me put on my ruffled dress, tied my hair together, took my hand, and we walked down the freshly washed streets. At every step, the wind fluttered mother's full patterned skirt that she later turned into a fancy dress costume for my sister. Mother had just turned thirty-two around that time, the same age I am now. We trudged up the cool staircase decorated with stucco, and I immediately started to whine when I saw the young, arrogant doctor. The whining turned into quiet sobbing, even though we didn't have to wait long; they took a cast imprint of my foot, wrote down my particulars, and let us go.

I don't know exactly where that building was, I couldn't have been more than five, but what stayed in my memory was that there was bright sunshine as we stepped out the door, and the summer sky gleamed a marvelous bright blue. We saw a little park across from the clinic, big enough to hold three swings and a sandbox. The place was deserted on a weekday morning; I felt it was my kingdom, only mine.

"I want to go on the swings." I looked up at my mother and ran ahead along the gravel path. I eagerly grabbed the chain, jumped up on the seat, and flew. I was a courageous child and swung up high. The thick foliage of the trees glided by my side with sparrows preening on the branches, the houses glided by with their windows wide open spilling the sounds of dishes, laughter, and radio music out onto the square, mother glided by together with the bench she was sitting on, and her smile glided by too as she looked up at me; she didn't say a thing, wasn't worried about me at all.

"You did that really well," she said finally when I ran up to her and hugged her. She stroked my hair, and I felt everything in the world fall into place, this is how things were supposed to be, sitting on this park bench in the sunlight with my mother, for as long as I wanted, the whole morning, and tomorrow and the day after tomorrow, even forever.

"We have to go," said mother and looked at her watch, irritated. She saw the astonished expression on my face, stood up, and smoothed her skirt. "You know I have to go to work. . . ."

I walked next to her silently, my head lowered, and only turned around at the exit to the park to make everything mine again, just for a moment—the path, the silence, the abandoned swing, and the gliding that had already congealed into memory.

Mother moaned and soon after woke up, touched my arm and brought me back to the doctor's room that was burning from the heat. "What do you think? Will she phone tonight?" she asked.

I knew she was talking about my sister, who had taken the plane to the Italian Riviera with her husband. I stroked her small hand covered with brown freckles.

"No. She usually doesn't."

"What do you mean?"

"This is her third honeymoon, Mother. I don't think she needs your advice."

"That wasn't what I meant, but . . ." Then her tone changed. "Are you jealous?" she asked, gloating.

I sighed and said nothing. I looked out the wide-open window. The wind whirled as big trucks passed by, pouring dust onto the burnt, grayish green grass. It was the fifth day of the heat wave; the long-petaled blossoms of the yellow roses were hanging their heads, scorched, along the massive iron fence.

Mother sat up heavily and I saw that her patience was over. "Where is this woman? She could have taken the needles out twenty minutes ago. . . ." She suddenly turned toward me and I felt her warm palm on my arm again. "You at least could give me a grandchild! But you keep being choosy until . . ."

"Mother, please . . . let's not get into that!"

I pushed her hand away and went to the other room to look for the smiling doctor. Skillfully and smoothly she pulled the metal sticks out of mother's thigh, said a few nice words, and we left.

"What should I cook for your father today?" asked mother as we walked side by side down the sidewalk covered with sand. I didn't answer and knew that she didn't expect me to. The dusty leaves of the trees quivered under the light gusts of wind, but there was no promise of the slightest cooling off, just more days threatening heatstroke and heavy, sleepless nights when you lie on the bed at the mercy of the weather and don't even feel like drinking anymore because your own sweat disgusts you.

I smoothed my skirt and looked at my watch. It was noon and that explained everything. At bright noon sunstroke trembles in the air like some pointy, vicious golden needle.

Translated from the Hungarian by Agata Schwartz and Luise von Flotow

■ □ ■ □ ■

FROM LIKE TWO PEAS IN A POD

Dóra Esze (Hungary)

October 15, Saturday

IN MEDIAS RES: YESTERDAY WE HAD THE PARTY AT ORSI'S, THE ONE they've been talking about for two weeks. So where should I start? . . . Orsi had been promising a big party, right? Well, she kept her word, to say the least.

I was really craving such an event. In the afternoon, I could already feel the desire to seduce someone creep up in me. So I did myself up the best I could. (Zozó didn't show up; he said he had to work on Gyöngyi a bit, and he can't do that when I am there.) I went on ahead. My heart rippled at the smell of adventure. (Two guys got on the tram; they stood next to me in the aisle. One of them casually commented, "You have beautiful eyes." "Thanks," I replied, just as casually, and nothing happened.)

There weren't many people at first. A few from the third and fourth terms, mostly couples (Schrőder and Lámi as well), Szabó, and a few of Orsi's girlfriends. We complained that there weren't enough boys, so Orsi made a few phone calls. So about two hours later Gyuli Fodor and András Zsoldos showed up, later Orsi's ex, Gábor Mészáros, who is, by the way, the older brother of her present boyfriend, Bucika. (Bucika didn't come. He's not a party type.)

At first there was a lot of conversation. We had something to eat; at Orsi's there are always excellent salads. Juli from 4E wanted to know what had been going on with me lately; I mentioned that I'd met up with Márta a few times (Juli had a crush on Márta's brother, Gábor Pelikán, two years ago), since Márta is now taking Dad's class.

And I told her about the so-called Don Juan–circle, at least what I know about it, that they're working on right now: Tirso de Molina's play, then Molière, a bit of Rostand and Pushkin, then Mozart's *Don Giovanni;* after that, Byron at length, because according to Dad, Byron's Don Juan is a genuine Don, though you could argue that his character is formed by the women who seduce him. The opera and Byron will be the climax, but if there's time left, they will also talk about *Onegin* and *Werther,* as a kind of postmortem. Juli was completely amazed: This sounds great! Wow! This is true literature. Why hadn't I told her about it earlier. She wanted to join. (I believe she already attended class today.)

Meanwhile the dancing had started. Orsi had one or two turns with András Zsoldos, then somebody put on totally different music, and Orsi withdrew to chat (or do something else) with her dancer. Maybe that was a sign. Oh yes, I left something out: at school, Szabó had grabbed me during one break as I was stepping over his bag. He grabbed me by the waist and pulled me close, asking if I was going to Orsi's tonight. The dirty louse did it really well, and the movement made me understand that for better or for worse part of the evening's programme had been decided. I felt quite happy about this, but was a little annoyed too because it doesn't hurt to explore new waters. Just a tiny bit annoyed, but enough to look forward to Palika Szabó with somewhat ambivalent feelings. (God! Who would have thought about a year and a half ago, when I was so crazy about him but he only noticed me on and off, that things would turn around like this!)

So, as I was standing in the kitchen, Szabó came looking for me, took my hand, and pulled me into the room where, besides Csaba Kúthy and Juli, there was only darkness and some romantic music. . . . I didn't say no. He pulled me close, we started to dance slowly, and this was followed by the other moves, no complaints from me. After the song (which glued our mouths together) we sat down in an armchair. He was very gentle. He breathed into my ear, whispering that I had no idea what a gorgeous woman I had become in only one year (why wouldn't I have any idea?). He said that this Fábris (he knows I hate nicknames based on my last name) sitting on his lap could not be compared to the chubby kid I was at fifteen, and my hair looked so great like this, I shouldn't ever get it cut, and the way I walked and danced, and my tongue, and my kiss, blah-blah-blah. It didn't feel bad, of course, but on the one hand Palika always makes this speech when we run into each other, and on the other, the feeling that I wanted something new, a new man, welled up in me again! I like this game with Szabó, but please . . . The decisive, separating move nonetheless came from him. When I said that all things considered I wouldn't want him to consider me his toy (an unusually silly speech! but it worked), he got offended and left. Honestly, I already knew when I sent him to see if the bathroom could be locked that he wasn't the one I wanted to explore there. (Though it wouldn't have been bad at all.) And then . . . then I really have no explanation why I did what I did next.

I can't remember if Fodor was already sitting at the table in the middle room when I sat down there or if he arrived later (to join me) (?). This guy is incredibly hip, my fingers were itching to touch him. At school, three-quarters of the girls would get down on all fours just to lick his footsteps. (Once, when I was still in first form, Mrs. Fülöpke, the cafeteria lady, said, "There is no other kid as handsome as Georgie in this school!") Last summer at Réka's place on Lake Balaton I chatted with him for about an hour, which was enough to find out that he thinks he is the center of the universe. Already there it crossed my mind that he should be taught a lesson. But if I take a deep look inside, I know I wanted to get even with Dió. Although that's stupid. That guy is pretty unimportant, even though I took the *way* he got up from me on Adrienne's bathroom rug pretty seriously. But once a thought sneaks in, it stays there. Especially if it slips in deeper than the conscious level. At the party last night I didn't know about this though. It would really be an exaggeration to say I did. But what I did was still pretty rotten.

As we were sitting at the table talking, I wasn't even sure I wanted to touch him. I only invited him to the other room because the music was horribly loud, and we lay down on the bed because that seemed the most comfortable place. He was talking about Regina, why they broke up, how much sex they had, and I must admit he sounded sincere. We're not really good friends; he didn't have to speak from deep within himself. It was his idea; I didn't ask for any details. I'm not sure when the decision formed in me. One thing I clearly remember though is that at one point while he was talking, I wondered what he might say if, without a transition, I leaned over and kissed him. It certainly wasn't a logical next step in our situation at that moment. Our lying next to each other was by no means sexual. And the way he touched me wasn't an erotic move at first either: it was about flesh on the thighs. I was sitting back on my heels, he was lying flat, and just to check me out, he ran his hand along my thigh, looking at me in a way that said, Well let's not forget that I was the one who proposed this gesture. Just as a comparison, he then gently pulled my hand down his thigh. It would be a lie to say that at this point he didn't desire me. And certainly I wanted him too, otherwise it would have been pretty difficult.

He put his hand on my breast before he kissed me. Our positions didn't change: I was leaning forward, my legs bent, no expression whatsoever in my eyes (I think); he was looking at me more and more intensely, his fingers under my sweater, then suddenly sat up, touched my lips, and pulled me down.

I was pleasantly surprised: his tongue is really hard, his embrace definitely masculine, good. And he looks such a softie! Meanwhile the voice in my head didn't shut up: how can I do it with *this* particular guy—but if the voice doesn't know that at that level it doesn't matter, and besides the list has to grow, I can't listen to it, sorry. What happened next I don't really remember. At some point, he went and put a note on the outside of the door. He asked me how I wanted to do it. I said that I had a rubber on me. He doesn't like them. Well, that's tough because we can't go on otherwise. He sighed and agreed.

I undressed him and took off my own clothes too (he didn't even notice—true, they usually don't, and they don't even have the slightest clue that this is my magic formula). We laughed a lot. For instance, when we moved with the sounds of the music filtering in from the next room, I rolled over on top of him and back down again ("Wow, that was fantastic. Let's tell them to play it again!"). Georgie Fodor did his utmost; he tried terribly to show off the lover boy hidden inside him. ("Little bird, little bird, where haven't you been kissed yet?") He planted little pecks of all sorts up and down my body. He's fairly well versed. And he was very satisfied with me. I was the one who ran faster though. When I reached the goal with the usual screams more painful than pain, he was awfully happy (his chest filled with an ancient pride, I think). He continued with a big smile on his face. But his smile subsided when I realized that if I carried on just so that he would feel good too, I'd be lying. So I didn't wait for him.

He was totally dumbfounded when I peeled away and started to get dressed. Everything went limp, of course. (I almost said, "See, the problem's solved," but something stopped me.) "At least . . . ," and then there was a hint that his whole being might find a spot, like a fountain, somewhere below my palate (not in those words though). You don't know, Georgie. You don't understand. You don't know how to handle these things. Bye, Georgie dear. (Not in those words.)

I headed toward the kitchen because I was hungry. There I was introduced to two newly arrived boys. The younger one immediately wanted to go for a ride. He didn't care who with, and he didn't even try to hide it. Who does he think he is?

By the way, Gábor Mészáros didn't care either. Initially, he was coming on to Réka pretty aggressively, but she rejected him even more aggressively. I, on the other hand, was somewhat interested in him, based on what Orsi had told me about him. About his body. I set him apart almost before I saw him. Funny, eh? I remember the moment he walked in. Probably every part of me knew right then. At least that's why I think I didn't chase after him: there was no need to rush; it would happen anyway. It didn't even bother me that he was after Réka. So when I walked out on Fodor and headed over to the kitchen, passing by the two new boys on the way, I literally sank into the arms of Gábor Mészáros, who grabbed me and pulled me close, because for a change there was a slow song playing. He was whispering something in my ear to the effect that if I were to leave, he would be very sad. His hand slid down over my butt somehow. As a response, I didn't stay passive either. What can I say? . . . Orsi hadn't been telling lies. I could hardly believe what I felt in my hand. The dance had no particular meaning. When it was over, I went back to tell Fodor what time it was because that's what he'd asked me to do before I closed the door on him. He was lying on his stomach and didn't react. Then he slowly started to rub up against the arm I was leaning on. I gently pushed him off and left.

I had to find something to eat. I put some spread on a slice of bread in the kitchen. Soon Gábor showed up and asked for permission to sit on my lap. He used a bottle of Traubi to turn off the light and didn't even get up. Gábor Mészáros's mouth was all salty. I felt thirsty from him. Lights. Water. Lights off. Kiss. Now me on his lap. But no magic circle appeared, not even later, no matter how hard we worked at it.

Beyond the kitchen there was a sewing room occupied just then by Csaba Kúthy and Juli. When they came out we went to use the freed-up space. You could take off the doorknob and use it from the inside or the outside. We put it on the windowsill.

I spent the next few hours in there with him. As a curiosity I would like to mention that there was no light in the room, at least none that I could find (this became interesting at the end when he was looking for his clothes but couldn't find them), and neither was there a bed. A tiny, tiny room filled with all sorts of stuff. Eventually we took possession of a heap of fabric. I can't remember a more uncomfortable place—but this wasn't a serious obstacle.

We couldn't go all the way, because I'd only brought the one rubber with me, and I don't engage in any unrestricted situation without one. But lots else happened. . . . His caresses weren't even the best part of it. It's hard to say what he did the best. Maybe biting—but that's not the best word to describe it. He was cruel on me with his mouth. Everywhere, everywhere! Cold chills kept running up and down on me; it was exhausting, more than painful: suffering, suffering, suffering was making my skin snap. I could barely endure how he attacked my neck, my breasts, the tip of my tongue, the fold of my thigh, my butt—but whenever he stopped, I was dying for more. Meanwhile he kept turning me over, like bread dough, which made me laugh a lot. He pretended to get angry, but this was part of the game and gave him reason to keep on punishing me.

When the dazed feeling I like so much is there (and that's the reason why I do it, I admit), I pay much more attention. But since I didn't feel on the verge of a precipice after the first kiss, nothing trembled between us later either. When I was walking my fingertips up his back, around his waist, above his butt, and he said hoarsely, "You got it," it was still the nicest thing I could be participating in.

From that moment on, I didn't leave him alone. He whined, implored, almost cried, shook with cold on all fours, asked me with chattering teeth to be a bit more brutal, sometimes burst out, "I can't take it anymore," and slammed his head against the bookshelf. But when he found the spot on my thigh, and I screamed, he howled in triumph: "Finally!"—and paid it all back with interest. He walked up and down on me like a cat, for endless hours. So, in the end, it wasn't his fault at all.

But whose was it? Mine? I don't hesitate once I feel the bubble has left me, disappeared, and the moment has come when playfulness dies in me, when my ideas don't turn me on anymore and the ideas of the other don't either. It doesn't bother me that at twenty-two minutes after one in the morning I still like the situation, and that at twenty-three minutes after, the guy whose nakedness I am holding in my hands stops being interesting. By the way, as I said, we had already been together a long time. Maybe I was bored. Bored by his shiny muscles and his cold, faultless skin. When I had definitely had enough, I announced I was going home. He must have felt the change himself, because without a word he started searching for his clothes (which he had a hard time finding). Once we were out, I couldn't find my shoes. In the hallway some guy called Marci was waiting for his friend whom Orsi was looking after right then, and he looked at me in a way that I could easily have completed my statistics—but there's a limit to everything. I couldn't stay in that apartment any longer.

On my way home, I wondered if I should consider myself soiled. But I didn't feel anything. No emptiness, no satisfaction. Now I feel good again, quite good. Quite good. I woke up at twelve thirty. Then I went over to Zozó's; we played dice a bit, and then I told him what happened last night. All he asked was why I didn't take the Georgie kid into my mouth. I thought about it and realized that I was probably afraid of failing. Because I had never done it. He asked me if I was saving that for someone who would be very important. I had never thought of that before and didn't know what to answer. In his life there have been several gestures of this kind that he's saving up—and I discovered again that he would give me all of them if we both felt that way, but only then. I didn't answer. He played *Turandot,* we lay down on the floor, and he caressed the secret spot on my thumb. Eventually I had to whisper in his ear that I adore him, and even though I knew I shouldn't, I hugged him. Of course he didn't hug me back. Because that will only happen when—and only if—only if both of us . . . very much . . . (Once I asked him what if he never finds a girl he can hug or if nothing ever develops between us where he could say, Nnnow! Then I'll die without it, he replied. I laughed at how sentimental he is, but perhaps I should have admitted the truth that it will happen, and it will happen between him and me . . . but he wasn't mad at me.) When I got home, I studied history all afternoon, because Fakir promised us a test for Tuesday: "One mistake is an F." (So I asked him, "Does that mean that five mistakes is an A, professor?" He didn't bat an eyelid. But he wouldn't be our adored, irreplaceable Fakir if he had!)

Translated from the Hungarian by Agata Schwartz and Luise von Flotow

■ □ ■ □ ■

A LITTLE BEDTIME STORY

Jana Juránová (Slovakia)

THE FAMOUS HUMAN RIGHTS ACTIVIST IS A LITTLE UNSTEADY ON HIS feet as he leans over the bed someone is sleeping in—probably one of the participants of the graduate summer seminar. This someone has an almost bald, shaved head, probably for image purposes. This he did not expect. The intellectual is leaning over a bed in a room whose door was not locked, at one thirty in the middle of the night, he is leaning over the bed in a very good mood, looking forward to sex, looking forward to how he is going to surprise the beauty who, all evening, had been tossing him deep, meaningful glances from her bewitching eyes. Suddenly a bright light shines directly into his face, this hasn't happened to him in a long time, the last time was during the interrogation when the secret police were still after him, he's already written several essays on the subject, it was quite terrible, they were sitting across from him, he couldn't see them, they'd been shining a light in his face, like in a bad film, and questioning him. Night. He'd been thinking about sex, and now there's this lamp. The intellectual shades his eyes with his hand. The baldy in the bed keeps opening and closing its eyes, it speaks a different language, English. A shaved head, like in prison, he doesn't like thinking about it, and he's not going to think about it, he wasn't really there long enough for them to shave his head, he wasn't there at all, he just wrote about it. He was at the interrogation, that's true, but the rest . . . empathy. It's a gift he has.

He won an award for everything he's written. Imprisonment, deprivation of liberty, totalitarianism, all kinds of unpleasant things . . . but why is this baldy lying in this particular bed? This is the room *she* went to, he had watched. She stayed around all evening after supper, right to the end, without a partner to take her off to bed, in other words, she was completely available. She'd given him a sign—what else could the fact that she hadn't gone to bed earlier possibly mean— she'd watched him and finally left the bedroom door open. So why wasn't she here? She'd had enough time to take a quick shower, he'd also freshened himself up a little, so where the devil is she? He's not that drunk! Where can she have gotten to? It's only a few steps from the bed to the door.

Baldy's hand is still holding the bedside lamp and pointing it straight into the eyes of the defender of human rights. He thought he'd have a pretty good time of it before his departure in the chauffeur-driven car at six in the morning and might even make it to the press conference in the capital later in the morning, might have to do without a shower, a coffee would be enough, and a cigarette to suppress odors of all kinds, and possibly a cognac as well. But instead of all these wonderful images, there's a bald head staring out of the bed, and god alone knows whether it's a man or a woman. What if it's a homosexual, there're a number of exotic specimens at this summer seminar, even men with earrings, which is something you just have to accept these days, after all, our good old Central Europe is opening up to the world, heavens, you have to accept all sorts of things. They'd all been so attached and interested, all evening, flattering him, almost gobbling him up, but after his demonstration of morality, professional dissidence, and suffering, he definitely did not want to climb into bed with a homosexual.

Baldy's hand is holding the bedside lamp, which tilts sideways after awhile and lights up Baldy too, thank god, it's a woman, her hand is reaching for her glasses, she screams, then relaxes visibly, but still keeps her sleepy myopic eyes open, there's a tiny stud in her left earlobe. Sybille is right, things have gone so far that you can't tell a guy from a bloody woman anymore. It's Neila, or whatever her name is, the one with the cropped hair who's interested in the dissidents of Central Europe, she's been doing interviews, helping make them famous, and is focused on him at the moment, going to ask him about the relationship between power and politics, and the political role of the intellectual, and the post-Communist outbursts of nationalism, and a bunch of other stuff. He knows all this, he could answer these questions without even hearing them, though he does have to be a little careful with this New York paper, can't make jokes about Jews or women or homosexuals, good thing political correctness, or whatever the hell it's called, hasn't made it here, shit, but what's next, here he is leaning over the bed of a journalist he's got a meeting with tomorrow, what if she thinks he's after her? What if she writes this up in her paper? Are there any witnesses? If not, then I'm out of here as fast as possible, before this awful creature points a camera at me. . . . What if she asks him about this in the interview? He could cancel the interview, but what's his excuse? What if she makes it public anyway? She's got him in her hand, god, these women, these bloody women, where's he supposed to go, doesn't matter, main thing is out the door, it's behind him somewhere, a quick turn, and *whpppp,* he's gone, nothing else counts, once he's in his room he pours down two vodkas, or maybe it's cognac or whisky, doesn't matter, it's some kind of hard liquor, and falls asleep. At half past five in the morning his chauffeur wakes him up, he doesn't bother washing, lights up a cigarette, and manages a bit more of a nap in the car. A day that is almost erased. He's almost erased too. But the night especially needs to be erased.

It's clear that this newspaper woman has got him in her power. He should find a way to wreck her reputation. Say she's a lesbian, for instance, maybe she is one anyway, otherwise she would probably have pulled him into bed with her, since he was right there. He'd heard she was married and had a kid, so why didn't she stay home with her kid—in stupid New York! What was she doing running after these dissidents in Central Europe, the former dissidents, why didn't she just stay home, what exactly does she want here? Does she want to sleep with a few of these Central European intellectuals or not? What exactly does she want? What if she was lying in wait for him in this bed, just to trap him? But how could she know that it was this room and this bed he would be heading for? She'd gone right after his talk, only taking time to set up the interview, and had disappeared, if she'd wanted to trick him she would have stayed longer, but he hadn't been sad to see her go, he didn't like her, such an unattractive, rational person that just squeezed you for all kinds of information, she probably was married and with a little kid, other men didn't seem to interest her either. . . .

But where had the other one gone, the first one, the one he'd been after? Didn't she want to do an interview with him too? Somehow he felt that was what she wanted, but he hadn't taken it all that seriously, hadn't even really listened, and thought she was just looking for a pretext, probably was just a pretext. They hadn't made any arrangements, he didn't give her an interview date, because he figured the date would fall into place, but not for a conversation.

He'd given Baldy a date though. He'd arranged for her to meet him in the capital the day after tomorrow to do a long interview, and afterward he was hoping to get away to the seaside for a while, give a few talks, and relax. But now . . .

Neila. It really was her. She'd been sound asleep, but suddenly awake again, gripped by fear and staring. She'd been so tired she'd gone right after the talk. Hadn't wanted to stay, there was no point. All day she'd been wondering how things were going at home with her two-year-old daughter and her husband. Were they coping? She'd phoned home, everything was OK. Then she spent the rest of the evening getting ready for the interview. In the middle of the night she woke up because she sensed someone leaning over her bed. Which was actually the case. At first she was terribly frightened, but when she saw who it was she was relieved. In Neila's shaved head the idea did not come up that this famous man might pose some kind of a threat to the rest of her body. She knew him as a defender of human rights, as a moralist who would never act in any way against his own principles. It was only in the morning that she wondered whether she'd ever heard him talk about this type of morality, but she couldn't remember. Why should you separate the one from the other anyway? To suffer for the truth and then rape someone in the night, that just didn't gel. He'd probably wanted to say good night to someone and gone in the wrong door. He probably didn't even know where he was. Maybe he didn't even know what he wanted. Just please don't puke all over me. When she shone the light in his face he said something in his incomprehensible Central European language, which meant that he wasn't there because of her because she could only speak English, and he knew that. He knew who she was, they'd arranged to do an interview for the big New York paper, they'd need an interpreter. So what did he want here at her bed? What time was it anyway? Two o'clock. While she was feeling for her lamp on the bedside table she'd been in shock, but when she recognized him, she was just perplexed. Shining the light into his face she saw two twitching, lightly swollen slitty eyes, like the eyes of a mole. He leaned over her with beads of sweat on his forehead and moist half-open lips, but then quickly turned and darted off toward the door on his short little bowlegs. He found the door right away. He may not have found the right room or the right bed, but he managed to find his way back to the door, and Neila was glad of that.

Only when he'd gone, did she realize that he could have fallen over on her. She would probably have been able to handle that, but only if she didn't go stiff with fear below him. He would probably have fallen asleep on top of her, and Neila would probably have been too embarrassed to wake him up. The next morning she would have been in a terrible state. How could she have explained why she was lying there with him on top of her? Luckily, things had worked out. He hadn't fallen over on her. Nothing worse could happen now.

But how was she supposed to do the interview with him now? What if he never again wanted to meet with her? What would they say at work? They wanted the interview; it was the trend at the moment. What she should do is just forget about him, and write a little piece on how he falls into women's beds dead drunk, but they'd probably not publish that. Her paper hadn't published that kind of a put-down yet.

Once the defender of human rights had slipped out the door in a fright, Neila sat up to see if Bora was in bed. She hadn't heard her come in, but had left the door of the room open for her as they'd agreed, because some of the doors in this old chateau were broken. If you locked them, they could get so jammed up you had to call night security, which was very unpleasant, and so Neila and Bora had agreed not to lock up—after all, who could possibly show up in the middle of the night?

Bora was there—at least it looked that way, there was a slight bulge under the covers in the bed against the other wall. They seemed to be moving slightly, but maybe Neila was just imagining this. Neila asked if she'd seen what just happened. Bora didn't answer. She was asleep. Neila left it at that.

In the morning Neila went to the bathroom just as the defender of human rights was getting in his car—he darted through the chateau gates the same way he'd darted out of her room in the night. Then he looked up. Neila sprang away from the window so he wouldn't see her. He quickly stepped into the car, and it drove off beyond the chateau walls.

She had decided to do her graduate work on this region, where the collapse of the Berlin Wall and the Iron Curtain had just finished resounding. There were all kinds of Don Quixotes running the government here, which was quite unlike other places in the world, and that was why people were coming from all over the world to take a look. The mail, the customs, and bus transportation did not work, however. But a particular phenomenon had survived that impressed women and gave men hope: this was the intellectual who could move the world. When Bora woke up, Neila briefly told her about the night visitor. Bora had a laconic response, "You'll have to get used to it. The mail and the customs and other institutions don't work in Central Europe, and that includes moral authorities. End of statement."

Ever since Neila and Bora have been enrolled in the summer course on democracy, they've shared the room and the bathroom. They share the housekeeping: bath, toilet, and floor. And the laundry. They admire each other's cosmetics, take a whiff of each other's creams and perfumes, and talk about what they're working on. They've been living in relative grandeur; their stay is coming to an end, a few closing talks, the last evening, and of course, the talk by this important local and at the same time Central European intellectual, a former dissident and defender of human rights. His personal motto: Always take the side of the oppressed. The talk was to be followed by drinks and lively discussions with the students until late in the night. The intellectual would be gone before Bora and Neila even woke up in the morning. He had a chauffeur.

Bora did not manage to set up an interview with him because he simply hadn't given her a date. She's a local, not an American, so it probably wasn't very interesting for him. Bora had hoped to still be able to arrange something after the talk, but then she'd given up; he was getting more and more drunk, but she'd decided not to leave the group because she didn't want to feel later that she'd missed something. She'd heard so much about him! And now this famous man is sitting there, telling jokes, showing off with stories about women, and tossing her the occasional meaningful glance. Bora had always thought men only brag like this when they're in their own company. Maybe he wants to raise some woman's expectations, hers or someone else's. Now and again he mentions his wife; with tears in his eyes he recounts how she helped him survive the regime. And at one point he says to Bora, "Such a pretty girl. Why would you want to take an interest in politics? It's a dirty business. All you have to do is sit there and smile; that suits you much better." Bora's interest in an interview with him is declining. In the end it's all gone. She's happy she didn't arrange anything with him and wonders why she's still sitting there at all.

The master is just coming to the end of a lewd joke that everybody's laughing at. Bora wonders how to escape from the ever-dwindling circle without the famous man noticing, since he keeps looking around at her. The door is behind him. Finally she says she's going to the bathroom and leaves. She steals into the direction of her room but then hears footsteps behind her, looks around, and there he is, with an encouraging and somewhat stupid smile on his face. So she makes straight for the nearest women's washroom. Surely he's not going to stand there and wait for her? No, the defender of human rights is gone when she comes out; there seem to be some remnants of cultivated behavior left in him, although the alcohol has soaked most of it off and rinsed it away, removing the incrustations.

Bora goes to her room. But this is a chateau, and a chateau has a lot of passageways, and she still doesn't know her way around after a month. She thinks she's taking a shortcut, but it doesn't work. She wanders around in the corridors and suddenly at an intersection lands straight in the arms of the famous and rather tipsy man. "Bora, I've been looking all over for you!" His eyes light up. The informal approach sounds like a lead-in to what is to follow. Luckily, the rest of them, in search of the master in these twisty corridors of the chateau, suddenly show up. Leading the way is Ivo, Bora's colleague, who admires and loves the master and is now a little afraid for him—anything might happen. They've come to make sure he's fine, and luckily they've found him, much to Bora's relief. Ivo and the others take the master under their wing and gently escort him down the passage to his room. At the door the master tries to fish the key out of his trouser pocket; it takes awhile. If he'd put it in his jacket pocket, it would have been easier—as it is, they stand around patiently waiting. The master then tries to aim the key at the keyhole. Finally, he graciously hands it to Ivo so he can open it up for him. They say good night—good night. "Where are you sleeping, Bora, Bora?" he mumbles. Bora doesn't answer and quickly disappears into her room.

For a moment she wonders whether she shouldn't try to lock up behind her, but then she decides it's not worth the trouble; the lock could get jammed and wake Neila up. Besides he couldn't even find his own door, or unlock it, so there's no point. She also thinks the famous man probably fell asleep before he even dropped onto his own bed. Meanwhile he's almost dropped onto Neila's bed! Bora keeps absolutely still; she hears the famous man babble something Neila can't understand. Something like, "Don't be afraid. I'm not going to hurt you," and then Neila points her bedside lamp at him and he gives a little cry. Neila strains her myopic eyes and stares at him, and then she puts on her glasses with the small round lenses and keeps the lamp trained on him. The defender of human rights shades his eyes and sways, unsteady. Bora wonders what might happen if the great man turned around and discovered the second bed. Would he try to find out who's sleeping in it? Would he pounce on her or drag her off to his room? Bora stays motionless. Finally, the famous man turns on his heel and finds the direct route to the door, which he quietly closes behind him. Bora imagines him scurrying down the corridors; she'd give a lot to see the look on his face. Neila asks in a sleepy voice, "Bora, are you there? Did you see that? He wanted to say good night to someone and got the wrong door." Neila sinks back onto her pillows and sighs. Bora doesn't answer. She should have locked the door. But then he would probably have pounded on it, and who knows how things might have turned out. The ones who pound on the door or phone all the time are the worst. This way at least she could be sure he wouldn't be back.

The defender of human rights hurries to his room, takes a couple of gulps from an open bottle, drops onto his bed in his clothes, and quickly falls asleep so he can forget everything. He dreams that American feminists have accused him of harassment and interrogated him with a light trained on his face. They ask him what he wanted in that room, and he doesn't have an answer. Actually, what had he wanted there? He can't remember a thing. And he decides that if this person from the New York paper ever gets in touch with him about this or comes to see him, he will say he had a blackout. And he'll do the interview with her as planned. He'll just forget the bed incident. What was that exactly? A lot of things happen in life. These things can happen to anyone; the main thing is that nothing happened.

Tomorrow morning he'll get into the car. The chauffeur will drive him to the capital. He has a press conference at nine. He'll have a coffee somewhere and feel better immediately. The chateau has high walls around it, with a courtyard inside. This reminds him of a prison yard. The defender of human rights gazes up at the sky. The prisoners' eternal yearning: he knows all about that, he's read a lot about that. He has true empathy. He loves the blue sky and the free flight of the birds. He gazes upward, and emotion wells up in him at the sight of the blue square. That's how the world looks for those who are imprisoned. It's still early morning, but he can tell it's going to be a beautiful day.

Translated from the German by Agata Schwartz and Luise von Flotow

■ □ ■ □ ■

DAY BY DAY

Etela Farkašová (Slovakia)

FEDOR, ONCE AGAIN MY DEAR FEDOR,

once again all my thoughts are with him; I turn them over in my
mind, speak them aloud, jot them down, I don't even bother to change
his name, I don't change anything, always the same name, always the
same likeness, the same story, because the reality is always (almost al-
ways) the same, (almost always) moving in a circle, repeated, day after
day; life in a depressing, endless circle (his, mine), ours together,
    it doesn't really matter where I start, but I don't change that either,
I keep returning to the same point of departure; a recurring point of de-
parture, you could say, some kind of (almost) unchanging focal point (of
his, of my) of our days,

every single day (literally, without a single exception) at about this
time I travel on the No. 117 bus, it is past the rush hour, so I usually
find my seat empty, I sit on the right side in the first or second row
from the front door, so I get a better view of the road (and so that I
can be seen from the street before the bus stops),
    there are usually not many people at the bus stop at this hour,
anyway, he stands a little to one side: in the burning heat, in pouring
rain, in storms and winter blizzards, he waits patiently, with a con-
centrated expression on his face, every single day,
    the driver slows down, I don't rush toward the exit, I prefer to get
off last, maybe I don't really want any spectators, maybe I wish to
prolong the moment when I remain a more detached observer scrutinizing the motionless waiting figure (although I know very well that

in my case the position of observer can be no more than a fleeting pretense, seen through long ago, cheating, illusory, because he and I, because we are two in one); *what weird memory?*

I get off and Fedor comes running toward me in his ungainly, awkward fashion (ridiculous maybe in the eyes of strangers),

he kisses me hard, I can feel the damp patches of saliva on my cheeks, he strokes my face, my arms, clutches my hands, M-mummy's c-come, M-mummy,

the refrain is repeated (again without exception, day after day): all right, Fedor, we'll greet each other when we get home, come on, my bags are heavy,

a mechanically recited refrain,

the fingers firmly hooked in my palm move toward the strap of the bag, I-I'll help y-you, let me t-take it,

well, what have you been doing today, Fedorko? (a senseless question, spoken equally mechanically), *a repeated symbol*

I ring him several times a day, just as he rings me about once every hour, I can imagine very well what he has done today, what he did yesterday, the day before yesterday, and what he will do tomorrow (my only difficulty is in imagining what more-distant tomorrows will be like: the tomorrows that will come in fifteen, twenty years, maybe somewhat sooner, maybe somewhat later; imagining my son without my presence, without my help and protection, without my words and touch, a vision of helplessness, desertion, one of my worst visions),

■ □ ■

M-mum-my, B-Bobby was ch-chasing E-eddie and they had a f-fight ag-gain t-today, little E-eddie was p-pecked f-five t-times, he tells me excitedly, *word formation?*

he hasn't learned to count to more than five, and even that required a tremendous amount of effort on my part, the same as with distinguishing letters, after considerable effort he learned to put together the five that make his first name, but signing his surname is beyond him, yet unlike me, my simple-minded son cannot only distinguish at a glance between Bobby and Eddie (to me two equally big, equally yellow canaries), but when we had a whole family of birds, he could reliably tell old Joey from little Suzy or cheeky Micky, no matter what the situation,

he prefers to talk to the canaries when he is alone in the room; I have secretly watched him a couple of times, I almost get the impression that he can communicate quite well with these dear little birds of his, m-my dear l-little b-birds, he refers to them with proud pleasure, th-they are j-just m-mine, a-aren't they? B-but I-I mean j-just mine

■ □ ■

the slowness—infinite, dawdling (sometimes, I suspect, rather deliberate) slowness, which suits his day, but which never ceases to irritate me (no admonitions help, sometimes when I hurry him up, raising my voice, he catches my hand, w-why are you so b-bad, and sometimes after such admonitions things slow down even more),

an idea of time that is completely different from mine, time, which, in spite of all my efforts, I still do not understand, filled in a different way, making a different kind of sense, dividing off our worlds (while I cannot understand his time, will I be helpless so far as everything else is concerned?)

he gets up at the same time as we do, but he is still lingering over his breakfast long after our departure (a great change for the better, he no longer demands our assistance throughout the meal, progress, we too have noticed some progress),

but that unimaginable slowness and caution, that has remained, it hardly changes at all, for the last few months he has been washing his own mug and plate, he places them on the table washed and dried, side by side, but he doesn't like to put them away on the shelf, his movements are uncertain and he often drops things, broken plates are one of those failures that destroy his confidence (only we two know how long it takes for him to get it back),

he doesn't know how to use the gas, an old lady from the next-door flat warms up his lunches, he clings to her although he finds it very hard to get used to strangers, after lunch they always sit for a while and chat together (one day I'd like to hear their conversation), then the old lady leaves and Fedor goes back to Eddie and Bobby, I always know exactly how long lunch took, because my son calls me just before he goes to ring the neighbor's bell and immediately after he has eaten, washed his plate and spoon, placed them pedantically next to his breakfast mug and plate (he hasn't learned how to use a knife and fork, he is afraid of sharp things, as he is of fire and electricity),

besides the canaries, we have Claudia the tortoise in our flat, when Fedor has tired of talking with Eddie and Bobby he lounges in an armchair and attentively watches the hexagons of Claudia's shell slowly move across the carpet (I suspect that what impresses him most about her is that unhurried, never-quickened tempo as a fundamental attitude toward the momentary importance of time); while the tortoise crawls from the window to the mahogany bench under which she has her hideout, another stretch of Fedor's empty, never-ending day passes by,

(but maybe I am mistaken): maybe for him it is not empty at all, in the flutter of the birds' wings, in the rustle of the tortoise crawling around the room, in the ticking of the old grandfather clock, in the muffled sounds coming through the half-open window overlooking the street, in the dripping of the water from the taps, in scenes he alone can see, in these he passes his time, different from ours, maybe he lives through exciting adventures I can know nothing about, time, in which he discovers some of the secrets that remain forever hidden to us, that sometime long ago, on the threshold of a child's awakening awareness, we may have sensed, but that we have meanwhile forgotten once and for all; maybe his day is far richer in feelings and sensations of a kind I shall never experience,

I turn my thoughts, my doubts, over and over in my mind, it depends on the criteria, after all (whether his time is richer, fuller, more exciting, but also more peaceful), but it is all guesswork, there is no certainty,

■ □ ■

the telephone is another thing that haunted Fedor terribly for a long time, we had been well on the way to teaching him how to use it, evening after evening I patiently helped him to dial my library, to give him the feel of it,

Fedor's memory lies in his eyes, his ears, his touch, his finger must have slipped or there was simply a problem at the exchange, instead of ringing at the library, the telephone rang in some unknown place and an angry male voice came out of the receiver, the boy kept repeating over and over again that he wanted Mummy, that he wanted to speak to Mummy, I can just imagine how insistently he repeated my name, which for some incomprehensible reason had infuriated the man on the other end of the line and he had cursed him viciously,

I found him red-eyed at home, he was so terrified that he hadn't even dared leave the flat and he didn't go to meet me at the bus stop; puzzled and depressed, he spent the whole evening telling me how a stranger had answered instead of me, he asked me what those coarse swearwords meant, he couldn't even pronounce some of them right,

w-w-where were you, M-mummy, he was still sobbing when already in bed, w-where were you?

I had a hard time to eventually calm him down and it was almost midnight before he fell asleep; after this experience the telephone was for a long time a source of even greater, even more incomprehensible and even more uncontrollable fear of places outside the home, of people in them,

the telephone, which allowed an anonymous stranger, an anonymous enemy to enter the walls of our home, and i-if that m-man had r-really c-come here, he kept repeating anxiously, I explained to him that, after all, that strange man didn't know our address, or even our telephone number when it came to that, it was just a wrong number, when that happened all you had to do was put down the receiver, nothing more, just put down the receiver and then try calling the library, the next time I would have been sure to have answered or the time after, it was silly and unnecessary to be so scared, after all, he was at home, safe at home,

it took us months more of patient practice before he dared pick up the telephone again,

■ □ ■

the world of Fedor's adventures, delights, as well as the world of his fears and anxieties (so far as I am able to perceive them, as I imagine and interpret them), he finds it very hard to suppress them, his real fears and those other ones, all lived through with extraordinary intensity, all written very clearly in his face, in his gaze, in the movements of his body, and above all in his speech:

the absolutely straightforward, open way he approaches others, an easy, too easy prey for ridicule and cruelty, but also for (sometimes equally hurtful) sympathy; an open straightforwardness combined with defenseless devotion,

from time to time I still make some attempt to hide it, to camouflage it, to teach my son some very simple subterfuge, for instance, how he should react when a stranger speaks to him unexpectedly in a tram or a shop, what he should say to welcome a visitor (a rare event, but they do come from time to time) and so on and so forth; the only trouble is that my son can't even remember, can't even learn such tactics, perhaps partly because he doesn't understand their significance, cannot see the point of them,

an open straightforwardness that pains me,

straightforward himself, he prefers to move in a world that is like that (which is probably why he is so fond of order, why he keeps arranging things in groups; why he loves regularity, repeatability, the unchanging daily routine, it accounts for his obdurate clinging to habits, even the most trivial ones),

a simple, orderly, stable world, into which you can see clearly: directly and without obstacles, a world that can be trusted (immediately a feeling of uncertainty returns, about whether my son's world is really like that, sometimes it seems quite the opposite, to me, to someone looking in from the outside, even though I would love to step inside or at least get as close as possible), all this I jot down,

to get near Fedor's world, no matter how,

■ □ ■

when he was born I only had four semesters to go to finish my degree in medicine, I awaited my child with naive pleasure, marriage and parenthood were common in our year, in my free moments I often played the violin, especially in the last few months, even though it wasn't comfortable; not that I didn't have much more urgent, important things to do, but I felt that music was at that particular time—in spite of my postponed exams—the most important thing for me, from time to time I fell prey to doubt, wondering whether I hadn't made a mistake when choosing my career a few years earlier, a mistake that could perhaps still be corrected: a feeling, which maybe really had nothing to do with my choice of profession, but with something else in my life, a premonition that something in it was coming to an end, that something in it was at that very moment being decided, a feeling that I would like to avoid something, correct some unknown mistake, stop that defective, wrong, erroneous something that was announcing itself so vaguely, but I just didn't know how, and moreover, I didn't know what,

one of my fulfilled premonitions,

my back aching, I stood for hours in front of my music stand, I felt I was only now beginning to understand many of the compositions, only now did they begin to mean something to me, but alongside that pleasure there was the ever-present premonition of an indefinite, unavoidable turning point approaching,

then for a long time I was lost to everyone, myself, and music too, and likewise the world was lost to me, it was reduced to the walls of our flat, to the routine of everyday care for that hopelessly dependent bundle of nappies, cloths, bibs, a bundle that, in spite of the utmost precautions, was forever wet, dribbling, or covered with vomit

lost; helpless to do anything about my feeling of being lost,

I couldn't understand it at all, there were moments when I no longer even wanted to understand it, what was more important than understanding the causes of the situation was to become one with it, submerge myself in it,

a completely new, unexpected and unforeseen situation,

my son and I, my simple-minded boy beside me, at every step, at every second, day after day,

my world, my life (really like this, from now on only like this?)

but the Bible says: blessed are the poor in spirit; is perhaps the spirit the same as the mind, the mind that does not and does not want "to know," because it does not want to have power, does not yearn for it, that is not calculating and does not want to be calculating and does not want to foresee, to plan, that does not want to subjugate, control, and manipulate; the

ETELA FARKAŠOVÁ

102

mind of a child, innocent and naive, is such a spirit/mind a precondition for what we understand as redemption?

■ □ ■

it was four years before Fedor learned to walk and another year before he was more or less able to form simple sentences, registration at a special school caused him enormous stress, strange surroundings had always aroused in him feelings of dread and unease, he was never any particular trouble in class, they were hardly aware of his presence, quiet, too withdrawn, too timid; but he just refused to communicate—with the teacher, with the other children, with anyone at all, when he arrived in the morning he sat down on his chair and clung to it until lessons were over, no toys or tricks could lure him away from it,

looking back at those years: Fedor and his hardly noticeable progress, I can see nothing, nothing else, it became the one and only measure of our time together, it was as if I wasn't there at all, I really was lost, I almost disappeared from the scene completely, what did remain in me after the first shock was this feeling of enormous responsibility, the feeling that I must be constantly on the alert, constantly at hand,

(and also: feelings of emptying weariness and loneliness, sometimes stronger than my pain), *Chance, unpossibility*

~~the idea that being stricken by mis~~fortune brings people closer to each other (maybe sometimes, maybe with some people); we two, Karol and I, were not able to transform our common misfortune into a sense of closeness, perhaps we could have been wiser, but we only knew how to be unhappy, each in our own way, blaming each other, irritability growing into angry hostility, later resignation, indifference toward each other, habit, waves following one after another,

■ □ ■

even now I sometimes find myself listening uncomprehendingly to people talking about their plans, hopes, undertakings, it seems absurd to me to link the future with any expectations whatsoever, for me time can never be a larva that changes into a butterfly, my time is only like shifting from one foot to the other, moving from one day to the next, now that Fedor has probably almost stopped developing the days are almost exactly alike,

an infinity of never-ending circles, squeezed into a never-ending network of never-ending mutually overlapping, interlinking curves, a space strictly and incorruptibly guarded by its own repeatability, there is no way out, no possible way;

   do I even want it to exist any longer, am I still attracted by what is to be found beyond that space?

■   □   ■

once, I've no idea how it could have occurred to me, I didn't get off at our bus stop, maybe I had an urge to see him through other people's eyes, or I longed for a brief respite to be able to get away from my own life at least for a little while, not to be involved at least for a few secret moments; and maybe it was just weariness brought on by the feeling of helplessness, injustice, by all similar feelings (only too familiar, too much a part of my life),

   it was time for me to return from work and my son was patiently, attentively watching the people getting off the bus, I was sitting right at the back, half hidden behind a newspaper, could I really have imagined that if I got off at the next stop, I should manage to escape, to change our fate, was I hoping that if I crossed the boundaries of a certain space or a certain routine, a happy, well-built young man would come to meet me and on our way home we would talk intelligently about the events of the day?

   from behind my newspaper I caught sight of the horrified expression on my Fedor's face, the real, naive, silly, dear, tender, awkward Fedor, who first cast a puzzled glance through the windows, then, in spite of the newspaper, caught sight of me and, wretched and terrified, ran after the bus, tripped and once almost fell, but didn't give up, running as far as the next stop, though lagging farther and farther behind the bus receding in the distance,

I would never do that again,

if one day I have to answer for my actions, I shall have to explain that, too, that attempt to see things for a moment through other people's eyes (or was it more an attempt to escape from reality or at least to postpone it for a couple of minutes; what could I have expected from it?), maybe I shall never have to explain it, answer for it, to anyone but myself,

M-m-mummy, y-you d-didn't kn-know y-you sh-should g-get off, Fedor, panting for breath, forced out of himself the moment he came running up to the stop, I-I w-was s-so f-f-frightened I-I'd l-l-lose y-you,

silly excuses that I had been absorbed in my newspaper, increasingly realizing how monstrous my misguided experiment had been,

and i-if y-y-you had g-g-gotten lost?

all the way home he kept patting me on my elbow, M-m-mummy, y-you r-really are . . . , there was reproach in his voice, M-m-mummy

he is scared to death of getting lost, he hasn't the least sense of direction, he doesn't know his way around even one part of the town, he can just about remember the streets in our housing estate, the only route he feels certain about and that he will take by himself and voluntarily is the route from our block of flats to the bus stop where he waits for me every single day,

■ □ ■

oh, yes, the Bible, more is involved than an attempt to interpret one of the Beatitudes,

entries in our family Bible begin with the year 1821, *on St. Samuel's day our first son was born,* and two lines down in the same writing, *the Lord God has blessed us with a daughter, Zuzana,* in between the dates of weddings, alternating with records of the births of further sons and daughters, all those Annas, Marias, Zuzanas, all those Samuels, Ondrejs, Jáns, and Michals, whose likenesses and lives are mostly only half-known to me or half-forgotten, but who were here and formed a kind of chain of related and differing traits in spite of the lost photographs and forgotten fates, they were connected to each other, they had passed on genes, traditions, memories, the last entry referred to me, my mother's clearly recognizable handwriting, tiny, pedantically arranged letters, then nothing more,

(an unenviable situation: a participant in interrupted continuity, a feeling that the women in the previous generations of this line did not know)

continuity, which had suddenly been interrupted, a chain with the last link out of joint, digressing from the orderly line,

■ □ ■

one evening I and my husband were sitting in front of the television, Fedor was feeding Eddie and Bobby, the television does not attract him, even fairy tales cannot hold his attention for more than a couple of minutes, but he came into the living room to fetch something and he crouched next to us, on the screen exchanges of fire between the Serbs and Croats were followed by shots of dead bodies in Jerusalem, an Armenian village where half the population had been massacred by Azerbaijanis, and glimpses of victims of a terrorist attack in London,

at first Fedor watched picture after picture, then he asked in a horrified voice, w-why is everyb-body sh-shooting at e-each other?

he asked in such a serious voice, as if at that moment he really had caught a glimpse of the natural laws of this world, because they are idiots, was Karol's reaction, abrupt and irritated, he had been in a bad mood all evening, as he almost always was when he stayed at home,

l-like m-me? Fedor blurted out, looking with distraught expectation from his father to me, reminding me of that unpleasant episode with the stranger on the phone cursing shocked and unhappy Fedor; calling him among other things an idiot, our son had clearly not yet shaken off the memories of this episode with the telephone, which had disturbed him so much,

but my husband spoke before I could, no, no, Fedor, he said, no longer so irritated, and gently pulled his son to him, it has nothing to do with you,

I had not seen such a gesture from my husband to his son for a long time, they stayed like that for a while, resting against one another, after years of living at home confined to the rooms, kitchen, the balcony with its flower pots (Fedor adores flowers, he has even given the geraniums names: the big open ones boys names, the small buds girls names, when he waters them he strokes them and talks to them), the tortoise's box and the canary's cage, Fedor's stuttering words, and my severed, tattered, mislaid thoughts, I didn't dare believe that I would ever again have my own world, I had come to terms with the idea that now that Fedor has been born I could only be a part of his strange world, it is perhaps paradoxical, but my son's existence seemed to absorb mine, not the other way round,

I have also heard myself express it another way in my mind: *Fedor's shadow takes up the space that is my life,* I immediately felt terribly ashamed of this thought, I really cannot allow myself to think in this way about the relationship between us or between our lives,

■ □ ■   *Oh No!*

I got my job quite by chance, a librarian friend needed someone to help her out, her mother had fallen seriously ill, and she couldn't look after her properly while she was working full time, at first I just helped out a few hours a week, later, when Fedor was able to spend part of the day at home by himself, I was taken on full time,

this change meant an awful lot to me, I threw myself into everything connected with the library with a delight that I had no longer expected to feel (Fedor generously presented me with two of his geraniums, Lojza and Gabika, to decorate my room at work: M-mummy, t-take th-them, at least y-you won't be s-sad there w-without m-me), the main thing, though, was the change in my own situation, in my attitude toward myself,

a couple of times when I was at the library, of course only when I was alone, I stood beside the flowerpots holding Fedor's geraniums, and when I had given them a good watering I tried speaking to them, just as I had seen my son do, I ran my fingers gently over the large, slightly wrinkled leaves and asked them in a half-whisper whether they were still thirsty and whether they were thriving in my room, occasionally, also in a half-whisper, I passed on Fedor's greetings, when

I leave in the morning he sometimes tells me in a very serious voice to give them his regards and then, when I come home, he checks whether I have kept my promise,

   it is a game I am happy to play, in order to get closer to my son; *this (also unchanging) desire of mine: to be as close to him, to spend as much time with him as is at all possible,*

but there are also days when, in spite of my newly discovered delight in the library, I cannot avoid feeling like a pawn on a strange kind of chessboard controlled by mysterious forces: just a couple of squares around me and no more, a couple of squares, that is all, the depressing confines of my future possibilities, unforeseen and yet in a sense predetermined moves, the notion of precisely apportioned squares (an alternative to the notion of my equally depressing infinity in circles),

   I wander around in these confines, I hang around in days that are sometimes without the least gleam of light, I grope in the dark, in hopelessness: everything essential is already given, this can never be any different; the future swallowed up by what has already happened,

   the whole of my present life and my future unwinds from one event, one single event: it would be possible to wind it back, *to return to the point of departure, concentrate it into one point—ALPHA—which is at the same time FEDOR,*

occasionally I pick up my violin, but more often I just run my fingers over the case, fingers that have long become insensitive, the music in them that at one time set the strings vibrating with such passion gradually disappeared, music doesn't sound quite the same as it did before, I listen to it but somehow *differently,* it is *different* music (above all, though, I am *different,* the *difference* is above all in me),

   or I open an atlas and let my eye stray over the maps, over places I had once wanted to see, their names are no more than a cluster of sounds, which needn't even be associated with any particular mental image, I have grown too-deep roots in my own world, the co-ordinates of which are determined by Fedor's existence, the other (external, non-Fedor) world has become remote, and that is how

I perceive it: as a distant world and, viewed in perspective, appropriately diminished, unimportant,

and if I have at least a little free time, I browse through magazines and books or I just walk slowly, lost in thought, between the short rows of bookshelves, but I'm not able to follow a continuous train of thought, or maybe I deliberately avoid it: what about, what for?

sometimes I jot down these scattered, tattered thoughts of mine (they are in fact not entirely chaotic, they all have a single focal point), I jot them down, as if this could help me, bring me relief;

moments of escape, but they might equally be attempts to go back in time, disconnected fragments of sentences, sometimes just individual words:

is anxiety expressed (written down) any less acute?

only those who have experienced it, only those who have actually gone through something like that themselves (involving their own children); anyone else, no matter how much they wanted to, no matter how much they tried, could not understand: not this and certainly not thus

■ □ ■

my experience as the mother of a simple-minded son had perhaps become the most fundamental part of me, it determined what I was, it was imprinted in me so firmly that it had made a new being of me, Me-and-Fedor, who was someone completely different than my onetime (onetime, which meant before my son's birth) Me-without-Fedor;

it was because of this irreversible change in me that I couldn't understand Karol, who would have liked to meet people socially from time to time, who stayed out with his friends or colleagues for the occasional celebration and then gave me an amusing account of it, it was stronger than my will, I simply couldn't understand him, just as I could not bear to have beside me a man whose body had not ceased to long for carnal pleasure, I would have liked to punish him by forbidding it, punish him and myself;

I hated him for every moment he didn't think about *that*, when he did not suffer like I did *because of that*, when probably involuntarily, following his instinct for self-preservation, his attention strayed from us,

DAY BY DAY

109
▼

if I had seen beside me an unhappy, utterly dejected man, one who did not forget for a single minute and did not allow himself to be distracted, I might have behaved differently toward him, and our relationship might also have developed rather differently, but I felt the devastation within me and I needed to see it in him, too, because it would have seemed fairer like that;

(will it be necessary to answer not only for what one did but also for what one did not do?)

■　□　■

whenever it is at all possible I spend Sunday with Fedor in the forest, these walks are some of my most beautiful moments: we sit in the grass and look for four-leaved clovers (I am always surprised how observant my son is on these occasions), we braid dandelion wreaths of various sizes, we watch columns of marching ants, or we just laze in the middle of a clearing with our faces turned toward the sun,

during that time when Fedor could take no more than a few uncertain steps and such trips were simply out of the question, I was sick with yearning for trees, streams, clearings in the forest, for the exhaustion following a daylong hike, for the physical exhaustion that would disperse all my cares, worries, pain:

to walk until I dropped, just walk, gaze at the green countryside around me, lose myself in it, breathe freely, become a part of it,

Fedor loves gathering flowers, on one such walk recently he picked an enormous bouquet of white dead nettles, M-mummy, I l-love you s-so much, he suddenly declared, stretching his hands out toward me as far as he could and dropping half the bouquet on the ground in doing so; he looked embarrassed, bent down and red from the effort, sought the words he needed, I l-l-love you even b-b-bigger, d-d-did you kn-know that?

it was time to go home, the evening sun was glimmering here and there through the top branches of the trees, we held each other's hands tightly, the limp dead nettles lay on the top of the wickerwork basket; there are such moments from time to time,

and then in the evening back home: Fedor falls asleep immediately, tired out, Karol as usual is still pursuing his own program; wandering

ETELA FARKAŠOVÁ

through the empty flat, hearing the neighbors moving beyond the walls, the telephone on the living-room table is silent, maybe all I need to do is pick up the receiver and dial a number, but whose?

ever since Fedor arrived in the world I haven't met any of my friends regularly (have I still got any friends at all?)

lying in bed, a picture lingers in my mind of grass, flowers, the sky with the setting sun, that most of all, the gradually disappearing rays, the light descending into the earth, leaving just a thin strip of watery yellow on the horizon that merges into the gray-blue background, growing darker all the time, that moment of extinction, which bears the promise of new light, the life cycle (no longer just my own), another of those cycles, a feeling of peace comes over me once more; I am in that green scenery, which has accepted me as part of it, with all that has accumulated in me: I am part of the greenery stretching for as far as the eye can see, it is almost as if I am no longer myself, with this particular appearance of mine, with this particular fate of mine, but one part of something indefinable, impossible to name,

the feeling of being part of a whole, it is no longer so important what I bring to it,

through the half-open door I can hear Fedor breathing, sometimes he lets out a loud sigh in his sleep, sometimes he utters a few incomprehensible words, maybe he is dreaming of a meadow full of oxeye daisies, of forest paths, and islands of white dead nettles, maybe he can also see before him the setting sun, suddenly in the silence of the flat at night, he laughs a clear, sonorous laugh, he sometimes does that, especially when he has had a pleasant day, I take this with me to my own sleep, that clear, joyful, somewhat convulsive laughter,

■   □   ■

I believe it was my mother who first uttered the sentence about finding comfort in religion, she somehow wanted to revive in me that image of a wise, omnipotent, but above all loving Father that I remembered from my childhood

but in my situation I had more need for a God with a woman's face, a Being who had to be neither wise and omniscient, nor omnipotent, just full of pain, so full that she almost became one with pain itself, able to feel the pain of others, too, to dwell in them,

understand them without a single word, without prayers for anything in particular,

a mother, whose child pains her and through her child the whole
world, sometimes I'm afraid that thoughts like these will bring me
to the edge of madness, to identify Fedor with the world is after all
absurd, I understand that, and yet it sometimes seems to me that
they merge into each other, for me, in my mind;

my simple-minded son and the world, which seems to me to be
less and less comprehensible, more and more deprived of meaning;
the thought about whether Fedor's sickness is really only the sickness
of my son (again, after all this time, I'm remembering the French
philosopher who wrote that strange history),

the search for dividing lines, which may not in fact exist,

sick Fedor in a differently sick world, a sick world and my differently sick son,

■ □ ■

I often catch myself looking for the likeness between us two; what
of me has been passed on to my son's face, similarities, where is my
share (no, I now think far less about guilt in the true sense of the
word than in the first few years), what share do I have in the childish-
ness and immaturity, the naivety and limited ability, the deformed
mind of my son; is it at all possible to define one's share?

I know from my student days: a defective chromosome arises either as part of the hereditary process or as a spontaneous or provoked
mutation, none of Karol's or my relatives (so far as we know) suffered
a similar defect, so we must look to probability, statistics, the law of
large numbers, or some would prefer to say—an unpredictable quirk
of Nature, of its uncontrollable powers, but why should I bother
now about the cause: known or unknown, it is the result that counts,
that is important, that remains,

■ □ ■

on one occasion an acquaintance of mine tried rather tactlessly to
express his sympathy, it was a long time ago, somewhere near the
beginning (my own personal, real way of counting the years is from

Fedor's birth, when I began to change, to become the person I am today), and to make his clumsy words even worse, this acquaintance said something to the effect that my love for my son was no doubt more compassion than true maternal love,

I didn't say anything, I didn't feel like explaining to him something that everyone must anyway discover for himself: we don't feel compassion for our own wounds, they only hurt,

■ □ ■

quite unexpectedly, the old lady who used to come to heat up Fedor's lunch suddenly died, he couldn't understand it, one minute she was and the next she was no longer; he kept ringing her doorbell, he wouldn't accept that our neighbor would never open her door to him again,

his first contact with death, the shock that someone could disappear, be lost, forever (Fedor's fear of getting lost became even more burdensome); confused, broken utterances, entangling themselves in two questions that for him merged into one, w-where is o-our n-neighbor, and when I try to explain, he continues, puzzled, taken aback, perhaps also a little offended, and who w-will I h-have l-lunch with n-now,

I didn't really want to take him to the crematorium, but he was so insistent that there was something he wanted to tell our dear neighbor, that in the end I gave in, my mother tried to talk me out of it, Karol just declared that in his opinion it was a ridiculous idea to take the boy to such a place, but I could do as I liked,

he did not cry, he listened carefully to the speakers all the time and stared in the direction of the catafalque, but on the way home he once more began pestering me with questions, that w-wasn't our n-neighbor, where i-is sh-she n-now, hm? w-where?

my subsequent attempts to explain that sooner or later people have to leave (weighing every word so that it would be as comprehensible and acceptable as possible to Fedor), that although it is true we don't know exactly when or where we go to, none of us knows that, simply one day it must happen, but that people leave behind something of themselves on earth, here, among us, I spoke as convincingly as possible, among those who loved them, we for example, would remember our dear neighbor, how they had prepared lunch together, joked together, and sometimes also been to the shops together,

he stopped asking, he didn't even respond to my explanations, we arrived home in silence, I arranged to change my shift at work, so that I didn't have to go to the library that day, I got on with the cooking, and Fedor withdrew to his canaries, he needed someone to talk to,

only in the evening, when we said good night to each other before he went to bed, did he come, snuggling up to me again and whispering, b-but you w-won't ever leave, y-you won't ever l-leave me, w-will you?

■　□　■

sometimes a very strange sensation flashes through my mind, that *all this* is just a dream, some kind of hallucination, limited in time, not definitive, as if all those years I had lived in a bad dream, all I had to do was wake up, step out of that dream labyrinth, free myself, and free him, too, him above all,

after all, Fedor cannot really be like this, *my son,* of my body and my soul, my son is normal, just like all the others, *the one here* is just his double, temporary, temporarily transformed, temporarily rolled up in this ball of misery, I feel that in reality he is different, this is all just an illusion (a memory of childhood frequented by fairy tales, the prince changed into a frog or the brothers who became crows), but it is enough to find the right word, the right key, the magic word that breaks the spell, or all it takes is a great sacrifice, the greatest of all, the sacrifice of endless patience;

I sometimes talk to him, to that other one, especially at night, in silence or to the accompaniment of music, I address him between the notes, I tell him all about my hard day, and I shake off a little of my loneliness, while the one sleeps beyond the half-open door, occasionally letting out incomprehensible sounds in his sleep, I talk to the other, the Fedor I carry within me, Fedor as I imagine him (after all, he could easily have been like *this*); with my confidant, who could it be if not he himself in his other likeness, who could understand me better, see into me better than him?

ETELA FARKAŠOVÁ

my divided son, split into two parts, about which only I know (and not always and not all the time); into my split, schizophrenic life, into my own splintered existence,

after such nights I observe my son particularly closely, how he clumsily spreads butter on a slice of bread, how he puts it into his mouth, a shower of crumbs falling onto the cloth, *where are you?* I think to myself at the sight of his misshapen face, in the night we talked together in quite a different way, you have stayed behind in my dream once more, in my longing, c-can I t-take an-nother p-piece, asks the one sitting with me at the table, eagerly stretching out his jammy hand toward the plate of sliced bread, you can, I tell him, but please be a bit more careful, don't mess up the cloth again,

eternal feelings of being split in two; without them I could probably no longer be whole, without these moments of escape into my imagination, to the fabrications of my fantasy (to hallucinations?), they have become part of me, they too,

and what if this is in fact that real love; I would probably have loved a healthy, normal Fedor more serenely and unequivocally, in any case with a simple, less conflicting, less divided (and also less dividing) love,

■ □ ■

one day when I arrived home I noticed that the margins of the newspaper were covered with clumsy drawings of misshapen figures, with outsize heads, undersize, deformed bodies, with eyes placed quite asymmetrically, sometimes even jutting out beyond the outlines of the head, at first I was very upset at the sight of these expressionless faces with grinning mouths, faces that meant nothing to me, that I did not understand at all, I realized that I didn't understand my son's face either, no, that's not true, I did understand his face, I was familiar with his expressions of pleasure, pain, and fear, but what was behind the face, what went on in his head, remained a mystery to me, I could only guess,

I picked up the newspaper, but did not devote as much attention to it as I would have previously, potato peelings slipped between my fingers onto the preelection speeches of politicians with the same indifference as onto the deformed figures in Fedor's drawings, just as

I was about to crumple up the pile of waste and dump it in the bin, Fedor came into the kitchen, M-mummy, w-what are y-you d-doing, d-didn't y-you s-see them?

yes, yes, Fedor, I saw them, I reassured him, you drew them nicely, you should do that more often,

b-but d-didn't you s-see us? (my attention was alerted, who "us," Fedorko? I stared once more at the drawing while he impatiently pushed the peelings away from the edge of the newspaper), l-look, that is y-you and th-that is us, c-can you s-see now? m-me F-Fedor and y-you,

it was only then that I noticed what was strange about the drawing: the bodies of the two figures almost merged into one, at first glance it seemed to be just one split trunk, from which four arms, four legs, and two heads were growing, I tore the margin off the paper and in the evening, when Fedor was already asleep, I tried to decipher the meaning of the drawing: the integration of the body, but the differentiation of the heads, so that was how he saw us two,

again the feeling that the most I could achieve would be to penetrate the world of my simple-minded son, a goal I did not know how to reach; again the idea of borders that sometimes seem impossible to cross,

■ □ ■

when reading an article by a certain woman psychologist who had discovered that children who were irremediably mentally disturbed preferred toys and objects that were large in size, I was seized by incredible joy and hope, because my Fedor is fondest of little bits of colored paper, cubes, broken twigs,

I carried this joy around with me for several days after reading this study, then it faded away and everything was as before,

■ □ ■

once our old neighbor had said to me, you know, everyone has their own Fedor, this was some years ago, when they were only just beginning to get used to each other at their lunchtime sittings, we didn't know much about each other then;

some are visible at first glance, she said, others only at a second or third, and then there are those that cannot be seen at all, they are so deep inside us that only we know about them, invisible, but those sometimes hurt the most,

(it's those my notes are about, I thought to myself, about all those visible ones and maybe even more about those others):

always the same, tattered, crumpled, mislaid thoughts, which come and go, occasionally transformed into notes,

these Fedor scribblings of mine

in old notebooks, on the back of Fedor's drawings and Karol's office papers, or in the margins of newspapers and magazines, on shopping bills,

sometimes I even jot down music instead of words, a few simple bars, almost always with the same motif, approximately the same rhythm, and more or less the same theme, on one and the same situation, on one and the same story:

we two, I and Fedor, together, inseparable, indistinguishable and (which is also very important) every single day,

with all my thoughts and feelings, when I meditate, speak or jot them down (and when I am silent too),

Me-and-Fedor, all the time and forever: in circles . . .

Translated from the Slovak by Heather Trebaticka

■ □ ■ □ ■

FAR AND NEAR

Daniela Fischerová (Czech Republic)

[handwritten marginalia]

I TURNED ON THE TELEVISION, AND WE WERE ONCE AGAIN FACE-TO-face. A man I had not seen in fourteen years was looking straight into my eyes and speaking insistently. I was protected by the one-way mirror of the television screen between us. The sound went off for a moment, and his words were incomprehensible to me. It was a perfect instance of déjà vu.

The program was a discussion of science fiction, and my long-lost friend, a literary critic, was speaking on the motif of "distance and proximity" and about various modes of resolution offered by that genre. Distance, he explained, isn't a physical condition, but primarily a state of mind.

"If I have the key to the gate," he said in the same deep, but dull voice with which he had instructed me in the past, "I am separated from the garden by a meaningless length of wire mesh. If I don't have it, I have to go around the back of the house, through the construction site, past the shed, and down the stairs."

The example was particularly apt, because I knew exactly which gate (construction site, shed, steps) he was thinking of. It was my gate, my garden. *[handwritten: ownership]*

The screen was big and showed his face in detail. We were just as close at this moment as we had been in the past.

This is a story about distance and proximity. It's not science fiction and it won't offer any new modes of resolution.

■ □ ■

When I was twenty-two, a serious young man appeared in my life. He was perhaps about thirty—I don't know, because I never asked. At that time he was a columnist for a cultural magazine, and he had read my work somewhere. We met in a coffeehouse.

From the first moment I was struck by a certain discrepancy in him. He was reserved and abstract in a way unlike any of the other men I knew at the time. He appeared unapproachable. And yet he sat closer to me than even the most aggressive men did. He didn't touch me. The whole evening he didn't attempt even one accidental brush, but instead, with his face very close to mine, he slowly and seriously discoursed on various themes.

I listened only very inattentively, because I found him unnerving. I don't remember anything from that first date other than the embarrassing feeling that he was unsmilingly scrutinizing my every wrinkle and pore, the powder mapped unevenly across my face, all the while talking with faint interest about sentence construction in the postwar short story.

Outside the window Prague swam in the evening gloom. Above the horizon a dark red stripe waved like a fluttering scarf.

"The stories that I don't understand very well are the ones I like best," he said. "And of those, my favorites are those that become clear to me several years after I've read them."

He wasn't referring to anything specific, but his comment certainly didn't apply to my stories. They attempted to be mysterious, but were as transparent as an aquarium and about as deep.

■ □ ■

I was confused by the mixed signals. Here was a person who, as they say in psychotherapy, invaded other people's space. He didn't respect the invisible membrane—noli me tangere—the circle drawn around each of us with holy chalk. Space is full of tension. We are separated by a whirling trembling force, which has its own intentions. Only love or aggression can penetrate it. In the embrace of a lover or an enemy it draws back, like a door operated by a sensor, and lets the intruder in. Each of us has a different-sized bubble of personal space. Mine is more than big enough. I hate slaps on the back, overfamiliarity, and trust. I sit in my space quite contented, somewhat disagreeable, and utterly self-possessed.

■ □ ■

Doctor M, as I called him then, also appeared quite contented, a little disagreeable, and above all utterly self-possessed. That self-possession was as taut as an inflated plastic bag. Remarkably, he rarely smiled. He never confided anything. I remember his scent quite well: he smelled of toothpaste. He was always fastidiously clean, and the impression that he had just stepped out of the shower was spoiled only by the dark pink stripe in the center of his forehead—some kind of birthmark.

For one brief moment we reached the very threshold of love, but it didn't bring us closer in any way. We were never on a first-name basis. He didn't have the key to my garden.

After that first encounter we began meeting sporadically and—as I would put it now—exchanging our mental waste with each other. We were two critics. No one would be able to pick out a young man and a girl from a stenographic transcription of our conversations. His indifference would have suited me well (in a period of odd deafness with regard to the world of feelings, when my unripe and undesired heart seemed as tough as cabbage) if it weren't for that act of violent intimacy committed against my bubble.

Borders foster action. Crossfire at borders and the carving of territory provide the raw fuel for history. All dividing lines in space and time give life to the impulse-driven zone of literature.

"Contemporary prose consists solely of monologue," he said. "Its growing incomprehensibility bears no relation to formal features, but is connected instead to a fundamental resignation to the idea that no one can understand. The author doesn't want to be understood, because he doesn't even understand himself. As proof he puts forth the idea that it's impossible to understand anything. The role of the omniscient author is passé. Our century has come to believe that knowledge always misses the boat. It doesn't resolve anything, and it doesn't protect anyone from anything."

DANIELA FISCHEROVÁ

As he was saying this he leaned in so close that my bubble, panicky, shot out its electric charge in self-protection, contorted, and adhered to his face like a death mask, like aluminum foil for wrapping food to put in the freezer.

"We are lost," he said with unusual gravity. "We aren't with ourselves, we aren't in ourselves, and we're never where we should be."

■ □ ■

I had already given up the idea that he might be hard of hearing. In fact, he had sensitive ears and more than once we had left a noisy local pub to wrap ourselves in a cocoon of silence, moving to some atrocious, empty, out-of-the-way bistro. There we conducted smooth, flowing, worthless conversations, safely distant from anything that might concern us, alone in the paper kingdom of literature. What we spoke of: "the archetypal framework of nature," "the mythical elements of reality," "the profaneness of the motif of coincidence and of every extreme situation." We spoke of things that existed and yet didn't exist and in whose pale veins flowed paper blood.

It would have been—if anything at all—a happy, sexless bit of nothing. Two hermaphrodite brains borne by an infusion of irresponsibility—ageless, outside reality, without a future. If it hadn't been for the fact that our bodies were so close, that the skins of our auras bristled with a crackling wave of sparks.

■ □ ■

He had the unmistakable image of an aging bachelor: a narrow intellectual humor and a certain tightness at the seams. He was married but he never talked about his wife—at the most he would mention her in a matter-of-fact way ("I'll be away, but my wife will send it to me"). I heard from other sources that she was a doctor, an anesthesiologist, quite a bit older than he, and supposedly very beautiful. I didn't think about her. She was and she wasn't.

■ □ ■

We were meeting more and more often, almost daily in fact. He began to walk me home (garden, construction site, shed, steps), but other than that our meetings in no way differed from the earlier ones—or perhaps only in a certain proficiency. We skipped over a stage of development. Within a year we were an aging couple, with its indifferent fidelity and utterly exhausted eroticism. He would wait for me at the college. We went to see films and exhibits. Everyone believed that we were lovers, but we were already listening to each other with only half an ear, and we were no closer than two stuffed lizards on a shelf.

Sometimes it seemed to me that everything was already behind us: the sobs of passion, the holy nights, the incidents of dragging each other around by the hair on the floor. That it had all happened long ago, in some other time, already forgotten. We were like two old people on a watchtower. The world lay deep beneath us; distant bare trees pointed up from the horizon like fringe.

Twice in my life I have experienced periods when the whole world of feelings, with its demonic sultriness, seemed incomprehensibly foreign, fabricated, affected, and messy. I was about ten the first time it happened: romance novels inspired me to unrestrained arrogance and high-minded amusement. This was the second time it had happened: not knowing why, for a year or two I escaped the magnetic pole of love, and its vibrations had no effect on me. Perhaps the third such period is upon me now, and this time it may last a very long while. Certainly this friendship, if it could be called that, was the best thing I could have hoped for. It removed the degrading stigma of solitude. We moved within a cloud of theory and talk. Thanks to this I was left in peace and didn't have to dance the tortuous mating dance of my generation. But I had no idea what Doctor M could be gaining from this odd relationship.

We said good-bye casually before Christmas, exchanged gifts (books for books, of course), and arranged to meet in January. We were so estranged that it didn't even occur to us to ask each other how we were spending the holidays. I stayed at home with my parents and then went to Budapest for a New Year's Eve concert.

The train scraped through the flat, unlovely landscape. Clumps of snow like curdled cream melted in the fields. For most of the night I dozed sitting up, and in the morning I was awakened by the slanting morning sun. The compartment was divided into two cubicles. In the sharp and unripe morning light a strange woman sat across the aisle from me. I hadn't noticed her before.

Her classical profile and indiscernible age suggested a beautiful bone structure. She was somewhere between thirty and fifty. She wore her raven-black hair in a bun and had a sharp, perfectly made-up face. She gave the impression that she hadn't slept the whole night, but had instead kept watch, tensely gazing into the darkness. Directors divide all female roles into blondes and brunettes, but not according to the color of their hair. Everyone knows what this implies. Ophelia is as blonde as vanilla pudding. Lady Macbeth could not be anything but a brunette.

I guessed she was Hungarian. It wasn't only because of her hair but more just the whiff of foreignness about her: it didn't seem possible to address her in Czech. It didn't seem possible to address her at all. Her bubble was like a concrete bomb shelter.

At the moment when I noticed her, she had just started to remove her rings from her long pale fingers. She had advertising-perfect hands, with fire-engine red polish on the nails. Slowly and with a certain single-minded attention, she removed the rings one by one (there were seven—one wedding band). She carefully laid them on the pullout table and then slowly and methodically began to rub an expensive scented cream onto her hands. The procedure took an unusually long time, and the woman gazed at her hands throughout, like a surgeon performing an operation.

I was fascinated by this spectacle. It was an ordinary gesture, and there was nothing unusual about a woman rubbing cream on her hands in the morning, but the tenacity of the act implied something strange. She put away the cream and put the seven rings back on. She didn't look around; she didn't gaze out the window. She sat for a moment, stretching her fingers. And then with nervous haste she began taking them off. She placed them on the table and again measured out a dose of cream. She rubbed in the cream and pressed her hands together. Her knuckles went white. With an indifferent expression she wrung her hands in a gesture of the most extreme desperation.

Suddenly the man next to her, whom I hadn't seen before over the tall seat dividers, stood up. He stepped over her legs silently, and because the armrest and the little folding table used up the nearly impassable space between her and the seat back in front of her, he had to extend his whole body over her. He didn't look at her, nor she at him. She didn't even retract her legs to indicate symbolically that she wanted to make it easier for him, and he didn't try in any way to pass by her more discreetly. Neither of them uttered a word of apology for invading the other's space. He crossed her like an obstacle in the terrain, and she rubbed cream into her hands. They were from different universes, subject to different laws. It seemed eerily crude, even though it was really nothing at all. But in that mutual indifference there was some kind of warning. The episode was both banal and key, overlaid with some mute and sinister evil. The man worked his way through to the corridor and walked quickly to the dining car. He didn't acknowledge me. It was Doctor M.

The woman's face betrayed nothing at all. She closed the cream and replaced her seven trappings of beauty. I recognized the wedding ring from his hand. I disappeared three cars away, and in Budapest I took care not to meet them even accidentally.

We met in January as usual and I buried the incident on the train far back in my mind. I didn't understand it, and I didn't want to understand it. I wanted a friend who would protect me from the world—one who would make no demands, as if he were a screen.

Prague was covered in snow that winter, showing her true face, her dirty facade buried underneath. As we walked out of the theater we linked arms—a rare gesture—because of the unusually deep snow. It was that particular, transcendent twilight moment. The snow had the gleam of a newly formed world. Suddenly, quite unbelievably, there arose the scent of violets.

Mythical elements of reality! The archetypal framework of nature! We cannot escape them—there is no way for us to run from them, and nowhere to run to. The emotion underlying those winter twilight moments, the animate silence of the twirling snow, the closeness of another's warm body. The beat of a lyrical drum when, in the dimming light and frosty air, the scent of spring flits past like a flying carpet.

DANIELA FISCHEROVÁ

The screen of snowflakes parted, and before us there stood a young man in a coat that was too flimsy for such cold weather, with a mass of tangled rusty curls hanging over his ears.

"Hi there!" he said to me, smiling warmly. I had never seen him before. M pulled me a little closer.

"So that's her?" the boy continued, speaking now to Doctor M, but not taking his amused eyes off me. "The writer?"

"Where did you come from?" Doctor M avoided answering him. His voice sounded strange—as if he were carrying a tray of long-stemmed wine glasses, carefully placing one foot in front of the other. "I thought you were gone. You said you were going away."

"I was just about to get onto my tram on Mir Square when the Holy Ghost stepped on my foot. So I guess I'm meant to be here instead. I told you I'm being guided."

"What were you doing on Mir? You're supposed to be somewhere in the outback."

"I guess not, since I'm here." He again smiled at me conspiratorially. "He doesn't believe that I'm being guided by a higher power. He never wants to believe me, I'm always in the right place—right where he needs me to be. Like a Saint Bernard."

"Hey, we're in a bit of a hurry."

We weren't in a hurry. All three of us knew that nobody was in a hurry. The young man wasn't tolerant enough to shrug this off and grimaced with patient distrust.

"He's lying," he said to me confidentially, "for no reason. He wouldn't even know how to explain why he's lying. He thinks I'm a misfit, an antipode, always looking at the world upside down. He's the antipode—but he doesn't want to admit it. It's the anesthesia, I think. Most of the time he's under anesthesia, right?"

Little clouds of mist flowed from both of their mouths, mingling long before they finished speaking, taking on an energetic life of their own. Doctor M was growing ever more nervous. Through the many layers of our sleeves I felt the invisible pull of an arm that had been leading me elsewhere, but he stood defiantly, as if that odd conversation were going to last until late at night. The young man suddenly pulled out a tangled chain on which was hanging a small key.

"I'll size you up," he said, winking at me encouragingly, as if he were promising me some sort of fun. "I'll size up the writer for you," he informed Doctor M. "You know I'm never wrong."

It was like a dream. An archetypal framework: the deepening darkness and the deepening whiteness of the snow, the illusion of isolation on an island of land, around the edges of which anonymous shadows slid past, a hot bunch of violets in the frost. All of this gave the episode some kind of hidden, cryptic meaning—an event banked away, earning interest for the future. Violets: the young man had a little woven sack of herbs hanging around his bare neck. Snowflakes melted on his rusty curls. He stepped up to me and unabashedly took my hand, turned the palm upward and began to swing the key over it.

"Don't be afraid," he said kindly. "I'm guided by the Holy Spirit. I would never hurt anyone."

The key, hanging between his thumb and pinky, began to swing slowly. Spellbound, I watched the increasing motion, which seemed guided by a force other than the boy's own will. His fingers didn't even move, but the key swung ever more wildly, until it was whirling like a dervish in ecstasy.

"She's OK," the young man announced considerately. He licked the key on both sides and then pressed it in his hand. "She'll be better in time, but not for you."

"That's enough—OK?" Doctor M replied in a flat monotone voice. "We have to go now."

The young man rightly ignored this information. He once again hung the key on his fingers, and it came to life and anxiously bucked like a horse, pawing at the ground with his hoof.

"Let go of her!" he demanded harshly. The arm loosened reluctantly. The key swung to and fro for a moment and then—as if it had found its own trajectory—began to whip between us with the sharp swinging motion of a pendulum.

"See?" said the boy kindly. "Hands off—the writer is not for you," He grabbed the key and turned to me. He looked straight into my eyes in a way that people rarely do. Throughout the odd and disjointed situation, he seemed so clear, so right, that he inspired neither fear nor the impression of intrusiveness.

"He's not the one," he declared intimately. He undid a button on Doctor M's coat and merrily tapped on his chest with a finger.

"Is anyone in there?"

Doctor M gazed over his shoulder and said nothing. The street-lights came on and a cone of light fell onto us as if we were on a stage.

"See?" the young man said. "He's not there. But where is he? He's afraid inside, because he's got an evil fairy in his heart. He's good, but the fairy tells him to do bad things. I give him good advice, but what can I do when he's not here? And when he is here, he's under anesthesia, so that he can pretend he doesn't hear me."

He stared at the key, set it on his palm, and held out his hand. The way small children give gifts. Time stood still for a moment, or at least slowed to a crawl. Everything froze—the snow halted in mid-air. Then Doctor M took the key and put it in his pocket. The pink stripe on his forehead glittered with frost. The young man laughed quietly and ran down the street, his rusty crest of hair quickly swallowed up in the snowy darkness.

■　□　■

Invisible violets, a dancing key, an evil fairy in the heart. Mythical components in a logic of facts. This is a logic of facts, or at least a logic of biased memory.

As soon as the boy left us we went off quickly and silently, no longer arm in arm. We often walked home in silence, so it was almost possible to obscure the reason that we were so intractably quiet that day. Confusion and cold were battling over me. I was overcome by shivering, and I wanted to get home as soon as possible. The twilight moment had passed, the snow stopped falling, and a pure winter darkness set in.

At the gate I found that I didn't have the key. It was useless to ring the bell in the empty house, but there was that often-used path through the construction site.

"Just so I know that you're home safe," he mumbled and we stumbled in the dark over frozen planks, torn cardboard, and the frozen desolate disorder of the empty lot. I clamped my teeth together firmly so they wouldn't chatter, and my face took on a resolute expression of defiance and irritation.

We found ourselves at the basement door to the house. I already had my hand on the icy doorknob.

"You wouldn't marry me anyhow," he said suddenly, without a question mark, out of the rhythm of our conversation, in a flat tone with little meaningful assertion. I was cold. I didn't want to know anything, didn't want to decide anything. My bubble had hardened with frost and wasn't letting anything in.

"No," I said, just as flatly. It was a reaction straight from the spine, merely a reflex, in which the mind plays no part. I didn't know why I was saying it. It was neither the right question, nor the right answer.

Doctor M nodded slightly and then symbolically raised a finger to his cap and left. I didn't wait until he had disappeared. In the house I found the key to the garden gate at the bottom of my purse.

■ □ ■

That night I had a dream in which Doctor M appeared for the first time. I am in the Budapest train station. The dream, as if working its way toward its climax, passes through a number of episodes, until suddenly I see railway tracks and an upside-down Doctor M walking over the ties, one by one, on his hands. There is an ecstatic expression, one I have never seen before, on his face, the dull light of dementia in his eyes. He is saying something imploringly, with a visionary's emphasis on each word, but I don't understand anything. I run along the rails and try with all my might to understand, but in vain: I hear a voice, but the words don't make sense. On the horizon a train appears.

With this the dream acquires a tone of horror and a sense of terrible and ruinous responsibility. The train is approaching. Doctor M doesn't pay it any heed and continues to speak in feverish ecstasy. An intense, sheer, and incomprehensible swirl of terror and love rises in me, the vortex of the bottomless absolute. The disaster looms closer and closer, until in a panic I cry out two words: "I know!"

I don't know what it is that I know. I don't know it either waking or sleeping, but I have to say it, because it's the only way to avert the catastrophe: everything rests on whether I know something. But it's too late, or else the knowledge is insufficient: the dream answers with a terrible clang of metal. I wake to hear myself screaming—I have a fever of almost 102 and an overwhelming sense of powerlessness.

Fourteen years have passed since that night. I am thirty-seven years old and married for the second time. I am certain that my life has never been, and never will be, more intense than it was at the moment of that scream. No joy, nor any suffering, has touched me as deeply. In concentric and ever-widening rings various joys and sufferings circle around me, but they mean less. No one was ever closer to me than he.

■ □ ■

I never heard from Doctor M again. I didn't understand why. I didn't know what had happened to him—I was totally confused. Somehow I wasn't capable of feeling pain—it was more like a loss of the ground under my feet, an odd vacuum without coordinates. I didn't miss him, I didn't feel his absence, but I couldn't get rid of him. He was and wasn't there. His absence was a different kind of presence, as when you know that an uninvited guest has fallen asleep outside your door. I didn't seek him out in any way. He had become a depressing specter, pressing on my bubble from the outside.

I met my first husband soon after that. We emigrated, and life took on a different theme for a time. I heard nothing of Doctor M. I married again and had two children. I returned to Czechoslovakia. The wind erased the trail. Fourteen years later I flew to Brisbane, in Australia, for a conference on modern literature.

■ □ ■

My body was raging with jet lag: two monster planes had overtaken time by nine hours. They had cast me into the near future; in Brisbane it was a summer afternoon, but for me a Czech winter morning was dawning. I didn't feel sick—although I had been warned that I could—but I had the confusing feeling that I was not there. I was nervously awake, but my body was still in a narcotic sleep. I had to look to find my hand and use my gaze like a remote control in order to get it into my sleeve. It was as if I wasn't there, where I was.

I showered and went out into the main room. My roommate, a Czech emigrant, was sitting on the table shaving her legs. I turned on the television so that I wouldn't have to watch her, and suddenly we were face-to-face once again. He was watching me from the screen. He was there and he wasn't, as always. The sound was low, and he spoke English. For a moment I didn't understand anything. He was speaking about distance and proximity. He used the word *wicket,* but he meant a gate—my gate, my garden.

"What show is this?" I asked the girl.

"It's not live—it's a video from last year's conference. It's on in all the rooms." She peered at the screen. "That man also happens to be Czech. He caused quite a stir here at one point."

She stroked her thick calf with the electric razor.

"Apparently in Prague he had cheated on his wife. The woman flew in with a pistol. She came to the hotel, somehow got into his room, and pow! But she must have been blind with rage. The man who cheated on her wasn't home. She got someone else by acci-dent. . . . Who was it now?"

She looked into the distance with the razor in her hand.

"Oh yes! The bellhop—some young redhead. The poor fellow was as innocent as a baby. Well, some people are just always in the wrong place at the wrong time."

She tapped her forehead with the razor disparagingly.

"And then she shot herself. She must have been crazy."

That piece of information had sought me out for fourteen years. It found me in Brisbane, Australia, on the top floor of the hotel Space. It had traveled at a speed of four kilometers a day. It hesitated like a blind turtle at the intersection of space and time, and fourteen years late, it jumped ahead nine hours. So now I knew, but what good was this information to me? It didn't yet concern me, or it had already ceased to concern me. Two different times were blending within me like a watermark.

"What's the matter? Jet lag?" asked the emigrant with the wisdom of an antipode, waving the buzzing razor under my nose. "I know how it is. I'm always flying somewhere, and I'm completely out of it. It's as if you aren't really here," she pointed to her chest. "Nothing matters to me. People talk, I listen, and I don't even know what they're saying."

"I know," I said mechanically. And then again, "I know."

Translated from the Czech by Andrée Collier Záleská

DANIELA FISCHEROVÁ

■ □ ■ □ ■

I, MILENA

Oksana Zabuzhko (Ukraine)

ON THE SURFACE EVERYTHING SEEMED FINE. THAT IS, EVERYTHING was indeed fine, or so Milena assured herself as she hurried home from the television studio those dark winter evenings (her face still stiff under the stage makeup she hadn't taken off yet and the feeble—at the thought of her husband, *I couldn't wait for you to get here*—smile of tenderness that of its own volition puffed up her lips into the little pipe of a kiss—*ah, you, my kitten*—breaking through the makeup, as if through the wafers of ice on asphalt that you had to watch out for all the time in the dark, even if they weren't there). Mincing cautiously over the invisible skating rinks, she would approach the building and, before going into the courtyard, would sometimes walk under the chestnuts that separated the building from the street and turn her head to search the windows with her gaze and determine which of them was lit to find out what Puppydog (Pussycat, Cottontail) was doing just then, not suspecting the joy of her approach. Most often the light was on in the bedroom, a washed-out blue on the lower part of the curtains: Cottontail was watching television. As he would jokingly put it, he was growing a tail: for some reason he would start to get an erection in front of the screen. And he would also say that he was watching for his sweet Milena.

Everything was fine as long as Milena was working in the news department. Twice a day she would appear before the camera with the moist light of "oh what a joy it is to see you again" in her eyes (because the viewers must be loved, as the director was always saying, and Milena knew how to do this; sometimes she even knew how to do it with her acquaintances, as long as she wasn't very tired) and read a text prepared by someone else, but that she occasionally improved upon, if not with words, then at least with her voice: Milena was unsurpassed at this or, to be perfectly honest, brilliant, and anyone who has heard her and remembers her from the screen will confirm it, so I'm not making anything up. With a voice like Milena's you could topple governments and parliaments in the evening and return them to their places of work by morning, and without any opposition from the electorate at that: her voice sparkled, shone, and spilled to overflowing in every possible hue and shade, from a warm chocolatey low-pitched intimacy to the metallic hiss of a snake, with an emphasis on the "s" (assuming that it is not just in stories that snakes hiss and that it is true that anyone who hears that sound must die). It even had a few shades that no one knew were possible, for example, the ozone freshness of dewy lilac at the start of the morning news (at half past seven), or ironic cinnamon spiciness (Milena had a particularly rich scale of ironic tones), or the kindly toastiness of a crust of bread that was reserved for government announcements, and if anyone considers everything I've been saying to be a metaphor, then they should try for themselves to pronounce after a day's training "President Kuchma met with the prime minister today" so as to make it sound sincere and even emanate domestic warmth, and they will surely grasp why Milena, a woman who was on the whole as helpless as a sparrow, was fundamentally feared by her colleagues and her bosses alike and why, even though she never took liberties and always tinged the news with the colors she was expected to (Milena had always been an A student, both at school and at university), the sweetly painful richness of her voice stubbornly pressed to the surface, radiating out onto her face barely discernible, coquettishly secretive mimicking little grimaces, which naturally made her especially attractive, but which did not always agree with the text that she was reading, so that it could appear to someone who had just awakened, for instance, that she was thinking of sneaking in a snort of laughter in a thoroughly inappropriate spot, which she wasn't really thinking of doing, or else some other utterly stupid thing like that. In short, Milena was feared and even considered a good journalist, and so someone in some oak-paneled office had taken it into their head to give her her own show. And this is where it all began.

Actually, suspicious symptoms had appeared earlier, too, in her news-department days. Insofar as the news was broadcast on channel thirty-something, Puppydog (Pussycat, Kittycat, Cottontail) had, with his own hands, nailed a specially acquired antenna (forty-five dollars, not including installation) to the outside of the window so that in the evenings he could watch his sweet Milena, because the building's common antenna got only the first three channels. Since then, lots of "nice shots," as Milena's photojournalist husband (who puffed himself up into a "photographic artist" on his business cards) called them, had started to appear on TV, and he was now in the habit of spending his evenings in the bedroom with the door closed, as if he were in a darkroom—the only lighting there was, if you looked at it from the street, a ghoulish blue rather than red—picking over the buttons on his remote and hopping from channel to channel like a bank manager calling up subordinates on the intercom, and when Milena would poke her head into the half-light of the bedroom to ask him what to make for supper, he would show her his teeth, from the bed, colored by the glow from the TV screen. After this they would often start making love. (Milena would turn off the TV at the critical moment.) Then her husband would go to the bathroom, and Milena would lie there face up and listen in wonder to the continuity of her life, thick as caramel, slowly moving around her in space.

And so one time when she came in from the cold, and straight from the hall into the bedroom, before she had even caught sight of the illuminated teeth, Milena heard a man's baritone greeting her from the TV screen with a booming, "Good evening, love." It turned out that some atrociously dubbed Brazilian soap was playing, and she and her husband had a good laugh at the surprise. Not long after, something similar happened to Milena's mother when she came for a Sunday visit. The two women's senseless jostling and tripping around the kitchen with their pots in an absurdist arrhythmic dance and their equally senseless jumpy conversation, all loose ends of interrupted sentences, cut off, dropped, and never picked up again, would tire her husband out quite quickly, and he would run off to the bedroom and lie low in front of the TV until the visit was over. Well, this time, his kindhearted mother-in-law, who was looking for him in order to enlighten him (she'd just thought of it) as to the proper way of sharpening kitchen knives (on a step in the courtyard), headed for the bedroom herself, and as soon as she had pushed open the door, from the twilight diluted by flashes swimming as if in an aquarium, a hysterical screen falsetto unexpectedly screamed at her, "Get out of here! Get out, I'm telling you! Do you hear me?" His mother-in-law forgot about her knives on the spot (then remembered them on the way home and telephoned from the streetcar stop, just when her daughter and son-in-law had turned off the TV because the tail, as its bearer had claimed, had grown quite big enough). And possibly the very next day, when Milena, worried because her period was late, pressed a button on the remote in the bedroom to take her mind off things, an unbearably brash little cartoon frog croaked out to her from the screen, "Don't cry, little girl. Let me sing you a so-o-ong instead," and a cheery little tune poured out, and an hour later Milena's flow started. It was then that she had her first evil suspicion: someone had taken up quarters in the TV set.

She didn't know yet who it was exactly, and later, too, she only thought she had found out, because, as I've said, this was all happening back in the news-department days, before Milena started her own show, which did so extraordinarily well in the ratings so quickly. If anyone has forgotten, let me remind you: Milena talked with jilted women. There were old ones among them and young ones, pretty and ugly, smart and not very (Milena rejected completely stupid ones): a peroxide-blonde translator—fat legs, a short skirt, a plastic doll's light eyes—talked about how many men were fighting over her just then, while a Ph.D. in chemistry, whose profile could have been called Akhmatovian if she had known how to carry it, aggressively insisted that at that particular time she was completely happy, and only at one moment did tears well up out of the blue, whereupon she pulled a handkerchief out of her handbag, fell silent, sniffled, and stuffed it back in again. Milena didn't cut those shots (not least out of some vague hope of moving the chemist's ex-husband to pity, in the event he was watching the broadcast). She had started with her girlfriends' friends—their classmates, hairdressers, and cosmeticians, friends from the nursery their children went to, and there's no end of occasions when women indulge in female confidences. Later, when the show was better known, the heroines came en masse themselves, just for the asking, and Milena simply marveled—sincerely at first, and then in a dull conventional way, in conversations for the most part—at the insatiable lust for publicity human suffering carries within itself, and aren't we all so afraid of death because that is the one thing you can't share with anyone?

She was proud of the fact that she was helping all those women to recut and resew (well, at least to rebaste) their suffering into a style they could wear, sometimes even quite smartly. This had happened to her on one of the first shows, which had subsequently brought in a whole cartload of letters. An awfully nice little woman, dark-haired with barely a dusting of gray, mother of two boys and boyish-looking herself, her hair almost in a crew cut and her shirt probably borrowed from the older one, a librarian, in other words, with no money to speak of, but with a classy sense of humor, went on, spreading out something invisible in her lap the whole time, about how she would be raising her boys from then on so that they wouldn't grow up to be like their father, talking in a calm and measured way that made the camera operators convulse with laughter behind their cameras, and it really seemed that the father was a real asshole if he couldn't appreciate a clever little woman like that. Granted, everything didn't always turn out so well, sometimes quite the contrary, and in ways you'd never even think of. Milena couldn't sleep for two nights in a row and took Corvalol and valerian with water when she found out that an ambulance had taken away one of her heroines because the day after the broadcast the stupid woman had gone and opened all the gas valves in her apartment. Everyone had a good scare that time. The director had even rushed off to consult someone about getting a certificate from a psychiatrist just in case, because you could tell the broad was a neurotic right off the bat, and her upper lip twitched on the right side, the camera brings out things like that like a microscope, there's no denying them. Here, evidently, Milena had got stung by her choice, but thank God, the whole thing had worked itself out. The dumb cunt had spilled her guts—who the hell wouldn't dump her? And why would you try so hard to get on screen, the producer spat out in puffs of smoke, if you can't even look in a mirror without your meds? Ah, stupid broads! Milena took quiet joy in this gracious verdict, that she was not the one being blamed, and then immediately felt ashamed of that feeling, and felt ashamed all day until her shame melted away. On the whole Milena was a woman of scruples, no matter what anyone said, and who would know better than I? So there.

That's what Milena's show was like, and she put it on, I'll say it again, with scruples. That is, she remembered well how she'd been taught at university that journalists must not show themselves, but their subjects, and if they wished to revel, if they wanted to all that badly, then not in themselves, but in their subjects. And she really did have a genuine interest in all those women and in peering over the fence into the abyss. As if to think what would happen if she ended up in their position herself, if her Pussycat took off one day and left her for good, which was somehow unnatural, even stupid, for her to think, much less imagine, as if your legs were unexpectedly to separate from you and scurry off down the street on their own, and leave you sitting on the sidewalk on your legless rear end, but still, what then, what would she be like then, and how would she feel? To try something like that on for size in her mind was so alarming and terrifying that it made her dizzy (like when you were a child and listened to stories about robbers while cowering under your bedclothes, or like violent erotic fantasies, when you imagine being raped by a platoon of soldiers).

Milena's pupils would dilate hypnotically on the screen, which, physiologists assure us, is in fact the main guarantee of attractiveness, and she'd cast spells to boot with her luminous voice, which ranged from the calming sensitivity of a sister of mercy (*Tell us, please, tell our viewers and especially our women viewers . . .*) to the angry, low-pitched rasp of solidarity of a fighting sister (*And you put up with all this for so many years?*), although sometimes she could not manage without the stealthy purring cajolement of the temptress when a broad would suddenly close up and wouldn't say another word, wouldn't reveal any more secrets, and she'd have to crack her shell as best she could. Why, sometimes Milena would even let out one of those lascivious low-pitched giggles of encouragement, practically indecent, as if in lovemaking, brusque and irascible, as if to say, Oh yes, my dear, oh yes, I've been there myself, well, and then what? That was usually how the most delectable bedroom morsels were gotten out of the heroines, after which the flood of letters and calls would rise to life-threatening levels.

Milena didn't really like herself when she resorted to tricks like that, but the tainted feeling was more than compensated for by the lamps of professional triumph, all lighting up at once—look what

I've done!—in which there were both beads of joyful sweat between her shoulder blades and captivated and envious looks from her colleagues—well, kid, you're an ace!—and that swelling sense of her own power, which comprised the main high, like the gymnast's from his absolute power over his own body: this way and that, I can do it any way. When she happened to be watching the show with her husband at home, then in those most drastic spots Milena, her sparkling eyes fixed on the screen, would unseeingly squeeze his hand white—*there, right there, there's going to be a tour de force in a second, listen!*—and, nervous and aroused, would giggle at every felicitous word that came from the screen, and he'd chortle, too, pleased and proud of her success. Their professional ambitions didn't overlap, and he had never photographed Milena, except well before they were married, back when they were dating, and even that was more as a pretext, because the static Milena was at a great disadvantage: her voice, her mimicry, the glint of quicksilver—that was her element, and not under any circumstances a stiff portrait, and Puppydog preferred to take pleasure in her live. For that matter he took pleasure in her portraits, too, and generally considered Milena a beauty, which was, of course, an exaggeration, even though there were others besides him who thought so, especially when Milena got her own show and nothing seemed to foreshadow any trouble.

Now they were planning to buy a satellite dish and install it on the balcony. This would come to about three hundred dollars, but it was worth it, because, although Milena conscientiously watched almost all her colleagues' shows, of course, Ukrainian TV couldn't satisfy her. Not that the Russian was any better; three-quarters of it ripped off from American models, while Milena was a patriot and always said that Ukraine must follow its own path. In fact, it would be worth buying a second set, because her husband preferred to look at "nice shots," and there are more nice shots, obviously, in movies, and he would mumble a recap of their storylines, in two or three quick sentences—who's who, who's with who against who—in Milena's ear, up to the point at which she came and snuggled at his side. His eyes glued to the screen, he would pull the duvet over her, gropingly tuck her in and gather her up to himself, tickle her cheek with his lips, and mutter, "This one here, the blond guy, he was abducted by aliens, but now he's come back." "Why did he come back?" Milena would ask absentmindedly as she pressed against him, staring by now in the same direction, and so, after a little more fidgeting, they would fall silent and, lying side by side, would sink their eyes in the screen, and the third person in the room and the apartment was that Panasonic, so that as time went on the idea of buying another TV even began to seem a bit awkward and bizarre to Milena. Wouldn't it be just like splitting their bed or apartment? "After all, intelligent people can always find a compromise, can't they, Pussycat?" Milena would say (which was to say: Pussycat would watch what interested her with her, and the rest of the time he would be free to amuse himself with his nice shots as he pleased), to which the smart Pussycat would call back cheerfully, like a soldier, "Yes, sir!" and just as cheerfully and resonantly smooch his sweet, smart Milena: compromise had triumphed. But late in the evening Milena herself didn't mind watching something more entertaining and thus distancing herself from the many faces and many installments of women's misfortune with which she now lived out almost all of her waking hours.

Altogether, that misfortune was quite strange indeed, made-up, dressed up, and coquettish. (Some of the women plucked up the courage for such a forced familiarity in front of the camera that she was embarrassed for them. When that happened Milena would yell out a categorical "Cut!" to the camera operators and, muting her voice, would spend five or ten minutes "chatting" the overly emotional young lady down to a more or less normal state.) And yet, and this is what is interesting, every one of them was genuinely suffering, sincerely and unaffectedly, and Milena had even thought at first that slighted women went to these tapings mainly in the secret hope of bringing back their ex or at least getting revenge on him. For there were those who asked Milena whether it was all right to address him directly, and then in millions of evening apartments there would resound from the screen ever so movingly, "Sasha, if you can see me now, I want you to know that I've forgiven you for everything, and I hope you're happy." Whereupon Milena herself would get a lump in her throat: at that moment she could actually physically feel the choral, gurgling sob of the female half of the nation spreading out in space—crescendo, crescendo—and a dark wave of public anger rising up (as if to smash an oppressive regime, as Russian TV used to say), swelling up, surging up at the unknown Sasha. "Bastard!"

millions of lips would whisper; millions of noses would sniffle, and for a fraction of a second the country would stiffen in an orgasm of human sympathy.

And this was all her doing, Milena's: she edited out the rest of the speech, because the speaker herself had not managed to stop with this exquisite opening. She had visibly been tossed about, like a car on a slippery road, and irresistibly drawn into the ditch—"Of course, you hurt me, and very badly. I still can't see how you could have been such a jerk, and after all I did for you"—throwing out ready-made phrases ever faster and faster, seething, rattling, and almost foaming from her bottled-up rage, predatory flames in her eyes, the hair on her head looking as if it would stand on end any second now, like that of a witch taking off in flight. In a word, the ultimate effect was completely opposite to the initial one. Milena's power was in presenting those women the way she saw them herself (better, of course, better!), and when she was unanimously chosen "show of the month" and in her own interview she said (focusing her attention on making sure that, God forbid, this didn't sound condescending) that to her heroines she was at once a girlfriend, a psychiatrist, and a gynecologist, this was clearly the absolute truth, which none of them could have managed to contradict.

And yet Milena had a vague feeling that this was not the whole truth: something still remained unexpressed, some exceedingly important ingredient, like yeast in dough, had been left out. And so, something similar was probably happening to them, too. Even as their single, all-devouring intention of calling out one more thing in their ex-better halves' tracks drove them into the studio, somewhere at the bottom of each of them there still stirred, as an amorphous dark spot, a far more incomprehensible urge: they were flying toward the light of the screen like moths on the porch at the cottage on those humid July nights toward the luminescent blueness of the old back-and-white Slavutych set, so that up close you could clearly hear the dry crackling of electrical charges or sizzled little wings. Did they (the women, not the moths, although who can know for sure what a moth thinks?) perhaps dream that by crossing over into that space beyond the screen they would get back the soul that a man had taken from them, and not just get it back, but get it back completely renewed, enormously enriched, basking in the glow of fame and raised up to unreachable heights above the lives they had lived until now, merged forever with the fantastic colored shimmering of all the TV movies at once, so that Santa Barbara, Dallas, the Denver dynasty, and the snow-white villas on the shores of tropical seas would all become their own, something that had happened to them, since they were there too, on the other side of the screen, and their everyday existence would be filled with perhaps even a kind of divine meaning? Milena knew only too well from her own experience this magic of the screen: the spellbinding effect of your own face in the frame, unrecognizable in the very first instant, multiplied by itself a hundredfold in all its barely perceptible movements, and how it envelops you in a ticklish warmth, like a foam bath, and you soften, you develop and expand, warmed by the energy streaming from the screen, unexpectedly so much larger than life that you are prepared to believe for a moment in your own omnipotence.

"An energy boost," Milena's husband would say. "Just go and read about lepton fields." (He would clip articles from popular magazines and put them in a special folder.) "Why do you think that back at the turn of the century the Inuit would break ethnographers' cameras and run away from them as if they were evil spirits?"

"A camera is different," Milena would fling back, her face still flushed and her eyes flashing, sensing that if this comparison were taken to its logical conclusion she would end up as an ethnographer and her heroine as an Inuit. There was no way that could please her, and so her husband would silently and agreeably switch to a different channel, one with reruns (all the more so as on Milena's they were already running the last commercial), and the TV would aim at them the typical squinty look of a Soviet secret policeman, a chekist, and as befits someone from the NKVD, he would say with paternal warmth in his voice, "I'm looking at you, and I can tell you guys are really good sports!"

Somehow both of them imperceptibly got used to the way the TV had gradually become an active participant in all their chats, why even, not infrequently, a counselor and a referee, and they stopped bursting out laughing when, for example, during an argument in which Milena, irritated not so much by her husband's imaginary jealousies as by the fact that she wasn't allowed to relax even at home, kept shouting (still flattered) that that Italian, the one her husband said she'd been making goo-goo eyes at over dinner all evening, wasn't worth a fig and that all she needed was some Italian, as it was she could barely drag her feet into bed, at that very moment an elegant, well-built gentleman was coming into view on the TV (which they now had turned on almost all the time) and saying judiciously, "My dear man, these days most Italian men are homosexuals, so this isn't going to give you much mileage," after which the argument fizzled and they started kissing (noticing occasionally out of the corners of their eyes that the same thing was happening on the screen, only now lying down). Most of the remarks on TV showed it to be noticeably more cynical than either of them. It would jabber perfectly calmly, as if it were talking about something self-evident, about things that either of them would admit to the other only in a fit of self-reproach. This was highly salutary, they both thought, because once you've heard something like that from the screen, you no longer have to be ashamed and to pretend. Milena, for example, would never have noticed on her own, or even if she had noticed, then not anytime soon, that her husband, even though he was listening and nodding patiently, was beginning to tire of her constant complaining about the studio head, who, although he wasn't finding fault, because there was really nothing for him to find fault with, was still probably the only person who had never once openly shown any kind of enthusiasm or at least approval for Milena, whereby he greatly shook our A student's courage, you could say he simply hobbled her, until she began to suspect that this demonstrative disrespect, as she saw it, concealed a behind-the-scenes intrigue, sabotage, a secret plot to take her show away from her, whereas Pussycat, on the contrary, expressed the assumption that the studio head simply had the hots for her and had chosen this way of keeping her in constant suspense, and so they kept dragging out this subject dully, always on the same point, and would perhaps have kept dragging it on until Pussycat lost his mind, until one evening the TV broke into a frenzy instead of him. No sooner had Milena started in on the studio head in the doorway, "He gave me a lift home, and what do you think, not a word about yesterday's broadcast, not a single word. No, I can't keep working like this," than she heard, "So unzip his pants and give him a blowjob." The cool advice came from the TV in two languages at once, French and Ukrainian, from an awfully vulgar floozie. Stunned almost to tears, Milena had shut up after that on the subject of her studio head.

Moreover, the TV seemed to intercept their thoughts even as they thought them, to abbreviate and edit them, sometimes even before they themselves set about thinking them through or elucidating their own true wishes to themselves. "Shall we hit the sack?" Milena's husband said as he put his arms around her and slid his hands down her back to her buttocks. She resisted a bit. "My script for tomorrow isn't ready yet." "E-ekh, my dear!" the TV intruded brashly, in the guise of a seasoned old broad from a Russian backwater. "How are you going to hold on to your husband if you don't keep putting out for him?" Hey, maybe that was true, Milena thought in alarm (a bit offended, though, at it being put so coarsely, and for Puppydog's sake, too: is a guy some kind of rabbit, heaven help us, for nothing else to matter to him?), but who can figure men out, no matter how long you live with them, you never know for sure, and so she finished that thought stretched out on her back, with her legs bent at the knees, as he was going into her heavily, without any rhythm somehow, and she wasn't getting anywhere, until she opened her eyes at last and gasped: riveted to her with the lower, mobile half of his trunk, he was leaning on his arms and supporting the upper half in order to see the screen over the bedpost, bursts of color running over his face, as in a discotheque, his eyes glued to it with a wondrous glassy look, and sweat sparkling on his upper lip. What? What is it? Milena wanted to shout, crushed by the weight of his body, which suddenly seemed to have tripled, coming down on her from above, by this humiliation, destructive as a steamroller, all the more destructive for its unexpectedness. Who was he with? Whereupon he moaned and came down, went limp, burying his face in her, now undeniably in her. Stunned, with mixed feelings of being laid waste and robbed, of sadness and reproach, she drew her trembling hand along his back, as if she were trying gropingly to put back in place the reality of her life, which just a moment before had vanished, disappeared into nowhere. "Who were you with?" she asked quietly, to avoid asking, What were they showing? because that would have been a direct complaint, almost a quarrel, whereas she was waiting for an explanation, a reconciliation, and apologies. But he didn't understand the question. He raised up his joyfully damp little mug in astonishment at her, glowing in full color. "What do you mean, who with? What's the matter with you, Milena? With you. Who else would I be with, girl?"

OKSANA ZABUZHKO

142
▾

Milena tried to forget this incident, squeeze it out, thinking that maybe she had really imagined it, like the studio head's intrigues. After all, immediately afterward, turning over onto her stomach, she had begun watching a very pleasant police drama with her husband, with lots of female corpses, and when he trundled off to the kitchen to get something to nibble on, as he always did after they had made love, and then came back and asked her something, she mumbled in response without listening, and twice, when he was too persistent, she even snapped at him, "Don't bother me!" In the end then, even if she had had to stand up in court, for example, even she couldn't have sworn with one hundred percent certainty what had taken place in bed and what had taken place on TV. All in all, this sort of thing happened to them rather often. In fact, the TV not only interfered in their lives but lived its own life, too, and an incomparably more vivid one at that, more festive, uniformly bright, and saturated on all nine channels at once, while the two of them each had maybe three or four (work, parents, friends) and only one joint one, and all of them, of course, were working in a slower and more boring way, with breaks, dark abysses, floating streaks of unnecessary moods surfacing from who knows where, and ghosts. Moreover, unlike them, the TV always had everything in order, and it was in an invariably chipper mood: each of its stories, however terrifying and bloody, always got a logical resolution; it never dropped anything in midstream in the cowardly hope that somehow everything would shake down all by itself, and it didn't leave behind any loose ends (relations that were not completely cleared up, unavenged life defeats, unrealized ambitions, unburied dead people, or any of the other baggage you take on in a lifetime!). It managed to put absolutely everything in order, to set out accents, and to insert titles and subtitles wherever they were necessary, so that it was actually a pleasure to watch.

There was nothing strange about it, then, that when Milena's husband had sold some wealthy magazine all the negatives he had shot in one lot and then the bastards had started dealing in his photos, and with no thought of sending him anything back, and he, like a pouty little boy, was telling Milena for the umpteenth time how he had once again seen a photo of his that day there and there, he had to repeat this speech umpteen times before Milena managed to tear her unconscious look away from the screen (on which a very nice

Canadian newspaperman was just deciding to sue his boss, who had cheated him) and noticed at last that her husband and the TV seemed to be out of sync with each other and were even almost contradicting each other, and kept asking, "What? What?" The dialogue that continued between them may have sounded something like this:

Husband: I'm saying that they swindled me, that's what!

Milena: So why don't you take them to court?

Husband: What court? Are you kidding? On what grounds? Why, they paid me over and above my contract. They threw me a bone, and now they're raking in as much as they want! (Milena steals glances at the TV.) With the taxes we pay if I were earning according to my contract, you and I would have been collecting bottles outside supermarkets long ago!

TV (in English and Ukrainian): There are no hopeless situations, man. We'll get the union together, we'll put our material in all the newspapers, we'll teach the beasts to respect the law!

Husband (confused): What trade union? What newspapers? What law?

Milena (shrugs her shoulders and turns back toward the screen).

And that, once again, is why it wasn't strange that neither of them noticed—and by the time Milena noticed, it was too late—what Milena's mother was the first to sense (and, as it turned out, the last), only, in her usual manner, she interpreted it the way she wanted to, and what she, who was still incapable of comprehending that a threesome in a home was, however you looked at it, a full set, what she wanted, naturally, was a grandchild. And so one morning she phoned and asked, with a happy girlish excitement in her voice, "Milena dear, I was watching you the whole time yesterday. Are you by any chance pregnant?"

"No," Milena said in surprise. "What gave you that idea?"

"Mmm, you seem to have gained weight. You were sitting there so nice and plump, and your face looked a little puffy or something."

For the second time in one day Milena, alarmed, weighed herself on the scale in her bathroom (a procedure she performed every morning) and even wondered whether the scale was broken, because her weight was, of course, stable—just like the day before, and the day before that, and the year before, and the year before that, and after all, if she really had put on a bit of weight, who would have been the first to tell her if not Puppydog? Just in case, Milena decided to wait for Puppydog. (He would disappear until noon into his darkroom, and Milena would leave the house in the afternoon, so for the most part they wouldn't see each other until evening.) In the meantime she rushed to review the tape of the previous day's broadcast with an elegant financier/economist, winning in every way, with a peppery dark Spanish beauty, who talked about how since her divorce she had been banging (she clung to this word insistently) only younger men and what a positive effect this was having on her self-esteem. Only this time, as soon as Milena saw her all-conquering financier appear in the frame, she fast-forwarded in irritation, greedily picking out just herself, especially the close-ups: could that idiot operator have screwed something up? (Milena knew that in three-quarter profile her face seemed wider and rounded in a homely way, and in front of the camera she usually didn't forget this.) But everything seemed to be the same. And yet it wasn't. Even if she was neither puffy nor, God forbid, plump, the on-screen Milena was nevertheless in some ungraspable way different, as if her bones had thickened and the shapes that were emphasized by her homey pose—her arm on the back of the chair, her hip turned up from the way she had crossed her legs, and her skirt pulled taut over it—had jointly weighed down into a grotesque, Toulouse-Lautrec-ish monumentality that the delicate Milena had never ever had. It was somehow over-free and irritating, maybe even arousing in its own way, but only to a taste that was indeed very plebeian. What's more, things were even worse as far as her face was concerned, which conspiratorially switched expressions in unison with what the irrepressible financier hadn't even stated or rather hadn't finished stating. From a professional point of view this was an extraclassy job, of course, insofar as it set the viewers off in the desired direction (for which the off-screen Milena, moved and shamed, could not in fact congratulate herself). At the same time, though, there were moments when it demonstrated an almost indecent satisfaction—flowing out satedly in a half-smile, the eyes ready at any second, it seemed, to get bleared (which only Milena's mother, obsessed with her own idea, could have taken for the distant "wandering" look of a pregnant woman!) until, as if she were really pouting, puffing up either with herself, or because she was pleased with the way the talk was going or, perish the thought, at her own and the financier's delectation in the muscular torso of her young bodyguard-chauffeur-masseur. Something dark and impure was looming in all this, its saturated slime poisoning the charge that Milena would usually get when she watched herself on screen. Her voice rocked like thighs swaying, an aroused, hoarse little laugh, a ticklish impurity. What had happened to her voice? Where did this vulgarity come from that was poured into it, dammed up like a stale breath? "What a slut!" cried the off-screen Milena harshly, as if slapping her hand, suddenly sobered, as if she had been drenched with water, by the sound of her own voice that had thus been renewed, and to this very same sound the on-screen Milena slowly turned to her that insolent mug of hers, shamelessly beautiful, blazing drunkenly from the studio lights, with its kiss-swollen slit of crimson lips, and winked arrogantly, even almost triumphantly, flashing a grin as if to say, And so, what did you think?

Breathing quickly and for some reason holding onto her pulse with one hand, the off-screen Milena pressed Stop and then Rewind with the other hand. This time the on-screen Milena, turning her full face toward her, stuck out her tongue at her, and between those dark glistening lips it really did look completely repulsive—pale, as if it were naked, and even twitching at the end. The off-screen one pressed the pause button to catch the wretched woman with her tongue hanging out: let her sit like that for a while! But she missed: the frame went by, and the on-screen Milena, suddenly brought to a halt, froze and gaped in surprise like a tarty doll feigning offended modesty. She even pouted her little lips for a "tsk-tsk," as if she were on the verge of saying, Bad kitty, you've hurt your sweet Milena!

"Hey, you're teasing me!" hissed the off-screen Milena, stung to the quick, covered with a slimy scaly cold. "You just wait a minute, I'll sssssssho-o-ow you!" She clicked the buttons, almost to the rhythm of her own accelerated heartbeat, forcing the on-screen Milena now to revive and expire by turns, now to twist and twitch in a cheery marionettish shaking, now to move in slow motion like a sleepwalker, forcing herself to raise her hand, as if under the pressure of a hundred atmospheres, but none of it was any use—the other Milena did not reveal herself in any other way and turned into a very ordinary screen representation, persecuted for who knows what reason, so that God knows how much time passed before the off-screen Milena, who was already prepared to drop her schizophrenic pastime (that is, agree with the other whore that she had really dreamed everything here in front of the screen), heard the ringing of the telephone from a distance, as if through a layer of water, and picked up the receiver, also in slow motion for some reason, overcoming with that one movement the pressure of all hundred atmospheres at once.

"Hello," said an unfamiliar man's voice, clearing his throat, pushing onto her from the depths of the receiver like a storm cloud. "Hello, I need to talk to Milena." Now she felt a chill inside, too. This was how it had been in the dreams about a bear that she'd had as a child from which she had always awakened with a cry of terror: the bear was coming nearer, giant and dark, and covering her with his shadow.

"Speaking." She tried to defend herself with her voice, reflexively switching on a silvery secretarial timbre.

At the other end, after a thoughtful pause (as if he were aiming for a precise hit), an answer, with feigned awkwardness: "Listen, pussycat. . . . Here's an offer for you. I'm tired of looking at you just on TV. In other words, call your girlfriend, the one from yesterday, and let's set a time; I'll come around. Don't get hung up about the price; I won't haggle."

"Who? What? How dare you? Who are you?" the off-screen Milena rattled off in outrage, at the same time as she was noticing with even greater outrage how the on-screen Milena, who could no longer sit still in her chair, had tensed up her whole body and started to play again. Her eyes flashing, with the impatient vibration of aroused giggling, she called out to the on-screen one, right in her face, in despair, just like an idiot, "I'll call the police!"

A nasty, authoritative laugh came out of the receiver. "No you won't, you fool. Better think about it, and I'll call back. I know where you live. And talk to your girlfriend. Don't worry. You'll like it."

"Go away!" the off-screen Milena shrieked, her voice completely squeaky now, but the receiver had been hung up anyway (whereupon she heard from who knows where snatches of the first few bars of Beethoven's "Für Elise" in an incredibly cynical, mockingly dance-like rhythm: pa-pa, pa-pa, pam, pa-ra-papam! gurgling out, as if they were drunk, then someone very seriously grumbled, "Sorry," and the dial tone started dripping noisily, like water from a leaky tap). The receiver lay down quietly on its rest, and the off-screen Milena, just as quietly, in a voice that was white with rage, said to the on-screen one, "I'll kill you," obviously with no idea of what she was saying.

Because really, well what could she do to the other one? Even in the unconscious fever of the first hours—run somewhere, explain something, and argue every which way, saying, take a good close look, that's not me at all (make a statement on air! even as absurd an idea as that had crossed her mind, imagine!)—Milena stayed lucid enough to be coolly aware the whole time, somewhere deep down: the other one, even though she was itching to tear her off herself, like mangy skin, was still far from alien to her, and not just in her external likeness. In her own way, that other one was even very effective, far more self-confident than the first Milena, less restrained (that's for sure!), and on the whole, ideally suited to her purpose. From a professional standpoint, it had to be acknowledged, she could not be reproached for anything at all, even though pent up inside Milena was a painfully vague recollection, following from the effort of trying to break out, that back when she was just starting the show, she had imagined her screen image to be different somehow—warmer, more radiant, or something. The kind of sincere women's sessions that go on in the kitchen nearly until dawn on the once-grasped-and-never-again-released crystalline-singing note of ever-deepening spiritual union: Sister, sister, the pain is subsiding; you're not alone in this world, your children are sleeping in the next room, and life goes on; we'll be wise, we'll be patient; these are precious moments, like music, like love, because you do in fact love her at these moments to the point of stiffness, of numbness, your head reeling a little from the intolerably burning height of her suffering. Here there is tenderness, and pain, and pride in our brave and silent woman's endurance, and a beauty that is unspeakable to the point of tears, and that later glows from both of the women in the conversation for a long time yet (until the crowd on the bus rubs it off): that's what Milena, who had known no small number of such evenings in her lifetime, strove to obtain from her heroines and from herself. In one of the very first scripts (someone had later cut these lines without leaving a trace) this was called helping-the-Ukrainian-woman-find-herself-in-our-complicated-time. Well, and what had come of it?

On the way to the studio (she didn't stay put to wait for her husband after all: she needed to be in motion, she needed some kind of action) Milena covered her head with her hands and moaned: a sticky and, most important, undeserved feeling of defeat was festering in her. After all, she had done everything the way she was supposed to, she had made an effort and put herself out like a madwoman, overworking herself so much that Puppydog had been reproaching her (recently, it was true, he had fallen silent), and now that odious creature was sitting in the studio, winking and hinting at something filthy, and what was most important, no one had noticed the difference! Well, yes, over the time of the show Milena herself had learned many new things, had grown professionally, as everyone said of her, and would no longer make fun, the way she used to, of her news-department colleagues, for really coming to life only when there were catastrophes, fires, or killings, and preferably atrocious ones. Even an idiot knows that if you want people to hear you amid all this wild noise of ours and not switch channels, then you have to either cuff them or tickle them in some intimate spot, and do it so masterfully, too, that they won't get jaded, that is, by changing your technique, and whoever says that's easy is simply envious and a failure, but! . . . There was, all the same, a "but." As the thought of that obscene complacent mug on the screen (oh, to smash it in!) washed back over her, Milena was blinded, as by a stroke of lightning, by a long tremor of hatred, very much like love, that ran down the whole length of her body. "What should I do now?" she mumbled to herself, ever so quickly, unconsciously speeding up her pace and digging her fingers into her coat collar, as if it were her enemy's throat: Milena was scared.

"Caw, caw, ca-a-aw!" She suddenly heard the cries above her. Milena raised her head: way up high, about halfway to the raw and empty sky that with springtime was already farther away, bare branches of trees were swaying in a feeble attempt at a Japanese drawing, a flock of startled ravens circling over them. "What a beautifully composed shot, and right to the point," she thought. "It's precisely on topic, and it doesn't need any editing." And so, from that moment, everything around her began unfolding smoothly, as on a TV screen, as if she had stepped out of herself into the space behind the screen, where nothing more needs to be decided, just watched. In the corridors at the studio, no one paid any attention to her, her preoccupied acquaintances hurried past, goggle-eyed and unseeing, and even in the stairwell not a living soul was lingering over a smoke. Here Milena remembered, with an instant unpleasant chill of humiliation, that she had dashed out of the house in a rush without her makeup, without even putting on lipstick, and she felt embarrassed, as if she were in her bedclothes. At the same time she was glad that so far no one had intercepted her and she could surreptitiously slip out, dash home, put on some makeup there, and then come back with a respectable face to meet the cheerful hubbub of greetings and noisy commotion of work switching on as usual at her appearance, starting with the guard by the turnstile down at the entrance and then racing like a flame along a safety fuse to the elevator and up, up, along the corridors, running along loops into offices. The strangest thing was that for some reason the simplest and most obvious solution hadn't occurred to Milena, namely, to drop by the makeup women and to rattle off to them, panting, "Oh, I've been running. As you can see I've completely lost my face, so put some Indian war paint on me, please," and even to visit with them a bit, smoke a cigarette; it was nice to take a break like that before starting work, especially because the girls liked her, followed her show religiously, and one, who was divorced herself, even boasted that she unplugged the telephone when the show was on so no one would interrupt. However, nothing even close to that dawned in Milena's confused mind, and she wandered through the corridors like a sleepwalker, an apparition, toward the service stairs: somehow she had decided that she just had to escape by the service stairs. As she walked she glanced into open doors, keeping her own face in the shadows, as if it were burned or something.

Suddenly the director charged out of a doorway right into her, his face distorted, and mumbled or hiccupped, in Russian for some reason, "Ex-excuse me." He wafted a sulfurous burning smell: a match, Milena gathered, noticing that a curl of gray smoke was unfurling above him as he fled into the depths of the narrowed perspective of the corridor. "The poor fellow's going to burn out some day," she thought, beside the point and without regret, for somehow she lacked not only regret but any feelings at all, as if the lightbulbs meant for them had been unscrewed, leaving only the speed at which frames were changing or, rather, she was advancing involuntarily from frame to frame, through a flashing tape. There was no way she could stop,

OKSANA ZABUZHKO

150

she had to keep moving, while any feeling, this she remembered quite lucidly, necessarily requires stopping and dropping out of the stream. Therefore, if one of them did by any chance come to life like a spark or a fidgety little flea, then she would immediately shake it off without stopping, letting it fizzle out all by itself and turn into ash in midair. Indeed, people sped this way and that, like comets, in intersecting sparkling cascades of tails as they burned out—more luxuriant behind some, more sparse behind others, whereby a constantly raised working temperature was maintained on the premises, and there collected over the years that fine, barely perceptible bluish gray coating on the walls, faces, and floor that studio guests sometimes take for a sign of plain smokiness, when in fact even though it is a smokiness of sorts, it is however far, far from being that plain. What a wonderful job I have, Milena thought with pride or, more precisely, with an embryo of pride. The embryo of pride flared somewhere behind her back like a firefly, brushing imperceptibly against her cheek, and sizzled up on the floor, without developing into a thought. Milena carried her gaze ahead of her rapidly, like a camera: the corridor was running onto her, constantly breaking in unexpected turns and flashing increasingly goggle-eyed faces to meet her, but the main effect was based on the fact that it was as if the camera were hidden, because no one saw Milena. Actually there wasn't any time to see her, either, because the film was advancing faster and more jerkily, and everyone was jogging or even galloping instead of walking. There now before Milena's eyes, that is, in front of her camera, the studio head's secretary, a long-haired blonde who was becoming short-haired as she went and then a brunette, miscarried, evidently a baby conceived just a minute earlier, which, with a gurgling froggish croaking that Milena found vaguely familiar, slipped out into the ashen twilight of the corridor and instantly disappeared, as if it had tumbled into the fourth dimension. "Could it be the studio head's?" Milena scribbled a question mark in her mind, the way she would have in the margin of a script, more for the sake of form, because she really wasn't in the least curious, and so the question took off after the wretched fetus that everyone had forgotten about. Milena did remember, though, that she was supposed to go out onto the service stairs and could only wonder, if the word is at all to the point here, why looking for them was taking her so long.

Suddenly the director popped out of a doorway again, now with a beard, using both hands to jostle ahead of himself, like a cart in a supermarket, two fat wenches, joined inseparably, as if they were making love, from which Milena concluded that one of them was in fact supposed to be her new jilted heroine, and the other quite the opposite, the rival home wrecker, and again she put an approving exclamation mark in the invisible margin. To liven up the show, it was a great idea, as long as they didn't get into a fight in the studio, although right behind them, wiping out any traces of them, there thundered past, in a fierce gallop, a sullen herd of men in identical dark gray suits with identical badges on their lapels. Milena didn't have a chance to look at them more closely. Some of the men were running, bending under the weight of banners with text that was running together in a blur, and the last one was actually carrying no less than the red-and-blue flag of Soviet Ukraine. But then dashing victoriously right after them, making echoes resound, came athletes melted together into a yellow-and-blue whole, only the first one, it seemed to Milena, who was by now a bit dazed from the onslaught of faces, was racing with a lit Olympic torch, and so the impression she was left with was cheerful and life-affirming after all. But here a shot of the gray sky and ravens was suddenly wedged in again: caw, caw, ca-aaw! The branches swayed up high. Where had the ceiling vanished to? She had got a double exposure, Milena managed to grasp, and forgetting about her unmade-up face, she grabbed the first prop that came to hand, a door handle that gave way at a light push and revealed in the doorway none other than Milena's own familiar studio: deep inside, cameras were all set for taping, and two chairs, lit up from all sides, stood on the set. One, for the guest, was still empty, while sitting in the other one, covering herself with the lid of her compact for one last look to check herself out, was some awfully familiar broad dressed in crimson, her knees roundly pressed together and put out ahead in a no less familiar way from under her skirt, like a shield. "Where have I seen her?" Milena fretted, noticing at the same time that the backdrop in the studio had changed, which is to say the show's logo, too: something like an ad for Revlon lipstick, with huge, moistly parted lips that promised either to surrender or to swallow you whole in one gulp, was hanging there now. And there was something else looming behind the chairs, in the unlit background, like a low couch or something, as in a psychoanalyst's office, but that she didn't get a good look at, because just then the woman in the chair took the compact away from her face, and glancing at Milena was her own face, that is, not hers, but that other one's, from the screen, only this time it was somehow improbably, simply not even humanly, even terrifyingly beautiful, as if from the days of silent films: the eyes flamed in dark rings, the lips blazed, the witch's eyebrows met on the bridge of her nose in a swallowtail, and her skin, matte with makeup, disdainfully immovable in the glaring light of the lamp, breathed with that heavenly peace that only the screen can really feign. "What have they been feeding her here to make her look like that?" Milena thought in the doorway, bewildered and still numb, while the other one looked at her in dissatisfied wonder, as if asking who the intruder was and even planning to clap her hands from her luminous height for someone to throw the pest out the door. "But this is my studio, and this is my show!" Milena almost cried out, on the verge of tears from the humiliation, and especially from her own looks, so out of place here, so plain she might as well be invisible, that instead of trying to argue with someone she could only run away, crawl into a hole, and not inflict herself on anyone's sight, because it was enough just to look at the two of them right now to say with certainty which one deserved a place in the studio—surely not this slattern by the doorway! But still, how did that scum dare, and where was everyone looking, the director, the studio executives, the viewers, after all? Since when did she have all the rights around here?

On this last thought Milena had to step aside to make way for a procession crawling in from the corridor like a wedding: the director—now clean-shaven again!—the camera operators, and looming somewhere behind them not one but two makeup technicians at once, and other dark figures. They were all leading, or almost carrying, a young blonde, barely conscious from emotion, with a pageboy haircut, with delicately raised cheekbones and a delicate sharp nose on which drops of sweat had soaked through the makeup. The blonde's eyes were still and glassy as if she were in a trance. They did not express anything themselves, only reflecting light from outside, and Milena—I have in mind, of course, the one who was standing by the doorway—was stung by a vague recollection of having seen eyes like that before, in someone close (familiar, warm) and of that moment being connected to something extremely unpleasant. The blonde pageboy was stepping unseeingly, as if her legs were folding under her, and she was on the verge of crashing down on her knees, stretching her arms out ahead of her with cries of ecstasy, because she was breathing quickly and her lips were moistly parted, practically like the ad on the backdrop, but it wasn't the backdrop that she was staring at so unblinkingly, like a calf at the sacrificial flames, but—Milena herself went numb, too, following her gaze—at that other one on the set who was now poised to meet her, like a panther about to leap, and was luring the new arrival with a smile so greedy, so evil, and yet so lush playing on her lips: Come on now, come on, closer, closer—as if she were drawing her to herself like a spider, step by step, along an invisible gluey tautly stretched hair, until Milena could hear it humming. Or maybe it was the hum of the switched-on equipment, hastily filming the blonde, who had already been caught by her blouse collar on the hook of the microphone, as she neared the set and raised up to the voracious witch in crimson—a crimson at once vibrant and fluid, as if it were filled with blood—her prayerful, incredulous hands, "Ave, Caesarina!" and as the other one leaned down with an impetuous twist of her torso, to hold her up, "Come to me, and I will soothe you," literally to snatch her, suck onto her because the poor thing was reeling, was ready to fall to the ground at the feet of her deity from a surfeit of emotion—no, she was really going to kiss her on the hand! "Music!" someone called out breathlessly, running past Milena in the dim light and just missing pushing her into the plywood cubes, boards, and other rummage stacked up against the wall. "Don't forget the music in this episode!" "Fuck off!" answered a nasal voice out of the dark. It was this sound that made Milena suddenly realize that something horrible was about to happen on the set, something so unthinkable even to her own imagination that she just had to switch channels immediately. And turning over in her mind like a mill wheel the mindless phrase, "What's going on, what's going on, what's going on?" Milena lunged through the doorway back into the hall.

"She's going to slaughter her." The next thought caught up with Milena on the run in the middle of the hall. "She'll simply lay her out on that couch and slaughter her, chop her into little pieces with a knife, and that foolish woman will expire with a humble smile on her lips. All of them in there, have they gone mad, can't they see what's coming?" She ran through the whole production in her mind and hardly had any more doubt that things were really heading toward some kind of ritual killing that had to be brought to an immediate stop. According to the script Milena was the one who had to do it, and that was why she hadn't managed before to find her way to the service stairs: now that it had been wound up, the plot was evidently unfolding according to the strict logic of TV. The revelation did not inspire Milena to decisiveness, or enthusiasm, and she tried to return to the terrible studio, but this turned out not to be all that simple. Once again the interminable corridor bored into her view, breaking out into dark flashes and turns, and people were running about. Suddenly she ran into the noisy throng of a whole company of leading Kiev actors, all of them in wheelchairs for some reason. They jostled her and pressed her nose up against a brass plaque that was cold to the touch (and covered to boot, like a windshield with breath, with a graying sticky film of that TV ash) and on which Milena, forcing herself to lean away, just from an instinctive revulsion, unexpectedly read, to her great delight, the words "Studio Head." "Why, of course, that's who's supposed to put a stop to this outrage!" With renewed zeal she managed to feel her way to the doorknob and burst in. The secretary wasn't in the reception area—she had probably stepped out for another abortion—the door to the office was unlocked, and the studio head really was in. Milena saw him from behind, with his back turned to his desk, a very wide oak table, about the size of a Soviet Khrushchev-era vestibule, grandly authoritarian, at the very sight of which Milena and, let it be known, not she alone, had always experienced a vague erotic arousal, marveling at the same time how authority can be so sexual even when represented by a table. At the moment, however, it was not the table that had her attention, but the studio head, to whom something strange was happening. Black netted wings, folded like a grasshopper's or a dragonfly's, were growing straight out from the stiff shoulders of his suit jacket. They were moving, preparing to spread, and the gray suit was jerking between them, comically flapping its rumpled vents. The next moment the wings moved decisively, letting out at the ends something that looked like bird beaks, and turned right before bewildered Milena's eyes into two outstretched woman's legs in net stockings and black pumps with pointed heels. Milena must have made a muffled sound because the studio head made one too. He looked behind him and froze in his unfastened trousers at the sight of Milena. Meanwhile, opening up to Milena behind the studio head was an entirely different sight that caused her to think, for the first time in her life, in a very agreeable way, "Hey, I'm going mad, nothing to be afraid of, it's even interesting." At first, a crumpled spot, a familiar crimson, flashed through her mind in a single strident smear; then something horrible flashed by in stripes, naked and hairy, and when she had a good look, it was her own unrecognizable face. She, that bitch from the studio, was now ensconced on the studio head's table with her legs triumphantly thrown up in a V for victory worthy of a rally, waving one of them in the air as if she were conducting an inaudible orchestra and watching Milena with no expression at all by now, as if she were an insect or something.

"Excuse me," Milena muttered stupidly, and the studio head, too, holding up his trousers, moved his lips in mirrored obedience, echoing her, but then he was impatiently pushed by a swinging black-netted leg with a heel, and a harsh cry rang out, like an execution order. Milena had never heard herself make such a sound as long as she had lived. "Well, what are you stopping for? Give me more! More! More!" The head ohhed, twitched, and coughed up his half-swallowed "Excuse me" over his shoulder in Milena's direction, and again two netted black folding wings squeezed and pinched him from both sides, and he obediently resumed trotting to that savage, unrestrained whoop of "More! More! More!" Also shaking, with a repulsive dry shiver from deep within her gut, Milena shuffled blindly out of the office and shut the door tight behind her: an utterly futile gesture, because the whoop was not in the least silenced thereby, but kept roaring in her ears, and the ceiling collapsed into oblivion from it, and there, flying up above the swaying black boughs, cawing, were the ravens. There was really nothing more to be done at the studio.

Just as soon as she understood that, right away Milena found herself on the service stairs: now the gigantic multistory digestive tract of the TV studio spewed her out easily, without any resistance. And the sleepy, very sleepy thought stirred heavily that maybe it was for the better (on the stairs for some reason Milena had started getting terribly sleepy). Maybe that's how it should be; why, that other Milena (now she was finally agreeing to recognize her, calling her by her very own name for the first time), that other one had gone farther than she herself, without her, by nature, would probably have dared. No, she certainly wouldn't have dared to act this way (her thought was interrupted by an exhausted yawn so wide it drew tears)—stopping at nothing, with no scruples, taking on all the dirt. She felt a relaxing warmth embrace and rock her: Let, let someone caring and strong do everything for her, and then she . . . later . . . later . . . later . . . , and now fully a queen and no longer the perpetual A student, like *some* people—she reproached herself for this in the tender grumbling tone her husband used—and dissolved into a smile, blinking her way out of her insuperable, deathly fatigue: to sleep, to sleep, pressed up against Puppydog, his broad barely furred chest, one sleepy hand feeling its ticklish growth and the other cradling his warmly swollen tail, Puppydog would put his arm around her, Mm-m, sunshine, my golden pussycat, calm her with the touch of his lips, a last bedtime kiss. "I love you," Milena would say to him from the far shore of sleep, and all the others, well, to hell with them and all their games, their shows, and all their insane broads. And that was what Milena dragged herself home with.

It was dark at home, and only a low, bluish gray light was seeping through the new stained-glass bedroom door into the front hall. Milena was astonished momentarily by the new door (when had her honey had time?) and by the whole ungraspable, disturbing feeling of unfamiliarity that one's own home evokes after a long absence (how much time had passed, anyway?), reached for the knob in the usual spot, was astonished once again, in the very skin on her palm this time, when she found it on the other side, groped about, and finally went in.

And saw.

That is, heard.

That is, simultaneously both saw and heard:

Milena (from the screen, still wearing crimson and her legs in the same victorious V): Give me more! More! More!

Husband (on the bed): Just a moment, Milena, hang on, love, hang on. . . .

Milena (from the doorway): No! Get out! What are you doing? You're mine! He's mine! (Undecipherable from that point.)

Milena (from the screen): Well, look at that! Look! Look! Oooo, what a turn-on! See? See? And now you do me, come up and do it, use your tongue, hear me, girl? Use your tongue, they all do me that way, all those manless broads, and they all rave from it, right on the air, the highest-rated show, two million letters a month. More! More! More! Use your tongue, I said, your tongue, there's no other use for you anyway. More! More! More!

Milena (from the doorway—she comes closer, takes the remote, and turns off the TV).

Husband (rabid): What? Who? Who are you?

Milena: I am Milena. Your wife.

Husband: Fuck off! (Grabs the remote and turns on the TV.)

Milena (from the screen, sitting in a chair raised high on the studio set): My beloved! My dearest, my sweetest viewers, and above all my women viewers, my brothers and sisters, I turn to you once again—I, Milena! I am the one who comes into every home to remind you that there is no earthly woe that cannot be conquered by the great force of our coming together! I am with you, my sisters. Anyone who feels lonely and abandoned this evening, cheated and hurt, come to me, and I'll satisfy you! I'll let you have a bite of my flesh and my blood, my sweet flesh and even sweeter blood, and your hearts will be filled with great joy, and you will be avenged on those who have hurt you; they will gnash their teeth and gnaw the earth in their impotent rage, for as long as they live they will never know the joy that is yours and mine, sisters! Here she is, my beloved sister who will be in the studio today with me and with you, here she comes now. Come, my dove (a church hymn starts playing), come, my sweet, my body is waiting for you, loving you, as no one has loved for thousands of years, oh come!

But she has no body, the other Milena suddenly thought, and it seemed that she had cried this out loud. "She has no body, do you hear me? This is all an illusion, a terrible fraud. This really used to be my body, and still is even now, and there is no other nor can there be." And, as if she were looking for proof for herself, she grabbed a knife, her husband's beautiful pocketknife, a Swiss knife with a tiny pair of tweezers and a bone toothpick in the handle that was lying open on the night table—but then it was possible that she was simply in great pain at that moment, realizing that she, too, had been jilted, the impossible had happened, dreams had come true, and she was finally united with the throng of all the countless women toward which she had been heading so unswervingly from the outset, and therefore unconsciously lunged to outscream one pain with another, louder, but easier one, as people often do when they thrust even rather different objects into themselves. The blade laughed blindingly in the teleblaze, its teeth wide open over the naked forearm, and then from the forearm there streamed, and ran, and even began to drip something inky dark, the color of a blank nighttime screen and with a shine like that of a metallic, grayish oily film, which crackled with sparks sputtering. . . .

And that, my beloved viewers, is the end of Milena's story, and it's almost time for us to say good-bye. May I remind you that I'll keep looking forward to your responses and that the authors of the most interesting ones, that is, those of you who suggest the most-captivating, boldest, most-dramatic stories for us to look at from your own lives, will be invited to the studio to take part in our up-coming broadcasts. The show goes on. Don't miss your chance! I am waiting for you—I, Milena.

Translated from the Ukrainian by Marco Carynnyk and Marta Horban

THE CYBER

Ljubov' Romanchuk (Russia)

"TO START WITH, SO WE CAN GET BETTER ACQUAINTED, I SHOULD probably set forth what I believe in, so that in the future there won't be any misunderstandings, innuendoes, or scores to settle. Absolute clarity in everything, that is a work norm I adhere to, and therefore in my new position I shall be revealing some aspects of myself that, it is possible, hardly anyone knows about. I'm not afraid of public opinion, and so I shall be absolutely honest. To some extent this analysis will help me too, to dot the 'i's' in relation to myself.

"So, let's begin with my assertion that I consider myself to be a positive individual. That is my right, and we can move ahead from there. So! What that means is: first, I, personally, live by reason; that's the main thing, and I consider people who give in to their feelings stupid. It should be clear, then, that it's utterly useless to try to make me feel pity. You can get through to me only by way of an axiom or a logically incontrovertible analysis. . . .

"I see that women, deeply emotional creatures that they are, have lost me right from the start. Well, it's your choice, my dears."

The newly minted department head brushed away a lock of hair that had fallen down over his eyes, straightened his glasses, and after checking to see whether his coat button, which was hanging by a thread, would last to the end of his talk, continued:

"Feelings are instincts that draw us closer to the animals, but reason—now that is a human being. Reason can explain everything, even feelings, if they are analyzed properly. Personality conflict and even relationship breakdown begin when one lets in unnecessary emotions and feelings that bring nothing but fatigue and disappointment. In any case, *logic is supreme,* and this is the most positive force in life. Clear, I trust?

"Then let's go on to point number two—which is: Everyone is equal. Anyone doubt that?"

"No."

"No need to. To me equality is not seeing any differences between men and women. I don't see them and I don't accept them. Why should women yield to men, even in morality? On what grounds? Personally I sympathize far more often with men, and I am of particular service to them in minor matters. Everyone should be equal, but not identical. Hence there is nothing more nonsensical than the harmonious development of personality. All people, both men and women—and this is point number three—are to be judged only according to their mind. Moral qualities are irrelevant, so far as I'm concerned. Only the mind, my friends, mind and logic. You know, the cleverest people are the cynics."

"So it follows that beauty means nothing to you?" a secretary pursed her lips in amazement.

"And just what is beauty?" retorted the department head with a wry face. "Beauty as such does not exist. It is something completely relative. You could say it is simply the formulation of customary views on what is good and what is bad. I do not recognize that artificial concept. You can train yourself, of course, in whatever you like: beauty, poetry, music. But what for? I don't want to train myself in anything, as a matter of principle. Expediency—okay. That's something that can be mathematically expressed, explained, calculated, constructed . . . but beauty—that, I tell you, is a nonstarter."

"Well, it seems we've missed the mark . . . ," mused a gray-haired senior lecturer in a velour jacket sitting in the front row, "missed it by a good long ways." It wasn't that long ago, he recalled, that he supported this young man's candidacy, arguing that there was no candidate more sensitive and responsive for the post. Yes, indeed, he had supported him. But then again, what had he, in fact, supported? There was only this strange appearance, something that made him different from other well-ensconced heads and deans, something loose and carefree. This strangeness had made everybody think that such a person would be liberal, open, and unsophisticated.

"Any questions?"

"What time is it?" asked the secretary.

"Time to gather stones together," the lecturer in the velour jacket answered evasively.

"Will you support the work of the department in the further development of the cybernetic intellectual structure that imitates human thinking?"

"Of course. I think it is both possible and necessary to create a machine that can replace people in all things—i.e., to reduce everything that is biological or energy-based to mechanics, copying and substitution. It may be difficult, but it's possible. What is a person? A mechanism, the sum total of their moving parts (molecules, cells, neurons); their thoughts, memory, feelings, and the sum total of their interaction. Consequently, a person can be reduced to a set of parts capable of reproducing and replacing all these reactions, and he will lose nothing in the process."

"What about a moral complex?"

"Everything is programmable, my dear. I am a materialist, a sheer materialist. I ask you to always remember that. And please, no complexes. Positive characters are always smart people and not sentimental moralists as some would have us believe. That is my rule of thumb—never to agree with what is generally accepted, since what is generally accepted is generally stupid. However, even though I hold nothing sacred and inwardly deny morality itself, I am in favor of always supporting it outwardly. Just to prevent chaos. Pure and simple.

"So, now, let's go on to the scientific part of our session. Science is a prime mover. It is supreme meaning and supreme justification. Is anybody going to be defending this semester?"

"My dissertation's almost ready," piped up a middle-aged research assistant. "New theories on the topology of space."

"Splendid. But get this: if you should introduce into your topology, into *our* topology, any dimension beyond the three that actually exist, I shall never speak to you again. I've had enough of all those artificial tricks. But what's happening there with the cybernetic structure?"

The lecturer in the velour jacket decided he should stand up. Putting his hands behind his back and watching the fall of the department head's mother-of-pearl coat button from jacket to floor, he began:

"You see, we have followed a completely different approach in this matter. The approach of the natural accumulation of data. Why all these new devices and cramming things into new data files, when the simplest approach has already been thought of—namely, experience? The experience of communication. Without that there won't be any structure. Some years ago we created a cybernetic fetus, capable of developing by analogy with natural embryos and absorbing all incoming data, including processing, storing, and classification. Our child has grown, not even suspecting it was a cyber. The programs have been working without interruption, and the behavior imitation has been absolute. And here is the result."

"What result?"

"You. Only time will tell how the experiment is to continue and the adaptation program is to develop. Excuse me."

Translated from the Russian by John Woodsworth

how interesting

■ □ ■ □ ■

FROM E.E.

Olga Tokarczuk (Poland)

THE SPRAWLING PARK WAS NOT VERY WELL KEPT. FOR ERNA IT SEEMED as if there were no end to it. Beyond the symbolic border of an old collapsed wall it led into a narrow strip of field and then into a forest, where one could go right through to the Oder River.

Nobody was looking after the ponds nestled between the high dykes, with their limpid, dark water. Maybe the ponds were deep, maybe they even reached to the center of the earth, where the waters from every sea, lake, pond, and river merged into a huge underground ocean.

Erna tried to visit the park as often as possible: this was the only place where nobody stared at her, pitied her, or tried to teach her a lesson. Katharine and Christine preferred wandering around the dusty back rooms of the house. They discovered a large fireplace with a mirror hanging over it. They declared the mirror was actually a hidden doorway to secret hideaways where "mad Gertrude" (as they called their aunt) kept precious memories of her past, and maybe even treasures. Only from time to time did the two girls go out to the playground, which Mr. Eltzner had built only last year. Erna too would see them now and then, when they stole eggs from the chickens. Why they did that, she did not want to know.

Erna would disappear into the park right after breakfast, always encountering the same question in her mother's eyes. "I'm going to see the little ducks," or "I've found some completely white violets," or "I'm going to get some fresh air" she would reply. Mother lowered her eyelids in the usual manner, as if to say: "You are free to go," and started talking with Auntie or one of her elder daughters. The park was Erna's privilege, a reward, a kind of payment for weeks of sitting still on the windowsill, from which the world looked so gloomy.

It didn't take long for Erna to inspect her territory. She made a tour of the ponds, watched the muddy river flowing, discovered a hilltop covered with clumps of white violets that looked as if they were turning gray. Later, she began to go beyond the limits of the park, beyond the strip of field, to the young, bright forest where often at summer's end you can find mushrooms hidden in the grass.

Then she would get up on the retaining wall and watch the river—vast, unsettled, and unending. The river breathed in turbulent eddies and murmured as it caught the tips of the overhanging branches. Erna didn't think of it as the Oder; this was not the same river as the one in the city, where barges plied to and fro. This one was simply called *She*—*She* was alive, young, powerful, and unforgiving. Erna gazed in awe at the double retaining wall that had been built to keep the river in its channel; she pictured the terrible flood Aunt Gertrude had talked about, when the water came right up to the farm, overturning trees, overflowing the dykes, and destroying the hitherto existing geography of the flatland.

Walking along the forested shoreline, Erna eventually came across the river's dead sister, an old backwater cut off from the river forever, a reminder of its past power. Now it was overgrown with duckweed, interspersed with water lilies. Over the water hung hot, humid air filled with the smells and noises of birds. This was a place of mystery, a place of transformation from the dead to the eternally alive.

Fallen leaves, broken branches, flower petals, all these fragile forms of life melted into the earth, disappeared into it, building it up from its roots, from the bottom of the planet, which is immortal. The transformation always took place quietly and without being noticed, but when you sat down on the grass and looked at the water, you could feel it.

Once Erna lost her way here. The place where she got lost was a headland surrounded by the waters of the old Oder. Wild lilac bushes grew here, their branches intertwined to form a real labyrinth. The light that reached inside took on the dark green color of the leaves. Dusk reigned inside the black lilac labyrinth.

During her lonely wanderings Erna drank in the world around her with new intensity. Her thoughts only now opened up to the world outside herself. Everything now was clear and distinct; things no longer cheated or deceived her. She no longer saw in them those vast, hypnotizing expanses and gradually stopped hearing excited voices within. Now everything within her was quiet and still. Every image fell like a stone into a well, reverberating with echoes of past associations.

"Erna is getting better." Dr. Löwe would smile. She was not hearing voices as much anymore and no longer saw ghosts. The psychiatrist was now obliged to close his most serious case, that is, hallucination.

Only once Erna spotted something strange in a tree near the playground, where the rest of the children were playing a chaotic game with constantly changing rules. It didn't have a form, but was some sort of stretched-out quadruple figure, something without shape, which could be discerned by virtue of its multiplication. For a while Erna felt an excitement, which passed when she could not find the words to fix the feeling in her memory. She then had a dream, the only one that she could remember from her stay at Kleinitz. She dreamed she saw a dwarf lying on his back. He was either sick or dead. She was amazed at how small and childlike his feet were. Apart from this sense of amazement there was no other emotion, but still the dream was disturbing to her, even frightening. She wanted to write a letter to Arthur Schatzmann, feeling bound to report her dream to him, but she could not recall from her memory all those polite forms needed to begin a letter. She also did not know how to tell him that she missed him, and this caused her great concern.

About two weeks after she arrived something happened to Erna, something that should have happened before this. When she went to the bathroom after breakfast, she noticed a splotch of red blood on her panties. She did not feel any pain; she did not have a headache or stomach cramps as she had expected from listening to the tales of her older sisters. She pulled up her panties and squatted. By and by she heard the twins trying to get into the bathroom, and so she had to leave. She walked past them without a word.

Mother was busy drinking coffee with Aunt Gertrude, so Erna went to Bertha and Marie's room. She didn't understand what they were smiling about. Bertha hugged her with unaccustomed affection, and Marie kissed her. Laughing and joking, they pulled out a linen belt with a pair of fasteners in front and back. They told her to pull up her skirt and fitted it around her hips. It was too wide, so Marie secured it with a pin.

"Here, these will be yours!" Bertha said, handing her a bunch of elongated pink pads, fitted with string loops at both ends.

"When they get dirty you have to wash them out thoroughly in cold water and put them out to dry. When your period is finished, you will have to boil them to get rid of all the spots."

Erna couldn't figure out how to put it on.

"You have to take off your panties!" laughed Marie. "Don't be embarrassed!"

Erna turned her back to them. She felt her cheeks burning. Her panties, which had dropped to the floor, were streaked with red blotches. She put a pad in between her legs, where the blood was coming out. She attached the loop to the front fastener, and Marie helped her with the one at the back. She felt as if she were in a harness, and the whole complicated linen contraption was squeezing her hips and crotch.

"So, now you are a real woman."

"Our little Erna is a woman."

Her elder sisters hugged each other and smiled at her with a new sense of affection. Erna was confused; she wanted to leave. She dashed over to the door and grabbed the doorknob.

"Wait, from now on you have to wash your dirty clothing yourself!" Marie called after her as she tossed over her panties.

Erna passed her mother and her aunt on the veranda and ran to the park. Every step reminded her of that peculiar contraption she was wearing. She felt it around her waist, between her legs, and even inside her. Now she felt chained, fettered, and closed in. She continued running, trying to get accustomed to this new set of clothing. Just the thought of feeling every step was strange to her. Before she was not conscious that she was walking, that she had legs and something else in between them—an aperture opening toward the ground, the opposite of her mouth. She was a tube on two legs.

She ran past the ponds, beyond the collapsed wall. She didn't slow down until she reached the forest, but even it seemed too bright, too transparent, for her to hide. So she ran on, to the scrub of black lilac, to the headland surrounded by standing water. She had to bend over in order to enter the labyrinth. She wove her way in between the clusters of bushes and finally sat down on the thin, leaf-covered grass. She was panting from running so hard; she felt weak and exhausted. Her breathing broke the silence that otherwise reigned here. To Erna it seemed as if it was not really her that was breathing but the silence itself, like a large creature rubbing against her body. She heard that rhythmic breathing that was hers and yet not hers, and it left her powerless. She lay down on her back. Above her she saw a dark green arch of leaves. It was right there over her head, and all of a sudden she wished the leaves would fall on her with their moist, smothering weight and take away her breath.

She lifted up her skirt and felt the contraption that was fettering her body. She loosened the ties and lay motionless for a while. Silence stared at her naked underbelly. For the first time Erna began to consciously run her hands over the burning, pulsating spot. She didn't know it was possible to touch oneself that way. Her body shuddered and swelled from one pass of her finger. She waited. She withdrew her hands and started to tear off the overhanging leaves. Crushing them in her hands, she put them between her legs like a compress in place of those belts, loops, and pads. She was overwhelmed by the suffocating scent of living plants, which touched her body both delicately and brutally, caressing her and pressing themselves against her. She covered her naked belly, breasts, and shoulders with leaves and smeared them over her face until she completely lost her breath.

Translated from the Polish by John Woodsworth

THE THIRD SHORE

Natasza Goerke (Poland)

"STOP PULLING FACES," PLEADS KALSANG. "WE DON'T KNOW THE hour of our death, and were yours to come, let's say, this very moment, you'd get stuck like that and that's how I'd remember you. And then I'd blame myself for the rest of my life: that I didn't rise to the occasion, that I didn't stop you in time."

Kalsang rises to the occasion, he stops me in time, makes tea. "Here you are, drink. It's a special tea from Tibet via Paris. A friend of mine bought it thinking with you." "Of you," I correct him. "And besides, I don't understand why the Tibetans buy their tea in Paris." Kalsang smiles, looks through the window. "See?" he says. "In this country December looks the same as July."

I've had enough. "Listen!" I yell at him. "How am I supposed to stop pulling faces when you talk to me in *koans*?" Now Kalsang pulls a face; he is surprised. "But, Treasure, I've only stated that in Denmark it rains all the time." I defend Denmark: "In England it rains even more. And if you want a change of climate, let's go to Poland—there are no Communists there now, nobody will deport you to China, and you can have everything: tea shop, the classic four seasons, there are even Buddhists." Kalsang looks at me, horrified. "I met Polish Buddhists in India. They marched around a temple chanting something. I thought they were an army platoon, but they were only chanting a mantra." "Don't be stupid," I say. "They must have been German Buddhists. The Polish ones are a bit like those in Denmark—they have beards too but they don't carry those little Fjällräven rucksacks, and they stoop more." "Maybe," admits

Kalsang, but without conviction. "Whichever," he sighs, "they didn't look happy." I smile. "Kalsang, Treasure," I explain, "the West is not Tibet. Here you're not born a Buddhist. Here you convert to Buddhism when you're really, really unhappy. One day you simply discover in yourself a space that makes you scared: you feel evil, more and more evil, while around you, just to make it worse, everyone's ever so good and saintly. So instead of making them sad, or being a pain in the arse and a source of anxiety, you start pretending to be one of them. Till something snaps and all hell breaks loose: you want to get hold of a nun and smash in her jolly face, you feel like shaking a cardinal out of his habit, throwing him into boiling water, and while reading aloud from the Holy Bible, closely observing him for behavioral changes. Of course, you don't do that, but you have to do something instead. You take to drink, you open a shop, or you convert to Buddhism." "And do you really want to go back to that Poland of yours?" asks Kalsang; he is very pale. "I don't know," I say, "but we can't stay in Denmark, can we? And from Australia or Canada everywhere else is too far." Kalsang reads the future from his beads. He counts them, rolls his eyes.

"We shall go to Tibet," says Kalsang and begins to hum. "It's the love song of the sixth Dalai Lama," he explains. "We used to sing it as children when tending yaks on the meadows." "Lovely," I sigh, "but I've really had it up to here with foreign languages, and besides, I'm not sure I could stand a country that has more Buddhists than Poland." "You would stand it well. Tibetans are simple people," Kalsang assures me. "And if you really want to complicate things, we can settle near a Christian community. You could practice your English, go to Mass, the nuns would give us rice and ballpoint pens." "In Poland you can have rice and ballpoint pens just as well, and you don't have to go to Mass for it," I shout and fall silent, while Kalsang pours milk into the tea and stirs very loudly.

"I'm going to meditate," announces Kalsang and leaves the room. "I'll send you some good vibrations, to calm you down. Later, we can go out for a walk," he adds. He shuts the door and begins to send good vibrations.

I pour out the tea and pour in the cognac. I feel sick at first, then blissful. I start drawing: all the Buddhists in the Chinese book get moustaches. "I'm turning them into Padmasambhava," I call out to Kalsang, who, I'm sure, has by now meditated out so much calm he shouldn't take it too badly. It's his book. He got it from me last Christmas. I got hand cream and a rosary, and talc to stop my creamed fingers slipping off the beads. Once I start praying that is, for at the moment I'm going through this weird phase in which instead of prayers my lips pour out obscenities. Obscenities are the words I always learn first with any new language. One day, by way of an experiment, I let rip in Tibetan. Kalsang's eyes nearly fell out of his head. Then he mumbled out a mantra and staring at me full of admiration asked: "Do all Polish women speak like that?" "Not all," I admitted. "Polish women are like Indian women: hypocritical, they hide in their clothes, which are not saris, true, but serve the same function—they simulate innocence." "That's a shame," laughed Kalsang, "for that's how Tibetan women swear, not in the presence of their husbands but with strangers." "As it happens, it's the opposite with Polish women," I sigh. "Their canons of femininity oblige them to be graceful, thus afflicting their expressive powers. In public life, the Polish woman opts for euphemism, but at home, when she lets her husband have it from the heart it knocks the stuffing out of him." "Hm," hmmed Kalsang, made me some tea, and went off to meditate. I stayed lying on the bed and, as always, started making greeting cards.

The world is full of holy days. Of New Year's Eves alone there are two hundred every year. I already have a nice pile of those cards; I just don't know who to send them to, so that I don't hurt anyone's feelings. For they are horrible cards—a reflection of my present state of mind. Collages are the best: Christ on the lotus, Buddha on the cross. . . . I can only send them to the Rajneesh commune; they think along similar lines.

"Listen, this book of yours," I call out to the kitchen. "May I cut it up? We'll send them mustachioed Buddhas!" After a moment's silence, Kalsang puts his head through the kitchen door. He says, "Before you throw a grain of dirt at Buddha you need to rise at least to the level of the first *bhumi*. *Bhumi* is a step on the path of *bodhisattva*. If you reach it, you can laugh at the sacred till you burst and you won't go to hell. But in order to laugh at the sacred, you have to meditate for a very, very long time—and not drink cognac." I hide the cognac under the table and make sure: "Was Christ a *bodhisattva?*" "If he acted for the good of other beings he was," says Kalsang. I show him a holy picture that my grandma just sent me. The picture is not a collage: Christ is lying in the cradle, sans moustache. "How tiny," marvels Kalsang. He places the picture on the top of his head. It's a blessing, and if you believe in it, it works straightaway. I think it really works. Kalsang rolls his eyes, smiles, and states with conviction, "Christ is a *bodhisattva*. Do you know his mantra?" I take a piece of paper and write down a fragment of the Our Father. Kalsang tries to read it; it twists his tongue. "Transcribe it into Tibetan," he asks. "I will include it in my prayers. Maybe Tibet will be free sooner and we'll leave Denmark." "Treasure," I cry, "stop messing things up! Christ cannot answer contradictory prayers. I've just asked him to help us settle in Poland." Kalsang shrugs: "Poland, Tibet—what's the difference?" he says. "The important thing is to leave here. If we agree, at least in this respect, they'll come to an understanding too and all will be well." "Who they?" I cry. "My God forbids other gods, and in your pantheon, there are so many of them that I'm sure to end up in some horrible hell. I'm earning that hell living with you. I'm pulling myself up by the roots from my native soil!" Kalsang grows sad. "But it's only one great symbol. We are different only on the symbolic level," he explains. "For in fact God is Buddha, and he won't mind if instead of the Our Father you say mantras."

I press on the Padmasambhava's forehead a stamp that Kalsang gave me last Christmas: it's a little swastika, in Sanskrit *su asti*, the ancient symbol of happiness. "Now, try and send it to Poland," I say. "You'll soon find out about the differences on a symbolic level." Kalsang nods and goes out to the kitchen. "I'll pray and all will be well," he assures me. And I feel that in a moment I'll go mad.

At the last moment I don't. I pick up my cognac and imagine that my cheek is being gently stroked by Piechocki. He's a guy I met once, years and years ago in Poland. His name is not Piechocki, of course, but I had to encode him somehow, to let him enter my memory in such a way that in case of my death, which may come at any moment, he won't be compromised. Now it's enough that I think "Piechocki" and straightaway I feel glowing warmth, that's how I've programmed myself. I talk to Piechocki all the time. I freed him of all his shortcomings and the man's grown so attached that he won't leave me for a minute. When Kalsang strokes me Piechocki turns up and instantly I feel more passionate. One could say—doubly passionate, for I love them both at once. I only have to be careful to keep my mouth shut, so that I won't cry out all of a sudden—Come, Piechocki, come!

It must be some sort of reaction to the cultural differences; the only touch of local color in this exotic life of mine. Piechocki is my entire childhood. It was with him that I smoked my first joint. He deflowered me on the Persian carpet when mother went to a congress of hiking doctors in Koscierzyna. Then he was a father who sent his teenage daughter to a convent school, and then, when he refined his taste, he became my professor. In his immaculate Polish he taught me about beauty. He would explain to me that beauty is in everybody and that everybody is a whole world, and that only an idiot could accuse the world of being ugly. The guy I've called Piechocki in fact spoke in a slightly different way, more convoluted and partly in Latin, but that didn't put me off. Simply, I cut out of my Piechocki everything that was unworthy of my projection. I communicated exclusively with the beautiful side of his complex personality, and just to avoid making it too ideal I brought his wife into action. Slowly, the tragic side of the story unfolded: I tore Piechocki between heart and duty. And when in the end he followed his heart, I decided to reward him and took him with me to Asia. Piechocki looked at me with Kalsang's eyes and whispered: He, I—it's only a difference on the symbolic level. So I took Kalsang back to Europe.

Now Piechocki is simply my shadow. He strokes my back with that subtle wisdom of his, reminding me discreetly not to escape into cognac, and when Kalsang goes off to meditate Piechocki starts praying. "Oh, Lord," he prays, "restore the little one to reason; bring a happy ending to this painful crisis in her identity." And when I listen to it, I get all confused and I begin to pull faces: now I have the face of Madonna, now that of Mahakala. My fingers slip off the beads; I knock over the candles, fall into the fire. "No, Kalsang," I cry, "I can't live either in Poland or in Tibet! Let's find a less religious place, a secular dimension where you live once, die once, and whence you don't have to go anywhere else."

Kalsang runs in and picks me up from the carpet. "What's the matter, Treasure?" he asks. "Have you been attacked by a demon?"

"No, it's simply confusion on the level of values," explains Piechocki through my lips, and he winks at me to keep my chin up. I do. "Kalsang, darling," I say, "it's nothing. My ego flooded out. For a moment I believed it was not a dream, that I really existed. But now it's all right," I add. I stroke Kalsang on the cheek and do a sit-up. I no longer exist; it was merely a funny crisis of illusory values.

Kalsang nods and murmurs, "Yes, egos are funny things. You have to be careful what you identify yourself with. If you feel like a mountain, then you'll start climbing yourself, and just before you die you reach the top and you notice the sky above your head. You want to soar into it, but it's too late and you die of anger. Such a state of mind at the moment of death does not augur a happy future. You may be reborn as a donkey or even a speck of dust on some terribly unpleasant mental plane." I start crying. Kalsang's eyes grow misty too; he identifies himself with a mirror.

It is like this: he reflects everything as it comes nice and clean, and likes every reflection. A Buddhist, as it says in the books, does not evaluate but loves everything. Kalsang makes tea. "You've been mother a million times," he says. "So now drink." I drink tea, grow silent. Behind my back Piechocki lights a cigarette. "What do you think about it?" I ask, waiting for him to embrace me, to say: Rubbish, you have only one mother and she should be loved. Piechocki pulls a face like a Russian icon, stubs out his cigarette. "I don't know," he says, and disappears behind the cross.

Piechocki, just like Kalsang, is a mirror. I asked him once, "Piechocki, do something with your facial expression, for if you die suddenly, I will remember you like that and shall try not to dwell on memories of you." And Piechocki says, "You grow distant; I can't look any different." I was at a loss for words. I asked, "Piechocki, darling, what's brewing in that noble skull of yours? You're the only root of my past, the nonexistent aspect of Kalsang, and without you I would've undoubtedly slipped into madness." "Return to Poland," whispers Piechocki. He fixes his black eyes on me and disappears with the cross.

That is, what disappears is the text on my screen, the text I've been writing about him all this time. Simply, the computer censored it and gobbled it up. A moment later Kalsang enters the room and asks, "How are you feeling? I've just had a vision that something bad is going on."

It is. Kalsang puts his hand on my shoulder. I close my eyes with all my might, but instead of Piechocki I see the pope. "Children, do not participate in sects foreign to our culture." The pope wags his finger, pretends he is smiling while the starving Buddha on the wall starts crying. "No, leave it," I tell Kalsang. "I feel rather feeble today, as if I were drained of all dreams." "It's wonderful," says the happy Kalsang, and embraces me more strongly still. "One has to look reality straight in the eye. You have to create projections like bridges: right onto the other shore. If you want, tomorrow we'll leave for Tibet."

I close first my eyelids, then my fists. "*Basta,* Kalsang," I announce. "*Basta!* My bridge has gone down the fucking river! I'm leaving!" Piechocki grows pale. "Where do you want to go?" he asks, his hands shaking. I make a face suitable for a departure and answer him: I'm going straight ahead. "I'm going to look for a projection that will lead me out of you and out of Kalsang. I shall find my own shore, and one I won't have to emigrate to. Buddha will die on the cross for the three of us, the only season will be laughter, and I, calm and peaceful, shall bathe in a million holy rivers while *bodhisattvas* together with the angels, all merry, cast their nets to fish for the obscenities in all the languages of the world."

"I don't understand women," says Piechocki with Kalsang's voice and completely confuses the plot. "Couldn't we have simply two faiths, two husbands, one moral system?" "Maybe you can, Treasure," I laugh. "Maybe you can, but I can't. I, like you, am the chosen people, except we're chosen by someone else, and that's our problem."

Kalsang knits his brow. "I think I understand," he sighs. "A demon has possessed you and you want to die." "I want to live," I say. I throw the rucksack on my back and begin to take my leave. I live leaving: Kalsang, Piechocki . . . I speak no tongues. . . .

Translated from the Polish by Wiesiek Powaga

THE THIRD SHORE

175

▼

■ □ ■ □ ■

THE MEN AND THE GENTLEMEN

Gabriele Eckart (Former East Germany)

THE NEWS THAT YOU WERE ONCE A STASI-INFORMANT COMES AS A shock, as though someone said you were HIV positive. You are out-raged, you gesticulate wildly, you cry, Impossible! And then you think, what exactly was going on, years ago, when . . .

You were cramming for final exams in your little room. You slammed your math book shut in frustration. Don't care if I only get a B. You took your favorite book of poetry off the shelf and began recit-ing out loud: Grant me a single summer, you lords of all, a single autumn, for the full-grown song, so that, with such sweet playing sated, then my heart may die more willing. . . . An escape you took every time the town and its daily routine threatened to stifle you. Just at that moment, there is a knock. The fat older man from the living room, the one who has been coming for meetings there every Wednesday with other men, ever since you were little, comes tiptoe-ing in. What crazy kind of stuff is that you're reading? He sounds as though his vocal cords are coated with flour. You explain; you pass him the book. He smiles. You know, sweetheart, this is one of the enemies of peace and socialism. He gives you a lecture, and then he says, Our state. This word makes me feel the way I do today when I hear black church music. He wants you to sign something? You nod, of course. But all you remember is the "pledge of secrecy." And your alias? The West German has to show it to you before you believe it actually existed—Hölderlin. And suddenly you understand why you haven't been able to read Hölderlin for years. I was surprised you didn't take your beloved collection of poems with you when you left the country.

Don't say you didn't know something was amiss. When you used to climb up the stairs with Mother and you wiped your feet on the floorcloth at Frau Meschwitz's apartment, she would say, "What an assortment of men again today," and Mother would blush as though she had secret lovers. But Mother never set foot in the living room on a Wednesday, not until all the men had gone. Instead, she spent hours unhappily clattering pots and pans in the kitchen. As soon as they left, one after the other, at ten-minute intervals (and Frau Meschwitz made sure they all wiped their feet on her floorcloth on the way down), Mother would open the windows wide as though they'd all been chain-smoking. Not one of them smoked. . . . How often did you press your ear to the keyhole? They're colleagues from work discussing an important project, Father said. He worked for the local council. You believed him. But why do they talk so quietly? No matter how hard you listen, the most you pick up is a name or two, locals, you recognize the occasional one. With time, they become a part of your life, just like school and the seasons. If a new face shows up, you show him where the key to the toilet is, and you say, Down one floor, it's the one in the back. They thank you. Everyone smiles, some are condescending, some are embarrassed. When you meet one of them on the street and you say hello, he appears not to know you, much to your surprise. But you get used to that too, with time.

At eighteen, says the West German, one knows what the term *state security* means. But you didn't know. You never watched Western TV. Not even the short form, "Stasi," meant anything to you. What about your classmates? They hardly talked to you. You were a loner. You wrote poetry. People didn't do that in a town like yours. Girls kept themselves busy with knitting or cooking. Or did they maybe avoid you because they knew what went on in your apartment? Frau Meschwitz's floorcloth was not the only one the men had to wipe their feet on. They virtually fought their way up the three floors, from floorcloth to floorcloth. You watched them often enough. And noticed the glances the other women sent after them. Then the women would stand in lineups at the baker's or the butcher's or wherever.

And whisper . . . It was a small town. What if someone had told you what the term *state security* meant and explained what was going on in your apartment. Would you still have agreed to work for them? Most likely, yes. At that time, yes. For you, the state represented what God means to other people. You wanted to be a party secretary. On election days you sang songs of proletarian struggle on the toilet, a floor below, with the door open. Until your throat was sore. While your father called on every apartment in the block to push people to go vote. If you hadn't moved away, you would probably have become a party secretary.

Two weeks later you're waiting at a flower shop. Not here, the fat man had said. He'd stroked your hair. Father never did that. And it won't be me; it'll be two of my colleagues. Don't worry; it won't hurt. You'll have some coffee and cookies and talk. Father nodded, sanctioning it. Exceptionally, he had a smile on his face. There was some kind of password that included the name Barbara, but you'd forgotten it. Already forgotten it. They believed you were you, though, even without the password. A girl, five foot six, with a red scarf, in front of the flower shop. The expression on your face: dreamy, if you believe what the files say. You have a report in the basket on your arm. Write up what it was like in Romania last year, the fat man had said. Why not? You immediately tore a page out of your math book and wrote it up. When the Moskvitch pulls up, they say something with the word Barbara in it, and you can't think what to answer; you pull out the report and hand it to them through the open window. Please get in, one of the men says, startled. He speaks your dialect, which is reassuring. This is your first report. In all there will be eight, written over the following months. On graph paper in blue ink. In one of them you list the names of 25 authors you met at a poetry seminar, and you give a three-line description of each one. Has a good/bad perspective on class issues. You include details. Forgot all about it, eh? the West German asks in a mocking tone. His knuckles rap the paper, cold black eyes drill their way into your memory. Forgot all about it? It is your handwriting. Yes, you say. This lord of creation waves the camera nearer. The machine latches onto the sections of text that are most painful for you. One person drinks a lot, and another has a copy of Solzhenitsyn on his bookshelf. Signed

"Hölderlin." Never in your life have you felt such shame. The most embarrassing thing is the language: a mix of baby German and party jargon. *The enemy of the working class* is your favorite term. You got fifty marks for those reports. Ten years later, during a search of your apartment, they take this sum back. You were surprised that they didn't take everything from the drawer of your writing desk, that they only took the one small sum. But you understood why. No excuse. You accepted money from the Stasi. You probably bought the four-volume Hölderlin collection with it. Cry, the West German commands. You would have done so without his ordering you to.

They took you into a new housing development. To an apartment where only men seemed to live. They sat you down at a round table in front of a window hung with a grubby curtain. They made coffee. They did not offer you the promised cookies. And they talked, about all the things you had already heard from the fat man. The enemies of peace and socialism. In contrast to the fat man, they addressed you formally. As far as I recall, you were flattered. You remember only one thing from the rest of the conversation, but you remember it exactly. Seven years later, or thirteen years ago today, it burst back into your memory. On the first day of a creative-writing seminar the participants introduce themselves. You hear one of the men's names. You feel frightened without knowing why. You react negatively to him. On the last evening, with everybody seated around a table in a café, you ask the seminar leader why you were barred from the course a year earlier. Without explanation. Three days before it was due to start. You'd even found a room in Leipzig. State security, he says. You hear the words. You know, meanwhile, what they mean. You have had the most painful experiences with them. In prison. Beside the course leader is the author you don't like. And suddenly you remember. Seven years ago, in that apartment at that table. You don't have anything to tell us? Well, then, we'll tell you something. We'll tell you how the enemy of the working class sneaks into the ethics of our young authors. They give the name of the man now sitting across from me as an example. Disloyalty, lies, alcohol. Please spread that around. Seven years ago, you say, I was ordered by the Stasi to spread rumors about you. I refused. But I must have believed the rumors because I reacted so negatively to you when we met. Instinctively, I didn't like you. I'm sorry. The course leader wrinkles his forehead. His eyes tell me, Shut up. Otherwise the gentlemen will be back in my office tomorrow morning. He means well. His wife likes what you write. It must have cost him something to keep you in the course this time. His warning glance slips across the young woman beside you, your friend. Today, you know why. You have seen her reports, signed "Galina Mark." What happened then, the man asks quietly. He doesn't look up from his glass. I broke off my contacts with the Stasi, you say proudly, setting your fist on the table. Twenty people in the room hold their breath. It is 1979. You are totally convinced that things are the way you say. In reality though, as you now read in your files, you were driven to the apartment a few more times before you managed to say no to them. Did you forget those trips? Waiting at the flower shop? No matter how deep you dig into your memory, you don't remember. The year 1972 was the darkest year of your life as far as your dealings with the state security are concerned. It seems to have been amputated from your brain. All you remember is saying no. But according to the files, you didn't even say no. You just didn't show up anymore. They waited for you in vain at the flower shop. In their German orderliness, they even wrote a report on the fact. It reads, The informant did not appear at the meeting place. On Wednesdays, when the men used to come, you went to Aunt Hilde's instead. You would much rather have served your state and done in the enemy of the working class, which is how they put it. You wanted nothing more. But did one "do in the enemy of the working class" by spreading nasty rumors about the married life of a young author who produced picture books that were even published by a state publishing house? Maybe he himself had refused to spread rumors about someone else. And so, logically, they were spreading rumors about him. What happened then? What about these reports on other meetings? A meeting in a car? Did you forget that too? your own voice asks. You were attending university in Berlin. The train journey was hellish, seven hours for two hundred miles, in cold, dirty, and usually belated trains. Yes, you said, after some hesitation, when the fat man from the living room phoned to offer you a ride; his colleagues had business in Berlin. It was so comfortable in their Moskvitch. You nibbled on apples, gazed out the window, chatted about everyday things, making sure not to go beyond the limits of daily banalities.

Today, you read that chatter, neatly typed up, on yellowing paper. It gives you the shivers.

Quite honestly, I don't understand you. You're an unknown quantity. It is unthinkable that I might be related to you. What schizophrenia! Not at eighteen, when you were writing those reports; you were centered then, sure of what you were doing. You wanted to do something for your state. But by the time you had been collaborating for two years, you knew what the term *state security* means. You are living in Berlin at the time. The Marxist-Leninist philosophy section in which you are enrolled is an ivory tower where you're concerned with the distant future. But you take streetcars; in the cafeteria you meet students whose parents are not state functionaries; Berlin is not a small town where everyone knows everyone else. Hardly anyone knows what kind of a home you are from. You seem trustworthy enough. People talk . . . and all of a sudden you know what the word Stasi actually means. It is something far worse than what you suspected a few years earlier when they tried to get you to spread rumors. You hear the word *Stasi.* It gives you a chill; your teeth chatter. But are the men who speak your dialect the Stasi? In 1974, a fellow student comes to see you, his face ashen. The Stasi are trying to get me to work for them, he confesses. Tell them no, you say. And you tell him that you threw them out two years ago because they'd asked you to spread rumors. That same evening you pack your suitcase and go to the secret apartment in Rummelsburg, where they are waiting to give you a ride home. Auerbach, 25 Karl-Marx-Strasse. Riding in the car, you lean back into the upholstery, nibbling on apples. You see one man's face in the rearview mirror. You think, He doesn't look like Stasi. You may be afraid of what people call the Stasi, but you feel very comfortable with these two. At least ever since you haven't had to write any more reports. Ever since they've stopped asking questions. Ever since they've left off with their rumors. You sneak a glance at the man sitting next to you. He couldn't hurt a fly, let alone arrest or interrogate someone. The word *Stasi* and these two men are two absolutely different phenomena. I would like to ask you something, you say. The black-haired man beside you turns his face toward you; the one in the rearview mirror widens his eyes with interest. You're not from the Stasi, are you? The one in the rearview mirror shakes his head. We're from the MFS, the Ministry for State

Security. The MFS? This is a new expression. Not quite though; the father of another student works for the MFS. You know him. He's a nice man. As nice as these two. The information is reassuring. It allows you to continue traveling with them. Can you imagine? you say. The Stasi is trying to get one of the students to work for them. I wonder how many people in my seminar are already working as informants. You repeat the word *informant* and shudder. The two men make no comment. A little later, and without your knowledge, they hand you over to the Berlin Stasi; you're a little too complicated for country folk. For a whole year you hear nothing. You're surprised they're not offering you rides home anymore; admit it, you're a little disappointed. I honestly think you would have continued taking your two rides per year with them, from Berlin to Auerbach, if they hadn't passed you on to the Berlin Stasi. I don't tell them a thing, you used to think. I don't give them any information they can use. But you did listen to them. And their talk settled in your mind. Whenever you met someone they had talked about disparagingly, you avoided that person. They influenced the contacts you made, and they planted their language into your mind, where it framed your thoughts for a long time. That language prevented you from writing anything that was not a reflection of the conditions around you.

So these are the people they call Stasi, you think, as the two men stand there in the doorway. Not the overweight elderly uncles that speak with a Saxon dialect and ask for the key when they have to go down a floor to use the toilet. The term *men,* used for the Wednesday callers, does not apply to these two in the doorway. The word *gentlemen* is more appropriate. You can't imagine them with grubby curtains in their conspiratorial apartment. At first glance, they seem to epitomize the late-twentieth-century secret-service professional. You have been expecting them for the past weeks, hoping they might have changed their minds. While you were in prison, you had agreed to work for them, because if you didn't . . . They had left it at threats. The sentence for attempting to flee the country was two years. They'd picked you up hiking in the Bohemian forest with a friend. And you didn't have return train tickets on you. It was three years since your dream of becoming a party secretary. That dream dissolved into nothing while you were in prison. At the very latest when you had to get undressed and a very ladylike lady in uniform looked into your rectum. You had no idea what she was looking for there. It was obviously part of the humiliation routine. Spread your legs and bend over. . . . A shock like that restructures your psyche in days. Shakes up the kaleidoscope. And the gentlemen standing there in the doorway with their smooth professional faces, these gentlemen are not your friends; you know that from your time in prison. You hate them. But you smile, and you let them in. Because you're afraid.

You were just having lunch, potatoes and cottage cheese. Don't you prefer roast rabbit? People who work with us can afford that. Thanks, you say, I like cottage cheese. They ask for tea. As you're putting the water on to boil, you see the can of rat poison on the shelf. You stare at it as though hypnotized until the kettle starts whistling. Then you obediently make the tea. One of them takes sugar, the other one doesn't. Good girl, their glances say. They watch every move you make. Your first book is about to be published. It's time we started working together, they say. The episode with the comrades from the south was just a prelude. I'm not suited to be a police informant, you say. I wouldn't be able to write anymore. Oh, please, don't use that word, would you, says the older gentleman, who wants you to call him Peter. We just want to have coffee with you and chat a bit. A leather face. A cynical expression around his mouth. You can see that he knows how to read faces. He can read your fear of him right now. He has the power to have you arrested again. There was evidence enough that you planned to flee the country. They listed so many good reasons during the interrogations you were surprised you hadn't come up with the idea yourself. The idea of fleeing will preoccupy you from this point on, though, until you finally manage an escape twelve years later. You're not willing to become a party member, says one of the gentlemen. Without party membership, your diploma will be utterly useless, you know. In this country, philosophy is a weapon in the struggle of the working class. Surely it would be better to continue your studies in the West. And besides, as they had discovered from reading the journal they confiscated after searching your room, you like to travel. . . . You like traveling, don't you, dear? says Peter. You're too afraid to ask him to address you properly.

THE MEN AND THE GENTLEMEN

He makes you his accomplice by using such informalities. You ask them to return your journal. All the other things in the rucksack were returned to you. What do you need it for, dear? He grins. You know what he's referring to and feel like slapping his face. In a short essay on the language that men use, you had cited the words of an acquaintance who compared a woman poet whose work you respect to a broomstick in bed. You had written out the names of all the people concerned. Peter visibly enjoys your embarrassment. We'll talk about it some other time, he says, thus ensuring that there will be another time. How is Frau . . . ? and he says her name. You answer what he already knows, I'm not answering any of your questions. He answers what you already know, In that case, let us tell you something. Listen. In contrast to the kindly uncles from the south, he doesn't gossip. He tells you about so-called ideological uncertainties in the woman poet's work, which stem from her secret relationships with enemies of the working class. And he gets you to say, Oh, yes, I think that's dangerous too. Which is partially honest. At this point you have only fallen halfway out of the heavens of socialist utopia, which you hold to be reality. At this point you are twenty-one years old, and you are caught in the middle, struggling the way everyone does who has lost their spiritual support. But you only talk to the poet about personal matters, like writing projects. That's when you take over the conversation. For two hours you tell them about your idea for a novel, making it up as you go along. You don't let them get a word in edgewise. Finally they glance at the clock. As they get up you repeat that you're not suited for what they want; you're not even a member of the party. All the better, says the older gentleman, shaking your hand with a smile. You look at him. Mephistopheles. The other one, the one with the baby face, is his servant. Don't say a word to anyone, the older gentleman places a finger across his lips. And at that moment you have an inkling of how you might get rid of them. Even if you don't have the courage to pour rat poison in their tea.

The worst thing is the letter. In the report that closes the "Hölderlin" file, the Stasi peevishly note that you did not supply any useful information. But you did give them that letter, and they passed it on, as they also noted, to those responsible. You still don't know why you committed this treachery. Out of fear, of course. But was it really fear? Wasn't it also a last remnant of your working-class conscience, lurking somewhere below the surface? The woman held some high position in the political power structure. She had an identity card that had opened some of the most secret doors to you. Driven by curiosity, you accompanied her through the rooms of the powerful. Men in armchairs, in front of TV sets, glasses in hand. They're watching porn films, she said; the pretext is that they have to decide whether to license them. What did you think? she giggled, then burst into laughter. Didn't you know? Before you left, she warned you. There are tight security instructions; all the mail for Berlin is being opened. So don't write to me. A week after the first visit from the Berlin branch of the Stasi, you get a letter from her. By mail. It informs you that the highest officials of the country are vultures. A few days later, another such letter. And another one. Six in all. They rip into the house like bombshells. You can't sleep anymore. Finally you package them, buy a train ticket, and hide them under your mother's bed. However, you hand one of the letters to the Stasi the next time they visit. They accept it. Was there only one? You swear you only got one letter from your friend. To your surprise they don't ask a single question about the woman. Today copies of all six letters are neatly assembled in your file. The accompanying text reads, She handed over one of these letters. Where did they get the others? Did they open the mail and photocopy them? Or did Father, alias Erich Schulze, hand them over? According to Mother, he came across the secret package while looking for the chamber pot. Why didn't they ask any questions? You had prepared an evasive but what you thought was a convincing explanation; you'd even learned it by heart so that you wouldn't say anything wrong. For the past eighteen years you have been salving your conscience with the idea that the whole thing was probably deliberately staged. Everyone you talk to says, Of course, that's what happened. Forget it. Still, no matter how forgetful you are—you even forgot your alias—you never forgot that letter. It gnawed at your dreams, a festering sore. You never really believed it was just staged. You knew your friend had weak nerves; you could tell from the way she laughed. You also knew that she was sleeping with a highly placed official whose wife held an even higher position and that the wife knew what was going on. A confrontation was imminent; your friend would probably be shoved a few steps down the ladder. The whole situation was choking her. A person caught in such a position is not careful. After you handed the letter over, you broke off the friendship. The woman called you. She invited you to dinner. She had exclusive tickets for a concert. Why didn't you go to her? Why didn't you say, I gave them the letter? Every time you think about it, you feel dizzy. You cover your face with your hands. You've been doing that for the past eighteen years. Why didn't you call her and say, I have to talk to you?

No need to get excited, says the West German. She was a party member. Meanwhile, the woman poet, the one who has called you a swine on his TV show, was a party member as well. You told the Stasi nothing about her. You didn't hand over any of her letters. He says you should not have kept a journal. You don't do that kind of thing in a dictatorship. He is obliged to consider your journal writing a form of collaboration with the Stasi. You shouldn't have let them inform on you either. After all, one can soon tell who is an informant. He is obliged to count the comments you made at the home of the informant, alias "Poet," as a form of collaboration with the Stasi. You nod your head humbly. On TV you ask the woman poet to forgive you. Secretly you think Anne Frank's diary must be a form of collaboration with the Gestapo then. Why don't you say it? The West German wields the same power over you now as the Stasi did then. He can't have you arrested, he can't starve you or lock you into a freezing prison cell without a blanket, but he can destroy your name. And what are you without your name? It means having to live without other people. It means contact only with rocks, trees, and sand. You're not cut out for the life of a hermit; you know that. You need too much love. And you're not intelligent enough. So, naturally, once you're in front of the West German cameras you behave the same way you did with the gentlemen from the state security. Obsequious, you handed them the letter. Obsequious, you answer every question the West German asks about your relationship with the woman poet; the Stasi asked me to do such, they offered me so much money, but I refused. While you're saying this, you read in his eyes which part of the sentence he will cut. But still you speak the sentence. He promised to be merciful if you complied. You know he was lying. But you're hypnotized with fear. You hand over the letter. In front of millions of TV viewers you accuse yourself of having informed on the woman poet for money. The media so much enjoys your self-accusations that they run the TV interview for days. You hear that the Stasi man whose name was Peter had to hold his belly, he laughed so hard at the sight. The West German has succeeded in doing what Peter couldn't do. Reduce you to nothing.

When you handed over the letter, it occurred somewhere beyond you. You hoped to get rid of your fear—that was the main thing. But then the torture set in. You liked the woman and she liked you. She hadn't done anything to you; in fact, in her rather awkward way, she'd tried to contribute to your political education. She'd probably wanted to warn you against taking up a career like hers. At a complete loss, you visit a fatherly friend for advice. He says, You lost your innocence today, but if you break off all dealings with those men, you may win it back again. This statement impresses you. You don't forget it. But how should you go about breaking off the contact; you've tried everything already, and they refuse to leave you alone. Are you supposed to grab them and throw them down the stairs? Together they probably weigh over 300 pounds. Tell everybody, he says. Let everyone know. Talk about it, especially when you're in the homes of famous people, in apartments that are bugged. You start making the rounds immediately. Every famous person you know. The Stasi keep calling on me; they want me to inform on you. The famous people are put off. Are you crazy? they say. Right there by the phone! You have to talk about it near the phone, you say in your defense. The Stasi have to hear. And it works. The gentlemen are furious the next time they call. You're slandering the state. That is absolutely prohibited. Suddenly they're addressing you formally. You interpret it as a good sign. When they leave, you discuss the visit with your fatherly advisor. He says, do a second round. Tell people you don't know, too. Your success is astounding. The usually controlled gentlemen from the Stasi are livid. Get out of here then! I don't want to talk to you again. You open the door. They leave your apartment without further comment. You watch them go . . . around the bend in the staircase. You catch a glimpse of Peter's face. Fear grips you; there's no mistake, he will take his revenge. For the next eleven years, until the moment you finally manage to leave the country, he turns your life into the theater of the absurd. One of his directives is the rumor that you are working for him.

Still you sing and dance for joy. And you tell everybody. You boast about it at readings. Whereupon you get no further invitations. At least not to readings in state venues. Later, the church offers possibilities. For the last years of the regime, the church acts as its artificial lung. Three months after this historic event you turn twenty-two. You're surprised by a birthday card from a married couple, both writers, who heard about your troubles with the Stasi in your second round of disclosures. All of your other acquaintances have been avoiding you since your "de-conspiracy," as the Stasi call it. This couple appears to be different. Would you like to come for dinner next week? Isolated as you are, you are grateful for the invitation. Roast rabbit (this should have been a warning) and an excellent red wine. You feel good; soon you're tipsy. Then you start chatting, and not just about your own affairs. Gossip. We all gossiped in those years; why not admit it before you start rolling out the criticisms. It made up for the life we were missing out on. Today, you read in your files that the man whose wife was such a good cook was a Stasi provocateur, alias "Poet." He'd been put onto you. They called it "skimming off the cream." They also regularly photographed the journal you kept hidden at a girlfriend's place. Over the next few years your political disillusionment, reflected in your public statements, took on such crass forms that they set up a control procedure against you. They declared you a psychiatric case and considered medical treatment.

It is during this period that Mother tells you the men don't come anymore. They don't use the living room anymore. On account of you. You expect to see Mother breathe more freely. But she seems more frightened than before. You don't understand why. Once, while you're out looking for mushrooms in the forest you have an argument with your father, and she suddenly shouts, be quiet, the trees are bugged here. She stands there pale and trembling, as though she were on her way to her own execution. The basket with the mushrooms drops from her hand. Then she points to the tops of the pine trees. Up there! Father laughs, Bugging devices in the trees—that would cost a bit too much just for this little enemy of the state. He points to you and then calculates what it would cost. . . . Brief images flick through your mind. Mostly images of fear. They hardly hurt anymore. The few that do hurt are those of former friends. There is hardly anyone who doesn't think you informed the Stasi about them. Since they all think you did, why were you stupid enough not to do so . . . and immediately you're horrified at the thought. Who am I? The informant "Hölderlin" or the enemy of the state "Ecke." The West German reduces you to the informant. He has the power to do so. Victors can rewrite the biographies of the vanquished. The fact that you fled the country doesn't count. Once an informant, always an informant. And society with its short-sighted logic now has an easy explanation for every detail of your life. Every sentence you wrote, you wrote on Stasi orders. Every breath you breathed, you breathed on Stasi orders. Every lover you had, you loved on Stasi orders. Every single step you took, including the last one, out of the country, you took on Stasi orders. Your friends say, That's nonsense; you know who you are. But who really knows who they are? Which one of the feuding siblings within you are you? Imagine that with what you know today you are once again sitting across from the two gentlemen who are sipping tea. It is 1975. They are saying as they did then, We can offer you an apartment with central heating in the Leipziger Strasse. A passport. The hard currency you need to travel. In return, we'd like you to keep us informed about the woman poet (the one who calls you a swine today). What will your answer be?

Translated from the German by Luise von Flotow

DANCE ON THE CANAL

Kerstin Hensel (Former East Germany)

NOW THAT A BIG, SMOOTH SHEET OF PACKING PAPER IS LYING AT MY feet, here by the left pier, I am happy, for the first time in years. It is no accident. Fate brought me this paper because I have been chosen to write. To do nothing else in this world, but to tell the story of my life; on this day I will begin.

Up on the bridge it is hot, the July day of the century. Air sweeps over the asphalt. If I squint hard, I can see silver and gray, car tires, women's legs, men's legs, children, dogs. Up on the bridge life sweats, the city boils. Here, where I am sitting, it is cool. The canal flows silently by. It is so hot that at times the water slows to a standstill, changes direction, or thickens to mush. Under my bridge, however, it is cool. I squat down, leaning back against the damp rock wall. My hair sticks to the back of my neck. I feel something cool run down under my shirt: bridge water. Above me, in the dark vault, dripstone and moss. The drops tremble at the tips of the stalactites a long, long time before they finally fall and explode on the stone banks or on my knee. Sometimes it takes days for a drop to finally fall from the ceiling vault. The bridge is always wet. Water seeps through the old stones, constantly. It's a good thing that I'm not sweating like the people up in the city, that I'm not scorched like the car tires, that I needn't be hounded and hurried until I'm parched. At work or on my way home.

I found a big blue sheet of packing paper and stole a dozen pencils from the place I call home. It's nice and shady here on this, the century's hottest July day, in 1994 in the city of Leibnitz, when I begin to write the story of my life. What was once an obligation I detested has now become a need. It's because this bridge, the one under which I am sitting, the last free bridge in Leibnitz, is *mine*. Because I claimed and conquered this bridge, because I now have a space of my own, I feel the urge to write. I make myself comfortable. My old jeans are protected by the two sheets of cardboard I am sitting on. That is all I have, and here is as good a place to begin as any.

I am writing under my real name Gabriela von Haßlau. They called me Goose and Ehlchen. Gabriela only when they hated me. The first thing I remember is a violin case. I received it on my fourth birthday. Brown leather on the outside, green velvet inside. I opened it and saw the instrument. I thought it was an animal, a dachshund under a magic spell.

When I gave a scream, Father yanked at my ponytail: "That's a violin."

Uncle Schorsch from Saxony was visiting us. He laughed: "Is she ever a silly goose, your daughter!"

Mother was embarrassed. Father spat it in my face, syllable by syllable: "*Vi-o-lin! Vi-o-lin!* Repeat after me!"

I was crying over the enchanted dachshund. Mother took it out of the case and laid it in my hands.

"Be careful!" said Father, and the bow stroked the dachshund's fur, which Father called "strings." "*Strings!* Repeat after me!" he said. The dachshund gave a whimper, and I cried more than ever.

Uncle Schorsch laughed and spilled cognac on his shirt. Mother disapproved and called on her brother to be quiet. "Let's just let Ernst be earnest." Uncle Schorsch snorted and chuckled into his handkerchief.

On the evening of my fourth birthday I stood holding the violin, the bow in my right hand. I scratched out a few cat sounds.

"F-sharp!" said Father. "And D-sharp!"

I curtseyed, just as they taught me. There was goose liver pâté, and music by Mozart from the record player. The villa was full of music and birthday smells. Uncle Schorsch was still laughing and spilling on his shirt whatever he found at the large table full of food and drink: cognac and Russian sparkling wine, pâté and salad. I learned to tell a dachshund from a violin. My father was a vascular surgeon.

On that particular birthday, he also talked about varices. That was his favorite word, *Varizen,* and I listened closely whenever he pronounced it. I liked that word, because I never was forced to repeat it. *Va-ri-zen!* There was never any of that. It was one of my father's words. *Mine* were words like *Violine, Pastete, Mozart.* Uncle Schorsch's words belonged to me as well: *Heiamachen, Ringelgehen, Muckschsein.* Father forbade Uncle Schorsch's words. They were apparently bad German, and in any case, if Uncle Schorsch didn't soon amount to anything more than deputy director of the Grimma consumer co-op, then . . .

Mother would interrupt: "You can't choose your family."

"Of course you can," said Father. And he added: "It's all about good form, good form. Christiane, repeat after me!"

Uncle Schorsch always left of his own accord, when his supply of laughter ran out. That was usually after Mr. Sandman's visit. We owned a television set and I owned Mr. Sandman. Ten minutes, and I had sand in my eyes. Uncle Schorsch would notice: "Your peepers are getting tiny, and your dachshund is right tired too. . . ."

"Violin!" said Father.

Uncle Schorsch said good-bye. In the time that was given me to sleep, Mother and Father fought in the family room. I pulled the covers over both ears and whispered, Violin, violin, violin. The next morning I was four years old and Father had already gone to work at the clinic. The sun shone through the big, old villa window. Mother rushed about, trying to mop up bits of sun dust. There were dirty tablecloths and some pâté left over from the birthday party. The violin case lay, brown and foreboding, on the console in the living room.

"You're going to take lessons, Ehlchen," Mother said.

I wasn't allowed to go to daycare, because Father was chief vascular surgeon and Mother, the proper *wife,* stayed home. I wasn't allowed to play out on the street either, because there was really nothing to play at on our street. And our villa had a yard, where I could draw hopscotch squares in the gravel with a small stick. *Himmel und Hölle,* Father called it. Uncle Schorsch called it *Huppekästel.* Bad German. I would hop all alone from hell into heaven, my left leg raised, my jumping leg too wobbly to get into heaven unpunished. It would land on the dreaded lines, outside of the squares, or collapse altogether. I would give up. Nobody would compete with me. Father made sure that I never fell into bad company. The only thing was, there was no company for me to fall into, good or bad. Under the back steps leading down to the laundry room, spiders had spun their webs. They lay in wait in the darkness at the back of the stairwell. I collected ants for them, beetles, and for a special treat, earthworms. I would place these little creatures on the front of the web—the spider would dart out of her hiding place, kill her victim with a single bite, and suck it dry. I fed the spiders every day, until Mother caught me and, with her mop, tore down all the webs and crushed every living thing.

I wore patent leather shoes, tights, a petticoat, a ribbed undershirt, and a green-and-red crocheted dress. Or a blue-and-white one. Mother braided my black hair into pigtails and tied them together with gold-colored elastic bands. Every night she ripped out the tangles with a brush and combed it until I whimpered from the pain.

"Think of the people who have varices," said Father. "They don't cry, either."

One day Mother cried. She sat on the red plush sofa with a bottle of cognac in front of her, Father's favorite drink. Mother drank two or three glasses and turned on a siren inside her. Mother was a stranger. I became frightened and wanted to phone Father at the clinic, but the siren stopped and Mother said calmly: "They've shot your uncle Schorsch. He's gone."

The word she used, *erschossen*, was neither mine nor Mother's nor Father's. It didn't belong to Uncle Schorsch either. It was simply there, spoken out of the void. It sounded like bad German. I shook my head and whispered into Mother's ear: "You mustn't tell anybody. It's our secret, right?"

Mother nodded and pulled me onto her lap: "You silly little goose," she said, "now you'll have to forget about your uncle Schorsch, and quickly."

I promised. That evening Father turned the television way up, and I heard it again, that word *erschossen*, and other words too: words about *power struggles* and *peaceful resolutions*. Mother's siren wailed. The bad German in our family died with Uncle Schorsch. Father decided to have a violin teacher come. Frau Popiol wore a curly red wig and a pinstripe suit, like a man. She came with her son Kurt, who was a retard. Mongoloid, Father said. Kurt would squat in the back corner of the music room. His head would bob around the whole time, and he would constantly bend his pale sausagelike fingers back at the knuckles. I would watch him closely. He might have been fourteen years old, and he fascinated me.

"Don't be afraid of Kurt; he is very nice," said Frau Popiol.

I wasn't afraid. Only his fingers bending back like rubber gave me the shivers. Frau Popiol made me stand in front of the piano and then took the violin out of the brown case: "What is this?"

I said nothing, because I knew that Frau Popiol knew that I knew. But she wouldn't budge.

"What is this?"

"A dachshund," I said.

Kurt clapped.

"You are learning to play the violin," Frau Popiol said and grabbed nervously at the red wig.

"Vi-o-lin."

"That's right."

I took the instrument obediently, played F-sharp, C-sharp, D-sharp . . .

"STOP!" the teacher cried out. I let the bow fall.

"You are a careless child."

"Yes."

"*You* want to learn the violin?"

"Yes."

"Not everyone gets this chance."

"Yes."

"How old are you?"

"Five."

"The right age."

"Yes."

"Do you know what a note is?"

"Yes."

"Yes."

"Yes."

She showed me how to hold the bow. Elbow turned out. Don't stiffen up. Fingers loose. Back straight. Elbow turned out. Head tilted to the left. Don't stiffen up. Fingers loose. Elbow turned out. Not like that. Yes, like that. Higher. Still higher.

The bow shook. I saw only Kurt, squatting in the corner, retarded and happy, slobbering, a monkey with a bobbing head. I wanted to know whether he would like playing the violin. The bow fell to the floor a second time. Frau Popiol gave a knock on the piano lid: "Where's your head, girl?"

"Vi-o-lin."

"Right, let's start with a rhythm test. Clap after me!" Frau Popiol clapped. I copied her and was clapping wrong by the second measure: "Hopeless, but your Father wishes it."

"I want to play with Kurt."

"I'll be back tomorrow. By then you'll know how to hold a bow."

Before leaving, Frau Popiol gave me a hug, kissed my pigtails, and her red curls mixed in with my dark braids. She kept kissing for a long time, until she reached my neck and the tickling made me tremble. Kurt bent his fingers back and Frau Popiol lifted him up out of the corner.

"We'll see you tomorrow, Ehlchen," she said. The word *Ehlchen* belonged to my mother.

The writing is going well. There's steam rising off the canal. Today the Leibnitz wool-dyeing plant let out some red. Yesterday it was blue, blue like packing paper. After three hours of writing, I take a break, get up off my cardboard armchair, stretch. I have to stay close to my bridge. Otherwise someone might come and steal it. I've already tried two other bridges, the Sonntagsbrücke and the Grüne Brücke. I was looking for shelter, a place to sleep, out of the wind. And every time—the cardboard was already laid out and I was wrapped up in my Caritas blanket—the Lords of the Manor arrived. Hey . . . you! That's our spot! Three men, old canal dancers, scruffy and scummy. That's what they said, that it was their spot. I didn't know. I took my blanket, my cardboard, and my plastic bag full of belongings. From the Sonntagsbrücke I walked to the Grüne Brücke. If there was one thing I knew since the first day I was homeless: it was forbidden in house and gate entrances. So on to the Grüne Brücke, out of the downtown area, where only a sliver of riverbank was to be had. But it was also taken—by a pack of hyenas, who chased me away: Go to a hotel! They stole my Caritas blanket and laughed with their rotted out, stumpy teeth. That one's from Social Services, piped a very young one, and the pack hissed and howled and yelped from one side of the canal to the other. Their turf was their turf. I learned quickly and found *my* bridge, between the wool dyeing plant and the old factory. It's called simply "Canal Bridge," Kanalbrücke, and it keeps the wind and rain away at night. The heat too, in this summer of the century.

I stretch out my limbs, stiff from sitting, and step out of the shade of the bridge. It's wonderful, to have written so much, and the world of my childhood warms over with the rust red offered up by the canal today. Summer shimmers over Leibnitz. I am free. Now that the inevitable ruin of my family is complete, I realize: for me, only one thing could come of it all, my independence. Sure, I'm all alone, and I'm dirty and wasted away enough not to be able to count on anybody any time soon—but what do I care about the disgust with which people approach me or the faces of pity they put on as they sweat under their burdens. As if they were better off. Nobody remembers my name or what I did or who I was or who I am. How wonderful. I certainly wouldn't have been called to write had the circumstances been different. I would just hang around and drink and stink. But I don't stink. I'm clean. I wash every day in the Schiller Park fountain, early in the morning, when the gate is still closed. Then, breakfast at the Caritas. Or I wash at the Caritas and eat breakfast in Schiller Park.

"I'm alright," I tell myself, "but I'm only alright because I'm writing." By noon I'll have covered the packing paper on both sides. I feel it flowing from within, a joy pulling, pushing through me.

I learned the violin. After two weeks of practice, I was holding the bow to Frau Popiol's satisfaction. To produce the first proper tone, I needed another two weeks. Only Kurt was enthusiastic. He would bend his fingers and grin, as his mother poured out her poisonous teacher's spleen. I wasn't musical. Father paid Frau Popiol well. In May of 1963 he was promoted to chief medical officer at the clinic.

On the day of his promotion Father was a human being. At breakfast he took me on his knee. He smelled of sports aftershave, a present from his varices patients from the West.

"*Hoppehoppe Reiter,*" sang Father, and the tips of his black moustache bounced. "Today is a big day, Ehlchen. Today I become chief medical officer."

Mother was cheerful too: "Now you'll have to be more earnest than ever, Ernst."

"I have a surprise for you, Ehlchen." Father lifted me up in the air and gave me a kiss. His breath smelled like the pharmacy. "Today you'll play your violin for the doctors at the clinic."

Father drank his cognac and left. I didn't want to. I was stubborn. Frau Popiol was called in for an emergency intervention. She hammered on: "F-sharp! C-sharp! D-sharp!" until she hammered it home. Mother ironed a white lace blouse.

"Don't shame us, child."

"The child *will* shame you, Frau von Haßlau."

"Why are we paying you, Frau Popiol?"

F-sharp! C-sharp! D-sharp! The dachshund howled, squeaked, whimpered.

"You're playing it wrong, Gabriela!"

"But we're paying you, Frau Popiol."

The time for the party had come. Chief Medical Officer Ernst von Haßlau met us at the clinic entrance. He stood before me big and white, smelling of other people's cognac.

"Wait in the septic area for now." The word *septisch* belonged to Father. I held the violin case under my arm and bit back the word *septic*. Mother smiled nervously, clung to her husband's arm. We walked through the echoing halls of the clinic, narrow, high corridors with sheets of ceiling paint falling away here and there. The old yellow walls stank of split-open, alcohol-scrubbed knees. The white varnish on the doors, with mysterious names, like Lab, Ultrasound, OR I, and OR II, was moldy and worn away. I heard whimpering from somewhere, from somewhere else the clanging of metal.

"Come on then, Ehlchen; they're waiting for us." I rushed and tripped along between my parents. The violin case dangled from one hand. I was afraid, as if I were going to get a big needle. The only thing I remember of the party is the blue hole. I stood, violin in hand, on a podium. In front of me, a room full of white people. I lifted the bow—and fell into the blue hole.

I came to on a stretcher, opened my eyes. Above me, Father's moustache, which trembled at the tips.

"Gabriela!"

A nurse came, fed me medicine.

"Do I have varices too?" I asked.

There was laughter in the clinic. Only Father didn't laugh.

"We'll find another teacher for you. You have utterly, utterly shamed me."

I lay on the stretcher in OR II. Over me now was the huge, round lamp. I hoped it would come crashing down and bury me. Utterly, utterly.

Bottles of cognac went round. The doctors said many words that didn't belong to me.

Because they couldn't find anyone else, Frau Popiol remained my violin teacher. Father sat in on several lessons and decided that Frau Popiol was strict enough, proper enough, ambitious enough, to teach me the violin. Only Kurt, whom Father found to be too much of a distraction, had to sit in the kitchen from now on. Mother stuffed him with cake.

I was so unmusical that Frau Popiol, after a year of vain efforts, gave up on me. During that last lesson, I played the song "Hänschen Klein" almost flawlessly; then I dropped the bow. That was it. Frau Popiol tore the flames from her head. Under the wig: white, shiny skin like polished chrome. The flames lay beside the violin bow. That was it. I shut my eyes and awaited punishment.

"Come here," said Frau Popiol.

"Vi-o-lin," I said.

Frau Popiol laid her hands over my closed eyes. I smelled rosin, sheet music. The hands stroked my nose and mouth, tenderly and stiffly and slowly and endlessly. Frau Popiol's fingers opened my lips. Dry and sticky from fear, they resisted. The fingers pried open my jaws, and through the tooth gaps of a six-year-old girl pushed violin-teacher fingers.

"Come!"

"Where?"

"Wherever you want."

I swallowed, bit down. Ungifted. That was it. Frau Popiol laughed. Now my eyes were open. They stared fascinated at the shiny white head.

"Come!"

A strange tongue against mine, a strong, mobile, strange tongue, that pushed through my teeth, felt its way around my little girl's mouth. Wherever you want . . . Frau Popiol's tongue went further, Frau Popiol's fingers went further, the blue-and-white crocheted dress.

I wanted to say something, sing something . . . unmusical . . . but you are well paid . . . Come! Frau Popiol lifted me up. She was a strong, incredibly beautiful woman. I floated in her arms, flew for fear, flew for happiness. That evening I told my parents how happy I was.

The violin was locked in its case. The case was stored up in the attic.

"Frau Popiol is sick," I heard my Father say.

Varices, I thought. Father will make her better.

"No, once and for all, no."

I never had to take another violin lesson. That September they put me in school.

The packing paper is covered with writing, front and back. Strange, how easily the words come to me. I have to protect this river inside me. I mustn't fall into the last hole, where there is no more freedom. Where I am now is nowhere near the end. I've earned myself a meal. What do I do, though, to defend my bridge. If those down-and-outs come, then I've had it. But why should they come today, of all days, when they already have the Sonntagsbrücke and the Grüne Brücke? My bundle of paper and my plastic bag full of belongings all tied up, I go eat. In the Caritas, former sportscenter "Cosmonaut Siegmund Jähn."

Translated from the German by Ryan Fraser

■ □ ■ □ ■

LADY WITH COWSHIT

Renata Šerelytė (Lithuania)

COW SILHOUETTES STOOD OUT BLACK AGAINST THE GREEN TWILIGHT in the sudden rain. The August meadow, missing its once-fragrant curls, lay cold and wet on the ground.

Along the side of the road, overgrown clumps of dog fennel leaned over ruts of brown water as if to dull mirrors. A few dark slashes faded into the coarse linen sky, as though someone had dragged an unwashed paintbrush across it.

Zita led her bicycle along the roadside, splashing loudly.

One corner of the sky—the separatist—shone deep and blue with white spots. Zita tilted her head back and grinned.

Careful! Cowshit!

Zita leaped over it, but had no time to steer her bicycle clear of it. One wheel followed the other through the soft lump. Zita cursed.

From the distant white village, peace flowed into the dark pastures. Somewhere a concertina creaked, yanked by amateur hands. When that sound stopped, a ghostly quiet fell, until somewhere a dog looking at tall potato plants lost patience and howled. Then someone opened a window and wheezed, "Shut up, beast!" The dying fields of barley echoed with chirping crickets.

Zita splashed along the muddy roadside, gripping the handlebars of her bicycle and listening to the screams of the night midges that spun circles overhead.

Far away, at the town line, an insolent motorcycle made a plurp-p-p and then roared onto the poorly lit road.

Zita clutched the handlebars and doubled her stride. She glanced down at her hands and grimaced: her thumb and index finger were bruised, her pinkie had a broken nail, and her palms were black.

Then, her foot slipped, and the watery mud from a puddle splattered across her faded pants.

The cat had been perched on a bench in the yard. Its amber eyes seemed lit from afar. The milk cans clattered; the cat leaped off her bench and languidly kittied-up to the well. Zita poured her some milk.

She led her bicycle to the woodshed; there, she lingered. She looked through the pile of wood chips and dried twigs; it reminded her of an empty anthill.

"These will outlive me. They will lie slumped, moldering, mixing with dirt, decomposing, but they will remain . . . while I . . ."

On the dark porch, Zita kicked off her galoshes. One of them slammed into the door, leaving a sloppy mark.

"Running off again?"

The door made an old-fashioned whine. Zita didn't respond. She painted her lips. Somewhat more garishly than she should.

"Don't come back drunk."

The screeching door closed, and a cough choked out from the darkness in the corridor.

Through the partially drawn curtains, Zita watched her granny walk across the yard, elbows stuck back, hands dangling awkwardly.

She suddenly became as thirsty as the bottom of the pond under duckweed. Zita yanked the curtain closed. The green twilight had painted the room in a peculiar light, and Zita thought she felt a stranger's presence in the room. No, he had already been there for a long time: obscenely panting, gazing at her with sullen distrust while sprawled on the bed. Zita pressed her lips together. Here! Take my flayed skin. It's my everyday outfit. Go ahead, use it to wrap your chapped feet like you would the corner of a blanket. It will certainly warm them.

Granny carried an earless pot through the yard. Smoke rose from the smokehouse; the gray stripe spread across the sky like ashes.

"Don't come back drunk."

Zita put a small shoe on her foot and stamped on the floor. Pbb-b-b! She blew noisily through her lips and turned to her mirror.

Her brother walked across the yard and turned toward the smoke-house. Cinders from the furnace sparkled through its dark windows. Then they vanished—the window was covered by a pale sheet. He was obviously going to bathe. Saturday.

That star-filled August night, after indulgences, two young guys dragged Zita home by her armpits. One was just a baby. . . .

"Those were bad spirits we drank," murmured Zita. "Bad . . ."

And she lowered her eyes, only to raise them again. Annoyed, she looked up at the dark sky. An aquarium. A Moorish aquarium.

Something had made a rumbling noise in the yard; the ground shuddered. It might be Kerzikiokas. Hopefully, he only needed to speak with her brother, to ask for advice or just to chat about work. Colleagues!

Zita wanted to laugh, but the darkness gagged her. He was just a baby with thirty-five years' experience at being an idiot who lived all alone out in the woods, far from humanity. . . .

And he's normally rather soothing—oh, sure, like a log pile covered with screaming crows beside a shrine. Or like a steaming cow pie in a pasture.

Zita cast an insignificant glance down onto her new shoes. Why did she put them on? They'd just end up in a ditch, where mud rots and dampness reeks. Where dark bushes stink of the bitterness of animals.

"Ugh, he did *not* know how to kiss." Zita shuddered.

But who could? No one, she sluggishly admitted and snuggled her forehead to the window glass. Maybe I shouldn't leave. . . .

Green darkness lay outside the window like water. Maybe everyone would drown—the little old woman, the rumbling dinosaur Kerzikiokas, and her father, who hadn't been home from town for who knew how many days now—maybe her brother would survive, bathing in the cookhouse, in the cozy splash of warm water, unaware of the green flood outside.

Should I stay . . . ? How could I think that?

But maybe?

Zita's gaudy lips did not move, but her eyes closed suddenly, as if someone had suddenly thrown sand at them.

The marred doors clinked; something plopped into the green twilight and landed with a light tap on the graveled bottom of the aquarium. In the smokehouse, her brother stopped to listen, stopped splashing. What—*who*—was that? He stopped to listen, then wiped a drip from his nose with his towel and bailed more hot water from the cauldron.

Darkness slunk up behind Zita and covered her tiny skirt with a piece of black velour to hide her naked legs; these took wide stallion strides forward, and the velour tore like a spiderweb and lay prone on the road. Darkness, like a poor old woman, began to fling herself from one side to the other, her elbows sticking out behind, her hands dangling awkwardly. Fog. The darkness stiffened. With steam from the bath, the darkness watched the fog rise from the fields.

Translated from the Lithuanian by Milda M. De Voe

■ □ ■ □ ■

PLEASURES OF THE SAINTS

Nora Ikstena (Latvia)

THERESA OPENED HER EYES IN A ROUND BED. WITH EACH NEW awakening, she was surprised to be lying there like a raindrop. And right next to her—Augustine, another raindrop in the round bed. Augustine was not awake. Since they never woke together, Theresa and Augustine had never met. They had only watched each other in sleep.

Theresa liked the moments of awakening. It seemed to her that a creaking lever was lifting a bramble-choked cover to release a stream of memory. She enjoyed the weightlessness in her head, where giant fragments of events roamed. She was awake; she could move, join, or even destroy these fragments. In sleep, Theresa was helpless—events took place, but she was forced to rush through and merely take note of them. She had awakened to tell Augustine everything. It was so good to see herself and Augustine in the round bed. And understanding that this mound of dry land was eternal, Theresa could forget her recent fear of getting blindly lost amid blossoming flowers and many-angled figures. Theresa could now touch Augustine and collect her thoughts. He slept so peacefully—this giant raindrop, Augustine. Theresa knew that he now wandered in the cosmos of flowers and many-sided figures, yet his face appeared luminous, and Theresa knew the reason for it—he could sense the small spot of dry land, his awakening, seeing Theresa. . . . Theresa kissed him—the long-awaited moment of contact—she felt how gently Augustine permeated her through her lips. At that moment she realized that everything she had experienced before waking had actually been

Augustine. And now she was kissing all of it, even as Augustine roamed and, perhaps, betrayed, sold, or murdered Theresa. But they were fated to it—two raindrops in this round bed. Theresa kissed Augustine, thus asking forgiveness for the night's events, which, though merely fragments, obediently filed into the order of recollection.

"Augustine!" was the first word that Theresa uttered. "I felt wonderful when, having wandered to the point of exhaustion, I discovered a bathhouse. Smooth shelves, a worn clay floor, wooden tubs filled with water moving almost imperceptibly below swirling vapors, a red-hot stove panting for the water's hiss. I stood in the doorway and watched its parched mouth. The thought of how desperately the stove longed for a splash of water irked me. Yet I was afraid to destroy this taut moment of suspense. I looked back. On the other side of the threshold, in the darkness surrounding the bathhouse, bright-green flowers glowed. I longed for rest, Augustine! I stepped into the mild vapors, dipped vessels into the water, and splashed the stove's hot stones, I dove into the steam and listened to the stove's satisfied gasps. . . .

"'Stop it. I'm out of breath,' I suddenly heard someone say. The steam gradually settled, and I noticed a naked Woman with short gray hair on the sauna's upper shelf. She was so beautiful, Augustine! Small drops of water glistened on her hot skin.

"'It's not so bad; the vapors tickle my armpits,' she said, banishing my confusion with a smile. I felt drained and miserable in my rags. 'You're like a cocoon,' she laughed and climbed down to help me undress. Her fingers brushed my timid skin. She poured water over me, and my sufferings and delusions, the rancid odor of life, oceans of sorrow, ashes of passions, fear of the truth, the satisfaction gleaned from lies, the insomnia of denial, the fevers of desire, fields of emptiness all flowed away over my eyelashes. . . . With the last drop falling to the floor, I gave a laugh.

"'In another moment you're going to be real,' the Woman said and gently cut off my long, wet hair. I didn't regret it, Augustine! I felt relieved watching the strands curl up and vanish on the hot stones. I forgot my timid body and kissed the Woman out of gratitude.

"'You are so gentle,' she whispered. 'I'd forgotten. You are from the gentle world, but life here is quite different.' I noticed that the moment of gentle peace was making her slow and sorrowful.

"'Do you know what it means to wait?' Her sorrow suddenly gone, the Woman nearly frightened me. She was addressing me harshly, hatefully, squinting her eyes, her eyelashes trembling. I wanted to tell her that I knew what longing for awakening was. But she did not want me to speak. She placed her hands on my shoulders and squeezed my shoulders together painfully. She kept me locked in her embrace and went on: 'Forever lying on the narrow shelf, listening to the stove gasp, relieving it from time to time with a splash of water, waiting for the white, humble vapors to climb up and tickle my armpits, making me laugh—an unnatural laughter that rattles my dry body. . . .' The woman breathed faster and faster, and it seemed that her eyelashes would flap their wings and fly away into dark space populated with green flowers and figures of countless angles. And then she let go her grip on me, smiled, and said calmly, 'I'm waiting for the Chestnut Baker. He comes rarely—when he's tired of standing by his huge stove. He lets me wash him, takes a nap, and makes love to me afterward. He almost never speaks, but as he's leaving, he always says the same phrase—"I'm going back to bake chestnuts." And I begin waiting for his next arrival, nurturing sinful thoughts; like destroying his stove, quenching the flaming ruins with tubs of water, laughing hideously in the scalding vapors.' The Woman was gazing into nowhere; everything had abruptly vanished for her, Augustine—the bathhouse, the stones, tubs, shelves, tickling vapors. She didn't see me anymore, either. Perhaps she was bathing the Chestnut Baker in an enormous lake? His stove was destroyed, but was he happy? He had no shop to return to. Was he to tire himself only by making love?

"'Can we watch him bake chestnuts and perhaps taste one?' I asked, wanting to protect the Woman from a mendacious nowhere. The Woman came back to her senses and gave me a look full of gratitude and sorrow. 'That requires courage,' she said pensively, but with an undercurrent of excitement. 'Courage, courage, courage,' she muttered, trying to encourage herself. Finally, she calmed down—I could stare at her incessantly, excitedly; the bathhouse and the vaporous solitude had taught her to solve dilemmas on her own. Up until I showed up in my tattered rags, the only phrase the Woman had heard was, 'I'm going back to bake chestnuts.' In the bathhouse, Augustine, reality was an illusion and vice versa—everything happened simultaneously; one could forget oneself and regain one's senses, but it was not possible to wake up because there was no distinction between reality and dream. The Woman emerged from her mendacious nowhere where a happy Chestnut Baker swam in an enormous lake, oblivious of the smoldering ruins of his stove. 'It demands courage,' she repeated blandly, 'but when will someone else like you visit me from the gentle world and propose such bold ventures?' The Woman took me by the hand, and we crossed the threshold to enter a corridor with a dim light at the end of it. 'It is from there that he comes. That glow must be coming from the coals of his stove,' she said, and we continued to walk. It was getting colder, and the light was becoming brighter—it certainly wasn't the light of any coals. Strange noises floated toward us. Suddenly, Augustine, we found ourselves in the midst of a mob of people, animals, things, lights, and noise. We were naked and confused, but nobody had time to notice us. We mingled with the heaving mass and smiled about what the glow of coals had turned out to be:

"... *The Merchant haggled over his wares, he knew how to buy and sell, he smiled his obsequious smile at anyone whose pockets had no holes, he was wealthy and amiable, he pinched the buttocks of chubby little girls and from time to time sang, 'Money rules the world, la-la-la-la, da-da-da-da, the Beggar a toothless limbless old man flicked his tongue like a sly snake crying every ten minutes out of habit, the Beggar who was a barefoot child earned his living by praying for mankind, his parents had recently been admitted to The True Fraternity—its members were busy maintaining Distance from the World with the help of a sacred drink, there was no time for anything else, the Minister had climbed on top of a gleaming car, yet he couldn't get up on his feet, he had very good shoes but their soles had no traction, but he had to stand up, stand up in order to announce with confidence and conviction—'I had a hard childhood,' at that moment the Godfather, who possessed wealth galore, purchased some sort of tomfoolery attached to a string in order to produce a popular play—free admission—with only two actors, one dialogue and an eternal catharsis—*

"*1st actor: Peter says the right thing!*

"*2nd actor: Peter has it right!*

"*A drunken Poet got tangled up in the words and wrote a poem about John Brown, the Poet who did not drink anymore was forsaken by his words, the Minister said he'd seen God, in the middle of the heaving mass he publicly promised his illegitimate children that they would inherit Transcendental Reality from him, having struck a thrilling pose the Prostitute lay in the middle of the square with her legs spread, she'd lost her job because she had not adjusted to a Bisexual Orientation, the Murderer cut his victim's ears off, thus depriving him of a last chance to hear the voices of the angels, the Vagabond was stirring up garbage cans and the rumors of the mob, mixing them together carefully, a cocktail like that was held in high esteem, being a Vagabond was his life . . . the Thief taught his trade to the Apprentice-Thief, after their first success they cut their fingers with a Korean knife, mixed their blood, and whispered a beautiful word they'd heard somewhere before—silentium—to each other, the Doctor was sitting in a glass cage but patients were describing their complaints with fine brushes and bright colors—they were hopelessly incurable, yet it was a beautiful sight, the Artist could not be distinguished since everybody was drawing. . . .*

"Such was this mob, Augustine, but its raucous qualities were in reality a thousand times more colorful. If they were given the liberty, they would swallow the whole universe, sucking in the green flowers, the figures with countless angles, and the tunnel we had walked through; watching the Chestnut Baker's deceptive firelight, they'd break into the Woman's bathhouse, upsetting the wooden tubs and replacing gentle vapors with a coarse trail of dust. We were still unnoticed by the mob and abashed at our nudity. Suddenly, the Woman rose up on her toes, her gray eyelashes trembled; despite the light, she opened her eyes wide. Augustine, can you imagine light-green eyes beneath gray lashes? I forgot that I was standing naked in a mob, I forgot everything. I tried to cement the Woman's eyes in my mind. But the Woman started walking, she was seeing smoke, she felt the fragrance of baking chestnuts. She had tried to wash this scent away so often, but it had resisted the wondrous qualities of her bathhouse waters. The Chestnut Baker was standing to one side, his eyes smarting, and snakes of sweat wound about his brow. He did not see the Woman. He was poking the coals under an old tin pan, attempting to keep the flame burning. The slightest movement would have caused the pan to disintegrate. The Woman squatted down next to him and blew on the coals. They glowed brighter, emitting a fan of flames, and the Woman ate hot chestnuts, singeing her fingertips. She watched the Chestnut Baker closely: his palms bore the red imprint of the poker; he was trying to protect his few remaining eyelashes from the hot smoke, but they fell into his eyes like the leaves of wilted plants. Having eaten, the Woman took me by the hand and we went back into the corridor. It was getting warmer and more comfortable. Back at the bathhouse, we sat down on the threshold. 'How miserable are those dark green flowers unfolding in the dark space around my bathhouse,' the Woman exclaimed. 'They cannot be picked, so I cannot make tea for the Chestnut Baker when he comes.' It was time for me to go, Augustine. I picked up my clothes, which were now clean and fragrant, and left. The Woman remained seated on the threshold, hating the green flowers that could not be picked."

Theresa stopped speaking. It seemed to her she had recalled a great deal. The fragments of events were obedient and let themselves be woven into words. Theresa smiled, imagining the events to be like hobbled horses neighing at pasture in the night. She had once been in a fragrant night meadow during her wanderings. She had lain down by a sputtering fire. A gentle incense with an unusual fragrance made her indolent and pliant; horses neighed softly, subdued by their ropes and the mist of incense. Theresa wanted to succumb to the temptation of the sputtering fire, not return as a raindrop to Augustine in the round bed. Yet, if ever there was an Eternal Return, it was Theresa's to Augustine. Momentous, perhaps beautiful, maybe even unforgettable wishes were dispersed in it like dandelion seeds. Therefore, Theresa was in the round bed next to Augustine, finishing her story. Augustine would wake up soon, but Theresa had to continue her wanderings. She kissed Augustine—it was the much-expected and everlasting touch—and she felt Augustine permeate her through her parted lips.

Augustine opened his eyes. He enjoyed that moment of awakening. Theresa breathed quietly next to him. Her eyelashes did not tremble; she was far away. So white was she, this huge raindrop, Theresa. Hesitating, Augustine touched Theresa's neck with his clumsy fingers. He drew labyrinths on the white skin; nobody could disturb him. He was awake; the events taking place in the darkness within him continued to unfold without his presence. Sometime and somewhere

Theresa would be joining them—was she murdering Augustine or saving him? Augustine knew he had little time to recount to Theresa the many events he had experienced. Yet he hesitated—his gaze lingering in her hair, the corners of her eyes, the sloping shells of her ears, the arcs of her eyebrows, the lines of her lips, the webs of her eyelids. . . .

"Theresa," Augustine started quietly. "My wanderings were a war. Something had happened to the chilly peace of the cosmos. It was full of fires, people fleeing, the noise of victory and defeat. The roaring songs of a feast could be heard—this is what it had to be like. Somewhere, living and dead bodies were being bulldozed—it had to be that way, too. I walked through the chaos in silence—how could I possibly speak to people who found happiness in destruction? They were cleaning the dark space enthusiastically; they felt alien, unhappy, unfulfilled. . . . Can you imagine, Theresa, their happiness was death, and it did not matter who died—divine temples or little children, old manuscripts or dusky, passionate women, painted sunflowers or fresh red irises, the countless strata of things, or old men who knew something about meaning and harmony. In this chaos of destruction, I met only one man with a zest for life. His marching in the streets was a motley, joyful vision.

"Flames, burning trees, blood—and suddenly, the shy sounds of bagpipes rise out of the smoke. The man's companions are playing their pipes off-key and are laughing at themselves, there are no women, they are drinking wine with abandon. The old man looks foolish. Two chestnut blossoms like horns in his hair, he was eating big, juicy, dark-blue plums. He appeared lighthearted in this world of devastation. Noticing my clean, white clothes, he waved to me and exclaimed joyfully, '*Urbi et orbi.* Barabas greets you, fellow traveler!'

"This is how I met Barabas, the cause of all the unfortunate mess. Barabas was kind; he invited me to join him on his journey to a place of peace. He assured me there would be enough wine to get us through the piles of bodies, stones, and smoking trees. I knew nothing about this man with chestnut blossoms in his hair. But he had bagpipes, he smiled, and I felt something more akin to joy than to the horror surrounding me. So this is how our journey commenced, Theresa. He gave a sly smile when he learned my name. You know, he treated me benevolently, as if I were a harmless lunatic, when I told him about our round bed, our separate awakenings, our dream stories.

"'Augustine, you come from a completely different world, so I can talk to you. It will make the trip shorter, although you are used to wandering alone. Drink the wine—you will never savor anything like it in your round bed!' Barabas stopped laughing for a moment and poured the wine with such gusto that it splattered redly on my white garments.

"'Khaaa-rrr-e!' Barabas gave a roar, his companions retreated with their bagpipes, and we started our carefree journey through the war zone to the place of peace he'd promised. He talked, and I have to admit that listening to him I completely forgot myself. Only the acrid smoke reminded me of what was going on around us.

Barabas's Story

"'I was born in a disgusting place. I was a strange infant because immediately I took note of everything—the dirty bed, gray rags, my mother's calloused feet, the crooked fingers of the old woman holding me, wet and feeble, and slapping my back to elicit a cry of recovery from the hypnosis of birth. When I started wailing, the old crone's face broke into a smile—of course, she had only a few teeth. My mother died; I remember that. She did not open her eyes; she just took a deep breath and smiled. My mother was beautiful though she slept amid rags and filth. I remember the old woman crying. So sad and disgusting was my birth. I became used to the old woman, so it took me a long time to find out what beauty was. When I was a child, I thought notched pots, thin soups, and half-baked simmering on the side of the stove were the epitome of love and perfection. The old woman never left me alone. She tied me to her and often went into the forest. We ate wild strawberries and the fresh sprouts of fir trees, chased snakes that dozed on the hummocks, let marsh tea put us to sleep, hid behind trees to watch elks eat beautiful death cups and survive; we sought frozen birds in the snow-covered forest, brought home ice-coated twigs that melted their beauty away in the warmth of our house, we gathered lichen that looked like the old woman's eyebrows, we fled from rabid foxes, cut saffron milk caps with the orange blood, scattered the dew from the grass, mourned flies devoured by a strange flower. . . . When I grew older, the old woman turned me out of the house, saying that the moment of my ingratitude was nearly at hand. I didn't know at the time what ingratitude was. I loved her very much and kept turning around and coming back, weeping with grief. But the old woman bolted her door and threatened to kill me if I did not leave. I knew what death was. Although my mother had smiled on that occasion, she had also disappeared. I did not want to disappear, so I retreated from the old woman's door. . . .'

"'Barabas had become pensive, somewhat sad, and it did not suit him on this merry journey. Then, it seemed his memories did a wild somersault. Once again, wine flowed generously.

"'Khaaa-rrr-e,' Barabas gave another roar. 'I almost grew sad, Augustine, over my own story! What can be more perverse in this kingdom of nightmares than sadness?' He halted and called one of his men imperiously. The man kneeled down, and Barabas climbed up on his shoulders. He rose above the others, stared around, and exclaimed, 'Vita brevis!' Standing in military bearing, his companions shrieked, 'Est!' For a while, the shouting continued—'Vita brevis!'—'Est!' Barabas was in high spirits; we continued the journey, and he continued his story.

"'When I left the old woman, I encountered expanses that made me laugh at notched pots, mushrooms, elks, foxes, and lichen. The expanses were inhabited by people, things, and ideas that tormented but could not destroy one another. Gradually, I realized that they did not want to be separated—like you, Augustine and Theresa. An eternal vigil hung over people; they returned from their short dreams with no memories. Being awake, they believed anyone who promised happiness. So I put chestnut blossoms in my hair, gathered my companions—who, though they played their bagpipes off-key, were faithful and cheery—and began to promise happiness. This is how my perpetual gaiety started. I ate, drank, devoted myself to the fine arts—my men cheered when I painted wings onto an ermine held by a plump lady, or an ear on a man who had cut his own off and gazed in confusion and fear at me from the canvas; I added black dots to a well-known music score, or I promoted symmetry by hewing off the other arm of a white sculpture. There wasn't a single woman who did not believe in my eternal love, which lasted as long as the meadow dew. You know, Augustine, if somebody happened along who asserted that happiness was not possible, people invariably chose me. They did not want to hear about suffering; they adored me fanatically, attaching themselves to me like the thistles in the old woman's hair. I can confess, Augustine, that blind faith is most difficult to stomach. I arranged another Feast of Waiting for Happiness and declared, "Happiness is death." And you can see how diligently they're preparing for it. I'm waiting for the silence to set in and then I will plant forests—the elks will come and eat the beautiful death cups and survive; the flower will attract flies, and they will die; I will gather lichen that looks like the eyebrows of the old woman.'

"Barabas finished his story; he was sad again, he did not drink any more wine, he did not call upon his men.

"'Where is that place of peace? Is it far?' I asked sad Barabas cautiously.

"'You want to reach the place of peace, Augustinius?' Barabas gazed at me with compassion. 'Escape by waking up; you can do it. My journey will be long: the silence will not come soon, and forests grow slowly.'

"'Khaaa-rrr-e!' I heard Barabas roar—wildly."

Augustine fell silent, he was tired of talking. He kissed Theresa—the long-awaited, perpetual touch. He felt Theresa permeate him through his lips. Lying next to each other, the two raindrops, Theresa and Augustine, breathed almost imperceptibly.

Translated from the Latvian by Jānis Ikstens and Rita Laima Krieviņa

■ □ ■ □ ■

THE MILL GHOST

Maimu Berg (Estonia)

AFTER THE CRITICS HAD LEVELED MY FIRST BOOK, I LEFT MY JOB AND went to the country. Despite the harsh criticism, I planned to devote myself entirely to writing. For living quarters, I obtained a room in quite good condition on the top story of an old water mill. The other rooms in the mill were empty, their windows and doors nailed shut with boards. The first months were spent putting the room in order—I had never had a place entirely of my own and I enjoyed arranging my room. But the disadvantages of living in a water mill became apparent quite soon: the room was damp, the murmur of the mill dam was more irritating than soothing. Because no one lived on the bottom story, my floor was terribly cold; it took me a great deal of money and effort to heat it. Before long, rats appeared in the empty rooms of the mill. Creating a great commotion at night, they ran, squeaked, and, crunching, chewed the wall as they tried to force their way into my room.

Influenced by the harsh criticism, I had obviously taken an exceedingly desperate step, given up amenities, a peaceful job, and a steady income. I had grown shy of people; it seemed to me that everyone knew me as a failed writer. In writing new stories, I tried to take into account the critics' suggestions in order to produce a work that would be sure to win praise, but that didn't seem to be succeeding. There had to be a great deal of blind anger, bitterness, and derision in the depths of my consciousness, the part called the subconscious. I wanted to write about goodness and love, but all the relationships among my characters were transformed into illness. I was incapable

214
▼

of depicting a single positive emotion, of endowing my heroes with nobility and spiritual grandeur. Only pettiness, jealousy, maliciousness, a desire for revenge and betrayal motivated my characters' actions. All those same evils of which the heroes of my first book had been accused by the critics. To the world, I myself must have appeared just as sullen, gloomy, and evil as my characters—why else didn't I have any friends? The critics had alluded to the similarity between my gloomy, self-assured person and that which I created. Arrogance and vanity were the evils for which the critics castigated me, as these had previously merited castigation in the Bible. My gait, bearing, gloomy derisive laugh, manner of dress—all this was contrary to altruism, humanism, and pacifism. A gloomy water mill was deemed the perfect place for the likes of me. It's unlikely that anyone would have believed me had I written about how my heart began to beat wildly upon seeing the bird cherries near the mill in bloom, or how I became intoxicated with their scent, with the nightingales' call, or how my eyes grew moist when, from my window, I saw the caution and love with which a young mother took her little ones across the mill bridge every day, or how a family of ducks splashed and paddled in the water. Surreptitiously, I slipped the birds food.

But they all nodded understandingly and knowingly when I sent a newspaper my new short story in which I described how I poisoned rats in the mill, and how I myself observed their agony. For this purpose, I had had a display window constructed between my own room and the empty mill room. (Let it be stated that I didn't poison a single rat, although I did indeed ask to borrow a stalwart female cat from the village, and this ended the rats' reign of terror within a few months.)

Although I didn't have many guests, nevertheless my novella did entice some of the more curious from among my former circle of acquaintances to the mill (as has been stated, I had never had friends), who, not distinguishing artistic truth from life's truth, wanted to see the display window between my room and the mill room. And why not the rats' agony as well, although they did not mention that. I said that the window was behind the curtain and that the view visible from there was too hideous for those good people. The curtain did in fact exist; it hid the moisture stains on the wallpaper. I didn't allow the guests to touch the curtain, and I noticed how one poetess, who cultivated beautiful poems about love and nature, tried to peek behind it. I shouted at her, she was startled to tears—soon afterward she wrote a poem about a morbid bat, a bloody nocturnal vampire, a clandestine killer. The poem, a new plane in the poetess's artistic creation, was otherwise very lively and figurative, the bat's Dracula-deeds were portrayed with bloodcurdling efficacy. The poetess was indeed talented. Only later did I hear that, after the poem was published, the people who came to visit me had nicknamed me the Mill Vampire, which was later replaced by the entirely more tame Mill Ghost, and even that soon went out of use—society was beginning to forget about me.

With the arrival of autumn, I noticed with shock that the money I had received from the book (its amount had been at least tripled in the fabrications recounted by my acquaintances) was almost gone, the excerpts and short stories published from time to time were insufficient to keep body and soul together; given the superficiality of today's reader, cultivation of long prose has always seemed senseless to me and has the unequivocal aroma of facile servitude. I was reminded of what one of my writer friends had said—never in his life, before or after, had he earned as much as he had for one variety show, which was performed throughout the country almost every week and which earned him five to six hundred a month. I could have tried it, in fact, although I had never cultivated that genre. It's true that some of my novellas had been referred to disparagingly as feuilletonistic. Perhaps I should now capitalize on this feuilletonism? But the path from writing to variety show performance would be long and arduous, all the more so because I hadn't even begun a humorous sketch yet. When I had money, I went to the kolkhoz cafeteria and ate a warm lunch to avert ulcers; and when there was no money, I bought some white bread and drank tea, sugar water, or lemonade along with it. Lately, subsisting only on white bread had grown tedious, and it began to affect my health. In addition, I feared I would be thought of as a parasite because I wasn't a member of any organization that would have entitled me not to work. The kolkhoz manager might also begin to regret his kindheartedness one day and realize that the mill apartment would do well for some young specialist oriented toward that enterprise.

Of course, I could have gone to work at the manor—a school held classes there now—but after all, I had come here to write. That is why I constantly forced myself over to the desk, rising from there only to get white bread and sugar water or, if not even these were to be found in the house, then to catch some sleep in order to quench my hunger. But the work did not progress. Or, to be more accurate, it did in fact progress, but in a manner diametrically opposed to what I expected. It didn't have the least bit to do with a variety show— feuilletonism had long since vanished from my novellas. They grew more and more morose and brutal; the characters were not only degenerate in spirit but in appearance as well. In them, sly hunchbacks plotted, a ruthless cripple functioned as a thrill-killer, a man with his right cheek disfigured by a large, purple birthmark stood beneath the windows of the women's sauna for days. In the stairways of the old town center and beneath its archways lurked rapists with seared faces; in the graveyard, a drug addict who suffered from elephantiasis terrified people; a cruel epileptic thrust needles under his wife's nails at night; and a blind hunchback sawed through wooden stairs in order to hear people fall and shatter. I tried to banish the demonic beings back into my subconscious. I began to write a story about a beautiful young woman, Linda, who had a nationalistic bent of mind, but already by the second page everything had returned to its old tracks—Linda turned out to be a lesbian prostitute who suffered from an incurable, evil illness and also passed it on to a lecherous leader of the people. The nightmares in my stories grew crazier and crazier. Despite this, from time to time I tried to sell a story. It's true there wasn't much demand for them, but, for some reason, the literary editor of one magazine for young people was taken with them, and every six months a small cluster of stories was published there. Later I heard that the magazine had been reprimanded for tenaciously publishing my stories, but, in the literary editor's opinion, the editor-in-chief apparently had prestige and the little tales were printed almost regularly. My concern over money was alleviated.

On the radio one evening I was listening to Schubert's music, which always affects me very deeply, occasionally even makes me cry. Listening to Schubert, I walk together with him in joyful places where nature is even more romantic than in the environs of the water mill. I am seized by anxiety, loneliness. I see pure, softly flowing rivulets, I hear roaring waterfalls, craning my neck I look toward snowy mountaintops, I lie on a scented, summer-warm meadow where thousands of bugs drone. I return to Schubert's lovely, romantic time when everything was beautiful, even death, grief, love's pain.

But that night a sharp knock pierced my Schubert-reverie. Because I had not had any visitors recently, that knock startled me considerably. I turned off the radio, dried my tears, straightened my clothing, and opened the door. At the door stood a man of some sort—medium height, with thick, dark, slightly curly hair. Small, curious eyes peered from between his high cheekbones. The man's face seemed familiar, but I couldn't remember where I had seen him. A khaki backpack was hanging from his hand by a single strap. "Juhan," said the man, and he stepped inside.

In the room he put down the backpack, then, taking long strides, he went over to the radio and turned it on. "Softly my songs beseech . . ." proclaimed a pleasant alto. "Schubert," said Juhan. He sat down in the rocking chair where I had just been sitting, listening to Schubert, and he grew motionless as he listened. It wasn't appropriate for me to disturb him. We listened until the Schubert was over, although I was no longer able to immerse myself in the music. When the announcer said in a toadish voice, "You have heard the music of Franz Schubert in a well-known interpretation," Juhan turned off the radio and pushed the rocker into motion. He rocked quietly for some time and I had nothing to say either.

Then Juhan's glance slid to the papers scattered on my desk. "You just keep on writing," said Juhan.

"Yes," I said, "I just keep on writing."

Juhan did not respond. The silence was embarrassing. After all, I could have asked why Juhan had come or whether, for instance, he wanted some tea. I had all kinds of herbal teas gathered and dried—wild thyme tea, chamomile, bearberry, linden blossom, peppermint, thyme, yarrow, caraway, cowslip, rose hips, birch bud, raspberry stem, black currant leaves, nettles, marigold, tansy. But I thought that it would be more clever to keep silent and to wait and see what Juhan had to say.

"And what do you yourself think of your stories?" asked Juhan at last.

"That's for me to know," I responded evasively.

"Are these the kind you want to write, in fact?" inquired Juhan. His little eyes watched me mockingly and slyly.

Suddenly I recognized him, but hadn't he already died long ago? Juhan's question hit the mark and forced me to answer honestly: "No, they aren't, but they come out this way."

"Right, right," nodded Juhan, "they simply come out this way."

Then we were silent again for some time. "Well, why don't you write? Time is fleeting," Juhan finally said.

"But it's not proper to write when there are guests," I thought.

"Have you invited me, in fact?" asked Juhan. He knew very well I hadn't invited him. I couldn't have invited him for after all I didn't know him.

"I didn't invite you," I said, therefore quite angry.

"If you didn't invite me, then you needn't take me into account, either. Sit at the desk, take a ballpoint pen and paper, and start writing."

I thought it over and found that Juhan was right. If he was forcing his visit upon me but demanding no attention or hospitality, it was probably best to act as though there was no one here, in fact, and to go on with my life as usual. All the more so because Juhan really had no business here at my place.

I sat down at the desk, put some paper before me, grabbed a ballpoint pen, turned my gaze to the window, and began to jab my nose. I became engrossed in waiting for an inspiration and forgot Juhan completely. In order to begin writing, I needed a cue. Lately I had constantly been getting cue words like "dead-end street, heretic, wart, main sewer line, submarine, Jew's harp, dysentery, swamp, intestinal parasite." From these I then went on to develop one story or another. Now, however, there rose before my eyes lilacs in purple bloom from the yard of my childhood home. There, too, was the scent of the large jasmine bush beneath our kitchen window, and little birds hopped among its branches. I remembered father and mother, sisters, playmates, and sunshine from my childhood glistened around me, warmer and brighter than all that came later. But I did not allow myself to be deceived. How many times had images of lovely places, beautiful memories, good people, noble scents risen before my eyes and entered my imagination, yet when I began to write them down, a heretic who had escaped from a submarine stumbled along a dead-end street, a wart on his neck, and, stinking of his intestinal parasites and dysentery like a main sewer line, he disappeared into a swamp droning his Jew's harp. That's why I didn't hasten to write about the lilac- and jasmine-scented sunshine, but continued jabbing my nose instead and waited for new cue words. "Jaan," I heard, and before my eyes rose my first love, a fair-haired, quiet, intelligent boy from our class. "Childhood, jasmine bushes, sunlight, Jaan," I repeated, but in fact no sensible story formed from these words. "The Alps, trout cavorting in a stream, verdant, fruit-laden orange trees growing beside a white highway, a lark's song, wild violets, Hortus Musicus . . ."

Everything beautiful and good swirled around in my head, and I felt nauseous. I crumpled up the empty paper before me on the desk—not even a line was written on it—and I threw it into the trash basket like a manuscript that had gone wrong.

"It's not coming?" Juhan asked from the rocking chair. I had utterly forgotten his presence. "Why strain yourself," Juhan said matter-of-factly. He got up, took his knapsack, and left, slamming the door shut. The rocking chair rocked, empty. I listened, my ear to the door, and although the mill's old wooden staircase usually creaked with every footstep, I heard nothing. No doubt Juhan was standing behind the door. I thrust open the door in order to catch him unexpectedly, but there was no one on the stairs or behind the door. I ran to the window; Juhan wasn't visible in the yard either. Fresh snow had fallen, there should certainly have been tracks in the snow, but I saw not a single track: Was Juhan in the mill yet, or had he left another way somehow? I ran to the yard, I called, no one answered, I circled around the mill—everywhere, the snow was pure and untouched, no tracks of any sort. I began to feel ghastly. I hastened back inside, locked the door, put on some tea water. I scattered some of my herbs into the pot and drank the strong, intolerably bitter mixture that boiling them yielded. That calmed me a bit. Then I sat down at the desk again to work. Since there is never a surplus of clean paper, I searched in the trash basket for the white sheet I had thrown there in despair at my recent creative slump and I smoothed it out. I remembered precisely that I hadn't written even a line down on the paper, but now I saw that the paper was filled from one end to the other with my handwriting. It was a beautiful, ardent, and slightly sentimental story about childhood sunlight, lilacs, and first love. Just the kind I had tried to write half a year ago. I revised the little tale and sent it to the editorial office of the young people's magazine with which I was acquainted. The editorial board sent back the story (although the board does not return manuscripts), and there was also a brief note: "Incompatible with our readers' concept of your style. Keep on as the Mill Ghost. Respectfully . . ." This was, of course, followed by the literary editor's signature.

I understood that my exile was over. That same day I asked the kolkhoz chairman for a truck, the driver and I piled my things on it, and I rode back to the city to my family. My short stories are having success, they will soon be published as a collection, and I've acquired friends.

Translated from the Estonian by Ritva Poom

■ □ ■ □ ■

FROM ALCHEMY

Kärt Hellermaa (Estonia)

THAT MORNING SARAH AWOKE TO THE RINGING OF THE DOORBELL.
It echoed loudly across her flat, louder than she had known a doorbell could ring. The noise cut through her head, befuddled by sleep as if there were no obstacle to the sound's penetration. Who wanted to disturb her so early in the day? Irritable and sleepy, and wearing her worn old nightdress, Sarah sneaked into the hall and peeped out the spy hole in the door. The corridor was empty; there was no one there. Sarah had been awakened on previous occasions by an urgent jangling only to discover that it was a false alarm, a sound at a certain frequency that confirmed almost with one hundredth of a second's precision her state between sleep and waking, fixed the moment when she was no longer asleep but not yet quite awake.

Of course she could imagine it was some incomprehensible sign, coming from beyond, coming from goodness knows where, projecting itself secretly into Sarah's life—but it could also be that her weary brain had sent a warning signal, switched on a little red lamp to draw her attention to overload.

The previous day unraveled before her mind's eye, backward and forward, open and shut, like a mechanical tape measure complete with locking device. The focus of the day was a person, a young man, whose contours were at first quite blurred, almost invisible, only in any way tangible by way of feeling. Sarah's instinct detected the vague outline that arose against a bright background, differing only slightly from it, an almost unnoticeably darker blotch with indistinct contours. At length, the vision consolidated and various details emerged, some more rounded, others more angular, while others again difficult to pin down. In the first place, the fresh childish face with its blue eyes, slightly narrowed in a smile, and the small, somewhat retroussé nose and lightly pursed lips. The young man had a short but slender neck, sloping shoulders that were at the same time soft and in no way broad, to which belonged, in all its illogicality—accentuating the slight asymmetry of the human frame in all its imperfections—a quite large-boned and ungainly body. The being that blocked Sarah's field of vision had a jacket with a fine check from whose sleeves protruded hands whose backs were soft-skinned, with delicate, well-shaped fingers, trousers with a crease, and straight legs leading down to shoes made of a good leather.

The expensive shoes certainly did not remain unnoticed by Sarah. They had to mean something—not only a decent income but also the need to look after oneself, the need to please! He was very good looking, that slightly vain young man, about whom Sarah now thought, avidly and incessantly.

The day came back on a number of occasions—the day had changed into a graphic image, a colored line, writhing like a snake— Sarah's mind kept stopping compulsively at the same spot, was obliged to dwell for ever longer periods on it, stopping with pleasure at some multicolored crossing point. The nodes had fastened themselves in her memory as tiny light spots and had formed a roguishly bright fallout. From these most important points a feeling of warmth and joy was emitted that diffused down Sarah's chest.

Yes, it was because of Henri and no one else.

Sarah had to admit that she had danced before the mirror that morning—naked before taking her shower—and had felt a new, intenser pleasure in regarding her body. While she was writhing ecstatically in front of the mirror to rhythmic music on the radio, life and strength flowed into her. Movement had always given her a feeling of well-being and enjoyment. There before the mirror she felt a strange sense of balance, sensing very clearly all that made up her body—her freshly shaven armpits, her belly with its lightly slack skin, the vaulting of her ribs, her relatively slender arms, her elbows whose skin had grown dry over the years and begun to wrinkle, her thighs full of those disgusting little bumps, her calves grown fleshy by much walking, even her large pink nipples and her pubic hair sprouting vulgarly—and this whole, which constituted her body, was simply the materialized citadel of a form of life, her home in which someone dwelt, her real self.

At that moment they were friends, her body and her real self, they existed alongside one another, in harmony and understanding.

She imagined herself dancing like this as Henri looked on, saw Henri gazing fixedly at her, the lustful desire of a young man appearing in his glance. Henri would no doubt be captivated by her mature temperament; her ardent passion would drag the man along with her! Why should Henri notice her thighs, worn weary with the years, why should he notice the wrinkles on Sarah's voluptuously bent neck! Unimportant blemishes of the skin, what were these to Henri!

She would have liked to see Henri's soft cheeks blush—oh, those childish cheeks covered with young, smooth skin—and feel his soft arms around her. . . .

How suddenly she could no longer bear the firm white walls that surrounded her on all sides—at work, at home, even on the street! How could she ever have thought that she needed them? She hated them now, so safe and harmless, giving a feeling of decent propriety, walls boasting of absurd discretion! They were torpid, tedious, and monotonous! An indolent, neutral, no-need-for-this white forest of white wall followed Sarah with depressing doggedness wherever she had business to do.

She had even had the walls of her flat papered white, in the hope that the white color would not be obtrusive, would simply help her recuperate, help her relax. White would seem right, because it didn't force itself upon you, did not strike the eye.

How foolish she had been! Sarah made a couple more frenzied gyrations in front of the mirror. The dancing, which in fact consisted of rhythmical jumping causing a dangerous swaying on the floor of the narrow entrance hall, was really too little for her. She would have liked to utter wild war cries—she didn't care what the neighbors might think—grab an aerosol can, and cover the walls of her flat with color. She wanted to put on a feathered Red Indian headdress and then whoop hoarsely and rush with distended nostrils into the woods to hunt. She would draw her bow and fire an arrow right into the heart of the first animal she came across. A hunter, that was what she had become! She was a very young Indian brave who had just undergone his initiation ceremony; the swiftest, most skillful and promising young man who, of an evening, would stamp out a dance of joy round the fire, with the rhythmic thump of the shaman's drum ringing in his ears, with a murmur of thanks to the Indian-faced gods on his lips.

She really would have wanted to be that magnificent boy, who had just become a real man.

My God, if Henri only knew what he had started! Sarah swayed on her feet, staggered like a drunk. Lightning flashed in her innards, a volcano full of burning lava was sputtering. She was in love, in love like a young girl! No, girls don't feel that hunger; they don't know what the flame of passion means!

Sarah had reached the large building that housed the editorial offices of the magazine, and similar enterprises, where both of them, Sarah and Henri, had been working for some time now; Sarah a couple of years more. Henri was not a complete beginner, though he had only graduated from university parallel to his job the previous spring.

His colleagues believed in Henri, as his articles, mainly political commentaries, were sharp and to the point. He was able to separate the wheat from the chaff, and his observations were usually pertinent. Henri had a capacity for analysis, and that was something important for their kind of work.

Sarah slowed her step, since she was afraid that every passerby could see immediately from her expression what an appalling paroxysm of feeling had seized her and what kind of hunger was gnawing at her vitals. She could do nothing about it. She was powerless to conceal it. As she climbed the stairs, Sarah's heart pounded in excitement and rivulets of sweat trickled from her armpits. She was in a real state. I'm crazy about you, was what she wanted to say to Henri, and she feared that she was going to do so as soon as she saw the young man.

Henri's image didn't leave her thoughts; he was now clearly visible in the depths of her mind's eye, swaddled in an invisible, big, warm, and dense cloud of a substance oddly familiar to Sarah. She wanted to wrap herself up in such a cloud, disappear into it. Evaporate! Sarah no longer wished to be herself; she wanted to rise, a cloud in the sky.

More than ever before, Sarah now wanted a pair of dark glasses, nearly opaque, that would hide her naked, loving eyes, their dark, glowing, thirsty pupils. Why didn't she have glasses like that?

When she reached the outside door, she very nearly turned back.

Nothing special had happened between them. Sarah had stood in front of the bookshelves in the editorial office, searching impatiently for some dictionary or other. Henri had passed by and had casually put his arm round her, given Sarah a slight hug, looked into her eyes, and muttered something indistinct, which Sarah promptly forgot. Then he had brushed Sarah's lips lightly with his own, as if in play, withdrawn in an instant, and gone back to his desk.

Sarah had stared after him in astonishment, maybe even shrugged her shoulders, and returned to what she was doing before she had been interrupted—not yet capable of grasping that from this moment onward—now that Henri, like a playful puppy, had approached his face to hers and put his arm round her waist—her world of white walls no longer existed, nor the Sarah that had hitherto belonged to them and resembled them. Both of them, both the walls and Sarah herself, had vanished, been swallowed into a vortex flinging off heavy colored splashes into the air, a vortex in whose depths roared something threatening and irreversible. It had all happened so quickly.

How could one fleeting kiss, which had hardly been a kiss, one faint touch of the lips change Sarah's life so profoundly? How could she have been so incautious, so foolish and romantic?

Could she not have imagined that she would come to work the very next day, knees atremble, only wishing for one thing: that Henri would come to meet her at the door, put his arm round her waist, and kiss her for a long time? That in their eager embrace they would completely forget their surroundings, and the people would momentarily stop work, then look politely the other way, burying their eyes in their papers, their gaze forever fixed on the screens of their PCs—and they, Henri and Sarah, surrounded by great silence, would kiss, just kiss while death waylaid them.

The unease rose, choking her. Sarah wanted to go to work only for a short while, enter the editorial office only to invite Henri and drag him out by the hand, a tail of flame behind them—such a streak of light that would be eternalized as a colored mist, like those stripes you see behind cars on dark streets in photos made of speeding cars, surprising with its attractive colors and mystery arousing curiosity. In such photos there was always something larger than life, time had been eliminated, as if the surface had been treated with a fine filter. Only light radiated, a lonely, illuminated flash of eternity.

The glowing red tail would not vanish from the stairs of the editorial offices; it would stay there for quite some time.

They would be in a hurry! They would rush like two crazy comets either to Henri's rented room or Sarah's flat, would storm beyond the speed of sound into any hotel, into any idiotic hotel room, between any nameless walls, the main thing being that there was room for them to intertwine their bodies undisturbed, where Sarah could infect Henri with her passion, hand over part of the joyful burden of the tenderness that had made her knees tremble on the way to work. Sarah would be quite frenzied, abandoned, and ravenous. What they would not do together in that room!

She could already hear her and Henri's moans of pleasure; the city would be booming and reverberating about them. Moans, kept in check at first and carefully smothered, ever swelling, growing almost into a roar, filling the firmament from edge to edge—people on the street not ultimately being able to hear the sound of their own voices—and no one, not anyone, understanding whether their cause was ultimate enjoyment or mortal anguish.

But it couldn't happen, that pleasure; such spirited *Liebestod* simply did not exist. She knew that never would Henri come with her and belong to her. She must not hope or wish for it!

Henri didn't even seem to be at work that day. Sarah, unhappy, melancholy, and pathetic, hung her coat up on the peg behind the cupboard. Her throat was parched, a desert dryness, scraping and hindering her breathing. She was now entirely dependent on Henri, clinging to him as if intoxicated. In her agonizing withdrawal symptoms she was a wretched drug addict, whose malady had developed so deplorably and become incurable. It had all happened so quickly. Too quickly!

That morning, Sarah had put her hands over her face and wept. She knew there was no hope. Henri was too young for her.

Henri would get married one day, take a suitably young woman who loved and trusted him. They would have children together and be happy. How would Sarah be able to stand this, to survive this? Sarah knew that Henri had a girlfriend, whom he often met after work; Henri never made any attempt to hide this—he was proud of his girl. Or was he prouder of himself—at having found a girl who wanted to be with him and waited for him? Maybe he wanted to share his joy with Sarah when he had kissed her between the bookshelves? Sarah felt herself to be the extension of Henri's girlfriend, a natural part of Henri's young lady. That was one way you could think about it. She had no reason to blame herself; she was in no way a thief or someone selfishly and recklessly meddling in other people's lives.

Calm down, she told herself on innumerable occasions. She should have forgotten the touch of their lips forthwith. It was a chance encounter, signifying nothing. Why did this one brushing kiss affect her so deeply, turning her head? Where had her common sense disappeared to? Sarah, normally so severe, introverted, and shy, had now gone and lost her self-control and was incapable of separating illusion from reality. Or didn't want to do so, the images, so beautiful and brave, excited her not a little. Blessedness sprang from them, like from a feather pillow. No one could take her illusions away from her.

The center of gravity of her world had irrevocably shifted to where it could neither be seen nor touched.

Sarah was like an inept understudy, suddenly confirmed to be playing a part without any preparation, helpless, who had to embody on stage some quite unfamiliar role. What performance, what play, what role was it that she, the amateur, was forced to play?

Henri was at work, after all! He was sitting in the far corner of the large office, reading. Sarah had simply not noticed him. Her heart began pounding wildly—a herd of at least a hundred foals was wildly galloping in her breast—and her hands shook so much that she didn't dare go to her own desk. But she couldn't betray herself! Sarah breathed in deeply, went out of the door, and strode off to the toilet. She spent some time there, putting on lipstick, powdering her blotched red face thoroughly, combing her hair carefully, and emerged only when someone began rattling the handle frantically.

She stood for a time in the corridor, to summon up as indifferent an expression as possible when she reentered the room—but had still not managed to move when the door opened and Henri appeared. The young man saw Sarah, greeted her, took a few steps toward her, and stopped. His face suddenly blushed. Sarah felt Henri's breath on her forehead and stiffened. She could hardly bring herself to greet him. Their eyes clung to one another. Sarah tried to hide her agitation—what agitation, it was panic—but nonetheless began shaking and knew that she could not utter a word. Silent and cramped, she made a heroic effort and used her last resources to summon up a smile. That was a mistake. Her facial muscles did not respond, instead throwing her face visibly askew.

Henri watched Sarah with embarrassment, on his face that childish mildness so familiar to Sarah, the same that had made the earth under her feet sway dangerously, then approached her and took her by the hand. His palm was moist. Sarah saw the transparent, moist and young skin of Henri's glowing cheeks, and feared that she would lose consciousness, would faint for the first time in her life. The situation was unbearable and frightful; she wanted to flee, at top speed, immediately; she wanted to lock herself in the toilet forever, to stay in the only refuge left to her! Then she noticed the fresh scratch near Henri's ear.

"You've cut yourself," she whispered, discovering that her powers of speech were gradually returning. Henri stood where he was in front of her and remained silent, though something throbbed gently in his face. Perhaps it only seemed so to Sarah. At any rate, the red of his cheeks increased and he blinked several times, as if thrown slightly into confusion. "You've hurt yourself," said Sarah, louder now, more bravely, and her voice had a slight ring about it.

Henri's hand had slipped while he was shaving that morning! He had cut himself, not deeply, but enough for the wound to be visible and draw attention to itself. Henri must have been disturbed by something before coming to work. While he was shaving he could well have suddenly thought about Sarah and the thought had made his hand jerk so much that he left a scratch on his face. But it could also have occurred unwittingly, because he was in a hurry, without any specific cause or reason.

Under the tiny scratch covered with clotted blood there was a reddish, swollen blotch, slightly proud. Sarah felt sympathy for him. She would have liked to have been standing at Henri's side when he was shaving in the bathroom that morning. She would have licked the seeping blood from his cheek, rubbed herself voluptuously against him, inhaled with pleasure the smell of blood. An elixir coming from Henri himself, that blood! Ah, she would have been thirsty and greedy, would have smashed the bathroom mirror to smithereens in her ecstasy; they would have rolled about on the floor in the blood and slivers of glass and given themselves over to ravishing one another!

Sarah would probably not even have noticed if the ground under her feet had opened in a hot rush and red and threatening flames of hell had gushed out of the dark depths, at first only scourging her legs and womb, then rising ever higher, the fire growing brighter and more powerful, flames now licking at her breasts and face, but she wouldn't even have noticed; she would have pressed herself so hard against the bloody-cheeked boy, clung instinctively to him, and drunk her fill, ever dizzier from his blood. Sweet, oh so sweet it would have been!

They were standing close to each other as before and looking at each other (again! I mean one another!) with embarrassment on their faces. Sarah could feel Henri's warm glow. Her heart was filled by a great, boundless sadness. A powerful and irresistible power gushed forth from Henri.

And now Sarah realized that the attraction lay not only in Henri's body. Sarah was looking at herself through Henri's eyes. This was hard to bear, very hard.

Then something happened. Sarah changed state, became an insubstantial, shapeless, contourless being resembling vapor, changed to a scintillating mist that slowly billowed around Henri, swaddling him. They, Sarah and Henri, were suddenly secretly scintillating nebulae, who melded into one another, completely merging in the large, bleak corridor, shimmering in all the colors of the rainbow, rising higher and higher, without hesitation.

A moment earlier, Sarah had indeed wanted to flee, to evaporate into thin air! Then the mists dispersed and the picture changed. Sarah was no longer standing in the cold corridor of the large, unfriendly building, but in the apple orchard of her long-deceased grandmother. She was only a child, not yet attending school. The apple trees were full of big juicy fruit—it must have been early autumn—and around the orchard stood a dense dark green hedge of firs.

That's how it had been during childhood; she remembered quite clearly both the orchard and the high protective hedge around.

The green color spread a strange peace. This peace gusted here into the corridor of the big house where she and Henri were standing as if nailed to the spot. Who was she now—still a child, a little girl skipping around in her torn skirt in her grandmother's orchard? But then who was this blotch-faced woman with a guilty expression on her face, who now, her body quite frozen and stiff, was gazing into Henri's eyes? What was eating the heart of this woman?

"Henri, telephone!" somebody was shouting at the door. Henri gave a start, but did not immediately let go of Sarah's hand. Only when he was called a second time did he make to rush off. That day, they did not meet again.

Sarah sat the whole afternoon in a daze at her PC. She couldn't get on with her work; only disjointed sentences would appear on the screen, random scraps of thought. She tried to understand what was happening to her, bombarded herself with questions, but nothing helped; she really could not comprehend her situation. She had never experienced anything like it before.

In her self-confidence, Sarah had thought for years that there was nothing new under the sun for her, that she had seen a thing or two in life! How naive she had been!

She had fallen unhappily in love, she had to admit to herself. Why unhappily? A heavy wave of passion roared in her ears; her blood was boiling, her head turning in intoxication, but she did not lose her sense of caution. There lay the difference. Sarah knew that the bliss would soon ebb. Someone within her was calling her in an icy, ruthless voice, telling her she was a comic figure, that she was deceiving herself, that she had fallen in love with the young boy like an old fool. Punishment for her caper would not be long in coming.

At the end of the working day, she was fidgeting in her seat. Even this chair, normally so comfortable, had turned against her and become an unpleasant air cushion, irritating and mocking her. On sitting down, Sarah felt clearly that she was no longer part of this world, she was now an alien who had to learn the social rituals of this world.

Ahead lay strenuous efforts whose extent were beyond her imagination.

Time could not be reversed. Time existed! In this lay the tragedy of her encounter with Henri. They could be near one another, feel they were in some way close, but between them were long years, which no one could erase.

Sarah had never before felt so acutely the importance of time. Henri was simply too young for her.

Their difference in age could be as much as fifteen years, or more. Henri could have been her son rather than her man. There was no hope for Sarah. She had to acknowledge that fact, paint it in large, clumsy letters on her white wall!

She felt a painful stab in her heart. She had to understand that she was indeed alive, her heart worked, but her flesh was fading little by little, her bones growing brittle, her limbs growing fat, her veins calcified and withered, her skin dry, growing wrinkled—on her elbows, her throat, her palms, over her whole body—and becoming looser, day by day.

Time belonged to the body, and her body had been permeated by too much time; the youth of the body was past. Only the spirit was still free and had to remain free, as Sarah hoped—the spirit, that great, sovereign being, sometimes tearing itself slowly away from the body and living by its own rules. The spirit would rise naturally above the obstacles of time. The body could not achieve this.

Sarah's spirit refused to admit that Henri was taboo for her. Inevitability did not interest Sarah's simple spirit, which time in no way limited, which could rove freely in the past, present, and future at one and the same time. For her spirit these aspects of time did not hold true; the spirit was above time and independent of it.

Sarah was quite familiar with how her spirit caused suffering to her flesh. This was an old habit. In the spring, Sarah was attacked by severe headaches. Fits akin to fainting numbed half her head and a portion of her body, and contact with her surroundings weakened to an almost dangerous extent. These fits, like dress rehearsals for death, could not be warded off by any pills or powders. By now, she had grown used to the tiresome attacks, sometimes lasting for days, and they no longer frightened her.

Sarah knew that on those occasions her spirit was trying to escape the body, longing to be free of it, to enter its own true state, its own invisible home. But her body would resist, not allowing her headstrong spirit the freedom for which it strove, not wishing to sacrifice anything.

In this way, the spirit had left a grand and independent impression.

The body was far more helpless. The spirit managed being alone admirably, but not the body. It tried to snuggle up to other similar beings—that is how it had been constituted—and subjugated the spirit, wherever possible, to suffer humiliation.

Henri had managed to tackle both, breaking Sarah's body's self-assuredness and bringing doubt to her spirit. He had shown her the true loneliness not only of her body but of her spirit too. When Henri gazed at her so clumsily in the corridor, Sarah had understood this very well. Nothing to be done about it. Now Sarah's spirit and her body were both desperately striving toward Henri.

Henri was the battlefield for Sarah's body and her spirit. Both were in trouble and gloating over the misfortune of the other.

Who was she, Sarah, anyway? What was wrong with her? On the one hand, it was quite clear: Henri had turned Sarah into a hot-blooded young girl, glowing with freshness, who could do nothing else but utter childishly besotted sighs and rest her hopelessly muddled head on the shoulder of her snub-nosed prince with bright eyes.

On the other, this was no mere bodily passion. The body had only given in first. Henri had first transformed her body—but body was not enough for him—next followed the spirit. Now Sarah was a prisoner of a delusion, which confirmed that she was someone else, some non-Sarah, whose youthful beauty was also proof of a new, unbreakable spirit. The hypnosis was no longer partial, but entire.

What could she do against this prison?

Henri's kiss the previous day had been just as dreamlike and ephemeral as a summer's day on some sandy beach, where the waves wash gently against the shore in the bright sunlight. Like the warm sigh of the waves over the green depths. Sarah could not suppress this thought.

The sun shone, the sea glittered, the beach was at peace in the light. The waves touched the slope of the sand, came and went, shimmered, glided, twinkled, approached and retreated, time upon time, again and again, the movements in an endless row, turned into one long uniform line, of one and the same succession, in one and the same unceasing rhythm. Nothing changed. It had been like this for an age.

It could be that the sea longed to melt into the sand, change into some third substance, neither sand nor sea, neither the one nor the other. Maybe the sand had wished to fuse with the sea, melt into the spume on the lustrous nape of the waves.

Everyone had seen the sea and the sand, but nobody knew how to look into them.

Sarah was the sandy strand and Henri the sea. Between them lay a well-defined boundary. Sea never turned into sand, nor the sand into sea.

No one could have convinced Sarah of the contrary.

Translated from the Estonian by Eric Dickens

NOTES

Why Do These Black Worms Fly Just Everywhere I Am Myself Only Accidentally

Previously published in Drago Jančar et al., eds. *The Day Tito Died: Contemporary Slovenian Short Stories* (Boston: Forest Books, 1993), 115–16.

24
taking the war from osijek to zagreb, rijeka
Osijek, Zagreb, and Rijeka are cities in Croatia.

20 Firula Road

Previously published in *Pro Femina: Special Issue on Contemporary Women's Literature in Serbia* (1997): 79–83.

35
a father who belonged to the Sokols
The Sokols was a sports-activities organization that originated in Bohemia at around the turn of the century. It had a Pan-Slavic orientation, which explains why someone who belonged to the Sokols would name their child Yugoslav (male) or Yugoslava (female). Yugoslavia originally came together as a union of the Southern Slavs (*jug* means "south" in Serbo-Croatian).

37
Jan Mayen and My Srem
Jan Mayen is a Norwegian island between Norway and Iceland. Srem is a region in the province of Vojvodina in Northern Serbia.

37
Ivo Andrić (1892–1975)
Bosnian-born Yugoslav writer who won the Nobel prize for literature in 1961.

The Story of the Man Who Sold Sauerkraut and Had a Lioness-Daughter

Previously published in *Pro Femina: Special Issue on Contemporary Women's Literature in Serbia* (1997): 38–41.

Everything's OK

Previously published in Daniela Crăsnaru, *The Grand Prize and Other Stories* (Evanston: Northwestern University Press, 2004), 50–56.

Far and Near

Previously published in *Chicago Review* 46:2 (2000).

I, Milena

Previously published in Janice Kulyk Keefer and Solomea Pavlychko, eds., *Two Lands, New Visions: Stories from Canada and Ukraine* (Regina: Coteau Books, 1998), 125–61.

140
a chekist
Cheka is a Russian acronym for the All-Russian Extraordinary Commission for Combating Counter-Revolution and Sabotage, established in 1917.

140
NKVD
Russian abbreviation for the People's Committee on Internal Affairs, a forerunner of the KGB.

From E.E.

The translator gratefully acknowledges Myron Pivnick for preparing a rough draft of the translation and Irina Pivnick for checking the final English text.

The Third Shore

Previously published in Teresa Halikowska and George Hyde, eds., *The Eagle and the Crow: Modern Polish Short Stories* (London: Serpent's Tail, 1996), 212–19.

The Men and the Gentlemen

176
my heart may die more willing . . .
Friedrich Hölderlin, "An die Parzen" (To the Fates), trans. Christopher Middleton, *Friedrich Hölderlin, Eduard Mörike: Selected Poems* (Chicago: University of Chicago Press, 1972), 10–11.

Dance on the Canal

192
Heiamachen, Ringelgehen, Muckschsein.
Loosely: "lullabies, ring-around-the-rosy, sourpuss."

192
I owned Mr. Sandman
Der Sandmann was a popular television show for children.

192
Himmel und Hölle
"Heaven and hell."

192
Huppekästel
"Hopscotch" (literally, "hop squares").

193
erschossen
"Shot and killed."

196
"Hoppehoppe Reiter"
"Go, Horsie, Go." A song sung to children when riding a cockhorse on someone's knee.

Lady with Cowshit

Previously published in Laima Sruoginis, ed., *Lithuania in Her Own Words: An Anthology of Contemporary Lithuanian Writing* (Vilnius: Tyto alba, 1997), 202–5.

Pleasures of the Saints

Previously published in *Review of Contemporary Fiction* 18.1 (1998): 55–64.

210
Urbi et orbi
"To the city and the world!"

212
"*Vita brevis!*"—"*Est!*"
"Life is short!"—"So it is!"

The Mill Ghost

Previously published in Kajar Pruul and Darlene Reddaway, eds., *Estonian Short Stories* (Evanston, Ill.: Northwestern University Press), 251–59.

220
Hortus Musicus
Founded in 1972, Hortus Musicus is an Estonian ensemble that plays baroque and fourteenth- to eighteenth-century European music on period instruments.

■ □ ■ □ ■

ABOUT THE AUTHORS

CARMEN FRANCESCA BANCIU has written three novels and four collections of short stories as well as radio plays. Born in Romania in 1955, she has been living in Berlin since 1991 and has published in Romanian and German. Her first, largely autobiographical novel in German, *Flight from Father* (*Vaterflucht*), appeared in 1998. Other titles include *Windows in Flames* (*Fenster in Flammen,* 1992), *A Country Full of Heroes* (*Ein Land voller Helden,* 2000), and *Berlin in Paris* (2002), a collection of essays, anecdotes, and short stories about life in Berlin through the eyes of a former citizen of Communist Romania. She is the recipient of numerous prizes and fellowships, including the Arnsberg International Short Story Prize in 1985. At the time, she was not allowed to leave Romania to accept her award and was also banned from publishing for five years.

MAIMU BERG was born in Estonia in 1945, and graduated from the University of Tartu with a degree in journalism. She has written a number of articles and short stories for magazines and newspapers. Her first collection of short stories appeared in 1987 and was followed by the novels *I Loved a Russian* (*Ma armestasin venelast,* 1994) and *Away* (*Ära,* 1999). Berg presently works at the Finnish Cultural Institute in Tallinn.

DANIELA CRĂSNARU is one of Romania's most distinguished authors. Born in 1950, she is a poet and short-story writer whose works include *The Grand Prize* (*Marele Premiu,* 1983), a collection of poems and prose, and *The Fallen Cork Tree* (*Pluta răsturnată,* 1990), a collection of short fiction, in which the story "Everything's OK" first appeared. In 1991, she was awarded the Romanian Academy Prize for career achievement in poetry. She was declared "Woman of the Year" in 1994 and is vice president of the National

Liberal Party. Crăsnaru is also president of CUORE, a foundation for needy children and orphans.

DIANA ÇULI was born in Tirana, Albania, in 1951, and graduated from the University of Tirana with a degree in literature and languages. Before her election as president of the Independent Forum for the Albanian Woman in 1991, she assumed responsibility for the publication of the literary magazine *Les lettres albanaises*. Çuli has participated in a number of conferences worldwide and has written several articles on literature and women's rights. She also wrote scripts for several artistic films and has published at least half a dozen novels, including *The Voice* (*Zëri i largët,* 1978) and *The Night Was Divided into Two Parts* (*Dhe nata u nda nëmes,* 1993).

LJILJANA ĐURĐIĆ is a Serbian poet, prose writer, and translator who was born in 1946. As one of the most significant poets of the Belgrade poetry circle, she has published three collections of poems, as well as two collections of short stories, *How I Loved Franz Kaspar* (*Kako sam ljubila Franca Kaspara,* 1988) and *Images from a Previous Life* (*Slike iz prethodnog života,* 1997). In 1995, she published a collection of essays, *Belgrade by My Mind,* analyzing political and cultural life in Serbia in the 1990s. She is one of the editors of the feminist magazine *Pro Femina* and works at the publishing department of the National Library of Serbia in Belgrade.

GABRIELE ECKART was born in Falkenstein in the former East Germany in 1954. She moved to East Berlin in 1972 to study philosophy. Her writings include *The Way I See Things* (*So sehe ich die Sache,* 1986) and *Seeing Things in a Good and Strange Way* (*Der gute fremde Blick,* 1992), both published by Kiepenheuer & Witsch in Cologne. Eckart left East Germany in 1987 and now resides and teaches in the United States.

DÓRA ESZE is a translator and one of Hungary's acclaimed young writers, born in 1969. Her work has been translated into German. *Like Two Peas in a Pod* (*Két tojás,* 1996) was her second very successful novel, published after *Raspberry River* (*Málnafolyó,* 1995). More recently, she wrote the novel *Let's Be Friends* (*Legyünk barátok,* 2000) and the soap opera *Steaming Elderflowers* (*Bodzagőz,* 2003). She lives in Budapest.

ETELA FARKAŠOVÁ was born in Levoca, Slovakia, in 1943. She studied at Comenius University in Bratislava and graduated as a philosophy and sociology major. She has published eight books of prose, including *Reproduction of Time* (*Reprodukcia času*, 1980), *Escaping Portrait* (*Unikajuci portrét*, 1989), *Day by Day* (*Den za dnom*, 1996), and *Hour of Sunset* (*Hodina zapadajúceho slnka*, 1998). Farkašová has received numerous literary awards and her short stories have been translated into several languages. She also helped to establish *Femina*, a club for Slovak women writers. She works for the feminist magazine *Aspekt* and is a professor of philosophy as well as a literary critic.

DANIELA FISCHEROVÁ was born in Prague in 1948. Her first play, *The Hour Between the Dog and the Wolf* (*Hodina mezi psem a vlkem*, 1979), was banned and as a consequence she could not publish or perform for eight years. Nevertheless, she continued to write, and some of her best works date from this period. Besides plays, including radio plays, she published *A Finger That Will Never Touch* (*Prst, ktery se nikdy nedotkne*, 1996), the collection of short stories from which "Far and Near" ("Daleko a blizko") comes.

NATASZA GOERKE was born in Poznań, Poland, in 1960, and studied Polish before moving to Kraków to study east Asian languages. She left Poland in 1984, obtained a degree in Tibetan from the University of Hamburg, and traveled in Asia, mainly in the Himalayas. Her collection of short stories, *Fractals* (*Fractale*, 1994), became a bestseller. In 1997, she published *Book of Pâtés* (*Ksiega Pasztetow*) and in 1999, *Farewell to Plasma* (*Pozegnania Plazmy*). Goerke, who lives in Hamburg, Germany, often writes articles for the Polish and German literary presses.

KÄRT HELLERMAA was born in Tallin, Estonia, in 1956. She graduated from the department of journalism of Tartu University in 1981 and has worked as a freelance writer and journalist since 1996. She has published several short stories and miniatures in various Estonian journals. Her first novel, *Alchemy* (*Alkeemia*), was published in 1997; her second novel, *Cassandra* (*Kassandra*), appeared in 2000. She has also written literary, film, and art criticism.

KERSTIN HENSEL was born in Karl-Marx-Stadt (now Chemnitz) in the former East Germany in 1961. She was a nurse before she studied literature, then worked in Leipzig as an artistic assistant for a children's theater. Since 1988, she has lived in Berlin as a freelance writer. She also teaches at the Hochschule für Schauspielkunst in Berlin. Hensel has published plays, articles in literary journals, and several books of poetry, including *No Clue* (*Bahnhof verstehen,* 2001). *Hallimasch* (1989) was her first collection of prose, followed by *Auditorium panoptikum* (1991), *In the Hose* (*Im Schlauch,* 1993), *Dance Along the Canal* (*Tanz am Kanal,* 1994), *Plaster Hat* (*Gipshut,* 1999), and the novel *In the Prison* (*Im Spinnhaus,* 2003).

NORA IKSTENA (b. 1969) studied Latvian language and literature at the University of Latvia. Her first book, *The Homecoming* (*Pārnākšana*), was published in 1992. She has also written several collections of short stories, including *Trifles and Pleasures* (*Nieki un izpriecas,* 1995) and *Misleading Romances* (*Maldīgas romances,* 1997), which have been translated into several languages. She is currently the editor of *Karogs,* a literary magazine.

JANA JURÁNOVÁ (b. 1957) completed her university studies in English and Russian in 1980 and worked for several organizations in Slovakia, among them the Literary Institute and Theater for Youth. She has published collections of short stories, including *Menagerie* (*Zverinec,* 1994) and *Only a Girl* (*Iba baba,* 1999). In 1989, she wrote the play *Salome,* which was staged in Bratislava, Slovakia, and Paris, and published in 1994. Juránová was one of the founders of the Slovakian feminist magazine *Aspekt,* and she is currently project coordinator and editor of the magazine.

ZSUZSA KAPECZ was born in Budapest in 1956. She has won several literary prizes for her poems and short stories. The collection of stories *The Angels Have Arrived in the City* (*Az angyalok már a városban vannak*) was published in 1998. She has also written a novel, *Life Is Great and Wonderful* (*Csudajó, gyönyörű az élet,* 2000).

ALMA LAZAREVSKA was born in Macedonia in 1957, and holds a degree in comparative literature and theater from the University of Sarajevo. She writes essays and prose. "How We Killed the Sailor" is from her award-winning collection of short stories, *Death in the Museum of Modern Art* (*Smrt u muzeju moderne umjetnosti,* 1996). Her other works include the novel *In the Sign of the Rose* (*U znaku ruže,* 1996), a collection of essays, *Sarajevo Solitaire* (*Sarajevski pasijans,* 1994), and a collection of short stories, *Plants*

Are Something Else (*Biljke su nešto drugo,* 2003). Lazarevska lives and works in Sarajevo.

SANJA LOVRENČIĆ was born in Croatia in 1961. She has published several volumes of poetry since the 1980s, and Croatian radio has broadcast many of her radio dramas and plays for children. Her collection of short prose, *Wien Fantastic,* was published in 1998. She is also a literary translator from English and French.

HRISTINA MARINOVA is one of Bulgaria's most renowned young writers. Born in 1975, she holds an M.A. in translation from the University of Sofia. In 1998, she won the Bulgarian national award for prose at the Shumen Students' Competition with her short story "Herbarium." She rewrote it for television, and this screen version was rated second at the annual competition of the Bulgarian National Television in 2000. Another short story, "The Smile of the Fishes" ("Usmivkata na ribite"), was translated into French and included in an anthology of young Bulgarian writers. Her apparently simple style combined with a shocking frankness has given her the reputation of a promising young author.

MIRA MEKŞI (b. 1960) graduated from the University of Tirana, Albania, with a specialization in French philology. She later studied Spanish and discovered her passion for Latin American literature. She has translated Ismail Kadaré's poems into French and a number of French and Hispanic authors (Borges, Cortázar, Duras, Neruda, Yourcenar) into Albanian. Her work consists of collections of short stories, including *Lips of the Unknown Woman* (*Buzë të panjohura gruaje,* 1997) and *Mountain with Spirits* (*Mali i shpirtrave*), and a fantastic novel *The Little Icy Planet* (*Planetthi i ngrirë,* 1997). She has also published children's books. Since 1994, Mekşi has been director of the Velija Foundation, which promotes Albanian culture. She is also the founder and editor of the literary magazine *Mehr Licht.*

LELA B. NJATIN is the author's pen name. She was born in Ljubljana, Slovenia, in 1963, and studied comparative literature and philosophy. Njatin writes novels and short stories; she has also written plays and designed costumes for theater and music groups. Her first novel, *Intolerance* (1988), received the national award for young writers and is now recognized as a prediction of the civil war. Other prose includes *Freeway, Far-Away Light*

(*Schnellstrasse, Fernlicht,* 1991). Her short prose has been translated into several languages, and she has held readings all over Europe. Several of her works have appeared in English translation, for example, in the anthologies *The Day Tito Died* (1993) and *The Veiled Landscape* (1995).

LJUBOV' ROMANCHUK is a young Russian writer with a Ph.D. in philology. She is a member of the Union of Russian Writers as well as of the National Union of Ukrainian Journalists, and currently works as a secretary and correspondent for the Ukrainian newspaper *Svoe Mnenie.* Romanchuk has published poetry, collections of short stories, and science fiction. She is the recipient of several distinctions for her short stories; "The Cyber" won the international competition of the magazine *October* in 1992.

JUDITA ŠALGO (1941–96) lived in Novi Sad, Vojvodina, Serbia. She published several collections of poems: *Along the Shore* (*Obalom,* 1962), *Sixty-Seven Minutes, Out Loud* (*67 minuta, naglas,* 1980), and *Life on a Table* (*Život na stolu,* 1986). She also published the novels *Skid Marks* (*Trag kočenja,* 1987) and *Does Life Exist* (*Da li postoji život,* 1995) as well as a collection of short stories. As director of the Youth Tribune, an alternative cultural and artistic space in Novi Sad, Šalgo was persecuted during the civil war in the former Yugoslavia.

RENATA ŠERELYTĖ was born in the village of Šimonių in the Kupškis region of Lithuania in 1970. She studied Lithuanian literature and linguistics at the University of Vilnius. Her collection of short stories, *Skinning Fish,* published in 1995, turned Šerelytė into one of the most promising young prose writers in Lithuania. She currently works as an editor, and her prose was published in English in the anthology *The Earth Remains* (2003).

OLGA TOKARCZUK is one of the most popular contemporary writers in Poland. Born in 1962, she holds a degree in psychology. She has published several novels and volumes of short stories as well as poetry. Her first novel, *A Journey of the Book People* (*Podróz ludzi ksiegi,* 1993), won the prize for the best book by a young author. She published her first collection of short stories in 1995. She has since published another collection of short stories, *Playing on a Multitude of Drums* (*Gra na wielu bebenkach,* 2001). Her most recent novel, *House of Day, House of Night* (*Dom dzienny, dom nocny,* 1998), was published in English in 2002 by Granta Books.

JADRANKA VLADOVA was born in Skopje, Macedonia, in 1956, and graduated from the Faculty of Philology. She is a literary and film critic and has published two collections of short stories, *Skarbo in My Yard* (*Skarbo vo mojot dvar,* 1986) and *Water Mark* (*Voden znak,* 1990), as well as children's literature. Vladova teaches literature at the Department of Literature of the People of Yugoslavia, University of Skopje.

OKSANA ZABUZHKO (b. 1960) has a Ph.D. in aesthetics from the Taras Shevchenko Kiev University, Ukraine. A Fulbright scholar at Harvard University in 1994, she has published several collections of poems, including *May Hoarfrost* (1985) and *The Conductor of the Last Candle* (1990). She has also written novels, including the best seller *Field Work in Ukrainian Sex* (*Polyovi doslidjennya z ukrainskogo seksu,* 1996), which won several awards and was translated into several languages. Her more recent prose, *Sister, Sister* (*Sestro, sestro*) was published in 2003. Zabuzhko also is a literary critic and the author of *Archimedes' New Law* (*Noviy zakon Arhimeda,* 2000). She lives in Kiev and works as a scholar at the Ukrainian Academy of Sciences.

■ □ ■ □ ■

WRITINGS FROM AN UNBOUND EUROPE

For a complete list of titles, see the Writings from an Unbound Europe Web site at www.nupress.northwestern.edu/ue.